THE VELVET COLLAR

by

C. P. MANDARA

Published by Chimera Books
ISBN 9781780803999

www.chimerabooks.co.uk

It is not death that a man should fear, but he should fear never beginning to live.
- *Marcus Aurelius*

The Velvet Collar

I made a bet with my newlywed submissive wife. I told her that if she could behave herself impeccably for a week, she could wear the trousers for a day. That included being able to dominate me. The bet was almost guaranteed to be impossible to achieve, and yet somehow she did it. It looks like I'm in for a fun night, doesn't it?

If that wasn't bad enough, Kyle has been spotted near our home. It scares me. I can feel the net closing in, and I'm still no closer to unravelling the pieces. We need to figure out what Redcliff wants, and fast.

In order to do this, I'm going to have to talk to my mother-in-law, who still isn't speaking to me. I have no idea what her problem is. She tried to kill me, not the other way around...

Chapter One - Kyle

"Kidnap her, lure Mark in, then threaten to kill the girl in front of him. That'll get him to sign anything we want him to, just in case he has a prenup." Michael wheezed for a bit after that, and the old boy didn't sound good. I didn't think the bastard had too many years left in him, but I'd said that about five years ago and he was still here.

"Why would I do that?" There was no way I needed an enemy like Matthews breathing down my neck wherever I went, so if I was killing Jennifer, I was killing her husband straight after. I'd play with them first, though. If they were going to die anyway, I could have a little fun with them.

"You're not actually going to kill her, you idiot. If we kill Jen our lives will end rather abruptly." Michael's sarcastic tone was not lost on me. "Actually scrap that; if either Jen's mother or father find us, they'll end our lives very slowly and extremely unpleasantly. We need to kill Mark. He's the key that will get us out of this mess."

"You think you'll be able to control Jen as soon as she inherits all the money?" I was sceptical. Although I didn't doubt dad would make some obscene threats if she didn't toe the line, she had more leverage now - lots and lots of money. With that came very powerful and influential friends.

"We've done it before, so I see no reason why we can't do it again. All it will take is a couple of perfectly placed warnings and she'll give us whatever we want. She doesn't have to know what the money's for. We can share the spoils between us." Dad then began coughing and spluttering, trying to clear his chest, and it wasn't until someone had given him a glass of water that he managed to calm down.

"What *is* the money for?" Dad already had bags full of the stuff so I couldn't understand what all the fuss was about.

"None of your fucking business. Just do as you're told," he snapped at me, and the tone he used pissed me off. All I did these days was run errands for him, and the rewards of being an obedient son weren't great. It was about time I got something worthwhile out of our arrangement. So if daddy dearest thought I was giving him any of *my* money, after I'd done all the dirty work, he was much mistaken.

Once I had Jen the rest would be easy - just as long as I could get away with it, and that remained to be seen.

"How are you going to make sure no one finds out?" There it was, the most important question I'd asked all morning.

"I have connections. We'll make sure you are out of the country with an ironclad alibi." Nodding to myself, I decided that was a reasonable plan providing it could be pulled off. I'd want details of his "alibi" and my supposed whereabouts, but we'd talk about that later.

"Anything particularly nasty you want me to do with the pair before I get rid of

Mark?" Dad always enjoyed a spot of torture. He loved to drag out the moment.

"I thought you'd never ask," came his slow, but brutally cold reply.

Chapter Two - Mark

"I adore being married to you, Mrs Matthews."

A very unladylike snort greeted my remark.

"Well of course you do. You get to tie me up, spank me, and generally drive me absolutely crazy and there's not a thing I can do about it."

She had a point. I currently had her pinned to the wall, and she looked very fetching in the cast iron shackles I'd had made for her.

"Thank goodness you came into my life when you did. I might never have discovered this marriage thing otherwise." I gave her a feral grin as I plucked a vicious rubber flogger off the wall.

"Exactly," she purred, blithely unconcerned by my wicked instrument, or maybe I should say the two wicked instruments that were currently walking towards her. At the moment we were both naked and very comfortable with the fact. "Marriage has been a wonderful walk in the park for you, Mr Matthews. You get your meals cooked, your shirts ironed, and your every instruction obeyed to the letter." She looked deadly serious for a moment, but I caught the light twinkling in her eyes, and it just made me want to whip my wife all the more. Oh, happy days. Naturally I had to have the last word, though.

"You burn food, you set *fire* to clothes, and you purposely disobey me in nearly anything that matters in order to get your ass tanned. This is probably why I avoided marriage for so long. You have no idea how hard it is to keep you in check."

I kept my face straight, but it was a hard-won battle.

"You like your food well done, shirts are extremely overrated, and at least I'm thoughtful enough to give you plenty of reasons to punish me. It would be even harder work if you had to come up with your own, darling." She batted her sultry little eyelashes at me, and the merest hint of a smile appeared at the corner of her lips. I swear she did it on purpose. My wife knew how to press all my buttons without even fucking trying. It was infuriating sometimes.

"You know I want to throw you on the bed right now and fuck you until you're a sobbing, screaming, hot mess?" I thought about for that a moment. "Actually, that's a lie. I want to fuck you every which way there is, every single second of every single damn day until there is no breath left in my body *or* yours." I ran the flogger gently up her stomach, and the annoying woman grinned down at me.

"You're quite the romantic, Mr Matthews. Too much more of that kind of talk and you'll start freaking me out. Now put your money where your mouth is and whip me until I've forgotten which day of the week it is." She eyed the flogger, as if to encouraging me to do my worst. My wife really was incorrigible.

"Am I freaking you out?" I grinned wolfishly at her but knew better.

"No." Her voice was clipped, and her eyes were still lustfully glued to my whip.

"Could I freak you out?" Yes, I was using delaying tactics to annoy her, and yes it was working.

"I doubt it. Unless you want to re-enrol me back at the ponygirl farm, we're probably good." She then wriggled her hips towards me as far as the restraints would allow and stared lustfully at my cock which was straining for attention. *Down boy, down. We have work to do.*

"I bet I could freak you out without even having to mention the words sex, kink or BDSM."

Jen wrinkled her nose at me. "This isn't where you confess to me that you're a World of Warcraft geek and that you secretly go by the name of 'Night Elf' is it?"

My eyes narrowed. "You really want to be whipped that badly, huh?" I raised my eyebrow at her, but my mouth twitched in amusement.

"For God's sake whip me already. You've left me on my own for a week while you were swanning around at some conference in Edinburgh, and now you're home you want to talk? We've been talking all week on the telephone," she wailed, "just let loose with that flogger and fuck me before I go crazy."

"Crazy, mad, bad?" That was our code for the intense, dark stuff. I just wanted to make sure that we were on the same page.

"Crazy, mad, bad. Mark, I've been waiting all damn week for this. Don't leave me hanging." Her voice was all breathy and ragged, just how I liked it. Christ, this woman could turn me on with the sound of her voice. Some dominant I was.

"Sorry, darling. I've just got to go grab something. Be back in ten mins." I swirled the flogger up her inner thigh and watched as her leg trembled.

"Mark Matthews, you dare pull that stunt on me and I'll..."

I didn't hear the rest of her sentence because I'd already left the room and swung the door shut. I did catch the resulting scream, however. A smug grin settled on my features at the thought of letting her stew for a while. When would Jennifer learn that she did not wear the trousers in this relationship? It shouldn't be necessary for me to have to demonstrate the obvious nearly every damn day. Honestly, the woman was going to drive me nuts.

I left her hanging for twenty minutes. I knew she'd go berserk, and that was exactly how I wanted her. If there was one thing I particularly enjoyed, it was tormenting my wife, and there were numerous ways to go about it. This time I was going to be particularly evil, but not in the way you're expecting. Oh no, I had another agenda this evening, and though I'd put off talking about it for the past year or so, it was time to bring it up again.

Rifling through Jen's handbag downstairs it took me a while to locate what I was searching for. This was mainly because Jen carried her whole life around with her in that bag, and if she could have fitted the kitchen sink in there, I'm sure she would have. Scrap that, Jen would have gone for a dishwasher.

Inside I found makeup, perfume, a diary, a cell phone, car keys, mints, earrings, a travel coffee cup, a pair of sunglasses, a purse, a book, an iPad, a cereal bar, and I'd barely touched the surface. Everything was placed haphazardly, and there was no rhyme, reason, or order to anything that was in it. How did the woman live like this?

Sighing, I emptied the bag on the floor, and by a long process of elimination finally found what I was looking for. I smiled grimly to myself. I was about to create World War III but this was important to me, so I needed to get it off my chest.

When I re-entered the bedroom Jen was ready for me.

"Mark, you're a complete bastard. We've been apart for a week and I'm desperate. You know this because we've been having phone sex for the last five days, and you've refused to let me climax every single time. If I don't have sex soon I'm going to explode, and you made this monster. I just want you inside me. Don't make me wait." She was almost wailing in need, and the sight was nearly my undoing. It would have been so easy to have taken my pants off and slammed into her up against the wall, but I meant to make my point tonight, and if I ended up going to bed with blue balls, that was a risk I was prepared to take.

"How much do you want to bet I can't freak you out?" My voice was dangerously low.

"Are we back to that again? Couldn't you have just said that earlier?" Jen sounded exasperated, as well she might. "I'll bet whatever you want. Now get over here and finish what you started, darling, else I'll start screeching, screaming, and crying - all of which you seem to be allergic to these days."

She was right. Tears don't usually bother me, but for some reason Jen's do. I can still spank her to the point of tears and not suffer too much, but if I know I've upset her until she gets to the point she's sobbing her heart out, I'm a mess. It's annoying, but I guess that's what this being-in-love-thing is all about. Ugh. I'd been bitten by the bug. *Concentrate. Let's get back to the situation in hand.*

"If I successfully freak you out, you will accompany me to Escape." Jen's face immediately turned frosty, as I knew it would. She had nearly died after our last visit there when someone had tried to poison her. We knew her father was behind the episode, but we still didn't know why. Although I'd made it my life's mission to find out, at the moment I was still none the wiser despite my best efforts on the project.

"I will not." She bit the words out one by one, and her eyes shot daggers at me. I sighed.

"I need to go, as they're honouring me with an award of some sort, and the instructions stipulate that I need to bring a partner. Would you rather I go with someone else?"

"You wouldn't dare," she growled. She was right, I wouldn't. There would be tears and everything.

"Just this one time, sweetheart, and then I'll pull out as one of the partners and pass it along to someone else."

"Can't you just say 'no'?" It was a reasonable question. I could just say no, but it wasn't as simple as that.

"There are a lot of powerful people in my sphere of influence there, and some close friends. I can't insult them by not appearing. Anyway, I haven't freaked you out yet so there's still a chance you might not have to go."

"And do I get a bet in return?" Jen's eyes darkened as she used them to glare at me full force. I almost took a step back under their vicious pull but managed to get a hold of myself.

"Absolutely." It couldn't be this easy, could it? I held my breath and waited for what would come next. The glare suddenly disappeared from my wife's face, and a cunning little smile replaced it. Uh-oh.

"I get to dominate you for an evening. Just one evening, darling. Shouldn't be anything to worry about. You're a big boy, right?"

My jaw suddenly locked itself in place, and it was my turn to scowl. "You're not playing very fair, darling." I picked up the flogger again and began caressing its rubber tails.

"Neither are you." That was a fair comment. Now how did I wriggle myself out of this one, while still getting what I wanted? Decisions, decisions.

"OK, but I have a condition for your bet. You have to behave yourself impeccably for a week as my submissive, without putting a foot wrong, and then you can have your night. If that's acceptable, we have a deal." There was no way Jennifer would be able to behave herself for a whole week, so I would never have to worry about upholding my side of the bargain, thank God.

"Why does there have to be a condition?" Jen was obviously going for the hard sell here, but I was having none of it.

"You get a condition on mine, too. If you don't freak out at what I'm about to do next you don't have to go." I held my empty palms up on either side of my body, to indicate our deal was a good one.

"Will you be using pain to freak me out?" Jen's eyes narrowed as well they might. I was fond of dishing out pain, but as it happened I wouldn't need to touch her for what I was about to do next.

"Nope. I'll be doing that later though, and you're going to love it." I grinned wickedly and tickled her left breast with the end of my flogger, watching as she danced and wriggled underneath its teasing trails.

"Fine. We have a deal. You do your worst." She then looked at me expectantly and waited.

Slowly I pulled out the thing I had stolen from her handbag. Jen immediately rolled her eyes, but to her credit she didn't go berserk on me, which was what she'd done last year when I'd brought up the subject.

"Are we really going to go through this again?" She gave me a look that should have been accompanied by a great big sigh and her hands on her hips. She then sighed, as if to prove me right, but her hands weren't going anywhere at the moment. I smiled smugly.

"No, we aren't going through this again. This year I am going to be crazy, mad, bad and flush all of these beasties down the toilet. As today is Friday you'll either have to go without sex for at least three days or risk giving me what I want. Either way, it will be hugely entertaining." My smile was big and wide, and yes, I know I'm a complete bastard. I'm also not above resorting to dirty tricks to get what I want.

"You wouldn't." Her horrified look spoke volumes.

"I absolutely would." I waggled the packet of birth control pills at her one more time, to let her know I was serious, and then began popping them out, one by one, into my hand.

"Mark Matthews, I am far too young to have babies. We've only been together for just over a year, and we've only known each other for about eighteen months. It's too soon."

"I'm getting old. It's not too soon. Besides which, one hundred years ago women were probably on their third or fourth baby by your age." I nodded my head encouragingly. She hadn't freaked out yet. "It's far better to have them while you're young. The medical profession also agrees with me." I winked at her.

"Mark Matthews, we were born in the twentieth century, where life expectancy is much greater than it was one hundred years ago, and the medical profession might be right, but I'm not ready to have babies just yet. Can't we wait a year?" There was a wailing note behind Jen's voice, so I was heading in the right direction. My visit to Escape was in the bag.

"That's what you said last year."

"But I want to travel the world." Jen was rattling her fists quite animatedly against her cuffs now, as she made her point clear, but I was ready for her.

"You can still travel the world - with our children in tow." I slid my hand under her sex and let her feel the warm heat of my hand, as our argument got firmly underway. I was all for distracting her if that meant I would get what I wanted.

"We need some alone time together," she moaned.

"We'll still get alone time because I'll hire a nanny." My stance remained firm.

"It won't matter because neither of us will have any sleep. Babies keep you awake all night." Jen had obviously done some reading on the subject. No matter.

"Only for the first few months, and if you're awake *all* night, and I'm awake *all* night, just think how much fun that will be." I slipped my index finger inside her pussy and watched her squirm. I was so hard right now I could have punched holes in steel.

"That's not how it will work, dear husband, and you're not the one who has to give birth." Jen looked at me meaningfully. "Things might never be the same again after a baby has come through there." Her eyes were staring down at my hand, the one that was now pulsing back and forth.

"That's what surgeons are for. They'll make sure it's all in good order when you're finished, sweetheart. I'll give them an excellent bonus to guarantee the fact, don't you worry." I nodded encouragingly.

"Ugh. You cannot be serious!" She then clicked her fingers as she came up with yet another argument. "There will be competition for my boobs. Have you thought about that?" Jen really was going to pull out all the stops in this conversation. I sighed.

"We can share. I'll have one, and they can have one. That way everyone stays happy." I began rubbing her clit and smiled wickedly when she whimpered.

"What happens if I have twins?" She only just managed to get her sentence out without stuttering, so I was definitely on the right track.

"They'll just have to take turns, darling." We have a thing about queuing for stuff in England, so I didn't see why it should be a problem. Best to get used to the general order of things sooner rather than later.

"They'll cry, they'll be sick, and they'll poop all over the place."

"I don't see how that's an argument. That's your domain. I'll do bedtime stories and walks in the park."

"Oh no you won't. It's an equal opportunities thing if we're having babies. You get to change diapers, too."

"Done. Now can we stop arguing and get to the fun part?" Jen was whimpering now, and if I wasn't much mistaken she was already close to climaxing. How good was I?

"There is no way..."

I immediately stopped what I was doing, knowing she was close and waved the packet of birth pills in my right hand as I walked from the room.

"You get back here right this instant!" she screamed.

"Now going to flush these monsters down the toilet. I'll be back in two minutes."

"You dare!" she screeched. It was official, my wife was freaking out.

"I dare." There were all sorts of screaming and hysterics as I left the room, but I didn't let it concern me. She'd calm down eventually. An orgasm or ten might help mellow her out a bit. That's why I'd made sure she was tied up before I began the discussion. She'd see things my way before long. I was sure of it.

It took mere seconds to flush all the pills down the toilet, but I gave Jen five minutes to calm down, just to be safe. Thankfully she wouldn't be able to throw anything at me unless she got out of those cuffs, and I'd made damn sure she wouldn't when I fastened them.

When I re-entered the room. I held up the empty packet in victory and said, "You're coming with me to Escape. You freaked."

Her look was mutinous. "You cheated, and when you get me down from here I am going to sever both of your testicles in..." I thought it best to interrupt.

"Then I am *never* going to let you down. I'll leave you tied up forever and make love to you ten times a day, every day until you relent." I kept a straight face and wondered what she'd say to that. A few seconds went by while she continued to glare at me, and then I added, "Twenty times a day then. Starting from today. I am giving you twenty orgasms before I will allow you any sleep tonight. Does that sound like fun or not?" There was the slightest twitch to her mouth, and I knew I had her.

"Mr Matthews, if you think you're getting off the hook that easily you're much mistaken."

"I can tell you you're not getting off yours until I unbolt at least four padlocks,"

I said with a sly look. She shook her head and rolled her eyes, but she was grinning.

"You are not out of the woods yet. What am I going to do if I can't have sex with you for the next three days? Do we have condoms? Please tell me we have condoms."

"You're going to think about having babies - so many babies that we don't have enough rooms for them all." I was really pushing my luck here, but in for a penny and all that.

"You have at least ten bedrooms in this house!" she squawked, while her eyes tried to disengage themselves from their sockets.

"So?"

"You can't rush me on this, Mark. When I'm ready I'll let you know."

"In that case I'll let you know when I have some condoms handy."

She screamed, and then I got the whip out, and she screamed a lot more.

By the time I'd finished with her that evening she'd said an awful lot of naughty words, but the majority of them were while she was busy climaxing under my fingers. I was pretty confident she'd forgiven me, but I was going to uncuff her one hand at a time, just to make sure.

Chapter Three - Jennifer

When I woke up on Saturday morning Mark was still snoring softly beside me. Slowly stretching my limbs out under the covers, careful not to wake him, I smiled to myself. Today I had a challenge. Obey my husband to the letter for the next seven days, and I'd get a chance to be on top for a change. I wasn't going to remind him about that until this afternoon, though. This morning I was going to have a little fun with him.

Now don't think for a minute that I don't adore being underneath my very talented husband. I am a submissive at heart, and ninety-nine percent of the time I'm very happy for him to wear the trousers. The trouble is, every now and again I have an itch that needs to be scratched. After being helpless underneath my father for so long, I wouldn't mind being in control every now and again. Not to the extent of those vicious ladies who whipped him silly, though. The thought of tearing someone's back to ribbons horrifies me, and if I ever lay eyes on that woman, Sophia, I'm going to give her a piece of my mind. Mark might have asked for it, but she should have known better. My husband was crippled with guilt. If he was already on his knees I see no reason why she had to grind him into the dust.

Frowning at the thought I slipped out of bed quietly. At least she hadn't killed him. I had my own mother to thank for that near miss. It had taken a good six months for me to forgive her for that, and even now we were still on shaky ground. We'd danced around each other carefully the few times we'd met up, and she gave Mark unpleasant glares whenever she thought he was ordering me around. This made him very nervous, so it was almost worth patching things up with her. But there was no chance of that just yet. I didn't understand her world, and I didn't want to. Until I had a reason to do so I would remain polite but distant. Hopefully we would have no more near-death experiences that way.

Approaching the Velvet Room, which had now become my walk-in-wardrobe, I wondered what I should wear to please my husband this morning. Mark had showered me with more clothes than Kim Kardashian, although most of them couldn't be worn in public. Seriously, I had more lingerie than the local Victoria Secrets store, and I'm not joking. Every time Mark went away he would always come back bearing gifts, and unfortunately the man went away lots. Often it was only for a day or two, so I can't really complain, but in the first year of your relationship all you really want to do is to spend time with each other. This week had been particularly hard, but thankfully he was working from home for the next few days, and I had him all to myself - hurrah!

Searching through my closet I flicked through coat hangers filled with Versace, Guerlain, Dolce and Gabbana, Alexander McQueen, Anna Sui and more. This morning nothing took my fancy. Hmm. How about just stockings and a basque? I was pretty sure it would grab his attention. Picking up a black La Perla basque that revealed more than it covered with all its mesh cut-outs, I then trailed lace-topped stockings up my legs before encasing my feet in four-inch stilettos. I'd had a year to get used to walking in these ridiculous shoes, and I was now getting rather good at it. All it took was a bit of practice. Attaching the matching suspender belt carefully, I surveyed myself in the mirror and nodded. Two could play at the birth control game. If he wanted to leave me unable to have sex all weekend long I didn't see why he shouldn't suffer at the same time.

Then I sat at my desk and carefully applied some makeup; nothing too bright, just a little peach colour for my cheeks and a pink tint for my lips. I was going for the barely-there look. After that all I had to do was pin my hair on top of my head, and I was ready to cook. If I could cook - which I can't.

Anyway, I went downstairs to the ginormous kitchen at Fountaine Bleu and wondered what sort of fare I could serve up for breakfast that wouldn't involve me setting off any smoke alarms. This was a dilemma, but it wasn't an insurmountable problem. I could do this. I could be a *Stepford Wife* and shock the hell out of my husband at the same time.

Opening the fridge door I stared at the contents inside it for a good minute or two, before admitting defeat. What the hell did I do with any of these ingredients? Closing the door and leaning my back against it I took a deep breath and tried to figure out another way to solve the problem. A bowl of cereal, perhaps? I could pour milk into a bowl, and I'm sure there were some cornflakes around here somewhere. Looking around the kitchen, which featured at least fifty cupboards, I nearly panicked, but then gave myself a stern talking to. When all else failed it was time to turn to Google.

Half an hour later I had made my very first omelette. Although I had no clue how to work an oven there was a whole section on microwave meals, and I knew how to operate one of those. Whenever my coffee goes cold I usually give it a thirty-second burst in there, so we were old friends. Turns out you can crack a few eggs into a bowl, add some cheese, mushrooms and bacon, whip it all together and pop it in the microwave for two minutes. Voila. You have yourself an omelette. Pop a little salt and pepper over that beauty, and you're good to go.

I'd just managed to grab a knife and fork and pop it on a plate when Mark's head appeared around the door. He'd just wrapped a robe around himself, and he looked edible. This was what I wanted for breakfast. Food was wholly overrated.

"Morning, darling." He rubbed his eyes sleepily, and then when he'd fully taken stock of the situation, said, "Holy fuck." The man then advanced towards me as if I was breakfast, and I wasn't having any of that. No way. If he wanted to fight dirty I was slinging the first round of mud.

"No, no, no, darling. Sit." I indicated the chair before him and pointed down towards my creation. Hopefully it was edible. I hadn't tested the theory.

He looked back at me, crestfallen, and then spotted the plate in front of him. "Holy fuck." He sat down heavily on the leather chair and blinked some more, but this time at the plate.

"You just said that." I nudged the knife and fork towards him, as if in encouragement.

"I know, and I'm not quite sure what has impressed me more." I gave him a dry look and then turned around and wiggled my naked ass in his direction.

"Why don't you think about it for a bit?" I suggested sweetly.

"I already have. I think we should just go straight back upstairs to bed." Mark's hand reached out to touch my ass, but I slapped it away.

"Eat your omelette. It's my first, and I made it especially for you."

"It actually looks edible." Mark looked at me with worried eyes but reached for his knife and fork. He gingerly lifted the underside of my creation and after inspecting it back and forth, turned towards me. "It isn't burnt." The complete shock and awe in his expression should have been insulting, but I knew first hand how bad my cooking skills were.

"No. It isn't. Eat up," I encouraged him.

"You aren't trying to poison me, are you?" My affronted look told him all he needed to know on that score. No one was poisoning anyone around these parts ever again. "Okay, okay, I'm sorry." He cut off a tiny sliver and popped it in his mouth. He then smiled. "This is actually not bad."

Charming. The man knew how to impress a woman. I tapped my foot against the floor as if reminding him I was still in the room.

"Sorry, darling. Thank you for going to all this trouble. I'm really impressed. It's a very lovely, albeit somewhat crunchy omelette." When I gave him a dark look he backtracked. "Very edible, though. Yum, yum, yum." To emphasise his point he began digging into his meal with gusto.

"Excellent. I knew you'd see it my way," I said, before proceeding to drop to my knees and shuffle towards him. There was plenty of room for me to dive under the dining room table, and as he was still in his robe I made short work of unfastening the tie.

"May I have my breakfast, Sir?" I purred, as his cock rose eagerly to greet me.

Mark coughed. "It isn't my birthday, is it? I'm pretty sure it isn't, but I just need to check."

I ran my tongue up the length of his cock, greedily, and a utensil clattered heavily against his plate.

"No, darling. It's not your birthday."

"In that case, have I been secretly transported to a parallel dimension or kidnapped by aliens?"

"Very funny. Do you want to chat or have me suck your cock?" Honestly, there was no pleasing some people.

"I suddenly don't have anything to talk about," he said, and then went very quiet.

Rolling my eyes from my hiding place under the table, I put the tip of his cock in my mouth and swirled my tongue around it. He tasted divine.

"I know you're rolling your eyes under there, which is another fifty spanks, Jennifer." My mouth opened in wry amusement as he shifted his legs wider apart to let me get closer to him.

"Do you want me to stop?" I said impishly, pulling away from him.

"Fuck no. I take that back. In fact, I'll remove five hundred spanks from your tally if you do a tolerable job."

Tolerable? Hmph. "Don't push your luck, darling. I accept the offer though." My mouth went back to what it was doing. Five hundred spanks off my tally of over twenty thousand wasn't really going to reduce it by anything meaningful, but I'd take what I could get.

Spending the next twenty minutes tormenting my husband was extremely enjoyable. At the start the poor man tried to continue eating his breakfast, but I was having none of that. After a minute or two of deep throating he promptly choked on his last mouthful, and I heard him lay down his cutlery in defeat. If I had been able to I would have crowed in delight. While life at Albrecht might have been monstrous, there were certain skills I'd learnt there that were invaluable. Wrapping my husband around my little finger with a few carefully placed strokes of my mouth was one of them. When he began making little noises of pleasure I knew I was nearly there. Now, it was my turn to be evil.

Stopping just before he reached the point of no return I let him go with a loud, sucking pop, and crawled out from under the other side of the table. Using a finger to tidy up the stray lines of saliva from around my mouth, I gave him a wink.

"Darling, I'd love to finish what I've started, but as you've tipped all of my birth control pills down the toilet I think we'd better play it safe for the next two days. A baby isn't just for Christmas darling. It's for life, and you need to do some research on the subject. When I'm happy that you're adequately aware of what you're going to take on, then we'll talk again. Until then, I've highlighted some prenatal classes you might want to attend and popped you an email with some reading resources. Enjoy the rest of your breakfast, darling."

Mark was already standing up as I flew from the room. There was a wickedly evil glint in his eye, which told me that if he caught me I was going to pay heavily for my sins. I figured I had a fifty/fifty chance of outrunning him and making it to a lockable bathroom, but now he was back to full fitness it would be a lot harder than it had been previously. Someone needed to stab him again - and no, I was not serious. I didn't want to go through anything like that ever again. It was a very dark time in our lives, and I'm quite frankly amazed that we both managed to come out the other side mostly unscathed.

Running up the stairs two at a time, as if my feet had rocket boosters attached to them, I managed to get to the top before Mark. He was only three-quarters of the way up, and I stood a fighting chance of making it to the bathroom. It was near the end of the corridor, so concentrating on pelting my way along the bleached wood floorboards I set my sights on the door handle. I had no idea what I would do when I'd locked myself inside there, and I'd have to come out eventually, but I'd think about that later. For now, I just wanted a little taste of victory.

Just as the handle came into view and I thought I'd nailed it there was an almighty roar behind me, and my world tilted sideways for a moment before I landed on top of my husband with a rather hard *thud*. It took my breath away for a minute, but when I'd recovered I did my best to pull away and continue my journey, only to discover that the man had hold of my wrist in a deadlock. Before he got a chance to say anything I said, "You started this." Rolling over to face him I scowled. "If you hadn't thrown my pills down the drain we could be happily bouncing up and down on each other right now."

Mark sighed. "I thought you were supposed to be behaving yourself in order to win your bet?"

"That hasn't started yet. I'm allowed a little revenge time after last night." I pouted.

"Says who?" He raised his infamous eyebrow, but a year under Mark's roof had taught me how to argue if nothing else.

"Says me. My bet doesn't start until this evening, else I'm not going to Escape with you. If you can cheat, I can cheat."

"Hmmm. So you want to play dirty, Mrs Matthews?"

There was a familiar twinkle in my husband's eye, and I knew I was going to regret this, but I said it anyway.

"Yes. I want to play dirty."

"Fine. You get a thirty-second head start to reach safety, but if I catch you, Mrs Matthews, you are going to be tied up and gagged for the rest of the day."

"Make it a minute, and we have a deal." I smiled with unconcealed glee. That would give me enough time to get a book and a glass before I imprisoned myself in the bathroom. Result.

"I think thirty seconds is more than enough time." Mark gave me one of his condescending looks, but I was having none of it.

"Take it or leave it, darling. I really don't want to go to Escape, so it's not a problem."

"You drive a hard bargain, Mrs Matthews." He eyed me up and down, as if loathe to let me go, but he finally released my wrists. "Fine. You get a minute and not one more second. Time starts now."

"Ooh, you..." I didn't bother finishing the rest of my sentence because I was already fighting to get on my feet and run as fast as I could to get away from the bastard. He was not catching me this side of seven pm. The bet was on.

Chapter Four - Mark

My bloody wife was a pain in the ass. Now I know that thousands of men have probably said the same words before me, and it's a bit clichéd, but believe me, my wife was more trouble than most. The woman always wanted her own way, she never did as she was told, and she went out of her way to infuriate me on a regular basis. I was going to need a flipping manual to keep this one in check, and considering I'd been spanking women for years and years, you'd have thought I'd have nailed this discipline thing down by now. The trouble was, I couldn't upset her. I swear I felt as bad as she did if I reduced her to tears with anything other than pain. It probably just needed an adjustment period while I coped with this living together under one roof thing. I was positive I'd figure it out - eventually.

Giving Jen far more than the sixty seconds she deserved, I listened as she sprinted towards our bedroom, probably to grab her smutty book by the bedside table and a glass of water. Then, as I suspected, she made a dash for the bathroom. This was a sensible bet, as there was a lock on the door. It wasn't going to save her from me, however, which was why I was in no rush to follow. It wouldn't do her any harm to have a bit of "me" time, anyway. I was shortly going to be pushing her body to the limit, so Jen might as well get comfortable for the time being.

Heading into our bedroom, I grabbed a change of clothes and then got into the shower. After that I went downstairs, marvelling that nearly all the stiffness in my leg had finally disappeared. It had taken a while to recover from last year's stabbing, but my darling wife and several microwaved meals had just about seen me through the dark days. But it annoyed me that Khalil was no closer to finding Redcliff's whereabouts. Wherever that man was hiding it was very far away, and I hoped to hell he stayed there. If I ever set eyes on him again, I wouldn't be responsible for my actions. There was no punishment in the world severe enough to deal with that vile bastard. Well, none that I could think of, anyway.

Heading outside, my thoughts returned to the matter at hand. Now, what would I need to get Jennifer out of that damn bathroom? Strangely, I had Leyland to thank for the answer to my little problem. He'd recounted his story of how he'd "interrogated" Marianna, over a couple of glasses of whisky, and the man had kept me royally entertained for just over an hour. Leyland also said he should have charged me for the episode, which sent me into a fit of hysterics, and I nearly laughed so hard I cried. Of course, I told him I'd given him his Christmas present for this year and that he shouldn't expect another anytime soon. Leyland took it well, considering. I nearly went ballistic when he told me he let Marianna go with barely a scratch to her name, but that was before I'd heard the whole sorry tale. Now I knew why she'd done my father's bidding I felt absurdly guilty. Was I that much of a monster she hadn't dared approach me? The answer to that question was indeed that I was, and I deserved to feel guilty. I told Leyland I'd take care of

Marianna and her little girl, but he informed me that he'd already paid all of their medical bills and that my assistance wouldn't be required. It was my turn to laugh again. Surely the pharmaceutical giant and general oddball, Leyland Forbes, hadn't gone and fallen for someone? By the furious look he gave me it was rather obvious he had. Considering my own sticky situation as of late, I decided I wouldn't rub it in. Much.

Anyway, to cut a long story short, he'd told me about how he'd got Marianna out of the bathroom with minimal effort on his part, and I'd stored that little detail away for future use. I hadn't expected to be using it quite so soon, but this would certainly put my wife in her place. It's time she knew there was no place on earth she could hide where I wouldn't find her eventually. Yes, I absolutely adore her - in case you were wondering - and haven't turned into a rogue stalker. At least, I don't think I have.

Grabbing a screwdriver, and a magnetic wristband so I could keep the screws safe until I wanted to put the lock back on later, I returned to the house, ready to wage war on my abominably behaved submissive wife. It was high time to show her who called the shots around here. Now I just had to plot some deplorable kind of torment, to make sure she behaved herself impeccably around me in future. It had never worked before, but there was always a first time, right?

"I know you're out there."

She might, but she didn't know what I was doing because I was being exceptionally careful to be as quiet as I could. Sitting still for a second, until she decided her ears were playing tricks on her, the screwdriver was back in action, tackling the third of four screws. My objective had nearly been accomplished, and I was feeling rather pleased with myself. If only everything in life was so easy.

When the final screw came out I wriggled the lock casing about with as much force as I could muster and tore it out of the doorframe. It was probably overkill, but it did the trick and my wife's shocked expression, as she sat in the bath reading her book, was priceless. Her face crumpled like a deflated balloon.

"How did you...?"

"No time for questions. Get your ass out of that bath and into the naughty room before I really lose my temper." My stern expression was in place, so she'd know I meant business.

She bit her lip, gave a little worried sigh, and grabbed a bath towel.

"No time for that," I said as I yanked the towel away, pushed her forward and spanked her ass. "Get moving."

She didn't need to be told twice.

Less than half an hour later Jennifer Matthews knew she was in trouble. She was in the bare concrete hole that I now referred to as the "naughty room", and I'd tied her ankles and wrists to the whipping post. Then I found a ball gag harness, featuring three straps that came across the face in a triangle shape, and I buckled it tightly behind her head. There was a point to be made today, and I intended to make it in style.

16

"Darling, I have a feeling I've been far too lax with you lately, and if you're accompanying me to Escape we need a refresher on what type of behaviour is acceptable."

The look she gave me was pure venom, as to be expected, but that turned me on, and she knew it. Wriggling about in her restraints also made my cock jump to attention, and I'd have to unfasten my jeans soon if she didn't stop bouncing around.

Gripping her chin tightly, to focus her attention, I stared straight through her with my darkest expression; one that would generally put the fear of God into any submissive. Any submissive bar Jennifer, that was.

"Your punishment, for the deplorable behaviour I witnessed earlier, is to be my pet for the next two days. That will mean lots of crawling, no talking, and you get to sleep on the floor." Letting that sink in, I wondered how she would take the news. Hopefully she wouldn't cry. If she cried I'd back down. *Don't cry, don't cry.* This would probably remind her of Albrecht, and I should have considered that before I made my threat. The trouble was she made me so mad I couldn't think straight sometimes. Honestly, what kind of Dom could deal with the trials and tribulations of marriage? Taking a deep breath I then said, "Do you understand?" I also crossed my fingers behind my back.

There was a distinct pause before her eyes closed and I braced myself for the worst. The fall out from this was probably going to haunt me for a week or two, so I prepared myself. Then the strangest thing happened. She dipped her eyes towards the floor and nodded. What the fuck!? Was she agreeing to this?

"Look at me." I needed to see the expression in her eyes. If she was upset I'd get her out of the restraints, take her into the bedroom and smother her with love and affection until I made her see sense. Hopefully she wouldn't be able to dismember any vital body parts before I got a chance to apologise.

When her head began moving slowly upwards, I searched around desperately for any indication that she was upset. So far there were no tears, no hiccups, and no snorts or sniffs, so I figured she would probably be angry with me. As her eyes finally connected with mine, though, they told me something different entirely. Her irises glowed with fire, and not the I'm-going-to-thump-you-kind. Jen was aroused at the thought of being my pet, and quite considerably so. I could smell the scent of her sex from where I was standing, so I knew she was wet, and when she drew a ragged breath slowly into her mouth, I realised that my earlier assumption had been incorrect. Women were truly odd creatures.

"Do you understand and accept your punishment?" As I still hadn't managed to get a response I asked the question again. She nodded demurely, with her eyes trained on the floor once more. She'd gone from panther to pussycat in less than sixty seconds, and the transformation was quite incredible. I wondered how long this could last. "Good. Just so we're clear if you want to dominate me as per our discussion last night, your time starts now. You will be a model submissive obeying my every command for the next seven days, or you will lose your bet. Do you accept those terms?" She wasn't getting other terms so she had two choices.

Unbelievably, she nodded again. Well, well, well. The challenge was on. I had seven days in which to make my errant wife misbehave. This was going to be the easiest bet I'd ever won. Nearly rubbing my hands together in glee at the thought of what I could do with her, my mind exploded with naughty possibilities. There was no question that Jen would wave the white flag at some point during the next few days, but I thought it might be nice to have a little fun with her for the time being. The thought of a meek-mannered pussycat crawling around the room servicing my every whim made me almost uncomfortably hot, and the peace and quiet of having her gagged was an added bonus. If I kept her tied up most of the time I'd barely even have to keep tabs on her. Oh, happy days.

"Okay then, my little kittykat, you have yourself a deal." One she was obviously going to lose because there was no way in hell I was letting my wife dominate me. That wasn't my problem though.

"So, before I find you a cute little outfit and get you kitted out, I definitely think some stripes are in order for your earlier display of disobedience. Strolling to the wall where I now hung all of my impact play toys, I let my fingertips linger on each one for a few seconds as I carefully considered what to do with my captive.

"Hmm, shall we start with the paddle?" I mused out loud. "No, that would be far too tame. I think we'll need something you'll remember for the next few days." My fingers moved to the next toy. "Perhaps the crop, as its sting is a little sharper." Although it sounded like a question, it wasn't. All I was doing was working my little submissive up to the point where she'd be creaming her panties off - if she were wearing any. At the moment Jen's eyes were glued to the wall, and I could see the rise and fall of her delectable breasts as she tried to control her mounting excitement. It was no secret that my wife liked a little pain. Although I'd taken it easy on her since the poisoning incident, I figured we'd waited long enough. It was about time to take it to the next level and see if she'd sink or swim.

"Actually, no, I think the crop is a little too tame for my liking this afternoon. How about we try something a little more challenging?" My voice was soft, but she heard me as my fingers continued to move along the line until I reached a leather, single-tailed whip. "Ah yes, a whip. There is nothing quite like the sting of being whipped properly, don't you agree, kittykat?"

Jen was almost hyperventilating with excitement now, and her eyes were glued on the whip that I was now freeing from the wall. I'd wondered for weeks if she'd be ready for this type of pain, but it was obvious she was. It appeared I'd been tiptoeing around my wife for far too long. I should have done this months ago.

When I got the whip down from the wall I walked behind her, trailing my fingertips across the top of her right shoulder blade. Her head followed me, watching, waiting, and listening for the first stroke. Frowning, I walked out of the room. She was not going to be keeping her beady eyes on my every movement. I wanted her unaware of where the next stroke was coming from, or what I was about to do next. Jen was going to anticipate each stroke, and she would need to rely on her other senses to make up for her lack of eyesight.

Grabbing a two-inch leather collar from my toy box, featuring a large stainless steel D-ring, I smiled wickedly to myself. Now all I would need was some black rope. Perfect.

When I walked back into the room Jen's head swivelled around to glare at me. My wife was an impatient little thing, but she'd just have to learn that I had my own timescale for our scenes. There was no rushing me.

Smiling at her and waving the new additions I'd brought in the air, her eyes zeroed in on them, looking this way and that as she tried to figure out what I was about to do. Putting her out of misery I came to stand in front of her, holding the collar up at eye-level.

"This is so you don't keep waving your head about everywhere, darling." Squeezing her cheek affectionately and ignoring the frosty look that was directed my way, I fastened it quickly behind her neck. I then held up the rope. "And this is so you can't look behind you."

Her look turned to one of confusion, but she'd understand soon enough. Attaching one end of the rope to the D-ring, and the other to an eye bolt in the floor in front of her, with just enough tension to keep her in place, I was satisfied that she was going nowhere fast. Her eyes were now trained upon the floor, and that was where they would stay unless I chose otherwise.

"Ready for my whip, darling?" A finger underneath her chin forced her to look at me, and though there was some of the fire I was expecting, there was a whole lot of heat too. Giving me a single nod of her head and a bucket load of sparks with her eyes, she assured me the challenge was on, and I could do my worst.

Nearly rubbing my hands together in glee, I happily obliged.

Chapter Five - Jennifer

Watching my whip-wielding husband as he began to lay down the law nearly made me climax then and there. I probably shouldn't admit this, but being gagged and torn down a strip turns me on in the worst way, and when he began to lay out the details of my punishment - well, let's just say my adrenaline levels went through the roof.

Since the poisoning incident Mark had been very careful around me, and while he'd delivered the odd spanking and flogging here and there, he'd also wrapped me in cotton wool. I've wanted to bring up the subject that I'm not breakable several times in the last few months, but I'm also aware he's still recovering from his stab wound, and I didn't want to rush him. It was a serious injury, and it took its toll for a while. In the last few weeks he seemed as if he was almost back to his old self, and I was hoping I'd get to see some heat soon. But it's kind of difficult to broach the fact that you want your husband to be evil every now and again. How did you bring that up in conversation? Thankfully it looked like I wouldn't have to. The expression on his face right now told me that I had a long afternoon ahead of me, and at the end of it my ass was destined to be bright red. I can't begin to describe the kind of exhilaration currently bubbling its way through my body, but it was incredibly intense. Even better was the knowledge that my husband felt certain I would lose our bet. While I loved the man to bits he was a smug, arrogant, and conceited bastard at times. If I had to go with him to Escape I was getting my end of the bargain. He would be mine for at least an evening, and boy, was I going to have some fun with him. The next seven days were probably going to test me to the limit, but I was ready for it. Bring it on, sweetheart.

After he'd collared me and I was pretty much forced to look at the floor unless I wanted to choke myself, he disappeared from view. It didn't take a genius to guess where he went. The man wanted me on my toes, unaware of where the next stroke would come from, and tension sprang into my arms and legs at the thought. A single-tailed whip wasn't a paddle, and it certainly wasn't a soft suede flogger. It was a mean and nasty beast, there were no two ways about it. The question was: could I handle it?

Breathing became difficult for a moment as I was whisked away to Albrecht stables and the vile presence of Kyle Levison. He'd threatened to take a bullwhip to me. Making an involuntary keening noise through my mouth I had a wobble.

Mark was standing in front of me in a heartbeat. "Jen, are you okay? Three nods of your head is your safe word. Remember? Do you need to nod?"

He looked very concerned, and I wanted to hug him for being so sweet. *Snap out of it, Jen, and focus.* Shaking my head slowly from side to side I took a few slow breaths and tried to remember where I was and who I was with. Albrecht was behind me now. I was safe here, and Mark wouldn't give me any more than I could handle.

"Are you thinking about Kyle?" Mark's face was dark. He knew me too well. I nodded in response and his gaze darkened further. "If I ever get my hands on that animal he won't be good for anything other than dog food by the time I've finished with him." Mark had his own demons to slay, as well as mine, with regards to that evil bastard. My father and Kyle had tried to kill him not so long ago, and when that hadn't worked they'd tried to kill him again with my help. I had a fantastic family, me.

"This whip is not a bullwhip. It's not long enough, for a start. It'll sting a little, but the leather is quite supple. It won't break the skin. It's going to hurt, and it might leave a few marks, but nothing permanent. Do you think you're up for this?"

I nodded. I knew that. What a time to have a wobble, huh? I'd entirely spoilt the moment, and I didn't know what to do about it.

"Do you trust me?" I nodded again. I would trust my husband with my life these days. We'd come a long way since Albrecht.

"Good. Remember your safe signal. I'll check in with you frequently, okay?" I would have smiled at that had I been able to, but I had to settle for yet another nod. Mark leant in towards me and kissed the top of my head. He lingered for a while, stroking the hair at the nape of my neck, before he reluctantly released me. "Let's do this, kittykat. We'll deal with our other monsters another day. They'll still be there tomorrow."

His hand then reached towards the inverted V of my legs, and his fingers slowly slid along my sex. They jump-started my libido pretty quickly, and bucking forward against the rope that held me, I moaned.

"That's better. You had me worried for a minute." He made come here signals with his fingers over my clit, and it felt amazing. Then he slid them between my labia and squeezed, making me gasp. He did it over and over until my legs began to shake. When I thought I could take no more he slid a finger inside me. Just a lazy, slow pulse, but he repeated it while his mouth was feasting upon my neck. It was as if I had gone from reality into a dream world. Mark could play my body so effortlessly. It responded to him like a flower to sunlight. Whenever he was near my petals would open for him, and I could deny him nothing - nothing. I'd even been prepared to kill myself for him. If that wasn't love I didn't know what was. When one finger became two, and two became three, I began sobbing into my gag. This man had turned me into a sex addict with a simple click of his fingers. Just the smooth timbre of his voice sent waves of pleasure through me, and he was using it to whisper sweet nothings in my ear, while his tongue lapped and licked at the delicate line of my collarbone. If Mark had asked me now if I wanted to have unprotected sex I would have said yes, so it was just as well I was gagged. My husband had completely corrupted me but in all the right ways. I was truly blessed to have found him.

"Are you ready to be whipped?" Mark's free hand came up to tweak a nipple, and I felt my eyes rolling about in my head. I desperately needed to come. Wriggling against my bonds, as if hoping that somehow they'd take pity on me and let me get closer to his fingers, I moaned again.

"Fuck. Seeing you tied up like this and utterly at my mercy turns me on in the worst way, Jen. I could look at you for hours. You have no idea how beautiful you are, young lady. What on earth did I do to deserve you?" He tugged at my hair as his lips sought my neck, but no matter how close he got to me it wasn't close enough. I wanted more. I always wanted more.

Releasing my hair he sighed, and slowly removed his fingers. I protested vehemently, but all he did was smile and tap my nose with his fingertip.

"Remember that these next two days are all about punishment, kittykat. They are not about your pleasure. If you please me I might take pity on you, but that is by no means assured. So you'd better make sure you're on your best behaviour."

He gave me one of his stern looks, that was supposed to send the fear of God into me, but these days it just turned me on all the more. Dear God, what was wrong with me?

"So, do you think you're ready for the whip? Or should I tease you a little bit more? Considering this is going to smart I think you should be primed for it. What say we go a round or two with the magic wand?"

Oh God, anything but that. I shook my head, not that it mattered. My husband was already off, searching for new instruments of torture, and there was nothing I could do but wait there, my poor clit pulsing with need as he planned new and utterly diabolical things to do to me.

When Mark finally did come back it felt like he'd been gone for hours, although logic said it could only have been a few minutes. Brandishing a rabbit vibrator in one hand and a magic wand in the other he looked extremely pleased with himself, as well he might. The asshole was going to make my life miserable over the next seven days, there was no question about that, but I'd have my fun. I just needed to breathe and accept my punishment like the good little submissive I was. Ahem.

"I found some wooden clothes pegs, kittykat. Don't they look lovely?" He opened his hand in front of my nose to display several of the mean and nasty looking things, and I let out a whimper.

Grabbing hold of my left nipple he rubbed it gently in his fingertips, teasing it softly to life. It was a dirty trick. In a moment the poor little nub wouldn't know what had hit it, but right now it worshipped each sweet touch that was bestowed upon it, standing proudly to attention as it begged for more.

"I love how responsive you are, kittykat. Your body blooms under my fingers, and I love watching you come to life as I play all of those sweet and extremely tempting buttons of yours."

So would I, if I thought there was any chance of getting an orgasm. Mewling as Mark gripped the first clothes peg and tested its jaws, I waited for the inevitable.

Bending his face over my nipple, Mark took the little bud between his teeth and bit down upon it, just a tender nip, but it was all I could do not to thrust my chest in his face. I was so aroused I would have jumped in bed with the devil. What was he doing to me?

"Hold your breath, kittykat. It's coming." Sure enough, two seconds later the mean bite of the peg came down upon my sensitive little teat and I mewled again in protest.

"I love those sounds you're making. In the next two days I want to hear lots of them, pet. As you won't be able to talk to me you'll have to figure out a way to communicate without words, but I have no doubt you'll come up with something, won't you?" His mouth was now bent down over my right nipple so thankfully he didn't see my scowl, but it quickly turned into a heated moan of pleasure as his tongue laved at my increasingly aroused flesh. He then pulled away, there was another sharp bite, and my body protested once more as the pain took hold.

"There, there." He cupped both breasts affectionately and placed a kiss on each, before letting go of me reluctantly. It wasn't for long. It took him only a few seconds to grab a vibrator, and then he was back to create as much mischief and mayhem as he could.

The man played with my pussy for hours, using every trick in the book. The rabbit came first, and he pressed it over all of my hotspots, which included my labia, my clit, and the tight little hole at my rear. Then he began pulsing it against me and inside me, shallow, tiny thrusts that did little except drive me insane with need. My hips were bucking up and down in torment, but he took no pity on them. When he'd exhausted the batteries of one toy he simply broke out the next, and when I saw the wand I wanted to cry. He knew it too.

"Three nods for your safe signal, Jen. Want to call it a day?"

Mark felt sure he had me because he stared at me for the longest time. He should know by now that I was made of sterner stuff. I would make it through my seven days, somehow, and if I passed out through exhaustion within that time I'd never let him forget it. Hah! Giving him a steely look I waited for round two to commence.

"Suit yourself," he said, clearly amused.

The wand was plugged in and switched on. The sound of the vibrations were audible in the concrete room, and my body shuddered in anticipation. He tapped it against his palm as his eyes roved all over my body. I'm pretty sure I melted into a puddle on the floor because my limbs suddenly felt boneless.

"Hmm. Where shall I begin?" There was no disguising the wicked glint in his eye, and I knew I was about to suffer far more in the next few minutes than I would when he began whipping me. Pleasure, or its denial, can be far more cruel than pain. Take my word for it.

Over the course of the next forty minutes or so, I won't tell you the number of times I desperately wished I could close my legs. Being strung up and splayed out is a fantastic way to turn a girl on, but you can have too much of a good thing. The wand had been pressed against every available inch of my flesh, sometimes in a long and sensuous dance, and other times as a mere whisper of sensation. Mark's aim, at a guess, was to make all my nerve endings stand on end for what was to come next. He didn't stop there, though. The wand dipped between my legs and with a generous helping of lubricant, slipped backwards and forwards in a heavenly dance. Keeping the vibrations on low, to begin with, he drove the wand in endless circles until I wanted to scream at him to stop. When he turned the vibrations up and concentrated his efforts in one place I wanted to scream exactly the opposite. I already knew I wasn't getting what I wanted, but that didn't stop a girl from a hoping, pleading and inwardly begging for a miracle.

The one really annoying thing about my husband was that he could read me so effortlessly. As soon as I approached anything close to an orgasm he'd turn the wand off and grin at me. How did he do that? How did he know? Was there some kind of secret tell I was giving him? It drove me insane.

After he'd played this prank on me five times I was utterly exhausted, and he knew it. I was hanging limply from my bonds, sweat pouring down my body, and I was trembling uncontrollably. If he wanted to whip me he'd better hurry up and get on with it because I was either going to pass out or fall asleep on him. I wasn't quite sure which.

Thankfully Mark had decided the same thing, as he chose that moment to disappear on one of his mysterious trips. If he was getting more toys I swear to God I was going to castrate him when I got my chance to tie him up. Let's see how he liked being on the other side of the fence for a change.

When he came back there was a carton of juice in his hands and a cereal bar. Unbuckling my gag he held a finger up to remind me there was to be no talking.

"Just a quick refuel stop, kittykat." He patted my head affectionately, and somehow I managed to stop myself rolling my eyes. I needed to remember that I was on my best behaviour for the next seven days if I wanted my prize, and I am never one to back down from a challenge. Right now it would be a good idea to

23

get into character and start purring. That would, at the very least, shock the hell out of him.

Downing the juice greedily, Mark then fed me bite-sized chunks of my snack. Licking his fingers, as well as my treat, I watched as he began to tease me by bringing morsels of food up to my lips, only to whisk them away again. Have I mentioned that my husband can be very trying on occasion? Maybe he was hoping for a reaction. Well, I'd give him one, but not the one he was expecting.

"Meow," I wailed noisily, watching the food dance away from me and looking pleadingly up at my tormentor, which was extremely hard to do with the awful collar around my neck.

"Huh." Mark looked shocked for a moment, and I resisted the urge to smile. If I had it would have been a great big smug one. "You can follow instructions," he said, almost incredulously. Looking at me suspiciously, he went on, "You're not actually looking forward to your punishment are you?" His eyes narrowed in on me, and watched me very carefully. "If you are it will obviously need to be changed."

No way. I could cope with being a pussycat, so I shook my head vigorously and began mewling for my next bite. If he changed it the odds were that it would be something far worse, so I decided to hedge my bets.

"Hmm." He popped the last bite into my mouth and then tapped his top lip with his fingertip as if considering what to do to me. I chewed slowly, a little apprehensive that everything was going to go south much faster than I would have liked.

"Nah. We'll stick with the kittykat punishment for now. I have a few things up my sleeve that I suspect you'll really enjoy." I suspected anything but. Still, better the devil you know, I guess.

"Right, we've messed about long enough. Break time's over. Let's get on with the show."

Chapter Six - Jennifer

My husband liked to work to music. When Mozart's Serenade No.13 began blasting from the stereo I knew I was in for some fun. At least the track was upbeat. I didn't have to worry that things were going to get too intense - yet.

When Mark came back into the room he was already unbuttoning his shirt, and that gave me every indication that this was going to be a long scene and that I should prepare myself accordingly. My gag was then reintroduced, and I closed my eyes as I tried to become the obedient submissive woman he craved. The one I needed to be for the next week in order to have my revenge. Surely it was a small price to pay for having my husband, the billionaire Mark Matthews, slathering at my feet? There was also a part of me that wanted to see what Sophia had taken from him. I was a little jealous of her power over him, and I wanted to be the one to wield that power. If he ever needed to purge himself again I wanted to be the one he would go to. I would not tolerate Sophia coming between us. Although I think I am openminded enough to be able to share my husband, if a scene required it, I wasn't prepared to share him with her. They had too much history, and she was a threat to my happiness. I'd make sure he knew it, too.

My thoughts were disrupted when the tail of the whip began to slide over my shoulders and snake down towards my stomach. Drawing in a shaky breath, I blew it out slowly through my nose and let the music carry me away. Bold and beautiful, joyful and playful, the notes blended perfectly with each artful line the whip made across my body. At first it was soft and slippery, creating nothing but whispers of sensation. It coiled around me, making the hairs on my skin stand up on end, demonstrating that though the whip was a beast to be feared, it didn't always have to represent pain. Mark gave me nearly six minutes of the sweetest torment for my warm-up, but he was very careful to avoid all my hotspots, some of which were now throbbing in torment.

When the music changed to Ode to Joy by Beethoven he became bolder. Now he used both ends of the whip, at first looping it around my right leg and running it up and down, before crossing the ends over and dragging it tightly up my skin. As far as sensation play went it sent ripples of heat flying through me, and my pulse began to accelerate. The man was a bastard for dragging his scenes out to the max, so I knew I could expect at least another twenty minutes of this kind of play before he would begin to deliver any pain. The anticipation was excruciating.

The music got darker as we continued. I had to suffer through Ravel's Bolero and Johann Sebastian Bach's Toccata and Fugue, amongst others, with the whip becoming increasingly animated upon my skin. Now I was treated to smacks and rough taps from the whip handle. They didn't hurt, but each was a jarring reminder of what was to come. When the first soft flick of the whip came at me I flinched automatically, but there was no heat behind it yet. Mark was still playing with me.

"Remember that safe signal?"

I nodded. I remembered it all right, but there was no chance I was going to use it. Mark then wrapped the whip around my neck, causing my adrenaline level to skyrocket, before he replaced his stern expression with a smile. The tail then slowly slithered down my throat as I glared at him.

"You are so easy to play, kittykat."

Yeah, just wait until it's your turn, asshole, I thought acerbically.

"Well, you'll be glad to know it's nearly time for the finale. Brace yourself, darling."

With that warning he disappeared behind me, and I almost winced as I heard the starting notes of Carmina Burana by Carl Orff. It was a song I loved and hated in equal measure. It was a masterpiece, there was no doubt it, and I couldn't listen to it without being in awe of the composer. On the negative side, it was one of my husband's favourite pieces to do damage to, due to the rather large bass drums used. He could usually time his strokes to perfection, which was awesome for him and diabolical for me, mostly because I knew exactly when each was coming. Sure enough he then cracked the whip in the air, and I tried my best not to brace myself for carnage.

All the way through the first few verses I was telling myself not to tense. That didn't do me the least bit of good, whatsoever, because when that high note struck it was an almost automatic reaction to brace myself for danger, and sure enough the whip cracked down with its own brand of fiery precision and delight. Over and over Mark brought that thing down to all sorts of dark, classical numbers that screamed danger and dire consequences were just around the corner.

Cursing over a thousand times in my head, every time the lick of the whip caught a nipple or an already inflamed piece of flesh, it nearly had me wailing in earnest. He knew just where to place the thing for maximum impact, and that included between my legs. He kept me on my toes guessing where the next lash would fall, but it always unerringly caught its target. Why oh why did I have to marry a perfectionist for a husband? It wasn't fair. How could he be so good at nearly everything he turned his hand to? There was no justice in the world.

The finale was about five songs long, and by the end of it I was sobbing. Each line across my back, ass, and thighs had a line crisscrossing over it, and every time a fresh welt landed it set my nerve-endings aflame. It smarted like wildfire, but there was no way I would safe word. All it did was increase my resolve to stay strong. Mark had me so off-balance by now I didn't know which way was up. One minute his whip was sinking into my flesh, and in the next his fingertips were skimming across my clit. I didn't know whether to laugh, scream or weep, so I did none of those things. Concentrating on sucking air into my body it was all I could do to breathe. My body once again hung limply from its bonds, and I had no energy left for anything bar the bare necessities. Mark would know I was getting close to my limit, so I had to trust that he would end this soon.

As The Hall of the Mountain King began to play a tide of pleasure was sweeping through me. The last three licks of the whip had been focused upon my clit, and I was having a hard time deciding if I wanted another stripe down there or not. Obviously it hurt, which was a good reason not to want one, but on the other hand it wouldn't take too many more strokes before I came all over the place. That was probably enough reason for him to continue, and he did until the song came to its abrupt end.

"All over, kittykat. You did incredibly well, considering we haven't done anything like that since just after we were married." Mark came to stand in front of me, and ran the pad of his thumb down my cheek before tracing the outline of my stretched lips, which were now protesting at having worn the gag for so long. "God, you look so beautiful like that. I could eat you up and come back for seconds." Bending into my neck, he inhaled my scent and pressed his erection into my stomach. I mewled in pain, though a different sort from that of his whipping. And he knew exactly what I was moaning about, for a ghost of a smile flittered across his lips.

Unbuckling my gag, a finger to his lips once more reminding me to be silent, he set about freeing my arms and legs from their restraints. It didn't take him long. When he'd finished he took a step back and pointed to the floor.

"Kittykat's crawl, precious, and this kittykat needs a bath before I show her the little outfit I've prepared for her. You are going to look adorable, just wait and see." As much as I doubted that, there was little for me to do but follow my husband out of the room and into the bathroom. He was at least right about one thing; I did need a bath. The thought of soaking in a tub of hot water would have put a smile on my face if I'd had enough energy to accomplish the task.

When we got to the bathroom I waited patiently on all fours while Mark was happily pouring some herbal bubble-bath under the tap, and a swirl of Epsom Salts followed. It was bizarre, but I couldn't remember the last time I'd taken a bath without him there beside me. Usually I'd just dive in the shower, but Mark always preferred to bathe me, lavishing attention upon me with the enthusiasm of a clandestine lover. I wondered if it would always be like this with us. I certainly hoped so. Every woman should be able to feel as cherished and adored as I did. Mind you, I don't think anyone should have to go through the rocky start I had to get here. I wouldn't wish Albrecht on anyone, but thankfully that was far behind me now.

"Nearly ready, kittykat, just popping a bit of cold water in so we get the temperature just right." Let me at it, I thought, dreaming about a long and leisurely soak followed by Mark's fingers all over me.

"Just remember that as you're a kittykat your bath will be completed on all fours, just like you are now." My mouth immediately opened in shock and I nearly said something very rude, but I reigned myself in just in time. *Don't respond. Just do as you're told because the end justifies the means.* Well, almost. Grumping silently in my head I obeyed orders to the best of my ability. Thankfully Mark had only run a shallow bath, so it was easy enough to step into, but it wasn't what I wanted. I'd been looking forward to a good soak, and Mark had suddenly spoiled my evening fun in an instant. I gave him a baleful glare, letting him know my thoughts on the matter.

"Don't give me that look. You earned this punishment so you can own it." He gave me "the look". "Or you could utter your safe word and make this nastiness all go away in an instant." That was followed by a wink. The utter bastard. So that was his angle, huh?

I winked back at him, smiled, and pulled a fist upwards, out of the bath, and began to lick it in the manner of a paw. I added a *meow* for good measure. Take that, asshole.

Mark sighed. "You're a stubborn little thing, aren't you?" His tongue was firmly in the left side of his cheek, and I couldn't resist a virtual fist-bump of satisfaction inside my head. "Well, if this is the way you want to play it, I guess we'd better get you clean, hadn't we?"

Plucking the showerhead down from the wall he then proceeded to half rinse/half drown me, before covering my body in a generous amount of shower gel. Grabbing a sponge he then lathered me up until I resembled a ball of cotton candy. Paying particular attention to my undercarriage, the infuriating man brought his hands between my legs over and over again. Resisting the urge to snap at him, I gritted my teeth and endured. I was already revved up to hell, so what difference did another round of teasing make? The answer to that question was quite a lot. By the time he'd cleaned all the soapsuds off and towelled me down I was a quivering mass of hormones that needed to be sated, and if he'd have let me I probably would have humped his leg.

"Feeling better?" Mark raised an eyebrow as he rubbed my hair dry. I gave him a strangled meow in response. He knew exactly how I was feeling because he'd gone to a great deal of trouble and effort to make me feel that way.

"Ahh, someone's feeling a little needy, are they?" He tapped a finger on the bridge of my nose, and I was tempted to bite it but restrained myself. Nodding to his question, assuming that was acceptable, I waited to see what he would say to that.

"Well, that's too bad. It's time to get you kitted out, kittykat, and there's no time like the present. Follow me." He pointed at the floor, just in case I was a complete idiot who had already forgotten the terms of our agreement. Smiling sweetly in response, I got back down on all fours and crawled as fast as I could after him.

We didn't stop until we'd reached the bedroom. Then Mark turned around with a smug grin, and it didn't take me long to figure out why. There, in the corner of the bedroom, was an adult-sized pet basket. It was fluffy and brown on the outside, with a red velvet interior. There was a big black paw print on the front of it, with the word *Kitty* stamped next to it. If that had been all that was waiting for me I probably could have coped, but there was lots more waiting for me in that basket, and I didn't like the look of any of it.

"Don't they look fun, kitten?" Perhaps my husband couldn't read my mind after all. Pursing my lips, I examined a few of the things in the basket out of the corner of my eye. There was a pink leather collar that featured a shiny silver bell, another ball gag, this time in pink, but featuring short silver chains with pink clips at the end. I had a feeling I knew what they were for. Pink leather ankle and wrist cuffs were in the mix, also featuring silver chains, and I didn't even want to think what those were for. There were also fluffy little pink mitts with tiny white rubber claws at the end of them, and pink booties featuring paw prints on the rear, and if that wasn't bad enough there was a headband with a pair of pink fluffy kitten ears, and of course the matching butt plug tail. Oh my God. He wasn't going to keep me trussed up in this lot for two days, surely? One slow glance up towards his face told me all I needed to know. He intended to do all that and more - much more.

"Sure you don't want to call it a day, kittykat?" He gave me a knowing look. It was the one that said *you know when you're beaten*, except I didn't because I was not going to fall at the first hurdle. I was made of sterner stuff. So what if I looked pink and ridiculous, crawling around on the floor for the next two days? Meowing, I shook my head and crawled between his legs, rubbing against him. My husband blinked in surprise when I looked up at him, and I mentally chalked up the first round to me.

We sat there looking at each other for a moment, each trying to weigh the other up, and none of us any the wiser. Eventually Mark cleared his throat, and it was back to business once more.

"Have it your way, kittykat. Now go on over to your basket and fetch me the headband. I think you're going to look particularly fetching in that."

Careful to keep my irritated sigh silent, I wiggled my bright red ass and did as instructed. Now that the cooling effect of the water had evaporated I could feel my skin begin to prickle and burn as the whipping marks started to make themselves known. Damn my husband. I was going to feel those beasts this evening and into most of tomorrow unless a miracle happened. Reaching my basket, I began sifting through the contents to reach the pair of ears he'd requested.

"Uh-uh-uh, kittykat. Cats don't fetch things with their paws, now do they?" Thankfully my back was to him, for there was another roll of my eyes while I took a deep breath and counted to ten. When I'd finished I rooted around the basket with my mouth, and eventually managed to pluck out the headband with my teeth. Then, plastering the most insincere smile on my face that I could muster, I crawled back and delivered the item into his waiting hands.

He patted me on the head for my trouble. "Good girl." Just you wait, I thought. Just you wait. Mark had a hairbrush in his hand when I returned, and he indicated that I should turn around by swirling his finger in a circle. I did so, and he brought me up into a sitting position before he began to tame the wet, matted mass of my hair. He was very careful not to pull on my roots, and for that I could be thankful, but the inactivity killed me. I couldn't sit still. My body was revved up to race, and it desperately needed to be let loose. Do not give in, I told myself sternly. This was exactly what he wanted.

When my hair was brushed to his satisfaction, twenty minutes later, I was told to retrieve the next item that would help with my transformation from human to pet. This time, Mark wanted the collar. We were going to work up to the good stuff, I noted dryly.

When I brought it back to him, I made him tug a little to get the collar away from my mouth. Making my displeasure known at the long and drawn out method of torture he was using, I once again smiled sweetly. Mark completely ignored me of course, which was a sure fire way to drive me from nought to crazy in less than two seconds.

Buckling it carefully around my neck, he then slowly surveyed his work. "You look utterly adorable, you know." He then gave the bell a swipe with his finger, and a delicate little tinkle sounded. I knew that noise was going to drive me nuts very shortly, but this punishment was only for two days. Maybe I could shove something in the little holes to stop the bell from jangling so much. Where there was a will...

"Now go and grab the wrist and ankle cuffs, darling." Sashaying my ass to and fro as I crawled, as if that might speed the proceedings up, I got the next item on the list. Two matching sets of pink leather cuffs, complete with short inter-connecting silver chains. Lovely.

"These should slow you down a little, don't you think?" Mark had me sit up again so he could fasten the buckles around my wrists and ankles, looking very pleased with his efforts. I could tell my husband was enjoying himself immensely, but I refused to let his smug demeanour get to me. Instead, I meowed to the best of my acting ability and batted my eyelashes. There was an answering twinkle in Mark's eyes, so I knew the battle was just beginning.

"Hmm, what shall we get next, kittykat? There are so many fun things in that basket of yours. Tell you what, how about I let you pick the next item? Off you go, kitten." He then smacked my extremely sore ass, and I scurried on my way to do his bidding, mewling in protest.

When I hobbled back over to the basket, thanks to my new matching set of cuffs, it was to find that there wasn't a lot left in it. Ooh, what was a girl to choose - mitts, booties, gag, or butt plug. It didn't really matter in the grand scheme of things because before long I'd be wearing the entire lot, but I decided I could put off a couple of items until later. My jaw still hadn't recovered from earlier, and my ass, well, that was another story.

Trailing the fluffy pink booties back in my mouth, I wrinkled my nose as bits of fluff invaded my mouth. Yuck. I was beginning to think that maybe I should have let Mark pick another punishment after all - then again, perhaps not. My husband had a rather wicked imagination, and sometimes it's better the devil you know.

"You're not very brave, are you, kittykat? You're just putting off the inevitable. You know that, right?"

That's right, asshole. Rub it in. It'll be your turn before you know it. Let's see how you like it when the shoe's on the other foot.

The booties were snugly wrapped over each foot and tied in place with a little pink ribbon. Have I mentioned I'm a girl who's not overly fond of pink? Anyway, by now I looked utterly ridiculous, but I was trying my best not to notice.

"Go on then, next item." Another vicious smack to my rear accompanied that, and I daren't look at my husband, who was trying his best not to laugh at me. The mittens were quickly drawn over my hands, rendering them almost entirely useless and I was just about to get ready for my next trip when Mark stood up and retrieved the last two items himself. Oh great. I was really looking forward to this bit.

"Have we saved the best until last?" Mark waggled the fluffy pink tail plug in the air. Lots more fur, all for me. Yay. Just to be awkward, I shook my head. "Eager little thing, aren't you, kittykat? What are the chances you're going to be begging me for sex before the evening's out?" You should be so lucky, I thought sourly. "Right, get your ass over the side of the bed, and we'll get the last few items fitted. Nearly over now, pet."

Sighing softly I did as instructed. He left the room, probably to grab some lube, so I had a moment or two to myself in which to recount my blessings, and thankfully they were numerous.

There were several perks to being Mrs Mark Matthews. The first was that I had an Amex Black Card at my disposal for all my material wants and needs. The trouble was I didn't really have any. Mark bought most of my clothes and shoes for me and constantly showered me with gifts. I think he still felt guilty about the poisoning incident, and this was his way of saying sorry. No matter how many times I've tried to tell him it wasn't his fault, there's this look in his eye that says otherwise.

I know he won't be happy until something is done about my father and Kyle, but until we know their whereabouts there isn't much we can do. We're playing a waiting game, and we both know it. We've had a year's respite, but I have a nasty suspicion that dad won't stay hidden forever and that we need to be continually looking over our shoulders right now. Mark has that covered too. At least one person follows me wherever I go, and more often than not, two. It drives me wild, but the first time I gave my minders the slip my ass took a full week to recover from the furious blisters it was given. The telling-off I received was almost as bad, and it made my ears burn, but the worst part was that he put me under house arrest for a week. Even though I don't actually go out that much, knowing I'm not allowed to is a total mind fuck. That was how I learnt that my safety is always of paramount importance to my husband, and any attempt on my part to disrespect this is almost certain to result in tears.

Last, but not least, is the sex. Any kind of sex with my husband is earth-shatteringly awesome, but the kinky stuff and BDSM sends my blood pressure off the charts. Since moving in with Mark I've discovered a whole new world of carnal pleasure, and I know, without a shadow of a doubt, that no man will ever be as perfect as Mark is for me. Yes he can sometimes be an ass, but he's my ass, and I love him to bits.

"I'm back. Did you miss me?" Talking about asses...

Turning my head around, it was to discover that my husband was now not wearing any clothes, and my breath hitched. There was only one thing I like more than a half-naked husband, and that was a completely naked husband.

"Shall we get you ready for that plug, kittykat?" His hands were once again on my ass, kneading and rubbing, and they felt divine. Solid warm heat seeped into me, igniting the fiery whip marks he'd left earlier. It was a little uncomfortable, but in a good way, and I relaxed into his fingers instantly. "Are you wet for me, precious?" It was a stupid question. I was always wet for him, but he checked anyway, sliding his index and middle finger deep inside me. "Ah, God, do you have any idea how much you turn me on?" I had an idea, and if it was anywhere near half as much as I was turned on right now, we were both in trouble.

It took Mark thirty minutes to get that damn plug inside me. Two fingers in my pussy turned to three, three turned to four, and then the plug was there, sliding inside my tight wet pussy like it had been made for it. He had me writhing all over the bed, bells and handcuffs jingling at each tiny movement I made, as he pumped the thing inside me over and over again, and this was just the warm-up! The real action had yet to begin, but I knew it wouldn't be long. Sure enough, a few minutes later I felt the cold slide of lubricant being applied to my ass cheeks. Mark even made that feel heavenly, sliding his finger up and down the valley of my ass until I was as slippery as a skating rink. Then it was two fingers in my pussy, while one was slowly being inserted into my ass, and that had me face-down in the duvet, chewing the bed sheets like a woman possessed. Honestly, I couldn't take much more of this without going mad. Mark knew, of course, but if there was one thing my husband was good at it was pushing my body to the limit. Unfortunately, it looked like he was going for an all-time record.

It wasn't long before all of Mark's fingers were inside me, stroking my inner walls and widening them to the best of his ability. Sometimes the strokes were short, sharp and intense, other times they were soft, delicate, smooth, and as slippery as silk. All served one purpose; they wanted to wear down my resolve. They were doing a damn good job of it, too.

When the plug pressed for entry I was more than ready for it. Almost squealing with excitement as Mark parted my ass cheeks, I breathed heavily as he began to slide the beast home. He took his time, of course. Tiny little pulses at first, to get me used to the idea, gradually increasing in length and breadth until they had me panting with need.

My clit was now a throbbing, painful mess. Mark knew this, and as a result stayed as far away from it as possible. I wanted to scream at the unfairness of it all, but I refused to give my husband the satisfaction. I would see this through to the end and make my point. When the plug finally slotted home I wanted to cry out for mercy. My body was now burning up with need, and I had a bad feeling we were going to end the evening at an impasse.

Pressing the fluffy tale close to my reddened buttocks, he rubbed it up and down my fresh welts and chuckled when I squirmed.

"You look adorable, kittykat." Mark pressed his lips gently to my back and moaned. "I swear I could eat you all up in a single serving." That was no exaggeration, as my husband regularly did eat me and no matter how long he dined upon my flesh, he always came back for more. "Right, back on all fours, kitten." Struggling to obey, I fought the soft mattress in front of me, until I turned my liquid bones around one hundred and eighty degrees. When I'd managed that I slid off the bed in exhaustion, but managed to obey his request. Lust poured forth from my eyes, but they were met with steely indifference. My earlier instincts had been right.

"Now, there's just one final item for you, but we're going to leave that until tomorrow morning because it's bedtime, sweetheart. Unless you want to leap into bed with me?" He then stood up and placed the pink ball gag back on the top of our chest of drawers, where it looked very incongruous, set next to a small Tiffany lamp and stained glass trinket box. I looked up at Mark for a long moment, letting the question hang in the air between us, before finally making a soft sigh of disappointment. That was all he was going to get. If he wanted to play dirty, that was his problem.

Mark stood there, for what seemed like ages, as if willing me to change my mind. I would not. This wasn't something he could manipulate me into doing, and the sooner he understood that, the better. Staring him down, I waited patiently for my next instructions.

"Fine. Basket." He pointed to the corner of the room and stormed off. I almost felt sorry for him.

It was long past time that my husband needed to realise that not everyone he met could be influenced by money, bribery, or power. These were not tactics that worked on me; I was not one of his employees. Mark might have had everything his own way for most of his adult life, but now he would need to learn to compromise and treat me as an equal partner. If he didn't, we were doomed to failure.

Crawling over to my ridiculous pet basket, I curled up in a ball and settled down to what would be a restless night's sleep, at best. Though this was a victory of sorts, it felt very hollow - and the war had barely begun.

Chapter Seven - Mark

I stormed out of our bedroom with balls that had shot past the colour blue and were heading straight for purple. Why had I started this? Initially it had just been a bit of fun to get my wife to consider the idea of having children again. Somewhere along the line I had suddenly turned into a big bully who wouldn't see reason. Jen was being the sensible one here. Well aware that I was being the irrational one, I cursed myself every which way to stupid. Jen and I had been apart for a week, and now, when I should have been fucking her silly, my blood was raging through my veins because I couldn't cope when I didn't get exactly what I wanted. Yes, I was acting like a spoilt child, and yes, I thoroughly deserved to feel bad. In a moment I would go back upstairs and apologise to my wife, but for the time being I needed a drink to calm myself down. One week was far too long to be apart from Jen, and I needed to start arranging my work schedules more efficiently, or better yet, hire someone to do all the unpleasant stuff for me.

The trouble is, as you've probably guessed, I'm not happy with the idea of relinquishing control - in any aspect of my life. That might be okay in the boardroom, but it wasn't going to work in a relationship. The thing was, every time we sat down to talk things got out of hand, and Jen usually wound up being tied up and spanked. For someone who was all about control, it appeared I didn't have very much of my own.

Grabbing a glass of whisky from the bar, and topping it up with a generous helping of ice, I made my way to the sofa and sunk into it gratefully. Taking a large swig of my drink, I wondered what would be the best way to extricate myself from this mess. Putting my head into my hands and rubbing my eyes, I sat there for several minutes, trying to force myself to relax. It didn't really help. The only thing that might work would be going back upstairs and trying to make amends with my wife. It was time to face the music.

When I entered our bedroom I turned to switch the light on, but then stopped abruptly. There was my wife, adorably curled up in her adult-sized pet basket, fast asleep. Why was I surprised? I'd given her quite the workout today, so she was probably exhausted, poor thing. Grabbing a big cream blanket from the laundry cupboard I gently draped it over her. Quickly getting ready for bed I figured I'd have an early night, and we could both clear the air tomorrow morning. I wasn't a monster, but sometimes I really needed to think before I acted. Getting what I wanted wasn't the priority any more. Having a contented wife who loved me, on the other hand, was.

"Kittykat's do not sleep in beds."

I rolled over to check my alarm clock and was amazed to discover it was nine a.m.

Jen spooned herself around my body, purred in my ear, and licked the side of my cheek. I laughed. I couldn't help myself. Rolling over I pushed her bed-head hair out of her face and tinkled her bell. She meowed and bit me.

"Ow." The look she gave me indicated that this would be a good time to deliver my apology. "Okay, I'm sorry. I was an ass. Sometimes I get carried away, and yes, I really overstepped the line last night. Will you forgive me?" She raised a very arched eyebrow at me, and that indicated I wasn't out of the woods yet.

"Fine. I promise never to do anything like that again. Ever. It's just that you'd look so fucking sexy carrying my child. I can't wait to have you barefoot and pregnant round these parts, and you already know how much I want to be a dad."

Jen pursed her lips and pointed at her mouth.

"Oh, sorry," I said. "Permission to talk granted." This was a first; Jen actually obeying instructions.

"Apology accepted. We can have a serious discussion about babies soon, but I'm not ready just yet, and you'll have to learn to be patient. Not everything happens exactly when you want it to, Mr Matthews." Although I knew that, it was still bloody annoying.

"I won't mention it again unless you bring it up first. How's that?" I wondered, somewhat sheepishly, if I'd stick to my end of the bargain. It sounded good though.

"It will do for now." Jen bit her lip, and that distracted me so much that I had to suck her face off for the next half hour or so.

When Jen finally got a chance to come up for air she said, "This kitten get-up has really turned me on, darling. What are we going to do, now that we can't have sex? You're driving me crazy," she whined.

"Who says we can't have sex?" I said, with a great big grin on my face.

She hit me. "Let's not start this again. You promised not to..."

"I'm not talking about that," I said, shaking my head. "Maybe we can't have sex in the usual way... but there's more than one way to skin a cat, darling. In fact, I've been getting that particular spot all nice and stretched, just ready to be taken.

"Mr Matthews. You are an animal."

"Actually you're the animal, but we're splitting hairs. Roll over on your stomach and grip the damn headboard." That was the last thing I said for quite some time.

The phone stopped me from lounging around in bed all day. It rang once, and I ignored it until they hung up, but by the third time I knew I'd have to answer it or risk having someone come round and start banging down my door.

"Give me five minutes to sort that out, and I'll be right back," I whispered to Jen, who looked absolutely shattered. I'd forgotten how many times I'd made her orgasm, but she'd probably had more than her fair share today.

"Take as much time as you need," she mumbled, dragging a great big pillow over the back of her head. "I don't think I can take any more." My mouth opened in shock at her complete lack of enthusiasm. This was totally unacceptable behaviour.

"We need to get that personal trainer back. Your stamina sucks, young lady." Pulling the bedcover back I gave her two sound swats on her already beautifully pink ass, and she yelped. "You get ten minutes rest, max. Make the best of that time, kittykat. Oh, and after I've finished what I'm shortly about to do to you, we're going out. Don't ask. I'll tell you later."

I just managed to get out of the door before a pillow came crashing down against it. The woman was pushing her luck. If she wasn't careful I'd make her go out in her kittykat attire...

"Hi Khalil, this is Mark."

I already knew something was up because Khalil would never ring me more than once unless it was a national emergency. Sure enough, his next words were, "Kyle's on the move."

Fuck. That made me suck in a breath. Here was the news I'd been waiting for, and now it was here it left a bitter aftertaste in my mouth. I wanted that bastard so bad I'd be hard-pressed not to rip his head from his neck when I saw him. I'd just have to hope I could contain myself, because that kind of death would be far too quick.

In a lethal whisper I asked, "Where?" I needed to know how close he was. If he was too close I'd increase the security detail I had on Jen. No way was that monster getting to her a second time.

"That's the strange thing. Technically he's in Canada, but my guys couldn't find anyone matching his description when the flight landed." Khalil did not sound happy, and neither was I for that matter.

"Doesn't bode well, does it?" My jaw clamped in a hard line.

"No. Watch your back. I have no idea where he is, but it would be wise to assume that he wants to get close to you."

"Still no idea as to why?"

"No, and that concerns me. Redcliff hasn't made a move either. No credit card pings, no bank transactions, no cell phone, no nothing." Khalil sounded frustrated, and that was rare. If there was any trace of him to be found Khalil would have it, so he was being very careful.

"If Kyle's on the move, he won't be far behind him." I screwed my lip up in distaste. This certainly put a spanner in the works. I would need Jen glued to my hip for the foreseeable future, and there were only so many novel excuses I could come up with.

"Any chance you could talk to Jen's mum? Maybe she'd be able to—"

"No, that's not happening." I cut Khalil off in mid-flow. His suggestion was sensible enough, but Jen's mum and I had a strained relationship at best. Damned if I was going to be in her pocket. I'd have to be really desperate, and I wasn't there yet.

"Think about it. She's your best bet. Not only does she know the man, but she has contacts we can only dream of."

"Not happening." I had my pride. Besides, if I told Jen's mum you can be sure that the next person to know would be my wife, and she'd only panic. We'd keep this under wraps until a definite threat surfaced.

"Understood. Right, well I'll keep you updated. That's all for now."

Putting the phone down on the table with a soft click, some of my enthusiasm for the evening ahead dimmed. At least Jen would be by my side the entire time, though. Until I knew where that bastard Levison was hiding I wasn't letting my wife out of my sight. Not even for a second.

When I got back to our room my kittykat was nowhere to be found, which immediately gave me cause for concern, but then logic kicked in. No one was in my house. We were safe here. Calm down and get a grip. Then I heard the roar of the shower and knew all was well.

Poking my head around the bathroom door, making my wife jump in the process, I said, "Since when do kitty cats take showers?" I gave her my famous *you're-in-trouble* look, but she retaliated by pressing all of her most glorious assets up tight against the shower glass, and I just leched at her instead. I was such a lucky bastard; every single inch of the woman inside that shower cubicle was mine, all mine. And I was never going to let her go.

"You told me we were going out. If we're going out I'm not a kittykat, and therefore I need a shower. No one will want to come near me if not." She rubbed her ass cheeks into the shower door, just to torment me. It was a spankable offence in my opinion.

"We are going out, but I've decided you are going as a kittykat after all. I think it will make the ride down to the club a little more exciting than usual. As to your smell, you smell of sex and me, and I love that delightful combination. As I'm the only one allowed near you that's all you should worry about, and showering is overrated." I don't know why I bothered continuing to talk after the first sentence because Jen clearly wasn't listening.

"What did you just say?" she asked me, abruptly turning off the tap.

"You are going out as a kittykat," I said. World War III was shortly about to start, but boy was I ready for it.

Jen opened the shower door, allowing a billow of steam to envelop the room, before slamming it shut behind her.

"Is this something to do with Escape?" she asked, not looking at me as she pulled a giant cream bath towel from the rack and wrapped it snugly around her body.

There was no point lying, so I sighed and said, "Yes."

"You are really pushing your luck this weekend, Matthews," she said, now looking at me out of the corner of her eye, so I guess that was an improvement.

"Obviously you don't have to come, but your end of the bargain will also be null and void if that happens." I winked at her, then turned and left her to chew on that one. Initially, the idea had been to take her along as my date, but now that the stakes had changed I didn't see why she couldn't be a part of the proceedings as well. If she said no, fine, we were both back to square one, and I could go to Escape on my own. It was a lot better than the alternative of being tied up, spanked, and possibly castrated by my wife.

The bathroom door opened in a blast of hot air, as Jen's wet hair swirled around the corner in a fit of temper. "Who will you take as your plus one?" While her voice was soft I didn't miss the deadly venom held inside that question. Hmm. How should I play this? Probably not the way I was going to, but what the hell...

"Sophia, of course," I said casually, before turning to walk down the stairs without a second glance. There was then a blissful moment of silence before all hell let loose. When an electric toothbrush crashed into the banister, a yard above my head, I had reason to be thankful my wife was such a crap shot.

"Over my dead body!" she screamed at me, and I wisely started running.

It was all sorted out over a cup of tea after I'd been brave enough to get out of hiding. When Jen got fired up it was always best to give her some space, and I did that by way of the man cave - otherwise known as my garage. You could change the entry code from the inside, which came in handy more often than I'd like to admit.

After I'd given her an hour I made my way back inside, but not before I'd taken appropriate measures to protect myself should anything else come flying at me. Holding a golf umbrella in front of me, I immediately inflated it as soon as I got through the front door.

"Truce," I yelled, waiting to see what would happen.

"You are not going with Sophia," came a disgruntled voice from up the stairs. Thank God. The woman had calmed down.

"Am I not? Who am I going with then?" Thankfully my wife's temper was usually short-lived. She normally seemed to explode and deflate reasonably quickly, but that wasn't always the case, so it was sensible to come prepared. I considered putting the umbrella down but decided I'd wait another minute just to be on the safe side.

"You are going with *me*." There was a pause, and then I heard the soft pad of her feet upon the stairs. I couldn't see anything yet, because the umbrella completely obscured my vision.

"For God's sake put that thing down. If I was going to throw anything at you I would have done it by now." The padding noises were coming closer, but as Jen didn't sound too annoyed I felt it was safe to put the brolly aside. When my eyes then trailed up the stairs my heart nearly stopped, for a vision of loveliness was heading towards me. I blinked stupidly for a moment, utterly enthralled, but somehow managed to get a hold of myself.

"You look incredible," I said, and she did.

"I found the extras you'd laid out on the bed. What do you think?" She smiled at me. Christ.

Jen had once again donned her kittykat outfit but had styled her hair in tight little ringlets that were pinned behind her head with a big pink bow. She had swapped the booties for pink, knee-high socks, and the mittens were replaced with a pink mesh crop-top that nearly covered her breasts, complete with arms and thumb holes, although the shoulders were cut out. A little pink tutu tried to cover some of her butt, and her tail poked prettily out of the ensemble. The only thing she wasn't wearing was the gag, and it trailed from her fingertips, the chains jingling with her bell each time she moved.

"I'm not sure I can take you anywhere looking like that," I said, and I meant it. I wanted to lock her up somewhere far, far away, and feast upon her until she screamed for mercy.

"That's your problem, not mine. What will we be doing at Escape?"

"Nuh-uh-uh," I said, waggling my finger. "It's supposed to be a surprise, so let's not get ahead of ourselves. Now come here, woman." I crooked my index finger in her direction, telling her that she needed to get her ass down the last few stairs quickly so I could get my hands all over her. Thankfully she didn't need to be told twice.

"This get-up has me dripping wet," she admitted, as my fingers sought for evidence of the same.

"So it does," I said, two fingers buried deep inside her. "How wonderful. Yet another thing I can torment you with, oh precious one." I gave her a wolfish smile as my fingers carefully tickled her clit.

"What do you get to dress up in this evening?" she enquired, as her tongue lapped at the stubble upon my jaw. It made me instantly hard.

"Black tie of course, what else?" I sighed. Hopefully my penguin suit had come home from the cleaners. I seemed to dust it off quite frequently these days.

"That is so unfair," she moaned.

"I'm not sure I'd look very good in pink," I said, trying my best to keep a straight face.

"You look fucking awesome in black, though," she purred.

"Give me that gag here, Mrs Matthews, and bend your ass over my leg. You are well aware that swearing is not tolerated around these parts." I gave her a dark stare to let her know I meant business.

"I was hoping you'd say that," she giggled. That was the last thing she said for some time.

Chapter Eight - Kyle

"How are you going to get your hands on her?" It was a reasonable question, but it wasn't one I wanted to answer right now.

"I don't want to get my hands on her just yet. First, I want to fuck with her." I'd been looking forward to this moment for a very long time, and now that it hovered in my imminent future, I was getting more than a little excited at the thought. The last time I'd had any real fun with Matthews was back in that abandoned old warehouse in London. That had been over a year ago. Since then I'd had a few mediocre interludes, but nothing that really whetted my appetite for destruction.

"Well, when you want to track her I can hack her cell phone, you can get someone to plant a chip on her, or you can drop a chip on an item of clothing or secure it in an accessory; something like a handbag or purse. You'll want an item that she regularly uses for obvious reasons."

Shaking my head, I growled. My tech guy might have been the best we could get at short notice, but he didn't have a clue. Who did he think we were working with here?

"Here's a news bulletin for you, asswipe. You are not going to be able to hack into any of the cell phones that either Mr or Mrs Matthews hold. If you'd done your homework, you'd realise Matthews runs **Zystrom, which currently produces the world's most sought after cell phone - the StrontiumX. You can't hack it. No one can even get near it. The technology is so cutting edge that only his employees are able to understand it.** While that may change in the next five years or so, it doesn't help us now. I'm not happy with a chip that gets stuck on something, either. Jen changes handbags almost as often as she changes her mind, and can often wear two or three in a single day. Clothes and shoes are even worse. How about we plant something on her? That way I can keep an eye on her for a few days and learn her routine." The idea was excellent on all fronts because if she somehow did get away after I'd captured her, it would be ridiculously easy to find her again. It would be fucking awesome if we could do the same thing to Mark, but he wasn't quite as gullible as my sister, and getting up close and personal with him was going to be difficult.

"Yeah, can do, mate," said the tech guy, who wasn't at all bothered about any of what I'd just said, "but there's one problem with that."

I do not like problems. Running my hands through the greasy mop of sandy hair on my head, I rolled my lip up in distaste. I needed a goddamned shower and some sleep. I'd had neither since I'd hopped on a plane yesterday. Tech guy had better hurry up before I got pissed.

"And that is?" My left foot tapped on the floor, and I was getting a little bit agitated. Too bad I needed this asshole. The Smith and Wesson in my back pocket was burning a hole in my pants.

"You'll need to get close enough to insert the chip, and then you'll have to inject her. Microchips are a lot smaller than they used to be, about the size of a grain of rice, but it's still going to sting when it goes in. You're not going to be able to do it without being noticed. Unless you can figure out a way to drug her, I don't think it's a feasible option."

Tech guy held up a tiny little capsule in his hand, and then showed me the injector that would be needed to slam it home. Hmm. Getting close to Jen these days was going to be a problem. Mark had a bodyguard with her at all times, and the last thing I wanted to do was get too close to her security detail. I'd need to be smarter than that.

What were the chances of finding Jen alone in a crowd somewhere? It wasn't a problem if there was Mark or a guard trailing after her at a distance, as long as the bastards weren't glued to her side. Now how was I going to find out what went on in Mark Matthews' social calendar? Smiling to myself, I tapped my finger against my lip as I considered who wouldn't mind doing the dirty on my arch-enemy. He'd have plenty of adversaries in the business world who would more than happily sell him out, but I needed someone who couldn't stand him. Someone like a disgruntled employee. Scratching my head, I frowned for a moment, but then it came at me like a lightning bolt. How about the fifty odd women that used to work for Mark but were suddenly offered redundancy packages on his marriage to Jen? They'd be pretty pissed, right? Ping. There it was. There was the answer I'd been looking for. Almost running for the shower, I decided I'd postpone sleep until later. The sooner I knew Jen's whereabouts the better.

Chapter Nine - Jennifer

When Mark helped me into the limousine, the butterflies in my stomach were threatening to escape. I felt almost sick with nerves, and I'd hardly had anything to eat today. Although I was well aware that Escape was a BDSM nightclub, and my attire probably wouldn't bat an eyelid, I think I'd have almost rather gone in there naked. Sensibly, I decided not to mention this to Mark.

"So, how are you feeling, sweetheart?" said my blithely unconcerned husband, as he settled down into his seat beside me. His hand crept up between my legs as I fastened my seatbelt, and I sucked in a breath.

"Terrified, excited, nervous, and sick. Roll all of those into a ball and start chucking it around, and that's about where I am at the moment." He laughed. "Relax. It's going to be fine. I was always told that if you fall off your horse, you have to get straight back on it again."

His hand continued creeping higher, past the crepe netting of my tiny pink tutu and towards the juncture of my legs. I could feel my skin prickle as his fingers gently caressed me.

"Whoever said that wasn't nearly poisoned." My tone was dry.

"Good point, but that wasn't down to the club. That was down to your weird and wonderful family, and my fingers are crossed we won't be seeing them again in a hurry." I had a feeling we would, but one could hope. "Besides, you have two of my men tailing you, so no one is getting close without my say so. There will be eyes on you the whole time. Please don't worry, sweetheart."

Putting his fingers up to my jawline he felt for the fluttering pulse in my neck and let out a low whistle. "Jeez, you weren't kidding, were you?" He brushed a swathe of ringlets away from my face and cupped my chin. "Look at me, Jen."

I did so reluctantly. My thoughts were all over the place. If I wasn't careful I was going to hyperventilate in a minute.

"That's it." His eyes centred me. "Deep breaths. In and out. Hmm. We just need to figure out a way to calm you down. You sit tight. Something will *come* to me in a minute." I almost laughed out loud, but his fingers were already circling my clit which was almost throbbing in pain.

"Do you think an orgasm might make you feel better?" he murmured in my ear.

"Stupid question, darling. Please do your worst."

He did all of that and more.

When we got to Escape I was once again dazzled by the myriad of white LED lights that decorated the skyline. They formed a cityscape on top of the large black building, and the lights were glittering on and off as if to announce something special.

Thankfully I was allowed to wear an overcoat as we were directed to the VIP entrance. It wasn't a great deal of comfort to me. I knew that as soon as we went through the black doors, it would be whipped away from me and I would have to face the music. The last time I'd been here I'd nearly died. A disaster like that couldn't strike twice at the same place, could it? As much as I knew I was being silly; I had a bad feeling about this place.

Mark took my arm as he led me along the roped concourse. There were hundreds of people lined up outside, and all of them were chatting animatedly. What was going on here tonight?

When I hit the black velvet carpet with the twinkling lights on either side of it, I took a deep breath and straightened my shoulders. I could do this. Arm in arm with my husband we walked towards the velvet curtain, and I gave a great big smile to anyone who cared to look my way. This was not going to beat me. Bring it on.

"Are you ready for this?" I gave a sideways glance at my husband and managed to smile. Although I didn't really know the answer to that question I was here now, and I intended to go through with my side of things. Besides, my curiosity had already gotten the better of me. The last time we were here I'd been walking across the Grand Canal in Venice; what would be waiting for me this time? It wouldn't take long to find out.

Elegantly attired girls dressed in wafts of black netting and lace parted the black velvet drapes and ushered us inside. This time the interior was dim, and another mass of glittering lights caught my eye. They were dotted all along a very familiar landmark - the Eiffel Tower. It appeared that we would be spending a twilight evening under the bright, twinkling lights of Paris. Oh là là.

Before I knew what was happening my overcoat was whisked away by another scantily-clad lady, and a glass of champagne on a silver platter appeared magically before me. Last time I hadn't even been offered one, although that may have had something to do with the gag in my mouth, so I was pleased Mark hadn't seen fit to insert the one he currently carried in his pocket.

"Can I drink this?" I asked, wondering if there was a catch. Mark didn't usually allow me to drink very much on our evenings out, so this was quite a novelty for me.

Mark plucked a glass from the tray and took a sip. He nodded his head in approval. "I would," he said in way of response. I didn't need to be told twice.

Trying my hardest not to guzzle the contents in one gulp, I let Mark thread his arm through mine and lead me across the floor. By this time I was extremely conscious of the pink tail dangling between my legs and my complete and utter lack of any real clothing. You'd have thought I'd have been used to parading myself around naked by now, but while that might be true around the house, it was rare that Mark would allow me out in public in anything less than a full burka. Okay, he wasn't quite that strict - but the Victorians could have learnt a thing or two from him.

Looking around at the milling crowd, I was pleased to find I wasn't the only "animal" in attendance. There seemed to be quite a few cats and dogs, as well as some horses, foxes, bears, and several other furry friends. Interesting. Was this tonight's theme? Of course, there was plenty of everything else in between, from hardcore top-to-toe leather, to bright and colourful latex. There were whips, paddles and floggers attached to belts and boots, all manner of restraints on ankles and wrists, and there were quite a few women who were completely naked, bar a collar and leash. I was positively overdressed.

"Still feeling self-conscious?" Mark's gaze was lazily assessing the occupants of Escape, much as I was, and there was a half-smile tugging at his jaw. My husband was obviously in his element, and though I was still nervous I figured I would probably have fun.

"A little," I admitted, but nowhere near as much as when I first entered.

"That's good. Drink your champagne up."

My eyes darted to Mark's. This was a first. Since when had he ever ordered me to drink?

"Spill the beans. What have you signed me up for?" My eyes took on a dangerous hue. If he expected I was going to be the star of the show like last time, he had another think coming. My eyes then took a sweeping glance around the building, as if scared that Leyland Forbes might suddenly hop out of the woodwork.

"Relax. I haven't signed you up for anything. You're here to have fun." Hmm. This was a first, but I was going to take him at his word. Walking down the Parisian street, towards the model of the Eiffel Tower, I saw delightful little French cafes, bistros, and patisseries. There was even a boulangerie, complete with a shop window full of baguettes and bread, the smell of which was incredibly enticing. Just like my last visit there was almost too much to take in, and I had no idea where to start.

"Johanna, Dominic, how lovely to see you again." Mark shook Dominic's hand as my head snapped upright to find both of his friends standing in front of us. Johanna was dressed in a similar version of my outfit, although she was in black and white, while Dominic was dressed in a black suit.

"I see you're heading the same way as we are," Dominic said, and he gave me a devilish wink.

"Don't spoil the surprise. I haven't told her yet." Mark pinched my rather raw backside and I shot up on a yelp. Everyone laughed.

"Do you want to head straight over to the main event, or do you fancy getting side-tracked for a moment or two?" Dominic then took my hand in his and brought it up to his lips, giving me a very flamboyant kiss. If he was teasing Mark it appeared to be working, for my husband's eyes suddenly glowed a dangerous shade of amber.

"What sort of diversion are we talking about here?" If I'd thought my husband's eyes were dangerous, the sound of his voice, which had now dropped a couple of decibels, was on another level entirely. On the other hand, Dominic's were almost dancing with delight, and he appeared to be enjoying himself immensely.

"Well, I was thinking we could head on over to the swap shop and..." The poor man didn't get to finish his sentence because Mark's face went purple and his hands clutched Dominic's neck dangerously tightly.

"Let him go," I said, shaking my head. "Can't you tell when someone's teasing you?" Dragging my husband's hands back down from their choke-hold I looked at him aghast. "Get a grip." I then turned to Dominic.

"I don't know why you're looking so pleased with yourself. You already know he's jealous of you. Don't pour salt into the wound." Last time I'd been at Escape, Dominic had been between my legs eating my clit and my husband had decided, for perhaps the first time in his life, that he wasn't prepared to share a woman. It was a revelation to us both. Dominic looked suitably chastised as he straightened his collar, and he then pulled a glossy leaflet out of his suit jacket pocket with the word Escape emblazoned upon it.

Clearing his throat awkwardly, he said, "I was only going to suggest that we all pick something fun to watch and go take a look see. Here," he said, as he thrust the leaflet in Mark's direction, "you choose."

Thankfully the tension in the room seemed to diminish, and Johanna and I sighed silently in relief. The anger drained quickly out of Mark's face as he perused the list of things on offer, and then there was a devilish twist to his features as his eyes lit up with delight. Crossing my fingers, I hoped that wherever we were going next would have nothing to do with me. I did not want any more tattoos, real or fake, nor did I want to be entering any "life or death" competitions. Where was another glass of champagne when you needed one?

"Right, follow me." All of a sudden Mark seemed to have gotten a new lease of life, and he was striding off, expecting all of us minions to follow - which of course we did.

No one had any idea where we were going, and Johanna and Dominic looked at each other oddly. Was Mark's behaviour strange? Yes, I guess it was. We'd been under a lot of strain lately, and it was probably to be expected.

Johanna linked her arm through mine and bent down to whisper in my ear. "It's nice to see Mark completely and utterly head over heels. Dominic and I never thought we'd see the day. What have you done to him?"

I blinked, totally taken aback for a minute. "Me? What I have done to him?" I repeated the question just to make sure I'd heard it right. Johanna nodded, encouraging me to continue. "Well, nothing so far as I can tell. He's still the same arrogant, self-centred, egotistical bastard..."

"No, no, no," she said, waving her hands about in the air. "That side of him will never change. What I'm talking about is how he is with you."

"Ahh." He was a pain in the ass most of the time, but I was happy to get someone else's point of view.

Johanna grabbed my hand and squeezed it. "He's in love. That's how he is with you. I've never seen him like this before."

"Oh," I said on a long note, the penny finally dropping. "You mean that."

"Yes, *that*," she said on a giggle. "The man is all loved-up. He treads carefully around you now, as if afraid he'll upset you. He's insanely jealous if another man even comes near you, and he looks at you as if he wants to have a million babies all at once."

"Oh God, don't talk about babies," I said, before slamming my hands over my mouth. Oops.

"So he wants babies?" Johanna sounded incredulous. My face must have said it all, for she then said, "Holy hell, you're serious."

"I'll deny it if you tell anyone," I said, giving her a warning look.

"Even Dominic?" The corner of her lip tilted.

"Especially Dominic," I said in a strained voice.

Our conversation was suddenly cut short as Mark took a turn to the left, diving inside one of the sidewalk café's called 'Le Jardin Des Cygnes,' or, roughly translated, The Swan Garden. It had a quaint façade, complete with some bright shutters and an awning, and some white, ornate cast iron chairs were positioned outside. They were already full of people, most of whom were sipping coffee or red wine. What on earth was going on in here? It'd had better be nothing awful, I thought grimly, else my husband was really going to suffer next week. Taking a deep breath, I clutched Johanna's hand tightly and followed her through the door into the darkened interior.

None of us realised at the time that we were being followed. We didn't discover that until much later when all of Escape's one hundred and nine security cameras were meticulously examined by experts. Of course, by then it was too late.

Chapter Ten - Jennifer

The room we'd entered looked a little like an auditorium, and we all shuffled down some wide steps and took our seats on plush red velvet chairs. Johanna and I shuffled about awkwardly, mainly because it was hard to sit down with a tail stuffed between your legs. I guessed we would get used to it. Anyway, whatever the show was it hadn't started yet as the red drapes were still drawn. The audience seemed excited though, and chatted in hushed voices to one another.

"Where are we?" I whispered over my shoulder to Johanna.

"Who knows? Mark has the program." She shrugged and kept her eyes trained on the stage. Curiosity was already burning a hole in my brain. Trying another tack, I turned to the other side to whisper the same question to my husband. I was less likely to get an answer from him, but maybe I could steal the brochure out of his pocket when he wasn't looking.

"Don't even think about it." My husband snapped his hand over his jacket pocket and arched the infamous eyebrow. This was usually a good sign that I should push no further, but today we had company, so I was hoping he'd be a bit more flexible.

"Please? Just a quick peek? Lemme look." Mark's hand reached out to caress the nipple closest to him before he squeezed it tightly between his forefinger and thumb. My eyes watered. "I guess that's a no, then," I whimpered.

"You guess correct. Now keep your eyes front and enjoy the show. You should know I'm also debating trying this out on you, should you misbehave, kittykat." There was a definite thread of excitement that whipped through his voice, which instantly piqued my curiosity. What were we about to see? My foot tapped anxiously on the floor as I impatiently waited for the curtains to rise. Turning towards Johanna for entertainment, I quickly turned away again as I saw Dominic's hands were between her legs.

There was a chuckle to my left. "Feeling jealous, kittykat?"

I was, but I was loathe to tell my husband that.

"Not at all," I chirped. "Just anxious for the show to begin." Thankfully someone must have heard me, for the curtains finally began to rise. Hallelujah. For a moment everything went completely dark in the auditorium, and I jumped as I felt someone's hands brush against my shoulder. Were they Mark's? It didn't feel right, so I instantly moved forward to shake off whoever might be there. Then the lights came up on stage and I saw that Mark had his hands in his lap. Frowning, I turned my head around, but all I found were two empty seats behind me. There was no one close enough to have touched me. Maybe it had been Mark after all. How weird. I didn't get a chance to ask him about it because the lights then began darting all over the place and everyone's eyes were glued to the stage.

When the moving spotlight finally came to a standstill it centred on a lone, naked girl, hunched up in a ball in the corner of the stage. She appeared to be shivering, but it couldn't have been because she was cold, as the auditorium was quite warm, and she would be even warmer under the bright spotlight. If I wasn't much mistaken, this girl was in trouble.

A master then strode on stage carrying a large chest, which he placed by his feet. He did not look happy. I almost felt sorry for the girl. Almost. If she was about to get a spanking, I was going to be insanely jealous.

When he thrust his arms out to the audience, all ears strained for what was to come next. "Ladies and gentlemen, welcome to the punishment room. This is the place where we chastise naughty slaves for their misdeeds. These aren't your usual run-of-the-mill indiscretions, either. These are gross misconducts of duty that have resulted in complete violations of their contracts. Slave, state your name and sins for the audience." The order was barked out, and the girl's head shot up in fright. The poor thing was very uncomfortable in front of a large crowd, but I guessed that was the point.

Looking out towards us she almost visibly cringed, but finally a very shaky voice managed, "My name is Filthy Slut, and my sins are many. I have been caught swearing and answering back. I have woken up late and forgotten to make master's breakfast not just once but several times. I have failed to follow instructions when out at our local munch. I have flirted with other men against master's strict instructions and the terms of my contract. I have been unrepentant when spanked, and I have been caught on camera climaxing without the permission of my master." She hung her head in shame, unable to go on.

"Oh, you did more than flirt, didn't you, Filthy Slut? You did much more than flirt. Go on and tell the audience the real reason you're here." That sounded ominous, I thought.

Almost quaking in my boots just listening to her recite that lot, I could hardly stand to hear any more. Oh lord. I hated to think what her punishment would be and hoped it wouldn't be more than I could bear to watch. Squirming in my seat, I waited, almost afraid of what she would say next.

"Yes, Master Carlisle," she whispered, dragging her head back upright, tears now pouring down her face. There was a pronounced silence before she finally managed to mumble something. Of course, none of us could hear it.

"Louder, slave." The command was barked out, and the girl's head jerked.

"I had sex with one of your friends without your knowledge, and behind your back, Sir."

Johanna's eyes flew to mine, as big as saucers, and she had her hand over her mouth in shock. I think we were both horrified at what she'd just revealed and scared witless for what might happen next.

"I don't think I can watch," I whispered.

"Me neither," she said aghast. Both Dominic and Mark then chose to give us a nudge, reminding us that we needed to be quiet.

"Yes, slave. You had sex behind your master's back, and without his knowledge, or so you thought. Did you think that kind of behaviour would be tolerated?" Master Carlisle was pacing up and down the stage now, his anger was almost palpable. The audience had their eyes glued to the front, and everyone's attention was firmly on the girl who was once again cowering in the corner.

"No, Sir," she whimpered, mewling harder when he took a handful of her dirty brown hair and yanked it painfully upright.

"Damn right it isn't, Slave. I have a mind to give you away. Perhaps one of the audience members would like you? Let's see, shall we? Anyone out there who would like an unfaithful slave in their household? One that can't even follow simple instructions? Any takers? She's going free." He looked up, his face sweeping from right to left as he surveyed the crowd before him. No one said a word.

"That's what I thought," he said, nodding his head. "No one wants an unfaithful, untrustworthy and lazy slave. The question is: what shall we do with you?" He looked at her with what could only be described as disgust. Tapping his finger against his cheek, he appeared to think about it.

"Spank her," shouted one man from the audience, unable to wait any longer.

"Whip her," shouted another, who apparently thought spanking too tame.

"Tie her up and deny her any release for a month," said a lady on the front row, making me mightily glad I was not the poor girl in question.

"Sensory deprivation for a week," said a gentleman from the back. After that the suggestions came thick and fast, and each was worse than the last. I hated to think what was going to happen to the girl, but whatever it was I had a feeling it was not going to be pleasant.

When Master Carlisle had had enough of our suggestions he raised his hands in the air and let them drop several times over, indicating that he would like quiet. We obliged. I think half of us were anxious to see what would happen to her, and the other half were positively excited. In any case, silence reigned supreme as we waited to hear her fate.

"Thank you for your ideas, ladies and gentlemen. It has certainly given me something to think about. I think I will spank my slave, while I consider all of my options. Could someone bring me a chair?"

A wooden, high-backed chair was raced towards him from a stagehand in the wing, and he took his place upon it.

"Slave," he said imperiously, "get your ass over my lap, now."

The girl scuttled over to do his bidding, moving as fast as a whippet. She must have been in love with her master, else she wouldn't have agreed to do this, but I wondered if he'd take her back after tonight's proceedings. How many people could recover from that? Was it a risk she was willing to take? I guess she knew she'd made a mistake and was trying to make amends in the only way she knew how. I couldn't help but feel sorry for her. However the evening panned out, she was doomed to suffer in some shape or form. Did she deserve it? It certainly seemed like it, but I was never one to judge until I'd heard the full story.

The first slap of Master Carlisle's hand rang out loudly in the auditorium. There was a pronounced wobble of the girl's butt cheeks, so I knew he wasn't holding back, but she didn't make a sound.

After that the spanks impacted with fury, and the poor girl's punishment began in earnest. For the first ten spanks or so the girl managed to maintain her position and poise, but after that she was wriggling all over the place, trying to escape the next wallop of her master's hand. I didn't blame her. Master Carlisle was giving it all he'd got, and we could clearly hear the sound of those spanks from where we were sitting, which meant they packed one hell of a punch. It only took another ten whacks before she was wailing, and quite honestly I didn't know how she managed to hold out that long. Her ass was already bright red, and the burn must have been pretty nasty by then. I felt sure she wouldn't have to endure many more, and sure enough, after a few more, her master stopped. You could have heard a pin drop in the auditorium, and everyone held their breath to see what would happen next.

"Go and fetch the paddle, slave." Oh my. She was going to be paddled, on top of the spanking? I reached for Johanna's hand, only to find it wasn't there. She appeared to be very preoccupied with Dominic's hands between her legs.

Mark's head bent down to whisper in my ear, "Feeling jealous?" Now normally I would be jealous of someone getting a spanking, but this was different. This was punishment, and it wasn't tolerable pain. This was heading into unknown territory, and it scared me.

"Hardly. He's going to fry her ass, and that's just the appetiser. I wouldn't want to be her for the world."

"Not of the spanking, you idiot. Are you jealous of Johanna?" Mark pointed between my legs, to make sure I understood what he was saying.

"Oh." My eyes sneaked back to Johanna, who was now almost slouching in her seat, in order to open her legs wider for Dominic's talented fingers. Her eyes were half-closed in pleasure, little sighs coming from her mouth, and she was completely unaware I was watching her. When my gaze drifted lower I saw glistening fluid all over Dominic's hands and a swollen clit that was lapping up all the attention. Was I jealous? Hell yes.

"Yes. Very," I whispered.

Master Carlisle had now got his slave to retrieve the paddle from his bag, and she was crawling back with it between her teeth. Positioning herself back over his legs without being asked, she once again assumed the position.

"Well we can't have that, can we?" I only just heard the murmur of his voice, as the paddling had commenced. The loud thumps reverberated around my poor head, and I nearly jumped each time I heard one. When my husband positioned his hand between my legs I nearly yelped in surprise.

"Shh. This will help you relax."

Hah. Good luck with that, I thought. Unable to take my eyes off the slave girl, I didn't think anything was going to ease my discomfort at watching her suffering.

Over and over the paddle crashed into her backside. This time she made no pretence at trying to remain still or quiet. She began howling almost as soon as he'd started, and her body wriggled so much Carlisle took a fistful of her hair in his hand to make sure she stayed where she was supposed to.

"How much do you want to be a bad girl right now?" Mark's fingers were working their magic, checking if I was already wet, which should have been a foregone conclusion. Shove me in a kittykat outfit, and I'd cream my pants almost instantly. Anything else was just icing on the cake.

"Not at all," I whispered fervently. And I meant it.

"I'll remind you of that later, precious." Burying himself in my pussy, he amused himself by pumping in and out of me with long measured strokes. I bit my lip, trying my best to concentrate on what was unfolding in front of me, but the distraction of Mark's hand was intense.

Meanwhile, up on stage the slave girl was pleading and begging forgiveness. Tears were dribbling down her cheeks, and her hair was a wet straggle around her face. Her ass was pillar-box red. Master Carlisle didn't pay her any attention. The paddle continued to come down with loud, regular smacks, and he did not appear to be in a merciful mood. When he finally finished and dropped the paddle on the floor with a derisive slash of his hand, my breath lodged in my throat. Surely this would be it? Surely she wouldn't be subjected to any more?

"Time to get the whip, slave." His hand struck her ass again as she was struggling to get off him. The crazed look in Master Carlisle's eyes scared me because he looked like he'd barely begun, and I didn't think this was going to end well.

The girl took her time getting the whip, and her movements were barely coordinated as she appeared to be swaying. I didn't know if it was from shock or pain, but she didn't seem to be in a good way.

"Will she be okay?" I whispered.

"Will she be okay or will *they* be okay?" Mark countered.

"Either," I murmured.

"Hard to tell. He's mad, and rightly so. If she doesn't take everything he has to give, I suspect the show will be over for both of them, so it will be interesting to see how this pans out." That gave me little comfort, but it was all I had, so I took it.

My eyes were glued to the whip as it weaved across the floor. Could she really take another round of this? Her eyes looked unfocused and dazed, her limbs trembling, and I knew that if I were in her place I wouldn't be looking forward to what was to come next. When she handed the whip to Carlisle's waiting hand he didn't even look at her.

"Face the wall, with your legs wide apart." It was another barked instruction, which was obeyed with faltering steps.

"Hurry up, don't make me wait, filthy slut." His accent was a clipped English one, but it sounded false to my ears. Like the man was trying to cover something up. It was probably me. These days I was almost suspicious of my own shadow. My father and Kyle were mostly to blame for that.

When the slave pressed her nose into the back of the stage wall a hush descended over everyone, and I swear I could hear the beating of my own heart as I waited for that whip to move. The first crack hit the air with some impressive acoustics, and the tail of the strap snapped back to surge forward, striking the poor girl's back. My head jerked at the sound, and Mark's fingers stilled on my clit as if he sensed I was upset.

"Are you okay? We can get out of here." His other hand reached for mine, and he gripped it tightly.

"No. I want to stay. I need to know what he's going to do to her." I needed to see this through.

"Suit yourself, but it's not going to pretty. I hadn't realised quite what we were letting ourselves in for here." Mark's hand started up again, notching up my adrenaline levels, although I didn't really need much help in that area. This time when the whip cracked I didn't flinch, but the girl did, her hands curling into fists against the wall, but to her credit she remained still. Though I didn't have a lot of experience with a bullwhip I have felt it once or twice before, and I know it's not for the faint-hearted, so for the next few lashes I kept my eyes tightly shut, concentrating on the slow, rhythmic pulses of Mark's fingers. I could feel an orgasm building.

"Are you close?" The murmured voice in my ear made me jump, but I quickly recovered.

"Yes." I didn't even think of lying. My husband knew me too well, and there were always consequences for misbehaviour. Some consequences I enjoyed, others were less friendly, so it was wise to err on the side of caution.

"Good. I'll slow things down for a moment until things get interesting."

That made me pause. "Things aren't interesting yet?" I opened my eyes to see Mark's eyes centred on the stage, and I wondered what I'd been missing these last few minutes. A quick glance told me that things had progressed quite quickly since I last dared to open my eyes.

The sound of the whip had stopped and Carlisle left the stage, but just as I thought the show was over he returned carrying a bag on his arm. It clinked and jangled as he walked, so I figured there was some kind of metal inside it. Restraints, maybe? What was he going to do to her now? I didn't think she could take much more, but I'd been wrong before.

Carlisle took his time walking across the stage, and it gave me the opportunity to examine him a little more closely. Until now my focus had been mainly on the girl, but I soon found myself curious about the man behind her. He was dressed in something that vaguely resembled a lion tamer's outfit, except it was all in black with bright gold buttons, and he wore riding boots.

Leaning forward in my chair, I noted he had sandy blond hair pulled back into a ponytail. He'd covered the top half of his face with a mask, perhaps to add theatrical appeal, and this nearly completely obscured his eyes, but even still, there seemed something vaguely familiar about him. Something I didn't like.

I wasn't going to dwell on it, though. Since the poisoning I'd been a little jumpy around people, and my psychiatrist had told me that was to be expected and that I would take a little time to heal. These days I seemed to see a bad guy around every corner, and though I would eventually convince myself I was just being silly, whenever I was around people I didn't know I had an irrational fear someone was out to hurt me. The doctor had convinced me it would pass eventually, and as Mark had a security detail around me whenever I went out, I was slowly beginning to feel a little more secure in my environment. Although it also drove me crazy.

Forcibly settling back in my chair, I closed my eyes for a second and let Mark's fingers take over. I needed to relax, and there was no better way to do that than to let my husband work his magic.

"You may be wondering what's in my bag, ladies and gentlemen." There was another jangle of sound, and my eyes reopened because curiosity won over relaxation.

Carlisle was striding up and down the stage, ignoring the slave in the corner as he surveyed the audience with a slight smirk on his face. This did not bode well. He seemed to be enjoying himself way too much. "Anyone hazard a guess as to what's in here?" He gave the bag another shake for effect, and I squirmed in my seat. Mark's lips were now on my neck, his fingers buried so deep inside me it was getting rather difficult to concentrate, but I was too engrossed in the story unfolding to let myself give in to temptation.

"I suspect most of you are thinking there are cuffs or chains inside my bag. It would be a good guess, but it would also be wrong. Besides, there would have to be a lot of them in order to fill this bag, and I only have one slave to punish, after all."

He had a point. The black satchel he had over his arm was a large one and made of heavy duty plastic. Whatever was inside was heavy and bulky. All sorts of possibilities were running through my mind, but none of them seemed very likely. I did some more squirming as my imagination got carried away, which seemed to please Mark no end.

Carlisle stopped walking and was in the centre of the stage. Opening the bag he used both hands to pull out a massive set of inter-connecting steel chains and straps. At first I had no clue what he was holding up, but after careful inspection I could see it was some kind of belt and bra. It didn't take me long to connect the dots.

"It's a chastity suit, ladies and gentlemen. This suit here, once fastened and locked, will completely prevent my sub from touching all her most intimate parts. It will also, more importantly, prevent anyone else from touching her. No one will have access to her unless they have this." He held up a small silver key that was fastened on a chain, which he then placed around his neck. "I intend to keep her locked up in this suit for the next month at the very least, or until I believe she has adequately learned her lesson. Then I may let her out, occasionally, but I don't expect that to be more often than once every two weeks or so."

His slave, who was by now staring agog at the steel contraption she was expected to wear indefinitely, didn't seem pleased by this turn of events. Throwing herself down in front of her master she proceeded to plead and sob for his forgiveness, asking for just about any punishment bar the one he had in mind for her. If it had been me I'd have probably walked away at that point, but she didn't seem to be going anywhere, which told me she was probably madly in love with the man in front of her. But if that was the case, why had she cheated on him? It didn't make sense.

Carlisle continued to ignore her, and instead addressed us again. "It's an ingenious design, ladies and gentlemen. The adjustable bands and belts all have their own padlocks, making any attempt at masturbation impossible, and the interconnecting chains will restrict her movement, ensuring that if she decides to run, she won't run far." He winked at us, but I paid him no attention. My eyes were locked on the girl in front of him who was still sobbing her heart out.

"So, what do you say, slave? Are you ready to accept your punishment or are you going to walk?" Finally, his eyes had turned towards the girl who was writhing hysterically in front of him, and it didn't seem like she would be able to compose herself any time soon. When Carlisle got bored of waiting for her to answer he shouted, "Enough!" It seemed to do the trick. She immediately stopped bawling and looked up at him with large brown eyes that were swimming with tears.

"What's it to be? Are you walking or are we going to get you fastened into this beast?" It was obvious she was between a rock and a very hard place because she looked completely horrified at the choice before her. Carlisle didn't seem to be a patient man though. "Answer now, or I walk. Your choice." He began putting the suit back in the bag and fastening the Velcro tabs, but just before he put the strap over his shoulder she caught his arm.

"Don't go." She shook her head and sniffed. Taking a deep breath so she could get enough air to continue, she then said, "I'll wear the suit." I had no idea how she could even contemplate wearing such a thing, but her mind seemed to be made up, for she nodded her head.

"Up you get then."

Putting the suit on was a laborious process. Everything had a padlock attached to it. First of all there was a collar, then a stainless steel bra, a belt, and wrists and thigh cuffs. Everything had to be adjusted manually before it was securely locked in place. The chains that would restrict her movement were everywhere. They trailed down from the collar to the bra, and from the bra they attached to the belt at her waist, and then down to the wrist and thigh cuffs. There was no way she would be able to wear clothes over it, and she was all but crippled for the time being. The short chain between the thigh cuffs would mean that she would have to shuffle her feet to walk, and even brushing her hair would be impossible, due to the way the arm cuffs were fastened to her belt with a similar short chain. The whole set up was diabolical in my opinion.

While Carlisle was carefully fitting each metal strap in its correct place and fastening each lock with a small gold padlock, Mark's fingers between my legs were going crazy. Concentrating on the pair in front of me was almost impossible, and judging by the squeaks of excitement beside me, Johanna was feeling the same.

"Stop it," I hissed at Mark, anxious to find out how this spectacle would end. That was my first mistake.

"Oh, I can't stop now, sweetheart. If I did I might have to put you in one of those suits myself." My clit was throbbing and begging for some kind of release, but Mark was too good. He knew exactly what kind of pressure to apply and how to keep me hovering on the edge of madness. Tightly pressing my legs together had no effect on him either. His hands refused to budge from their mooring. The man was an ogre.

"You and whose army?" I growled, and I meant it. Watching the thick silver belt come down tight across the slave girl's pussy sent sparks of something hot and molten deep inside me, and I swear anyone trying to put me in one of those things would probably get their eyes torn out.

"I bet I could get you into one of those," Mark murmured in my ear. I rolled my eyes. Thankfully it was so dark there was no chance he'd be able to see it.

"I saw that." His teeth latched on to my neck and gave me a small bite.

"Saw what?" I replied, the picture of innocence.

"The eye roll. I can read minds. Remember that." *Yeah right.*

As the steel bra was attached firmly around the slave's chest and tightened, I hitched in a tight breath and began to see stars. I was about to come, and there was nothing I could do to stop it. Even after a year of being under Mark's tutelage, I still couldn't get over the shame and embarrassment of climaxing in public. Maybe one day I'd overcome it, but that day was several years away.

"Stop overthinking. Just let go."

"No." I pinned my legs tighter together around his hand, and he laughed. Johanna chose that moment to orgasm beside me, and her muffled squeaks and moans further enflamed the fires that were burning me up from the inside out. Nearly cursing aloud I checked myself just in time and swore a strip of very fine cuss words silently in my head. Score one for me - finally.

When Carlisle was happy he'd adjusted the suit to perfection and was confident his slave had absolutely no access to the more delicate parts of her anatomy, he made her parade up and down the stage for the amusement of the audience. Her short, mincing steps looked painful and awkward, and it was clear the suit was going to be a challenge for her. Arms had to be forward at all times, head held high, and due to the chains and belts between her legs, she had to be very careful how she walked. Even small distances were going to be a challenge for her in this new outfit.

"How does it feel, filthy slut?" Carlisle was enjoying himself, that much was clear. There was now a kind of maniacal madness in his eyes that I didn't much like. I was starting to think his slave had made a very poor decision in her choice of partner.

When she looked up at him with a terrified expression, almost cowering as he towered over her, I wanted to yell at her to run. Unfortunately I did no such thing. Mark had just tipped my body over the edge and I was in the throes of orgasm, so it was all I could do to make sure I wasn't screaming the place down for another reason entirely. Clamping my lips shut and trying my best not to wriggle around I kept my eyes focused on the couple in the spotlight, and held my breath.

"Well?" he repeated, anxious to hear the answer to his question.

"It feels awful," she finally managed to wail. "Tight and restrictive, heavy and hard." She lifted her arms and legs experimentally as if hoping the suit might fly up and leave her. It did no such thing. She had probably just signed up to spend months in the cumbersome contraption, and it looked like she had only just realised it.

"Well, that's too bad," said Carlisle, "because I think I like that look on you." He nodded to the audience and gave us a wolf-like grin. "What do you think, ladies and gentlemen? Is it a good look on her? While some of the women yelled no, the majority of the crowd shouted the opposite. It seemed he'd worked us up into quite a fervour, one way or another.

"Yes, I thought you'd like it." He then held up the small key for all to see. "I think she looks amazing. So much so, that I might want to keep her like that forever." He nodded, long and slow. Johanna and I, who were slowly coming down from our post-orgasmic highs, nearly choked.

Carlisle looked about in the big black bag and quickly pulled out a pair of pliers. Johanna turned to face me with a quizzical expression, and I was equally clueless. Obviously, we weren't thinking very clearly at that point because I'm pretty sure

Dominic and Mark knew exactly what was going to happen next.

Placing the key between the jaws of the pliers, Master Carlisle proceeded to chop it in half. The shocked gasps of the audience rang around the auditorium just before the lights blacked out.

Chapter Eleven - Mark

"Relax. Those guys are actors. They've been leading you on a merry dance the whole time."

My wife looked like she'd just seen a ghost, and I was trying my best to calm her down. I probably should have told her what to expect before we entered the room, but where would the fun be in that? At the moment Jennifer looked ready to commit murder, and I didn't think Johanna would be far behind her.

"What? That was all staged?" Johanna shook her head in amazement for a moment, before a slow smile replaced her frown. "Well - they had me. Did you realise it was all an act, Jen?" She was still holding my wife's hand and hadn't let go of it since we'd left the theatre. I wanted it back but was too polite to say so.

"Oh my God, I've been nearly in tears watching that, and now you tell me it's all pretend?" Uh-oh. It looked like I was about to get my wife's hand back, but not in a good way. I got ready to duck. "Mark, you complete bastard. I believed every single word in there." Ducking did no good. Jen lumped me in the stomach, and I winced.

"Darling, your spanking tally is not looking good," I said tightly. "How many are we at now? Twenty thousand, two hundred and fifty?" I gave her a fierce look to let her know I meant business.

"You've just added two thousand. It was twenty thousand and fifty yesterday," she said, her eyebrows furrowing downwards.

"You got two thousand for hitting me just a second ago, so let that be a lesson to you." That was accompanied by another look.

She rolled her eyes and was about to say something before I said, "Twenty thousand, three hundred now. Want to earn some more?" I brought out the gag that had been burning a hole in my pocket. "Tell you what, before you say anything else that is almost guaranteed to get your ass in trouble, what say you wear this for me?" It wasn't really a question. I had it in her mouth before she could utter a sound and I made quick work of fastening the buckle behind her head. Lots of garbled complaints followed, but it made little difference by that point. The deed had been done.

Dominic cleared the air. "What do you want to do now?" He looked at Johanna with amusement and bit his lip. I didn't know what he was laughing at. His partner looked equally mad, and if he wasn't lucky, he was going to get some in a minute.

"Well, I thought we'd venture over to the main event, seeing as we've got the girls all dressed up," I said. Dominic put a finger to his lips to prevent himself from laughing. Johanna obviously had no idea what was going on, for she gave him an odd look.

"Don't look at me like that, or you're going to get some of what she's having."
He held up a black ball gag, almost identical to the one I'd placed on Jen, bar the colour. Great minds thought alike. I resisted the urge to smirk.

"You wouldn't," she said, backing away in a hurry.

"Oh, I absolutely would. Now be a good girl and do as you're told. I think you and Jen are very much going to enjoy the next exhibit. It's going to be right up your street, so to speak." Dominic put a finger to his lips, cautioning Johanna not to speak, and amazingly she obeyed him. We then ambled over to the main arena, grabbing another glass of champagne on our way, which of course Jen couldn't have, much to her great displeasure. I pretended not to notice. Besides, in a few minutes that would be the last thing on her mind.

Before we knew it we were back in cardboard cut-out Paris again, ambling along Parisian sidewalks with not a care in the world. Someone was playing the accordion, and there were a few street vendors around discreetly trying to entice us into their "shops". We were not interested this time around. Making a beeline for the main arena, which was located down some steps under a glimmering pyramid, near a very authentic Musee Du Louvre, we descended into darkness again.

This time it didn't last long. As soon as we reached the last step and pushed aside the black velvet curtains, bright lights assaulted our eyes, and for a minute no one could see a thing. Blinking the bright glare away, it didn't take long before the massive room revealed its secrets - and there were quite a few of them.

My eyes weren't concentrated on what the room had to offer, though. I wanted to see what Jennifer would make of it all. Would she want to compete with all the others, or would she prefer to stay by my side? Did I mind which option she chose? Good question. But no, tonight was her night as much as it was mine, and I wanted her to have a good time. Please let her enjoy this, I silently begged.

Jen, who had now managed to refocus her eyes, was looking around the room as if someone had told her there was a psychopath on the loose. It wasn't fear exactly, more apprehension, and I could understand that. This was probably a lot to take in all at once.

"It's a pet show. The biggest human pet show in the UK," I said, waving my hand around in a large arc. "Owners bring their pets in to be examined and judged. Some complete exercises, others just stay in their cage. It all depends on what they're comfortable with. In this room we have ponies, dogs, cats, wolves, foxes, bears and many more. They are all here to play." Would Jen share their enthusiasm? "Don't worry. As promised, I haven't signed you up for anything." I crossed my hands together and performed a slicing motion, so she could relax for a second. "Just take your time and have a look around."

Jen pointed to her gag hopefully, but I shook my head. "Pets aren't allowed to talk. If you can't be trusted to be mute, you wear the gag. Now go and have some fun. I'll be right behind you." It was all the encouragement she needed. Taking Johanna's hand, they explored the room together, while Dominic and I trailed behind them.

The first exhibits were cages upon cages of cats and dogs. They had all been placed upon tables for easy viewing, and not a single one of them could keep still. Most of them had been gagged, just like Jennifer, but there was still the odd little mewl and snuffle as we walked around them. No two pets were the same, of course, and Jen found each and every one of them fascinating. Some wore makeup, some had studs, and some were chained by their leash to the bars of the cage, while others sported wrists and ankle cuffs attached to eyebolts at the bottom. There was a lot of bondage tape going around in various colours, and this was generally applied by folding ankles up to buttocks and wrists up to shoulders, to make the human subjects closer resemble their chosen animal. A lot wore specially designed shoes and mittens, and a few of the females had clothing similar to Jennifer's; little skirts and bra tops that revealed more than they hid.

A couple of the cages also contained food and water, and we watched the pets munching and drinking with their noses scraping around their food bowls. Jen wrinkled her mouth up at this, so I saved that little snippet of information for future use. It would probably prove a useful punishment one day.

The exhibits were numerous, and we had only seen the front half of them after a good ten minutes' walk. When we finished the line and went down the rear of them, things got far more interesting. Well in my opinion, anyway.

I've always had a thing for pert backsides, and row upon row of them is a mouth-watering treat. Especially when most are recently tanned and blushing a most pleasing shade of bright pink. The multiple tails were quite something to behold, too. There were all sorts of differing thicknesses and lengths, some fur, others plastic or rubber. Some were stuck up high in the air, while others had their tails firmly between their legs. Jen and Johanna were fascinated.

"You can touch them, you know. They're going to be judged later, and this is the warm-up session. There will be hands all over them examining their form and posture, so you might as well have fun. I believe they enjoy that sort of thing." I winked at Jen, and she didn't need to be told twice. The bars of each cage were more than wide enough to insert a hand into them, and after a cautious attempt or two at petting and stroking a few specimens, Jen and Johanna soon got into the swing of things.

As was to be expected, they delighted in teasing the poor caged beasts. A tweak of a nipple here, a smack on a backside there, the occasional light fumble between their legs, and it wasn't long before the pair of them were lost in fits of laughter. Dominic and I let them have their fun. We'd be having the last laugh soon enough unless I was much mistaken, but we'd wait and see.

"You can make them climax if you want to, girls. They are on display for your amusement. Similarly, you can tease them mercilessly and leave them hanging; it's your choice." Up until now the women had been cautious with the displayed pets. They'd been testing boundaries and getting bolder with each new toy they found. So as soon as they'd been given permission to do pretty much anything they wanted, their eyes lit up with mischief and I felt sorry for the next line of caged beasts. I had a feeling they were in for a rough ride.

Johanna and Jen spent the next half hour in tandem, using their hands and fingers to make as many animals squirm as they could. That meant four hands in one cage at a time, exploring as they tweaked, nipped, stroked and danced over every inch of exposed flesh they could find. Tail plugs were being pumped in and out, nipple clamps tugged and tightened, and they showed no preference between cocks and clitorises as their fingers ran riot - especially after they discovered the strategically placed bottles of lubricant that were dotted all over the place.

As the room around us began to fill with likewise-minded patrons, the girls became more and more aroused. Their nipples started to stand, their cheeks took on a rosy hue, and two sets of pupils became very dilated. I could already see a thin trickle of fluid seeping down Jen's legs, and I knew, without having to look, that her sex would be swollen and pulsing. This was what I had been hoping for, and sure enough, she now had that hungry look I love. Soon I would have a question for her, but for now I was quite content to sit back and watch her work. I had to admit that I was pretty fired up just watching the pair of them play. Just a few more minutes and my wife would be where I wanted her. Well, I hoped so, anyway.

Jen and Johanna had more fun tormenting their subjects than doling out pleasure, although they did their fair share of both. They listened with rapt attention to every little squeak, moan, and whimper. Their fingers tugged hair, squeezed clits and gripped cocks. Squirming, shuddering, and bucking hips were the direct result of their actions. No one was immune to their charms, and it didn't much surprise me. They were both incredibly beautiful women.

"Shall we spoil their party?" Dominic looked over at me and raised his eyebrow sardonically. I already knew that he'd signed Johanna up for a stint in a cage. He assumed I'd done the same for Jennifer, though no such agreement had been made.

"Let's," I said, by way of reply. I'd talk to Jen and see what she thought. My gut instinct said she'd want to take part in this, but she was still wary of Escape, and that might put a spanner in the works. I wasn't going to push her.

Beckoning Jennifer over, it didn't take me long to remove the gag, but I cautioned her to be silent until we were outside the room once more. Inside, it was strictly forbidden for pets to talk, and there didn't seem any point in us being disqualified before the games began.

"That was fun." Wiping a line of drool from the corner of her chin, Jen cracked her jaw a couple of times to loosen up her mouth, before looking up at me. When she did I sucked in a tight breath. Her eyes were sparkling, her face lit up with excitement, and I could feel her body humming with need. Wanting to take her into the nearest dark corner and fuck her senseless, I somehow managed to control the urge. There were no secret corners around these parts, and if there were, they were already occupied.

"I'm glad you enjoyed yourself." My voice gave nothing of my arousal away, but my wife could read me by now. She was far more astute than most people gave her credit for.

"You look like you want to throw me over your shoulder and find the nearest cave, darling." She batted her eyelashes at me as if encouraging me to do my worst. If we were in a slightly less public place I might have taken her up on the matter, but I wasn't happy being caught with my pants down in here.

"Oh, I'll be doing that later, kittykat, rest assured. Right now, though, I have a proposition for you. An entirely optional proposition before you go nuts, so don't look at me like that." I held out my hands as if to assure her I meant no harm. It did little good. I'd stolen her happiness away, and she now looked like she wanted to murder me.

"You said that..."

"And I meant it," I butted in. "This will be your choice. I wasn't going to ask you, but Johanna has already been signed up for it, and I thought it would be polite to ask if you wanted to give it a go too. If you don't, that's fine. You can spend the evening glued to my side, just like we agreed. Just hear me out, okay?"

Jen's face dropped, and she looked down towards the floor. It made my heart sink ten stories, and I rushed to comfort her.

"Relax. I mean it. We can go home right now if you want to. Right now." I lifted her chin up, so she had to look at me. As soon as she did she would know I was serious, and sure enough, she nodded. "Do you want to go home? I can have the limo waiting for us in two minutes." Jen put her finger on her bottom lip as she thought about it. My fingers twitched inside my pocket, hovering upon my cell phone, should the outcome be negative. I didn't think it would be, but I wanted to get her out of here immediately if it was.

"No. Talk." The lure of mystery and a little bit of curiosity get them every time. Jen knew if she left now I wouldn't tell her any details of what was about to happen, and she was absolutely correct. The only way she'd find out was by playing the game. My wife knew the rules of engagement; she'd lived with me too long.

"There's a competition for the best pet. You get your own cage, lots of wandering fingers, and the occasional orgasm if you're lucky. You also get to be tied up, gagged, and spanked occasionally. It might not be your thing, but I thought I should at least..." I didn't get a chance to finish my sentence.

"I'm in."

Atta girl. "Are you sure? I'll be watching from a distance, and I still have security guys in the building, but I want to make sure you feel comfortable here. If not we can go home." While I might have been pressuring my wife into this purely so I could gawk upon her in a cage, I didn't want her to feel like I was pressuring her - if that made sense.

"I'm sure. Now I know why you put me in this outfit, and it would be an awful shame to waste it. How do they judge this event?" Jen's eyes narrowed in on me, and I knew she was fully engaged with the task. I then got a little bit worried. If she was counting on beating the opposition, she had very stiff competition.

"Do you want to enter this to win?" If she did, I was about to dash her hopes.

"No." Well, that was succinct enough, I suppose.

"Well, why do you want to enter the competition? You don't have to do it to please me." I was pretty sure that wasn't the reason, but I thought I'd make sure.

"I'm not doing it to please you." She gave me a lazy grin. That was *my* favourite look, so I was not amused.

"Then why are you doing it?" I was genuinely intrigued. What on earth was going on in my wife's head now?

"Because I want to beat Johanna." She gave me a cheeky wink and began walking back down the steps to the arena without a backward glance. I shook my head in utter confusion. I would never understand females. Thankfully, I didn't have to in order to remain married to one, so that was a bonus.

It didn't take long to get Jennifer in a cage. When we'd re-entered the arena Johanna and Dominic were nowhere to be seen, and my wife was so anxious to join her she nearly screamed out loud when she saw the queue of people in front of us.

"If I'd known you were this keen to get tied up and caged we could have done it at home, and I'd have thoroughly enjoyed a couple of hours of peace yesterday." Maybe I could get one for the bedroom. It would be a nice feature, I thought.

"You're not funny. Now you've got the idea in my head I'm excited. Too excited to wait," she said, in a delightfully sultry voice.

"Well it's a good job I have VIP privileges then, isn't it darling? We get to jump the queue." I couldn't see why anyone would be in such a hurry to get locked inside a small cage, but then, I wasn't a female. As previously said, females are funny creatures.

Pulling her out of the long line I walked her up to the front, where the cages were lined up and waiting to be filled, and showed the attendant my card. He gave me a handful of padlocks and told us to pick a cage. He also said that if we needed any help getting strapped in, he'd be over right away. That wouldn't be necessary. I was more than capable of locking my wife away in a small prison, and the wrist and ankle cuffs she wore would make the task even easier.

"Sometimes it's very nice being married to you," Jen murmured in my ear. We were standing in front of the cage she had picked, and just waiting to be handed the key.

"Only sometimes?" If I got a cheeky answer in reply, I swear I was going to leave her in that cage a lot longer than necessary.

"Fine. It's always nice being married to you. Except when you think I've blackmailed you. That wasn't fun. But thankfully we're over that now," she whispered, knowing damn well she wasn't supposed to be talking.

She had a point. I'd let her off on that score.

"Mrs Matthews, I think it's about time we get your gag back on so you can squeeze your butt into that tiny little cage, else you're going to get disqualified before the games even begin." The pink rubber ball was already in my hand.

"What are you trying to say about my bu..." That was all she managed to hiss. A firm shove of the ball against her lips and pleasant silence returned. It wouldn't for long.

"I love your butt. It is the perfect size and shape, and there is no other butt in the world I would swap it for." I kissed her forehead to try and dismiss any further arguments. Even though Jennifer was gagged that wouldn't stop her, believe me. This would be a good time to distract her with something.

Taking one of the silver clips attached to her gag, I began teasing her left nipple with my thumb and forefinger. It bloomed into life with little effort, and a few well-placed nips soon had it standing so proudly to attention it could have almost saluted me. Squeezing the jaws of the clamp open, I then placed it over the poor nub and watched Jen closely. A flash of shock or pain crossed her face, but this quickly turned into something else. Her eyes went dark, and her lashes fluttered at me. I knew that look. It would serve her well for an hour or two in the cage, I thought. Attaching the other clamp in a similar fashion, she rubbed her face up against mine and almost purred. Mrs Matthews was getting into character pretty quickly, and I have to say, it suited her.

"Right, enough of that young lady. You have an adoring public to please. It seems you have picked a very tiny cage, and you're going to have fun wriggling into it. Have a go, if you don't believe me." My finger pointed towards the floor, indicating that she should get on her knees and start crawling inside. She was down on all fours in a flash, and I nearly choked. The woman could do what she was told, after all. Interesting.

Jen sat there for ten minutes trying to get inside the cage. The window simply wasn't wide enough. No amount of shoulder rolling or contortionist moves would let her get inside the four small walls, and short of dislocating both shoulders, there was no way she was going to accomplish the feat. I already knew this, of course, but it was good fun watching her wear herself out. Finally, I decided to take pity on her.

"Do you want to know the easy way to do that?" Sitting back on her haunches, she gave me a look that said something along the lines of "you are a complete and utter bastard", but I have to confess I kind of liked the look by now, and I secretly think she did too. Let me put it this way: Jennifer Redcliff wouldn't have adapted well to a man who didn't challenge her, both inside the bedroom and out.

Pulling the back door off the cage with one heavy tug, I revealed a large square that she would have no difficulty getting into. It was attached by a few metal clips, but these could be secured by padlocks later if I so desired. Mind you, if I did that no one would be able to spank her, and I was very much looking forward to watching that.

There was a long groan through the gag, and she gave me another of her looks, but she didn't waste any more time as she crawled forward. When her ass was securely inside I grabbed the first couple of padlocks and secured her wrists and ankles to the sidebars of the cage. Picking up the back panel, I then reattached it to the metal clips. Perfect.

"You look utterly edible like that, you know. I might have to get one for the bedroom. I could lock you up every time you misbehave."

Jen rolled her eyes.

"That's another one hundred spanks, young lady. Behave yourself. Speaking of those..." I pulled the back off her cage once more and delivered twenty perfectly positioned and quite firm spanks to her ass. It wasn't nearly red enough after them, so I administered another twenty amid much squawking and wailing. Only when I felt the proper hue had been attained did I reattach the bars.

"You can't be the only one in the line who looks like her master's gone soft on her, can you?" I gave her a wink and walked off. I wouldn't go very far, but I wanted to watch her from a distance and make sure she was enjoying herself. Although I didn't think I had much to fear on that score, I also wanted a drink. A stiff, single malt would make me feel much more at ease, and then I'd go and find Dominic. I had a feeling this was going to be a very entertaining evening.

Chapter Twelve - Jennifer

As soon as Mark walked away my cage was hoisted up by some kind of mini forklift device. Seeing two large prongs come straight at me was not a pleasant experience, but thankfully they went underneath me and not right through me. I was then rattled and shaken for a good ten metres until we came to an abrupt halt in front of a large raised block which already had the name *Kittykat* inscribed on it in the form of a bronze plaque. Had I been that predictable or had Mark just been hopeful? I was almost offended.

The forklift prongs then began to lift me upwards, and I felt very vulnerable, rocking about in my little cage. Were the appropriate health and safety protocols being adhered to? I certainly hoped so. We'd probably had enough scandal in the family for at least the next ten years, and falling off a pedestal dressed as a deranged kitten wasn't going to be a fun A&E experiment.

Thankfully the guy on the end of the wheel seemed to know what he was doing. He got me up on the pedestal with little fuss, and before I knew what was happening he'd already driven me off and left me to my fate.

After I'd been safely installed up high, the first thing I did was test my restraints. It was what any sensible girl would do. In times of emergency, you needed to know exactly what you had to play with. I had four very securely fastened wrists and ankles in leather cuffs that were going nowhere. Unless someone had a padlock key or a pair of cutters, I was stuck. Thanks to Mark, I also knew that the back of the cage could come off, allowing a lot more access to my body than I had previously figured. This could be a problem. Hang on, this was what I had signed up for. There would be lots of hands all over my body doing exciting, dangerous, wonderful things. Hopefully, they would also drive my husband crazy, which should mean that as soon as we got home, I'd get slammed up against the wall and fucked senseless. When Mark was driven wild by insane jealousy, sex was amazing. Scratch that, sex was always amazing - but let's say it was even better than usual, and that's saying something.

I snapped out of my daydream fairly suddenly as I saw a flash of movement in front of me. Catching the glare of light upon shiny black plastic, a woman in a black catsuit loomed into view. Uh-oh. It looked like I had my first customer. Let's hope she was friendly.

"Oh, darling. Come over here. This one's all dressed up in pink!" She clapped her hands excitedly, almost making me jump as she bent her head down to peer into my cage. It was a unique experience. I almost felt as if I were an exhibit at a zoo when her partner came round to stare down at me too.

"She is adorable, isn't she? I wonder if she's up for hire?" My eyes darkened beneath their hungry, scrutinising eyes. I was not up for sale, and if Mark had put me up for sale he could wait until he was sixty before he got any babies.

"We'll have to ask. I'd love a pet, even if it was only for a day. Can you imagine the fun we could have with her? I could brush her hair, take her out for walks, dress her up, and torment her senseless. Oh yes. I want this one. Can I have her?"

I could see her partner, a handsome gentleman with short, wavy brown hair, rolling his eyes upward. He was clearly used to indulging her, but I think I saw some intelligence in those eyes too. At least, I hoped I did.

"How about we look around all the exhibits first, just to make sure she's the one? We haven't even looked around half of them, darling." He tapped her on the shoulder and pointed her in the direction of the rest of the pets lined up.

"Good idea," she squealed, "although I don't think I'll change my mind." She wandered off, skipping past me, but the man stayed for a while longer, eyeing me with unconcealed amusement.

Finally, he bent down to talk to me. "Don't worry. She doesn't know you're Mark Matthews' wife, so you'll have to forgive her. My girlfriend doesn't have a hope in hell's chance of getting you for the day, but I'll let her dream for a while longer." His hand reached in the cage, and he gave me a soft pat on the head. "Though I can see why he's so taken with you. Matthews is one lucky bastard." With that, he was off.

My heart rate had just about calmed before another pair of feet came into view. These shoes definitely belonged to a man, and as I looked up to spy a black suit, another one could be seen just behind him.

"What's this one, Leonard? Another puppy?" A very proper and posh accent assaulted my ears. Did he have to shout? I might be mute, but I most certainly wasn't deaf.

"No. This one is a kitten, dear." Ah, a gay couple. The second man's voice gave it away, being a little on the effeminate side. And a little derogatory, too. What was wrong with kittens? Then it clicked; they were probably mostly girls.

"What's wrong with kittens?" his partner asked. Great minds thought alike.

"Nothing. I just prefer cock."

Don't we all, darling, I thought.

"You can still have some fun with kittens. Look at this one - she's absolutely gorgeous." A hand came through the cage to finger the pink bow I was wearing upon my blonde curls. It reached down to tinkle the bell on my collar. "We could hire a puppy and a kitten, and watch them get up to naughtiness all day long."

What was all this hiring business about? I wondered if Johanna was going to get hired out. I then wondered if I'd be jealous if she did.

"How about we hire a puppy and a wolf?" Amber eyes peered into my cage as a

62

pair of lips wrinkled in disgust. "Oh, she is too sweet for words. All this pink makes me nauseous." He waved his arms about as if there were a nasty stench in the room.

"You are entirely too predictable. It's good to spice things up a bit." The fingers reached for a nipple to discover they had been tightly clamped.

"Oh, God. You are simply too divine for words," the man cooed, rubbing his finger over my clamped teat repeatedly. I bleated through my gag and batted my eyelashes adoringly at him.

"Don't get too attached. Matt says she's Matthews' wife. You've got more chance of shagging the Pope." The fingers I had so been enjoying were removed in a split second. "Jesus Christ, why didn't you tell me that before?" The pair moved swiftly on, while my blood boiled. Did I have leprosy or something? Was I now the most untouchable woman in the land? It appeared so. If I didn't get someone's fingers on me soon, I swear I was going to burst.

Thankfully I didn't have to wait long before more revellers walked by. This time they came in their hoards, one after the other, and then several at once. One minute I was craving attention and in the next... I was overwhelmed by it all.

Fingers were now all over me, petting and stroking, nipping and pinching, and sensation flooded my body as if a dam inside me had burst. This is what I had been longing for, but when it happened all at once it was almost too much to bear.

"She's dead cute."

"Isn't that Mark Matthews's wife?"

"If this is the only chance I can get at sinking my fingers inside her, there's no way I'm not going to take it."

"Is she wet?"

"Can you make her come?"

All this and more flitted past my eardrums at the speed of light. It didn't concern me in the slightest. My attention was firmly centred on my body and the mass of fingers crawling all over it.

Some had their hands on my head and were burying themselves in my silky ringlets, others were fascinated by the bright pink ball in my mouth. A few ladies found my pink knee-high socks very entertaining, especially when they pinged the elastic around my thighs. A group of men behind me had their mitts all over the mesh crop-top I wore, and were trying their hardest to get their hands on my boobs. All these actions I could just about cope with. There were plenty more that I found a whole lot more challenging. These would be the fingers that were flicking my nipples through the heavy silver clamps I wore, and the ones that were tugging at the straps of my gag and getting tangled in my hair. Then there were the fingernails digging into my inner thighs as they scraped a path upwards, and the ones that were squeezing my clit repeatedly.

If that wasn't enough, someone had almost buried their hand inside my pussy, and yet another had gotten hold of my tail and was having enormous fun pushing and pulling the damn thing. I didn't know whether I wanted to scream or beg for more. The pleasure/pain aspect was all-consuming, and if someone had asked me to recite my name, I think I'd have drawn a blank. There wasn't much I could do, really. I rattled about in my wrist cuffs, testing each strip of leather to its limit, but nothing budged. Trying to rock the cage had little effect because I'd been placed in an indented, rectangular groove upon my pedestal, and that meant I was going nowhere. There was little left to do except submit to all these people and let them have their way with me.

As soon as that thought entered my mind my body did its best to consciously relax, and that was when I started having fun. My discomfort at being surrounded and swarmed upon morphed into something else, and that was desire. Earth-moving, mind-shattering, brain-numbing desire, and it exploded in shocking waves all around me. Suddenly the fingers that had been so obtrusive only a second ago were now adored friends, actively doing my body's bidding. I'd gone from being repulsed to entranced, and all I wanted was more - much, much more.

Thankfully the fingers obliged. If there had been only one or two pairs of them, maybe they would have just teased me, but there were honestly too many to count, and they were insistent, working me over with great enthusiasm and vigour. My first orgasm crashed over me within three minutes, and the second didn't take much longer. Three, four, five and six were all achieved within forty minutes, and after that I was crying for mercy because I couldn't take any more.

"Ladies and gentlemen, move aside please. The honourable judge, Gordon Watters is required to examine this pet for the next few minutes, so please stand back and give him some room." This was good news, on the whole. It would give me a few precious minutes of respite in which to hope and pray that Mark would rescue me from this monstrous onslaught. If I didn't know better, I'd bet my husband was watching me from afar and laughing his head off. What he didn't know, was that I would have the last laugh. After I'd been made to climax ten times, there was no way he was getting any of the goods later.

Gordon Watters was a portly man, probably in his mid-sixties, and judging by the smell of his breath, he was very fond of beer. The gentleman wore an expensive suit, an even more expensive watch, and his left eye had a slight twitch that was slightly unnerving. I assumed he enjoyed his job around these parts because he showed no hesitation about getting his hands on my body, and when they were there, it seemed almost impossible to get them off again. Already well aware that I probably wouldn't like what he had to say about me, I tried to hum a little tune silently in my head to ignore him. That worked for about the first five seconds, and then there was no blotting him out. His voice got louder and louder until I was almost wincing at each new word, and each sentence was worse than the last.

"Well, what have we here, gentlemen? A fine specimen, this one, methinks. Quite young. I'd say she was probably the right side of thirty." I nearly choked beneath my gag. He was out by a few years, and I was not amused. Initially his hands began examining me from the top of my neck, all the way down to the curve of my spine, in long sweeping motions, but this was just the start of his examination. His hands were hot, clammy, and a little stiff in their movements, which I didn't much like, so I straightened my spine and pretended to ignore them.

"Not particularly responsive, although quite smooth and finely toned. Her owner obviously takes her out for regular exercise." I bristled a little, and swayed my hips in annoyance, not that it had any effect. "Reasonable muscle definition, lots of enthusiasm," he said, as he reached my nipple and gave it a fierce tweak that elicited a loud groan from me, "and very nice to look at if you like that kind of thing." *Charmed, I was sure.*

A finger was inserted underneath my top lip, pulling it up sharply. "Nice teeth, full lips, she's the kind of pet that would always look better gagged." A sarcastic glare crossed my features, and I couldn't wait to hear what he had to say next, and oh joy, I didn't have to wait long. "I'd say she probably has a feisty temperament, is often difficult to handle, and rarely does what she's told."

Had this man been talking to my husband? Either that or he was a Clairvoyant, which seemed extremely unlikely.

Mr Watters then began sauntering around my cage, examining me from every angle, which for some reason made me extremely nervous.

"Reasonably nice outfit, acceptable ass, and good presentation overall. This puts her in the top twenty percent. Are you writing this all down, Mrs Dennison?"

A lady in the background who wore a big pair of tortoiseshell spectacles suddenly jumped half a mile into the air, and her mousy brown hair went flying in all directions. The clipboard she had been holding fluttered in her hands, but she somehow managed to catch it, to the detriment of her glasses which were now somewhat crooked. Taking a finger and propping them back securely where they belonged, she said, "Yes, Sir. It's all here."

Mr Watters barely noticed. He was nodding to himself absently, his eyes glued to my body, and we all sat there wondering what on earth was going to happen next. Thankfully, Mrs Dennison helped us out.

"Are you going to spank her next, Sir? There's a box here for that." There was a slight wobble at the end of her sentence, and I couldn't help but wonder what kind of power this man held over her. She appeared to be scared witless of him, and I suspect she had good reason - although what that was, I had no idea.

"Yes. What a good idea. Could I have the paddle, please?" It was no sooner said than done. Mrs Dennison had the paddle in his hand before I could blink, and the back of my cage was being yanked off soon after.

"Push that backside out, kittykat. Show us how much you enjoy a good spanking. We always add a few extra points for the most enthusiastic pets."

I did as I was told. There was still a spark of competitiveness inside me that insisted I beat Johanna, and I was guessing I probably hadn't done very well so far.

"That's it. Lovely work. Nice pert buttocks there, gentlemen, wouldn't you say?" There was a chorus of mumbled agreement from behind me, but I just wished they'd get on with the job at hand.

"She's still wearing quite a pretty rosy blush from earlier, too. We like that, Mrs Dennison; note it down, darling." There was some furious scribbling going on as Mr Watters began examining my ass in detail. "Tail in the proper place, firmly wedged," I squeaked at that point, "and she's a lot more responsive down this end." Rolling my eyes at his assistant, she quickly looked away from me and continued scrawling with her pen.

"Well, enough of that. Let's begin." Mr Watters didn't believe in warm-ups, and the first ten smacks of the paddle had my eyes smarting with tears. I then got ten seconds of recovery time before he started the next round. This was nothing compared to what Mark usually doled out, but tiredness was probably getting the better of me. When he started his third round of spanks I wanted to mewl out loud in protest, but I managed to restrain myself.

"You can make some noise, kittykat. We like that. It means extra points." I would have slammed my head into the bottom of my cage had there been room. As it was, when Watters started round four I made as much noise as possible. It felt good. Yelling helped channel the pain, in a weird and wonderful way - even through a gag.

"Lovely. We're done here. Oh, wait, just one more thing." Watters slowly sauntered around to the front of my cage, and peered down at me with a smile on his face. I hoped that was a good thing. Then he put his fingers in the bars in front of my face, and I nearly broke both my wrists and ankles trying to move backwards as fast as humanly possible.

"Calm down, kittykat. I just need a 'meow' before I move on. Rules are rules." He needed what? Seriously? The gag on the back of my head was unbuckled, and the ball removed. It seemed he was serious after all. Everyone waited expectantly for me to say something. I decided to step up to the occasion and after swallowing a couple of times, came up with a very cat-like "meow" that any feline would be proud of. I then decided to up my acting skills by adding a bit of a purr. The gag was reinserted, and I had no idea whether I'd performed adequately or not.

"Lovely. Let's move on, Mrs Dennison."

My five minutes of stardom was short-lived. The fingers were slowly coming back, and I wasn't at all sure I could cope with a second round. As it turned out I was being pessimistic. This time I didn't draw in large crowds like before. They must have been following the judge. Now it was mostly couples or small groups that had come to gawk at me, and most of them had no interest in making me orgasm - quite the opposite in fact. These people were out to torment, tease and terrify, and they were doing a reasonable job of it, in my opinion. In less than ten minutes my clit was on fire, my nipples felt like they had done ten rounds with a heavyweight boxer, and I couldn't remember the number of times I'd been spanked. Whilst Watters had refitted both ends of my cage after he'd examined me, everyone now knew how easy they were to remove, and several opportunistic souls had done precisely that to get much better access to my ass. This meant I was receiving regular spankings, usually at the same time my clit was being played with. Now I don't know about everyone, but I find it extremely difficult to come while being spanked. I can't relax. So it didn't take long for me to become extremely frustrated, and irritated with everyone and everything. If I'd had the use of my mouth I would have let someone know, but unfortunately there wasn't much

I could do, tied down as I was, except swing my hips from side to side, which generally amused everyone, and let out the occasional grunt. Although I didn't regret my earlier decision in entering the competition, I made a mental note to get more details about what I was letting myself in for in future.

"Ah, there you are." My head snapped round instantly. Holy hell, I recognised that voice. With a sinking feeling in the pit of my stomach I watched Carlisle come round to stand in front of me. Oh shit. Having just discovered how awful the man was, I didn't feel very comfortable with him anywhere near me. It didn't help that I was virtually nailed down to the bottom of my cage.

"Do you recognise me, Petal?" Oh, no, no, no. That had my attention. Petal had been my name when I'd been transformed into a pony girl at Albrecht stables, against my will, I might add. Trying to escape from its confines had been one of the most horrible ordeals I had ever experienced, and by the looks of it, the fun and games weren't over yet. Unless I was much mistaken, Kyle Levison was standing in front of me. He'd swapped his English accent for his native American drawl, and the sound chilled my blood. My eyes flared when he squatted down to peer over me, and I hoped to hell Mark had figured out who he was and would come running. It was a slim chance, though. I'd only figured it out because he'd practically thrown his identity in my face.

"What a shame you can't talk, Petal. Don't get me wrong, you look awesome caged up like that, but I'd love to hear what you thought about my artwork on your back. I can still see the scar, although it's healed up rather nicely. What a shame. The next time I get my hands on you I'll do a much better job. You have my word." The beast winked at me, and I nearly lost the contents of my stomach then and there. "Yep, that's right. I'm coming for you. We've had to wait a while for the heat to die down, but now that it has, you're mine. Dad sends his regards by the way. He says I can do pretty much whatever I want with you when I snatch you."

Why was he telling me this? To scare me witless? If that was the case, it was working. Kyle Levison was never getting his hands on me, though. Now I knew he was after me I was staying in Fountaine Bleu under lock and key with a whole army of armed guards around me until the bastard had been caught.

Kyle moved slowly around my cage, leering at my body from all angles, and my insides churned. What was he up to now? His hand reached underneath me, pinching a swollen nipple, and I yelped. I couldn't help it.

"A bit sore, are we?" The other nipple received the same harsh treatment, and it brought tears to my eyes. When his hands reached the scar on my back, I winced, and it was all I could do to stop myself from trembling madly. I didn't want him to feel my fear, but there wasn't much I could do to stop him. When his fingernails dug into the scar tissue I squawked loudly, but there was no one around to witness the noise. They were all further up the line, hanging on Watters' every word. Kyle had timed his moment perfectly. Fantastic. I was stuck with a sociopath/psychopath, and I couldn't do a thing about it. There was a nip on the inside of my right thigh, a pause, and then another nip on my left, which was even more painful. My eyes watered as I craned my neck, trying to see what the bastard was up to.

"Don't get all agitated on me. I'm nearly finished, Petal." His fingers snaked between my legs and caught my throbbing clit. Bile climbed up my throat once more, as I felt him squeeze the poor nub between his knuckles. "Oh, the things I want to do to you, Petal. The things I want to do..."

I did make retching sounds then. I couldn't help myself. I began trembling like a forest in a storm force gale, and once the shakes were upon me I couldn't stop them. Surely he'd go now. If anyone walked around and saw me like this he was going to be in trouble. But Kyle didn't worry about things like that. Pulling off the end of the cage, he slowly caressed the bright pink globes of my ass, as if admiring the damage. He then gave each cheek five, unbearably hard spanks, which did reduce me to tears, before quickly placing the cage back together and almost sprinting off.

"Just remember I'll be back before you know it. There's no way you can escape me, Petal." I screamed my head off at his retreating back, trying my best to attract someone's attention, but there wasn't a soul around to hear. As soon as Kyle was out of sight I dissolved into fits of tears and waited for someone to rescue me. Coming here tonight had been a bad idea, and all I wanted was to go home. Right now.

It didn't take long to discover why Kyle had scarpered. When Mark came running around the corner, only a minute or two later, my relief must have been immediately evident in my eyes because I've never seen him move so fast. He got the cage door off, speedily removed my gag, and then demanded to know what had happened.

"Were you watching?" My voice was wobbly, but it worked, thank God.

"Yes. When you started to shake all over I knew something was wrong. You looked like you wanted to vomit at one point. Was it because of what had happened in the auditorium? I recognised Carlisle." Mark was making short work of releasing the padlocks on my cuffs, and I couldn't wait to be free of my awful prison.

"Carlisle wasn't who he appeared to be," I choked out. "He was American." My nerves still had the better of me, and there was no point trying to form long sentences yet, but I knew Mark would be quick on the uptake.

"You've just seen Kyle? Holy shit. I knew there was something off about the guy. How on earth did that bastard get past security?" Mark looked like he was about to murder someone. His eyes had gone black, and there was a tense air about him. I felt exactly the same way. This was terrible news for both of us.

"He says he plans to kidnap me." Another short sentence, but it got straight to the point.

"Over my dead body." Mark freed the last of the cuffs and pulled me from the cage, encircling his arms around me. It was exactly what I needed. Now I could breathe again the tears began pouring in earnest, and I couldn't stop them.

"Shh. We won't let him win. He just wants to scare you. You're safe now. You're with me. I will never let anything happen to you." I looked up into my husband's eyes, and I wanted to believe him. There was plenty of conviction in his expression, and I knew he meant every word he said. The trouble was that Kyle was a loose cannon, with plenty of funds at his disposal. He had no scruples, was more mentally unbalanced than Willy Wonka, and just as crazy. That man was the type of person who would never give up, and there was no question that both of our lives were going to be made miserable until someone caught him and put him where he belonged - behind bars.

Mark held me for what seemed like an age, but when I could finally speak again, all I said was, "I want to go home."

Chapter Thirteen - Mark

As soon as Jennifer had calmed down enough to sit on her own, I rang security. Describing Carlisle to the best of my ability, I gave them an adequate description but was well aware that Kyle would have changed out of that costume by now. The man wasn't completely stupid. Then I rang Khalil and told him about the incident. He wasn't surprised. Thankfully, he was already way ahead of me and assured me extra security would be waiting for us on our return home, and that Jen's security detail would also be upgraded. Promising to do all he could to find Kyle's whereabouts, I left it at that.

"Let's get you home." I reached my hand out to Jen who was now sitting at a table in one of the French bistro's that lined the main street. She was wearing my dinner jacket while carefully sipping a large glass of red wine. I figured she needed it.

"No."

That was not the response I'd expected. Her voice had a mutinous tinge to it, and I wondered what was up now. "A few minutes ago, you told me you wanted to go home." Unless I was going crazy she had just changed her mind. Women. You can't live with them, and you can't live without them.

"You need to get your award, and I refuse to let Kyle win. He is not going to scare me. We will stay, and we will enjoy ourselves."

Jen had a face as black as thunder, and didn't look as if she was enjoying herself, so I had to ask, "Are you sure?"

"Yes. But I would like to get out of my costume now. Is there any chance of that happening?"

"Absolutely," I said. That wouldn't be a problem. They even had their own wardrobe in this place. "But are you sure you're sure?" Jennifer growled at me, and I wisely made no further comment on that score.

It didn't take us long to find the wardrobe department downstairs. Madge was on duty, and she seemed genuinely happy to see us.

"Ooh, Mr Mathews! What a treat. I haven't seen you in ages. How was the wedding? You two make the most dreamy couple. I have to admit I did swoon over the photos a little."

Resisting the urge to snort, knowing full well how "dreamy" our nuptials had been, I put on my most sincere smile and thanked Madge for her kind comments. She was a sweet old thing. Nutty as a fruit cake, but lovable and harmless, nonetheless.

"Do you mind if Jen borrows something for the evening?" I knew she wouldn't, but it was polite to ask anyway.

"No, dearie, not at all. You pick what you like, honey. If you need any help getting into it, just give me a shout." She wouldn't. If there was any chance of me getting my hands on my wife's body, I took it - and trying on clothes provided the perfect opportunity for this. Once upon a time I had hated clothes shopping, but these days it was growing on me. Letting Jen sift through the pile of rails, happy as a kid in a candy store, I decided to pump Marge for information.

"Did you see a guy in here earlier? Someone with long, sandy blond hair, quite tall, might have had an English or American accent?" It was possible Kyle had brought the suit with him, but I doubted it.

"Oh, you mean the man with the mask, and the ridiculous suit with the flashy gold buttons?"

Bingo. "Yes, that's the one. Did he say anything to you?"

"No," Marge frowned at me, "and he was quite rude. Just waltzed away with his outfit without even signing the ledger. I chased after him, but I was too late. He seemed to just vanish into thin air." That was a feeling I knew all too well.

"Was he on his own?" If he came alone, I would feel a little less uncomfortable than I did now. If he had a group with him, we needed to head home.

"Yes. There was only him. The man was in an awful hurry. There was a major scuffle before he went on. The regular guy who was supposed to come in and do the punishment performance was suddenly taken ill at the last minute. It was all very strange." I bet it was. Didn't that explain a few things? Kyle was up to his usual tricks. Either he'd overheard us or watched us entering the tent.

"Darling, what do you think of these?" Jen had found several outfits to her liking, and her eyes were sparkling with enjoyment once more. Thank God.

"They are all wonderful, princess." They were long evening gowns, and each one would probably make me want to eat my wife more than I already did; and let me tell you I was ravenous right now.

"Which one do you like best?" Ah, so she wanted to please me. I was all for that.

"The red one, princess. It'll make you look like Jessica Rabbit and have men drooling so badly they'll need to come and mop the floors.

She grinned at me. "Will it have you drooling?" There was a calculating look in her eyes that I adored.

"Even more so than I am already? Yes, I'm pretty sure it will. Need some help?"

"Yes please."

Madge grinned at me. "Want a carrier bag for the kitten outfit?"

"No, that's going in the bin." I shook my head. It would remind us both of Kyle, and that wasn't something we needed.

"Suit yourself. Go have fun." I'll be out back if you need me. She tapped her nose as if to tell me our secret would be safe with her and then walked off. I bit my lip to stop myself from grinning. Was I really that transparent?

Jen then piped up from behind the changing room curtain, "Can I have some help with the zipper, darling?" Duty called.

It took a long time to get my gorgeous wife sheathed in the red dress. It had all manner of fasteners and clips that needed to be done up, and my fingers just weren't cooperating as they should. They seemed to take regular detours of their own accord, beneath the soft, shiny skirt of her dress, to seek dalliances with sweeter pastures that resided beneath.

"You're wearing no panties, princess. I do so love it when you don't wear panties."

"Are there any available?" Giving Jen an affronted look, I shook my head.

"This is a BDSM club, darling. No one wears panties in here. They've been outlawed, take my word for it." She sighed, but her eyes were still sparkling.

"Are you going to let me come or are you just going to torment me silly?"

I had one hand underneath her dress cupping her breast, and the other was working furiously between her legs. If there was one way to make her forget about Kyle, this was probably it.

"Torment. We can't actually have sex here."

"Says who? There's a curtain on this cubicle, and I am so fucking desperate to have you inside me I might actually get down on my knees and beg - though that might be difficult as this dress is pretty tight."

"Young ladies do not swear," I said in a stern voice, but I couldn't remain cross for long. She'd just told me she'd beg for sex, and that always made my day. "I don't usually get my pants down in public," I murmured in her ear. "I have certain standards to uphold." I didn't, but I was going to make her work for it. It was almost too good to be true, so it was time to take full advantage of the situation.

"So don't take them down. I'll just unzip them for you." She was nuzzling at my neck and thinking was now rather difficult. There were probably a dozen reasons why I shouldn't do this, but none of them immediately came to mind. Jennifer was as good as her word though, and in five seconds flat she had my cock in her hand. These days she had more enthusiasm for sex than I did, and that was saying something...

"Steady on there, Mrs Matthews. I distinctly remember you saying something about begging."

"Do you want the long version or the abbreviated version? I only asked because I've been teased rather mercilessly in the last couple of hours and I'm a bit desperate."

"Only a bit?" I should think she was a bit tired, too, after the umpteen orgasms I'd seen her having, but you'd never know to look at her. "All right, we'll go with the abbreviated version." Obviously I'd much rather have the longer version, but I was a gentleman and all that.

"Great." She got down on her knees, probably ruining the dress in the process, but neither of us cared much about that, and I was almost holding my breath anxious to hear what might come next. It wasn't often my wife offered to beg for sex, so I made the most of the opportunity. "Please darling, I need you *now*. I've been desperate to have that lovely big cock inside me for the past hour, and it is all I can think about. I am so hungry I might explode, and if you don't fuck me in the next five minutes there is a very real possibility I might die. Please let me..."

Jennifer lost the power of speech as soon as my cock was buried inside her, which was a shame, but I couldn't wait any longer, and Madge wasn't going to give us all day. Burying my teeth in her neck I took a moment to whisper, "That was the abbreviated version?"

"Oh yes," she moaned, and for a moment I wasn't sure if that meant "your cock is awesome", or "yes, that was the abbreviated version". Thankfully she clarified the matter a few seconds later. "I could have gone on for hours if necessary."

Hmm. Grabbing hold of Jen's hair I yanked it backwards sharply, watching her body arch in response. Burying myself in her to the hilt I threw her against the back wall and did my absolute best to wreak havoc on her intestines. Judging by the moans she made, and the amount of times her fingernails scraped down my cheek, my wife didn't mind in the slightest.

Madge coughed loudly when she re-entered the room, which was jolly sweet of her, but entirely unnecessary. We'd both climaxed, and I'd managed to get Jen back in her dress and just about made her hair presentable. Her rosy cheeks were a dead giveaway about what we'd been doing, but Madge already knew what that was.

"We'll get the dress dry-cleaned and pop it back to you on Monday if that's okay?" I grinned at Madge. I couldn't help myself.

"Hey, you run this place. You do what you like." She waved her arm in the air and grinned back.

As we left the room I distinctly heard her chuckle and mention something about newlyweds. It almost felt like I was sixteen again.

Jen and I sat with Johanna and Dominic while we were waiting for the awards ceremony. I had already told the pair that she wasn't allowed to go anywhere alone, and after explaining the reason why both of them were understandably concerned. Trying my best to direct the conversation away from some of the more unpleasant parts of the evening, we spent a pleasant half-hour in a little bar, Les Caves Antoine, sipping several different wines and trying out a large platter of French cheese. It took the edge off things quite nicely.

"Isn't it about time we took our seats?" Dominic looked at me and pointed to his watch. Looking down at mine, I realised that an hour had flown by with me hardly noticing.

"You're right. We'd better head on over there." Throwing down some cash for the bill, I held out my hand to help Jennifer out of her seat. She rose gracefully into my waiting arm, and looked absolutely resplendent in her scarlet gown. Honestly, I couldn't wait for the awards ceremony to be over. Why hadn't I listened to Jen and stayed at home? All I wanted to do was strip my wife completely naked and have my wicked way with her, tucked up safely beneath the sheets of our king-sized double bed. The colour red looked incredible on her.

"Oh, how did I do in the pet thing?" Jen turned around to look at me quizzically.

"How the hell should I know? We scarpered from there together," I said. She looked crestfallen for a moment, and I wished I'd thought to take a look at the results.

"You beat me." Johanna looked around and smiled. "You didn't win, though. There were a good thirty or so before your name was called, but you were in the top fifty. That's pretty impressive when you consider how many were in there." She beamed at Jen and grabbed her hand, giving it a squeeze. "Well done."

"Thanks." Jen seemed pretty pleased with that, so all was good. "Did you have fun?" Jen bit her lip as she left my arm to begin whispering with Jo. I had no idea what they were talking about, but they were giggling an awful lot. Perhaps they were comparing notes.

The awards ceremony was being held in the second largest room at Escape, in the *Atrium*. There were lots of twinkling white fairy lights, plenty of black velvet chairs, a clear plastic pedestal, a microphone on a raised dais, some dark velvet drapes, and the crucial red carpet as the centrepiece. The back of the stage currently had a film projection of glitter exploding everywhere, in case you didn't get the general idea of what was happening.

"Are you excited, Mark?" Johanna seemed in awe of the surroundings, fairly hopping with glee. I had no idea why. These award things were usually as dull as dishwasher.

"Oh yes, very excited," I lied, hoping I'd injected enough enthusiasm into my voice to be somewhat believable.

"Do you know what the award is for?" Jen turned on me questioningly, as I led her towards our seats, and I had to confess that I didn't. I had no idea what I was up for, but if I had to have a guess, it would probably be something along the lines of Long Suffering Idiot. Having ploughed a lot of money into the Escape venue, I hadn't been entirely sure it would pay off, but luckily a few years down the track and we were back in the black. I could now sell my share in the company for a healthy profit, and pass the dubious honour of overseeing the place to someone else.

"No idea. Isn't that half the fun of an awards ceremony?" Walking past several people who had already sat down, we finally found our seats. The Atrium was already over three-quarters full, and the last few stragglers were making their way quietly through the double doors.

When the lights dimmed everyone went silent. I couldn't wait to see who'd be hosting this year. It was usually some leggy, six-foot-tall blonde, so Jen would probably be super jealous when we got home, fall out with me, and then demand angry break-up sex. After a year of being married to her, I suspected she wasn't all that jealous. I think she just liked being slammed up against the wall while I dominated her to within an inch of her life. Either way, I was fine with the idea.

The loudspeaker rang out. "Ladies and gentlemen, welcome to Escape's annual awards ceremony. This year your host is Leyland Forbes." Fucking hell. That was one way to spoil my evening in less than twenty words. That man had better not come anywhere near Jennifer dressed as she was, or I might be responsible for a whole new set of medical bills.

Leyland came on stage looking fabulous, of course. What the ladies saw in him I had no idea, but for some reason they loved him. He got those ridiculous gaga eyes as hormones everywhere went crazy. Thankfully the disease was only limited to the female sex. Although we were now technically "friends" after he'd helped me find out what Jen had been poisoned with last year, we were not best buddies by a long shot. My evening had officially gone sour.

Sitting there, listening to Leyland waffle on for a good half hour or so while the girls were rapturously entranced, left me daydreaming about Jen in her red dress. It was a very pleasant daydream, and it was completely X-rated. When Leyland eventually called my name, Jen had to poke me in the ribs to get my attention.

"It's you. You're up," she hissed. I huffed and got to my feet, pretending to be as surprised as everyone else had. Then the loudspeaker blared out once more, and I nearly tripped over my own feet.

"Bring your lovely wife with you, Mr Matthews. This award is for both of you, as it happens." Keeping my smile carefully plastered to my face, while swearing underneath my breath, I thanked the gods that Jen had had the foresight to change before coming here. If she'd still been in her kittykat suit, I would have strangled Leyland on the spot. Helping Jennifer up, we walked arm in arm up the stairs to the stage. Grabbing Leyland's proffered hand I shook it, but then the asshole went into the swoop for my wife and got a kiss on the cheek. My smile darkened.

"Do you know why you're here this evening?" Leyland asked me, and there was mischief dancing in his eyes. If I didn't know better, he'd asked to host this evening, and that meant trouble.

"Because I've won an award?" I asked dryly.

Leyland gave me a killer grin. "How did you guess?"

Thanks for that, Leyland. I had managed to figure that out all by myself. The crowd tittered.

"Don't keep us waiting, Leyland. An award for what?" said Jen, elbowing me. It was a warning for me to play nice, but I took no notice.

"Hang on and let me find the card." Leyland dug into his pocket and made a good show of trying to locate our award. When he'd finally got the right one in his hand, he cleared his throat and stared at the crowd.

"So the moment you've all been waiting for. Why have we decided to honour Mr Matthews this year?"

Don't push your luck, Leyland. I can still bury you, even though I've given you most of your shares back.

"This award is for the couple most likely to split within a..." Leyland didn't get a chance to finish his sentence because I'd nicked the microphone.

"Behave, Mr Forbes. As I'm part owner of Escape, I'm entitled to have you thrown out on your ear if I wish." Was it wrong that I really wanted to exercise that right at the minute? He just had to push me one millimetre further, and I'd

74

crucify him.

Leyland snatched the microphone back.

"Would you do that?" his mouth opened in mock horror and he even managed a few *ahhs* from the audience.

"I wouldn't need much of an excuse," I confessed.

He nodded as he thought about this, and then turned to Jennifer. "You aren't thinking about leaving him, are you?" He bent down to whisper conspiratorially, "I've heard he's an ogre. If you want to come live with me, you need only say the word."

Jen rolled her eyes, and for once I thought the move most appropriate.

"Leyland. My husband might be an ogre, but only in the bedroom department." She shook her head as if talking to a naughty child and gave him a fierce frown. "Why is it you love winding my poor husband up? I already know there's another lovely lady in your life." Leyland blinked at her stupidly. Strike one for Jennifer.

"You do?" He almost stuttered. This was fantastic.

"I can tell when a man is in love, Mr Forbes. Enjoy it. Some of us only get one chance at true happiness, so remember to embrace it with open arms." She then patted his back, which I was unhappy about, but overall I was pretty pleased with the result. Especially as Leyland stood there on stage, completely dumbfounded for a moment or two, before somehow managing to regain his composure. Grabbing the microphone once more, he held it up to his lips and gave Jen one last sneaky look.

"I'm only joking folks. The award is for Escape's most dramatic couple of the year. Give them a round of applause, ladies and gentlemen." I stood there, just about managing a smile while Leyland passed over a gilt statuette of a loving couple embracing. I desperately wanted to bash him over the head with it, but a warning look from my wife convinced me not to. Somehow I even managed to thank him.

As we walked off stage I hissed under my breath, "Leyland, one of these days I am going to..."

"Shh. He'll hear you," Jen whispered, and gave a giant tug on my arm.

"That's the whole point," I muttered darkly, to whoever would listen.

Thankfully Jen and I were in agreement that we should now go home. She'd had enough of the day's events, and I needed to have jealous, angry, make up sex, to convince myself my wife was not in love with Leyland Forbes. Dominic, the annoying bastard, was still having lots of fun at my expense.

"Shall we go and get our coats?" Honestly, the sooner I got away the better. Everyone agreed that we should, but Johanna and my wife insisted on going to the toilet first. What is it with women and their obsession with lavatories? Maybe one day I'd find out, but for now I just nodded my head. As long as they were going together, and women *always* went to the toilet together for some unknown reason, all was well.

"Did you know he was going to do that?" Dominic was still on the subject of my number one favourite person, and I really wished he'd shut up.

"If I'd know he was going to do that, do you think I'd have gone up there willingly?" I motioned for one of the cloakroom attendants to come over so I could show them my ticket.

"You'd have to go up there to receive your award. There was no way you could avoid him."

"There is always a way." A national emergency, a work-related incident, or I could suddenly have been taken ill - so many possibilities. "Anyway," I said, changing the subject quite abruptly, "did you and Johanna have fun this evening?"

"Hell yes," Dominic said fervently. "Most fun we've had with an audience in a while. Jo loved the pet play scene. How do you guys come up with these ideas? Every year it seems to get better and better."

"I don't come up with them personally, although I do have to sign off on them. We have a panel of people for that. They have lots of enthusiasm, drink lots of coffee, and they talk all day. They do seem to produce results, though. I think they've outdone themselves this year. It's a shame we couldn't have stayed longer." The cloakroom attendant chose that moment to return with our coats, and for the time being I hung ours over my arm. It was far too hot to put mine on. Searching over my shoulder for Jen, I wondered what they were up to. Having visions of them sharing a cubicle together and doing naughty things to each other, I had to shake my head sharply to dispel the images bouncing around inside. Perhaps I was one of those sex addict types you hear about in the newspapers. Maybe I needed therapy.

The next thing I knew there was a commotion behind me, and Johanna came bursting through, her face white as a sheet. My stomach dropped and bile rose up my throat. There was no way I wanted to hear what was about to come next.

"Jo, honey, what's wrong?" Dominic took her arm and let her catch her breath, while I looked around frantically.

When Jo was able to speak again she only said two words. "She's gone."

Chapter Fourteen - Mark

This couldn't be happening; lightning did not strike twice in the same place. I could not be that unlucky. Grabbing Johanna, I asked her to take me back to the place where she'd last seen Jen. Meanwhile, I got Dominic to put a lockdown on the joint. No one was getting in or out until I found my wife - and I'd better find her, or there would be trouble.

Following Johanna quickly, I learnt that she'd disappeared while inside the ladies. How was that possible behind a locked cubicle door? Although I had no idea, I intended to find out.

"Did you hear anything? Do you know if she unlocked the door? Did anyone come in? Were there people here already?" My questions came thick and fast, but thankfully slow enough that Johanna could understand them.

Putting a hand on my arm, she said, "There was no one in here when we went inside. As soon as we'd locked the cubicle doors, though, a group of ladies came in, and I heard them chatting. When I came out I waited for who I thought was Jen, but when the door opened, a lady with bright red hair came out. When I asked her where Jen had gone, they said a man with a mask had come in and taken her. One of them said he'd gagged her, which they hadn't thought anything of, and then hustled her out of the room. They'd just assumed the pair were off to do a scene somewhere."

"Did anyone see where they went?" My heart was racing so bad I could barely hear myself speak.

"No. I asked, but all of the group were still in here when I came out."

"Shit. She could be anywhere. Where would Kyle go in order to get her out of here? Or maybe he has already." I slumped against the wall as the reality of what had just happened sunk in. What should I do next? Call the police? They were the last people I wanted to be involved, but if he had taken her outside I needed to get them involved.

Walking back towards Dominic and the front desk, I decided to talk with the manager and get an announcement out. If Jen was still in the building, I wanted to make it impossible for Kyle to get her out.

"Are you going to call the police?" Dominic had a grave expression on his face, and I knew exactly what he was thinking.

"Not yet. I'm going to get together a group of employees and friends and do a full search from top to bottom. I'm also going to get the security footage reviewed. If she can't be found, then we'll contact the police, but it's unlikely they'll be able to do very much at this time of night."

He nodded. "Johanna and I will round the guys up and get a search started. Is there anywhere we won't be able to access without a key?" Thinking ahead, that was Dominic.

"Not if you take the manager with you. There are only a few rooms that are locked, and he'll be able to open them for you. I wouldn't put it past Kyle to have bribed someone for access. The security we've installed here isn't the easiest to break into, but I want everywhere checked, just in case." Dominic didn't need any further encouragement. He marched off, and I knew that if Jen was anywhere to be found, he'd find her.

Muscling my way into the back office where I knew the cameras were kept, I quickly apprised the security guy of what had happened, and he was happy to cooperate. I'd go through the back tapes later if I had to, but right now the most important thing was to find out if Jen was still in the building, and I hoped and prayed she was. Kyle wouldn't have been able to take her out of the front door without someone recognising her, and I'd have thought at least a couple of people would come forward after I'd made my announcement on the loudspeaker. That had been a difficult decision, too. It took me what felt like an age to figure out something appropriate to say. Although I suspected it had been a kidnapping, I had no actual proof as of yet, and if I started waving words around like that I'd have droves of people heading to the exit door in a panic. In the end, I just asked that if anyone had seen Jennifer Matthews recently, they should contact the front desk immediately. As yet we'd not heard anything, and that couldn't be a good sign. How did you hide someone in a room full of people?

After the poisoning incident last year, poor Jen had been in the papers a lot, and her face was well known around these parts. There were also a lot of people in the building who knew that I was very protective of my wife, and if she'd been walking on her own with a strange man for any length of time, it should have raised a few eyebrows. So far, it hadn't, and that had alarm bells blaring in my head. The bastard must have disguised her somehow. A hood perhaps? Or a cape? Unless he'd got her out of that red dress she would be very recognisable, and if he had gotten her out of it, his days on this earth were numbered.

I scanned the security screens with the utmost attention to detail. There were so many people in the building; it was like trying to pluck a drop of water from the ocean. Crowds and crowds of them flittered across my gaze, my eyes repeatedly zigzagging from left to right as I tried to pick up on anything that might be of use. I figured I was looking for a cape or a big coat with a hood. While she wouldn't exactly stand out like that because there was a little of everything crazy in the building this evening, she should be easier to spot. Three times either myself or the security guard caught something which could have been Jennifer, but on closer inspection wasn't. So far, there was no sign of Kyle either. He'd also have changed by now. I had no doubt he'd worn the mask to abduct Jen, so I'd know exactly who was behind this, and he was a guy who lived off the fear of others. When I got my hands on him...

"That one, there." My eyes zeroed in on a tall man with long hair trailing just past his neck, with a female of about Jen's height dressed in a ridiculous Red Riding Hood costume. They were in the main street, heading towards the Atrium, and I knew for a fact there was a fire exit in that room. It was alarmed, but Kyle might not care about that now he knew we were looking for him. They then turned to enter one of the sideshows, maybe to hide for a moment, but when another camera captured the faces of the pair I knew instantly it wasn't them. Goddamit. I wanted to slam my fist through the monitor in front of me, though it probably wouldn't do much to release the fear and anger that were currently burning a hole in my gut. Keep your calm, Matthews. I warned myself. There was no way I could go to pieces; Jen's life was in the balance.

Scouring the screens between us, we managed to get through all the rooms once, without finding a thing, before they began repeating themselves. This time, I vowed to look more carefully. There was something I was missing. Even if they'd hidden in one of the sideshows they'd have to come out eventually. They couldn't stay put forever. All this time I was nearly mindless with worry that Kyle might have somehow already got her out of the building. It was unlikely but possible. If he had someone on the inside or had paid off one of the employees, he could already be several miles away by now. But worrying myself silly wasn't productive, and it wouldn't get Jen back. *Concentrate.*

"Wait. What about these two?" The security guy, whose name tag read *Dan* pointed to a couple in Escape's underground parking lot. The man was wearing a heavy overcoat and had a beret on his head. The woman was dressed in black. She wore a cape that nearly covered her from head to foot - perfect if you didn't want to be noticed in a hurry.

"Should they be out there?" My eyes narrowed in on the pair. There was no one else around. I was pretty sure the only people allowed in that garage were the staff or valet parking attendants, and those two looked like neither.

"No. I'm calling security." Dan immediately picked up the phone and punched in a number.

"Liam, can you get to parking bay 216 ASAP? We think a woman has been taken hostage." Dan turned to me. "He's on his way after he's called for back-up. Is it likely this guy will have a gun?"

I shrugged my shoulders. He shouldn't have one. The general public had to pass through metal detectors in order to enter the building, but that meant nothing. If Kyle did have someone on the inside he could have a stash of weapons for all I knew. "Let's just say he knows how to use one, so go in prepared just in case."

"Roger that."

Meanwhile, the pair were marching over to a bright red Tesla Roadster, and I knew that if they got in it I'd very likely never see my wife again. My Mercedes is nippy on the road, but it can't beat one of those.

"You can't let him get in that car," I whispered, horrified.

"They won't get away," he said, and though he sounded certain of the fact, I wasn't so sure. There didn't seem to be anyone else about, and unless someone managed to get there in the next twenty seconds, Jen was gone. Pacing away, in front of the security footage, I had never felt so helpless. I would have run to the parking lot myself if there had been any chance I could get there in time. Unfortunately it was across the other side of the building, and even if I sprinted it would be at least five minutes before I could get to it, probably more with all the people milling around.

"Don't worry, we're going to spook him," Dan said. Pressing down on a big black button he spoke into a microphone on his desk and said, "All security personnel, please head out to parking bay 216 immediately." It reverberated back across the room, so I knew it had been a loudspeaker announcement. The man with the beret on whipped his head around and I could tell instantly that it was Kyle. Tugging on Jennifer's arm he practically dragged her the last few yards to the car, and I have never wanted to kill someone so badly in my entire life.

Dan then switched the emergency lights on in the lot, flooding it with an almost blinding glare, and Kyle lost his grip on Jen for a moment. She took full advantage, giving him a swift kick to the shins to try and break free. He clung on to the fabric of her cloak for a moment, but as the garment wasn't tied on she let it fly off her, running as fast as she could in the other direction. Several security agents burst through into the lot, and Kyle had to deal with the idea of self-preservation. He didn't have time to run after Jen if he wanted to save his own hide. Sure enough, the man turned his head back towards the Tesla and jumped inside. Seconds later the car engine whirred into life, and he sent security guards flying everywhere as he blasted out of the parking lot, as fast as his wheels would carry him. This left me frantic for a moment. I couldn't see Jen on the screen, and there was a chance he might have run her over or worse.

"He's just burst through the barriers at the exit." Dan switched the cameras over, so we could see the tail of his car escaping. There was no way he'd have had time to pick Jen up, thank God, but that didn't mean she was okay.

"Anyone set eyes on Jen yet?" My voice was a whisper, but thankfully Dan heard me. Picking up a walkie-talkie which was charging on the side of his desk, he said, "Anyone got eyes on Jennifer Matthews?"

There were a lot of "negatives" that flew back in the feed, and my heart dropped with each further one that was relayed.

"Search the entire parking lot and report back as soon as you see anything." Dan looked back at his security screens and frowned. "We'll find her, Mr Matthews. She can't have just vanished."

Sitting there in silence I scanned the screens yet again, looking wildly from side to side, hoping against hope to catch a glimpse of Jennifer. What the hell had happened to her? Having visions of her lying sprawled out on the tarmac of the lot floor, leaking blood from all angles, all I wanted to do was throw up. If that bastard had killed my wife, I wouldn't be responsible for my actions here on in.

"We've searched the parking lot from top to bottom, boss - it's clear." Fuck. Where was she? Could she somehow have been inside that car? Please God, no.

"Do you think she might have run outside? Or would she try and re-enter the building?" Dan was asking sensible questions, but my mind was mush, and it took several seconds for me to get my head around the simple issues.

"She shouldn't be able to re-enter the building, as the doors leading out to the parking lot are normally sealed closed from inside." If she was running around outside clueless and Kyle somehow managed to catch up with her... All these thoughts were spinning around my head, and my blood pressure was going to go through the roof."

Dan pursed his lips and continued staring at the series of screens in front of him. "Normally I'd agree with you, but they must have come through a door to get into the lot, and if it was left open, she might have gone back through it."

He had a point, but it was a slim chance at best, and I didn't want to get my hopes up. Watching room after room flash by on Escape's security cameras, I realised it was probably time to call the police. If Jen had run outside, she'd have managed to get someone's mobile phone by now, surely? She was sensible enough. Mind you, Kyle would have also scared her witless. People did funny things when they were scared. The question was: what would my wife do?

She'd be back in the building creating a commotion somewhere. I didn't think it likely she'd have run outside. For one, Jen was wearing a sleeveless dress and it would be cold out there, and for another, that was where Kyle was heading. If the door to the main building had been left open, she'd have run back through it to have the protection of a lot of people around her. Did Jen know that Kyle had driven off, though? If she didn't, there was every chance she might be hiding somewhere, not wanting to come out until it was safe. There was one more option to try before I decided to call the police.

"Can I borrow the loudspeaker for a moment?"

Dan looked surprised, but nodded and passed it over to me.

"Could Mrs Matthews report to the front desk, please? Mr Levison has now left the premises." That would get everyone talking for sure, but I didn't care. I just wanted to see if my wife was safe. Dan and I sat there for a minute or two, looking glumly at the screen as nothing happened. Picking up my cell phone, I took a deep sigh and wondered what the hell I was going to say to the police this time. The last thing we needed was another scandal, but if Kyle had somehow managed to get Jen, then they needed to be involved as soon as possible. I didn't have much faith that they'd manage to find her, but any chance was better than no chance.

"Wait. What's that?" Dan was suddenly looking at his computer screen very intently, as a flash of red streaked by. Whoever it was, they were running as fast as their legs could carry them, but there were too many people in the room to keep track of the lady for any length of time. Though neither of us had managed to see her face, there was a good chance this might be Jen. For a moment I dared to hope.

Dan's expertise came in handy as he knew what direction she was heading in and which cameras stood a good chance of picking her up next. We found the lady in the main street next, knocking people out of the way as she made a beeline for the front door. Although she was moving fast, I was sure the dress was Jen's. Although bright red was a favourite colour for women at Escape, there weren't many floor length dresses going around, and the lady was clearly hampered by some very high heels - ones that I distinctly remembered Jennifer putting on.

"It's her," I whispered.

There was another tense thirty seconds or so before someone charged up to the front desk and demanded to talk to me. Jennifer's voice was unmistakable. Rushing out to greet her, she flung her arms around my neck and buried her face in my chest. Picking her up, I hugged her to me for the longest time as the horror and fear of the last hour slowly leaked from my body. She hadn't been kidnapped. She was here - right here - and I was never letting her go.

"Oh thank God," I whispered. "For a moment there I thought you were gone."

"So did I," she whispered back with a face as white as paper, "so did I."

Chapter Fifteen - Jennifer

There was a reason I had taken so long to get back to Mark. When Kyle had raced off in his sports car, I knew damn well I wasn't running after him, so there was no chance of me heading outside. I'd rather have camped out in the parking lot for all eternity. Remembering the door we came through, one he'd had a keycard for, I thought I'd try that first. It might be locked now, but it was worth a shot. Thankfully it was still ajar, so I crept inside and closed it behind me, hearing the satisfying click of the lock. Although Kyle might still have the keycard, I suspected he'd be long gone by now, and for some reason I felt safer behind a closed door. Now I just had to get through to the other side. We'd had to come through two doors to reach the parking lot, so on the way back I'd just assumed the other door would also be left open. It wasn't. On closer inspection I realised it was a fire door, and it had clicked softly shut behind us. This now presented me with a rather unpleasant dilemma. I couldn't go forward, and on retrying the door handle behind me, realised there was no chance of me going back, either. Shit. This meant I was now trapped. Usually I'd do what any girl worth her salt would do in this situation, which was scream the place down, but Kyle had gagged me, and padlocked the thing to the back of my head to make sure I couldn't remove it.

Using my voice was not going to be an option. On the upside, I still had the use of my hands and feet, so I hammered on the door which led back to Escape as loudly as I could. For the best part of ten minutes I slammed my palms into the thick wooden door, and I didn't draw any attention to myself whatsoever. Either there was nobody nearby, or it was so noisy no one could hear me. The door might have been soundproofed, too.

Telling myself not to panic any more than I was already, I tried to think this through rationally. Someone would find me eventually. All I needed to do was stay put and try and stay calm. The trouble was I knew Mark would be going crazy. The longer I was holed up here the more he would worry, and he'd have everyone in London scouring the streets for me before long.

Sighing, I decided to try the other door out to the parking lot. I knew there were a few security guys out there because I'd watched them try to storm Kyle before he took off like a bat out of hell. They'd probably all scarpered by now, but it was worth a go. Preparing to hammer on the door once again like a demented demon, I braced myself and gave it a go. My hands stung like fire by now, but if it got me out of this room, then I was more than willing to pay the price.

Another five minutes went by, and I didn't hear a peep. Just about ready to give up and call it a day, I had the shock of my life when the door began to open. It was one of the security crew who'd heard my banging just as he'd completed his sweep of the parking lot. When he burst in we both looked rather startled, and I jumped back with a squeal of shock. It took us a few seconds to get a hold on the situation.

"Are you Jennifer Matthews?" I nodded feverishly. Pointing to my gag, and turning around so he could see the lock on the back of my head, he nodded in understanding. "There's a pair of bolt cutters in the cupboard. They'll cut through that. Gimme a min." True to his word, he grabbed a key ring around his waist and opened a cupboard on the far wall. Rattling around for a bit, he eventually got a pair of cutters out and went around the back of my head.

"Ma'am, I'm going to try my best and not get any of your hair stuck in this, but I can't promise, okay?" More nodding. Right now I didn't care if he cut most of it off, as long as he got rid of the thing. Thankfully, with one sharp click, the gag was gone.

Pulling it out of my mouth as if it were on fire, I said, "Yes, I'm Jennifer Matthews. Can you get me through that door? My husband will be frantic, and I need to get back to him ASAP."

"Sure thing, Ma'am. I'll be right behind you."

He unlocked the door for me, and that was it, I was off. Running as if the devil himself were after me, I lost the poor security guy in seconds. Not caring who I had to push past in order to reach my goal, I stumbled my way towards the front desk, often almost headfirst.

When I finally reached the reception of Escape, Mark was nowhere to be seen. What now? All I wanted was a friendly face, and I needed one ASAP. I wasn't above yelling, either.

"I need to speak to Mark Matthews. Is anyone out there?" There was no immediate response, so I cranked the volume of my voice up to painfully high and ear-shatteringly nasty. "Please let there be someone out..." I didn't get any further. Mark was rushing towards me like a bullet, and the reception desk flew open like it had wings. Before I knew what was happening, he'd picked me up and crushed me to him in a death grip, and even though I could barely breathe it felt damn good. For the next minute or so, all I did was bury my face into Mark's neck and count my blessings. Life was extraordinarily precious, and even more so when you thought you were about to be tortured and tormented by a completely deranged nutter. It was a narrow escape, but I'd made it - just.

We left for home as soon as we could bring ourselves to untangle our limbs. The embrace had been a long, life-affirming nod to each other, but both of us needed more - much more.

Thankfully Mark was way ahead of me, and the car had already been brought around the front of Escape just as the thought entered my head.

"How do you do that?" I looked up at my husband questioningly as we left for the night, receiving numerous hugs from well-wishers and a fierce squeeze from both Dominic and Johanna who had nearly been sent mad with worry.

"Read your mind?" Mark had his arm locked in mine as he marched me smartly to the car. I had a feeling I wouldn't be allowed out of his sight in the near future, but it was a price I was willing to pay. Kyle had nearly scared me witless.

"Yes."

"Easy. I have supernatural powers. I'm also the most amazing guy in bed this side of the Milky Way. Just so you know." He waggled his eyebrows at me.

I bit my lip to stop myself laughing as he helped me into the car. While I knew he was trying to lighten the mood, making sure I didn't dwell too heavily on the events of this evening, I couldn't help but think back to what had just happened. It had been close - far too close. It was going to leave an unpleasant taste in my mouth for some time to come. Still, I should probably play along with him. It wouldn't do any good to let Kyle run rampant in my head, and the man had done enough damage already.

"How far away is the Milky Way? Just in case I need to test the theory?" Turning towards him, I gave him my most innocent look.

"You, young lady, will never, *ever* be testing that theory, and the Milky Way is two point five billion light years away, so unless you want to die enroute, I wouldn't recommend it."

"Maybe Zystrom will have to have a side-line in aerospace engineering. If you put your head around the problem, I sure you could get me there quicker than that."

"Don't count on it." Mark grabbed my hand and squeezed it. "You are never getting away from me, Mrs Matthews. Divorce will not be an option, and I will follow you like a bloodhound wherever you go."

"I think there are laws against that kind of thing," I said.

"If there are I'll be sure to change them." He probably would, too. "Anyway, do you want to talk about what happened? I'll understand if you don't right now, but at some point we'll need to go over it, just to see if there's anything we can use against him. The sooner that man is apprehended and put behind bars, the better. I can't bear to think of him anywhere near you." The feeling was mutual. I never wanted to set eyes on that man again.

"If I talk, what's it worth?" Since I might as well get this mess over with, I didn't see any reason in putting it off, but it made sense to see if there was anything in it for me.

"My, my, what a greedy girl you are, Mrs Matthews. What do you want?" Mark stared at me over the wheel, and the black silk of his bowtie shone under the streetlights, as did the matching material on his lapels. I wanted to rip it all off and devour him then and there, but I'd learnt long ago that sex in a car was awkward, not to mention a little dangerous. Hmm. What did I want? Sex, as soon as I could get my hands on it, that was for certain. Not the kinky variety this evening. I was too desperate to wait to be tied up or spanked. All I wanted was rough, gritty, pin-me-down-and-make-me-like-it sex. Although...

"How about some female domination, darling? After all I've been through, the least you can do is let me take charge for the evening." I injected just the right note of whining into my voice, making it sound like a plea. There was a good chance this could work if I played my cards right.

"Over my dead body. We said you had to behave for a week. It has not been anywhere near a week yet. You have to earn that privilege." Although his voice was gentle, there was a thread of steel through his voice that indicated there was no point arguing. On the plus side, I was still in the running for my night of fun, as long as I obeyed my husband's every word. How hard could that be?

"I'll settle for some of the rough stuff, then. Can you work with that?" I blew him a kiss before placing my hand on his crotch - and what a very firm and hard crotch it was.

"I think I can work with that, Mrs Matthews. By the way, if you decide to torment me on the way home, I'll get my own back in the bedroom. It's only fair, darling." His eyes twinkled with mischief, and I knew he meant what he said. The trouble was, I had never been one to back away from a challenge.

"Promises, promises," I whispered, stroking the tips of my fingers down his straining length.

"Talk." His voice was gruff, sexy and full of sin. Smiling to myself, my inner kitten purred. I was going to enjoy this.

"Fine. Where should I start?" I knew exactly where to start, but I wanted to hear him bark something sarcastic at me. That turned me on, too.

"I find the beginning is always a good place, Mrs Matthews, so stop stalling."

Squeezing his cock gently beneath my fingertips, I heard him suck in a breath before he turned towards me and gave me the evil glare. Fine. My sordid tale was about to begin.

Kyle managed to get me out of the ladies toilet without the merest whisper of a protest by posting an A4 sized sheet of paper under my cubicle door. It read *Open the door silently and don't say a word, or I'll kill your husband*. Yes, there was a chance it could have been a hoax, but when I saw who'd signed it I knew there was no point taking that risk. Then a shoe came underneath my door letting me know he meant business, as well as a flash of a knife.

All sorts of things went screaming through my head at that point, most of which were concerned with getting my ass out of there, but nothing sprang to mind. I was in a small cubicle, I wasn't likely to get past him, and if I did, there was every chance he'd stab either me or Johanna. If that wasn't bad enough, there was a chance he had my husband stashed away somewhere, and I wouldn't risk his life for anything, although he'd probably kill me for that sentiment later. Judging from the look Mark was now giving me, I figured our late night sex session was going to be intense. Oh well.

Anyway, the message got me out of the cubicle with very little fuss, and as soon as I set foot outside, Kyle pressed a black ball against my lips and pushed it with bruising intensity. I had no choice but to open up for him, and as soon as I did he yanked my head back and fastened the buckle. When I heard the snap of a padlock shortly after, I knew I was in trouble.

"If you move an inch out of line, or try to escape, I will call the man who is currently holding Mark and tell him to kill the bastard. All it takes is one misstep, Petal, and you'll be one of the youngest widows on the planet. You think about that." He took his cell phone out of his right breast pocket, to show he meant business, and then replaced it. Next thing I know, he's dragging me out of the ladies and Johanna is none the wiser. What do I do now? What can I do? The answer is nothing - not until I know for sure that he doesn't have my husband. In the back of my head, I'm almost positive that he hasn't managed to get his hands on Mark, but who's going to play Russian Roulette with that kind of information? Let's say I get it wrong, and he makes that call; Kyle is just the type of sick bastard who would get his kicks doing something like that.

Herding me around Escape like a stupid sheep, I could feel Kyle getting off on his power trip. Every time he looked my way he had this smug grin on his face that made my insides shrivel up and die. Knowing what the man was capable of made my abduction ten times worse. Stumbling blindly along, seeing nothing because my body was completely overtaken by fear, I was surprised when he ducked into one of the little side streets and pushed me down some steps into a darkened room. Able to ask no questions, I just stared morosely around me, trying my best to figure out what might come next.

"Is this the girl?" A man came out of the gloom and stared at Kyle. He was tall, with dark wavy hair curling at his temples, and he was big. When I mean big, I mean he had muscles rippling in all the right places, most of which were covered in tattoos.

"This is the girl," Kyle confirmed.

"You want me to measure her up, now?" Big Guy looked me up and down, and his lip curled in disgust. If I hadn't felt small enough already, he'd just reduced me to dust underneath his shoe.

"No, I want you to dance the can-can." Kyle gave the man a withering look. "Of course I fucking want you to measure her up. That is why we're here, right?" Big Guy didn't look at all put out as Kyle's ranting continued. Ignoring him for the most part, he went to a drawer at the back of the room and rummaged around in it, finally withdrawing a tape measure.

"Bring her over here then. Let's get this over with." Big Guy crooked his finger, indicating that I should walk to him, but not wanting to go anywhere near the thug, I stayed put and pretended not to have seen a thing.

"Get your ass over there before I pull my phone out of my pocket and order the world's quickest execution." Kyle shoved his booted foot up my ass, and I went stumbling forward. Angering him further would be a bad idea, and what kind of damage could a man do with a tape measure, anyway? I might as well get this over with.

"Legs shoulder-width apart, arms out," Big Guy barked. Obeying orders, I wondered what nastiness Kyle had planned, and whether Mark and I would get out of this mess alive. As the tape measure snaked around me, my limbs began to tremble in fright. Trying to control a body going into meltdown was impossible, but Big Guy didn't care a whit about my distress, continually barking at me to stand still. This just made me jumpier.

When he'd finished writing all his measurements down, Big Guy turned to Kyle and asked, "How soon do you need it?"

Kyle shrugged in response. "As soon as possible. How quickly can you get it to me?"

Big Guy chewed his lip as he thought about it. In a week, I should think. Shouldn't take much longer."

"Make it twenty-four hours, and I'll give you a whopping fat bonus cheque." Kyle held out his hand and waited to see if Big Guy would take him up on the offer. He did.

"There might be a sleepless night involved, but I'll hold you to your word on that." They both shook hands vigorously before Big Guy disappeared out back. The room then plummeted around thirty degrees, as I wondered what Kyle was going to do next.

"Do you want to know what I've got planned for you?" Kyle's eyes lit up like fireworks, and it was clear the bastard was enjoying himself. In response, I shook my head. All I would do was panic, so he might as well keep it a surprise for later.

"Too bad, because I'm going to tell you anyway." He grabbed my chin and brought my face towards his, forcing me to look at him. His fingers dug in sharply, squeezing my cheeks painfully tightly as his eyes bored into mine. "I'm having a little chair made for you, Petal. One with many different restraints, which will let me do numerous nasty things to you, while you have no option but to sit there and take it. If I'm not careful, it might even kill you. There's nothing I enjoy more than watching people suffer. I think I get that from dear old Dad." His grip tightened as he drew me closer to him. "I'm going to enjoy playing with you, Petal." Wincing as his words cut straight through me, I tried to wriggle out of his grip, but his hold on me was far too tight. "Yes, I think I'm going to really enjoy myself this time. Dad's given me a lot of cash to make sure the job's done properly, so we're really gonna have some fun, you and I. You won't believe some of the things I have in store for you, girlie."

While Kyle was busy telling me about the nice things I had to look forward to, my face had gone paper-white and I was hardly breathing. My heartbeat felt like a drum inside my chest, and I have never wanted to run so badly in my entire life. The only thing that held me there was the phone inside Kyle's right breast pocket. Maybe if I made a grab for it, I could get help somehow. My fingers twitched beside my waist. All I'd have to do was reach up, ease it out of his pocket, and then smash it. With any luck, he wouldn't know the number off by heart, and it might give me a few hours to try and find where he had stashed my husband. As my hand reached up impulsively Kyle smashed it back down again with his fist, as if he'd been expecting it.

"I wouldn't, Petal. Even without the phone, all it takes is a nod from me to one of the guys, and you'll be known as the black widow for the rest of your life. I'd only need to kill a couple more of your partners, and no one will go near you. Sound like fun?" I shook my head and lowered my bruised hand. He smiled. "Glad to see you're not completely stupid."

He grabbed hold of my shoulder and steered me towards the door, opening it just a crack so he could see outside. Pulling his phone out of his pocket he dialled a number and pressed it to his ear. "Is the coast clear? Good. How's our man doing? Well, if he gives you any trouble, you put a bullet in his head. Yeah." I whimpered at that, and Kyle tugged me sharply, warning me to shut up. "All right, gotta go. Speak later."

Tossing a cape at me, he barked, "Put that on and make sure the hood's up over your head." When I'd complied, he pulled a beret out of his pocket and shoved it over his own. With that, we were off.

Kyle's arm guided me through the throng of people outside, and he smiled broadly at anyone who crossed his path. Most of the people we saw weren't interested in us; they had better things to do. This was a big night for everyone here, and if they weren't walking with purpose they were laughing and chatting with their friends. Hardly anyone spared us a glance, although I tried my best to catch the eye of anyone that cared to look in my direction. Before long we'd parted ways with the main crowd and were heading around the back of the Atrium. Guessing that Kyle had an exit plan in mind, I waited to see how he intended to get us out of there. All the fire doors would be alarmed, and though he could just walk out of the front door, there was a chance he would be spotted.

An announcement then sounded through the hall, asking that I approach the front desk. For a second I felt elated. It was Mark's voice! Kyle didn't have him after all, the lying bastard. Screaming through my gag I tugged at Kyle's arm to get away, but his hold had tightened into a death grip. At least my disappearance had been noticed, and they were looking for me. There was no way Kyle could use the front door now. My optimism was quickly quashed when Kyle held out a keycard and pressed the handle of the fire door. It immediately opened for him. No alarm, no bleeping, not a single sound could be heard. Either someone on the inside had switched it off, or the keycard had overridden it. Either way, we were heading outside, and that was bad.

"Don't even think of running. I have a gun in my back left, and I'll put a bullet in your brain." Kyle had a key for the next door, which he produced out of his pocket and swiftly unlocking it, we found ourselves outside in a parking lot. There was no one about at this time of night, and besides, there was no access to the public from this side of the building. It was unlikely we'd see anyone. Fuck. This had all been too easy. He'd snatched me from right under my husband's nose, and in five minutes I'd probably be miles away. What could I do? As he pulled me along in his vicelike grip I look around wildly. Please God let there be someone about. Anyone would do, I just needed a distraction.

We were headed towards a bright red sports car. Trust Kyle to pick the flashiest car he could find for an abduction. Sometimes I almost credited him with intelligence, but right now he was certifiably insane. There was no way I was getting in that car with him. The police wouldn't have a chance of catching it.

As my brain frantically tried to come up with a plan, or anything that might help me get away alive, blinding lights suddenly hit us from above. For some reason the emergency backup had come on, on top of the regular ones, and that was all the distraction I needed. Tugging ferociously at Kyle's arm I gave a swift kick to his shin, and in the confusion he let me go for a second. That second was all I needed. Sprinting off in the opposite direction far faster than my legs wanted to carry me, I was met with a snag. Feeling Kyle's hand brush against the cape that had been draped around my shoulders, I simply pulled my shoulders back and let the thing fly off me.

Adrenaline pounded through me as I did my best to beat the world land speed record, but realistically, I knew it wouldn't be long before Kyle caught up with me. I have never been much of a runner, and even my best fear-fuelled attempt wasn't going to keep him off my back for long. Just as that depressing thought hit me, a handful of security guards came bursting through the door we'd just vacated, giving Kyle a headache on a grand scale. Did he come after me, or save his butt? I was counting on the latter, and I ran around the outer perimeter of the parking lot until my lungs felt like they were bursting. Making sure I didn't go anywhere near the exit lane, in case Kyle decided to stop and yank me inside the car, I tried my best to run in the opposite direction. I didn't care where I was headed, I just wanted it to be as far away from him as possible.

Hearing the mighty roar of a car engine being revved up to the max, I took cover behind a large white Range Rover. If he had no clue as to my whereabouts, that had to be a good thing, so I sat as still as a mouse and tried not to breathe. As it turned out, Kyle wasn't interested in me at that point. He left the parking lot as if his wheels were on fire and I sank to the floor as the shock of the evening crashed down upon me. Drowning in self-pity for a few moments, I then realised that Mark would be worried sick about me somewhere, and I had to get back inside the nightclub and let him know I was okay.

I sighed and slumped down in my seat. The retelling of the tale had sobered me up from the exhilaration of my escape, and depression was quickly setting in. Kyle Levison and my father would not give up until they had what they wanted, and until then, my overprotective husband would have me under house arrest. Don't get me wrong, I didn't want to be going anywhere on my own at that moment, either, but a girl liked to have some freedom every now and again.

"Don't worry. We'll get them. It's just a matter of time. We can't let them win."

My husband grasped the hand that was still in his lap and gave it a tight squeeze. I squeezed back, but it was a little on the lacklustre side. Kyle had come so close to winning this evening, that I should be screaming and crying right now. Actually, I had no idea why I wasn't, although I knew it wouldn't do me much good.

"Do you still want me to torment you when we get home? I'll understand if you just want to go straight to bed."

"Oh hell yes," I said, horrified at the prospect of missing a night of the good stuff.

Mark shook his head. "When are you going to get it in your head, Mrs Matthews, that I do not tolerate swearing? That's another fifty spanks added to your tally. By the way, if you want an extra long foreplay session this evening, I'd get back to what you were doing if I were you."

I looked at Mark, flexed my fingers and grinned. Did I want an extra long session of foreplay? Wasn't that just prolonging the inevitable, while he had lots of fun and I suffered immeasurably?

"Of course, if you don't want an extra long session, I can be finished within about two minutes, five if you're lucky - but I can't guarantee you'll orgasm in that time."

"Why you..." Punching my husband on the arm as hard as I could, given the short distance available in the car, I wisely didn't let the tirade of swear words out that were rattling around inside my head. Unfastening Mark's zipper, I grabbed a tight hold of his semi-erect cock in my left hand and set about doing as much damage as I could before our ride was over. I planned to have him pleading and begging for a blowjob before we got indoors, and I was going to give it everything I'd got.

Chapter Sixteen - Mark

Jennifer now had her mouth, lips, and occasionally teeth upon my cock, and this was not a good combination when I was driving. It was my own fault. After twenty minutes of teasing, my boxer shorts were a dripping wet mess, and I needed relief in the worst way. When she offered her services to solve this problem by means of an orgasm, I automatically declined, however. Road safety is a very serious thing and anyone who says he can concentrate while on the receiving end of a blowjob is having a really bad one, that's all I can say. Jennifer didn't take no for an answer, of course. She was stubborn like me in that regard. I sent lots of threats her way to curb her enthusiasm. Fifty strokes from the paddle, flogger, and crop was a good start, I thought, but that completely fell on deaf ears. I then threatened to torment her with oral sex for an hour, and that turned into two when she wouldn't stop. That had no effect on her either, and I was a little bit disturbed that I wouldn't be able to carry through with all these threats, but that didn't stop me from making another. My last and final warning, which came with a blinding flash of light, was that if she didn't behave herself right this instant, she would have disobeyed me and that would mean an end to her night of dominance. As I fully expected her to continue, I figured I'd at least solve one problem. These were baby steps for me. Although I'd had my fair share of women in my time, I'd never really had any meaningful relationships, and no one told me marriage came without a handbook. There were so many pitfalls you could easily fall into without realising it, and trying your best to avoid tears, hysterics, and dismemberment was a delicate business.

I noted with a frown that Jennifer had removed her mouth from my cock and was now sitting upright with her hands in her lap. Was it something I said? Glowering, I looked at her, and said, "What are you doing?"

"What I am told, Sir." She had a little smirk playing around her lips, and I wanted to strangle her. Frowning harder, I inwardly cursed my own stupidity.

"Well, that's a refreshing first." Except that it wasn't.

"I thought so, too." Jennifer pretended to look out of the window. In fact, she was looking just about everywhere but at me. As it was nearing midnight, and everything was shrouded in a thick coat of black, I didn't think she was paying as much attention to the landscape as she would like me to believe.

"Why *are* you so desperate to dominate me?" It was a question I needed to ask. Sophia had pretty much choked me off the idea of female domination for life, so there was little chance she was going to get her way, but any insight into the workings of my wife's completely erratic brain could be useful.

When she didn't answer my question immediately I looked at her, but she was still pretending to be studying the landscape. "Jennifer. Remember you have to do everything I ask of you in order to get your night. Are you refusing to answer my question?" My voice was dangerously quiet.

"You are using the dirtiest tactics, Mr Matthews." Jen turned around and gave me a sullen look. She then fingered the soft silk of my bowtie that was still tied tightly around my neck and began to loosen it.

"Are you disobeying me?" I think I was going to enjoy this game. We would have to play it more often.

"No. I'm just taking my time obeying you. There was no time limit specified, so be patient. I've had a rough evening." That shut me up for a minute, but it was more to do with the soft flicks of my wife's fingertips around my neck. How could even that tiny act be arousing? Seriously, the effect she had on me was nothing short of cataclysmic. When she'd unravelled the bow she pulled it from my neck with infinite slowness, rubbing the thin sheet of silk across my neck as she did so. I growled. She then took the tie up to her nose and breathed in my scent, and that made me growl all the more.

"I love it when you go all alpha male on me." Undoing the top two buttons of my shirt she opened my collar, and I had to admit it was a little easier to breathe. "Feel better?"

"Answer the question," I barked. Yes, I was a little upset that her mouth was not still upon my cock, and yes, I was probably taking it out on her, but she'd started this.

"You won't like it..." she trilled in a sing-song voice. That made me mad. Now I really needed to hear that answer. Taking a quick moment to wonder whether my wife was playing me, and rather effortlessly at that, my eyebrows furrowed. Jennifer wasn't stupid, I already knew that, but perhaps I'd underestimated her level of cunning. Maybe I needed to readdress that at the earliest opportunity.

"Fine. You are disobeying me and the night of femdom is officially off. Don't say I didn't warn..." As I was spitting mad at this point, for all manner of reasons, my tone was now lethal. It had the edge and menace of a serial killer, with the firm tone of a headmaster. I was quite proud of it. Letting the last word hang in the balance I waited for my wife to interrupt me, and sure enough, I wasn't disappointed.

"Okay. Okay. There are several reasons. Firstly, every now and again I wouldn't mind getting my own back. You are always in a position of power, and every now and again I wouldn't mind a little slice of that. Secondly, it would turn me on something fierce to have you at my beck and call for the evening, and judging by most of the females in Escape, I am probably not alone in this fantasy. Finally, I want a little of what you gave Sophia; your devotion, your complete and utter surrender, and your trust. If you want to be dominated again in the future, I want you to come to me. Though I am not a jealous woman by nature, if you go and see her again I will not be responsible for my actions." Jen's fists opened and closed, and I could see that her temper was up. Well, well. My kittykat had claws.

"I see." Funnily enough, I was more inclined to let her have her evening, now I knew the reasoning behind it, but don't get me wrong, I wasn't that keen.

"I don't think you do." Jen absently fingered the outline of the glove box in front of her as she considered her next words, and I knew I wasn't going to like this.

"Imagine me in bed with another man. Imagine that. Now I know that wasn't what you did with Sophia, but you were halfway there. The thought of what she did to you makes my blood boil." Jen banged her fist against the dash, and I looked

91

at her in surprise.

"I am never going to imagine you in bed with another man. There would be an almost certain jail sentence if I was forced to do that." I got her point, though, even if it was moot. There was zero chance I was ever going back to Sophia. Those bridges had been well and truly burned. "I give you my word that I will not see Sophia in any context but as a friend from now on. Does that stop your need for domination?" Pulling into the driveway, I was relieved to hear the crunch of gravel that indicated we were home.

"No. I still want my night, but it does make me feel a little better." Jen offered a small smile in my direction.

"Do you know what's going to make me feel good this evening?" As I came around to undo her door, helping her out of the car, I relished the feel of her soft, silky skin against my hands. My wife had better not be tired. There was no way I was going to sleep until I'd had my fill of her.

"No, but I have a feeling you're going to tell me." Jen wrinkled her face up, as she wondered what I would say next.

"Having you do everything I say without question. I won't even need to tie you up and gag you. This is going to be bliss. It might almost be worth getting my ass spanked for." The wolf was back.

"You're incorrigible." My wife waggled her eyebrows at me, and said, "Do your worst, darling."

Honestly, that wasn't a very bright thing to say to a starving man. The woman deserved all she got.

Two hours later, my wife was a hot mess. In that time I'd tested her newfound "obedience" to the limit. The first thing I did was ask her to take on the role of stripper, in order to tease me. I thought she'd instantly refuse and put an end to all this nonsense. To my surprise, she did no such thing. In fact, I think she took it as a personal challenge because what happened next nearly blew my mind.

Putting on a playlist, mostly by hip-hop rapper types I had never heard of, she began unzipping her dress. The words "Drop it like it's hot" kept repeating themselves ad nauseam, but thankfully I'd gone mostly deaf. My eyes were glued to Jen's gyrating body going up and down and round in circles. The red satin of her dress shimmered in the dim lighting of the room, and when she beckoned me forward from my spot of the edge of the bed, I was quick to comply. Rubbing up against me, she began unfastening the buttons on my shirt, and it was fucking incredible. I could feel her breath on my neck and the faint remains of Chanel No5 on the air. Having come to associate that smell with my wife, it didn't take long for the scent to become intoxicating.

When the dress began riding up over her legs, exposing the silky smooth, gently tanned flesh of her thighs, my hands were all over her.

"Uh, uh, uh," she purred, waggling her finger. "You're not allowed to touch strippers." The woman then dared to raise her eyebrow at me, and that definitely sent my blood pressure through the roof.

"Unless you haven't noticed, I make the rules here, and you obey. If you do as you're told you'll get your night - but only if you play by my rules - and they say I can touch you as much as I like," I growled. Already aroused to breaking point, there was a good chance I was suffering just as much as Jen was. Sure enough, that dress of hers took a good twenty minutes to come off, and as I already knew she was wearing no underwear beneath it, my cock went wild. Inch by slow inch, the satin bunched up around her waist and my fingers were stroking, kneading, and embracing her flesh in every direction. They moved all over her legs and had particular fun with her ass, which, judging from the little mewling sounds she was making, was still a bit sore from earlier. Then, when I saw her pupils go dark, they moved between the juncture of her legs, finding hot, sweet nectar to dive into. I coated my fingers with it. Applying it liberally all over her clit, Jen really began to dance, and she was a little less coordinated as the dress started to rise higher. Letting her amuse me for a while longer, my fingers continued to dance on her clit, hopefully getting her just as aroused as I was. Eventually losing patience, I tore the rest of the dress off her and threw her down on the bed.

"Stretch your arms up and grip the headboard. Then don't move, okay?" She nodded, her lithe arms reaching up to grab two metal poles.

"Now stretch those legs wide, darling. I'm ordering you to keep them like that unless directed otherwise, and I may be some time. We clear?" She nodded at me and did exactly as I said. Her lips were already deliciously swollen from my kisses, and her face was hot and flushed. Wanting to run my fingers through her long blonde tresses until I had buried them in there so deep they would get lost, I positioned my body on top of hers, holding most of my weight on my arms so I wouldn't suffocate her.

"You are wearing far too many clothes, darling," she purred. An animalistic look of passion shot from her eyes to mine, and the woman looked almost feral.

"I forgot to mention that you aren't allowed to talk, either." Was that too evil? Probably, but it was too late to worry about that now. I wanted her trapped inside her own little head, unable to beg for release, and entirely at my mercy. Today I was in charge, and I damn well wanted her to know about it. So for the next hour I set about covering her body with my fingers, lips, and tongue. No part of the delightful canvas in front of me went untouched, but some parts got more attention than others - a lot more attention.

Somehow Jennifer managed to obey my commands to the letter, even though I was extremely careful not to let her come. Continuously edging her to the pinnacle of orgasm, only to deny her at the last minute resulted in lots of squirming and writhing, and plenty of moaning and groaning, but no talking. My wife was deadly serious about this night of dominance, then. It seemed Sophia had really gotten under her skin.

When Jennifer's body began trembling as the strain of doing what she was told was almost outweighed by exhaustion, I debated telling her she couldn't climax unless she dropped the whole issue. Thankfully, I quickly realised that was going to punish me, too, and I figured there were better ways to tackle the problem. Right now, I just wanted to slam into her until we both saw stars. It was time to revoke the no speaking rule.

"You get ten seconds to beg me for an orgasm. Make it good, or you're going to sleep without one. Your time starts now."

Jen's eyes widened. "You wouldn't."

"Ten, nine..." My wife got with the program fairly quickly after that.

"Please bury that wonderfully hot, hard, cock inside me, darling. I am so wet for you right now that I think I'll explode with the first stroke. I need you to slam into me *so* hard. If you let me come, I'll let you have anal every day for the next week..."

She didn't need to say any more than that. My body was already tormented beyond belief, and promises like that were kerosene on a city-wide blaze. Rocking her body underneath me, I gradually increased the pace of our lovemaking until I really was slamming into her, over and over again - and it felt utterly incredible. She was so tight, wet, and utterly perfect in every way. But she had been wrong about one thing. Jen came on stroke nine, and I let her ride that out for a good five minutes or so. That's the kind of considerate, caring guy I am.

After we'd finished our epic sex session, Jen promptly fell asleep on me. Admittedly the day's antics must have exhausted her, but honestly, where was the chitchat all these women wanted? Here I was, bright as a button, and all I had was snores for company. Mind you, perhaps that was my reward for a job well done; peace and quiet. I smiled to myself and cuddled up close to my wife, who mumbled something or other unintelligible. Probably keep your hands away from me you bastard or some such nonsense. Too bad, because that wasn't happening anytime soon.

When her breathing had softened to a barely audible whisper, I felt it was safe to creep out of the bedroom and grab myself a much-needed glass of water. Being the gentleman that I am, I also brought one back for her. She'd need it in the morning.

Looking at my watch, I wondered if I could call Khalil, or whether it had better wait until morning. It was just after one a.m., so I figured I had better wait. Although it was kind of an emergency a few hours would make no difference, and Khalil would probably need all the sleep he could get when faced with this new problem. Damnit. Where had Kyle come from? And where was Redcliff hiding? I very much doubted the old man would be in the UK. He would be in a sunny beach location, living it up without a care in the world. When I got my hands on him...

Sighing, I did my best to put all the drama out of my head. Right now, I just wanted to lay my head down somewhere soft, and preferably somewhere within inches of my wife's. Creeping back between the covers, to a somewhat rumpled, if not wonderfully warm bed, I pulled Jennifer's body back into mine. Sinking into a deep and dreamless sleep, I thanked God and anyone who would listen that I still had my wife beside me.

"What do you think?" The clock above my office desk said the time was approaching ten a.m., and I'd been chasing calls all morning. Most of them were work related, but I'd finally got through to Khalil, and I desperately wanted his opinion on Kyle's antics last night. Relaying the story that Jennifer had told me, doing my best to leave nothing out, I was met with silence until I'd finished. That unnerved me. It meant he was worried.

"I think Kyle's playing with you, and I think you already know this." There was more silence. Trust Khalil to hit the nail on the head first time.

I sighed. "He never really meant to abduct her last night, did he? It was a scare tactic. If he'd wanted to take her he had ample opportunity to do so earlier, so why mess about?" This confirmed my suspicions.

"Exactly. He wanted to prove that he could do it, and he wanted to toy with you a little. I think he's planning something else." Khalil did not sound happy.

"Anyone planning to kidnap someone in a bright red Tesla isn't really thinking ahead. Was it ever found by the way?"

"No, but it was recorded stolen. It was an impressive theft by all accounts, too. You don't break into one of those on a whim." This was another statement from Kyle. He had money and brains behind him.

"But how the hell did he know where we'd be?" The guest list at Escape was encrypted for a reason because no one wanted that kind of information to become common knowledge. Some of us didn't mind disclosing our identities, but the majority preferred to remain incognito.

"Either he has someone watching your place, there's a hacker in his midst, or he knows someone on the inside. Could be a combination of any of those, too."

"No car can get close to this house, so he can't be watching our comings and goings." The thought made my blood go cold. Just supposing he was, it would only be a matter of time before he went for my wife a second time.

"He doesn't have to watch your house, and this isn't some cop show where all they do is stakeouts. These days you just have to install a hidden camera somewhere or make sure the exit roads to your property are monitored. It's going to be relatively obvious if it's you. Your Mercedes would be quite easy to spot." Fuck. I hadn't considered that.

"How can I find out if he's done that?"

"You want me to send a team out to check?"

"Yes." Right now, if possible, although I didn't add that. Khalil had my back, and he'd be on it as quick as was humanly possible. The thought of that bastard keeping his beady eyes on my wife's whereabouts made me physically ill.

Putting my hands over my mouth, I sucked in a deep breath and tried to process all this.

"You'd be surprised at how easy it is. Modern technology has come a long way in the last twenty years or so. You can plant GPS tech on virtually anything, and you'd never notice it was there unless you were looking for it. Make sure you check through everything she was wearing last night."

"Already taken care of. All of it is in the bin." Well, bar the red dress, and that was going in the bin now I'd torn it to shreds. Madge would not be amused.

"I'd advise you to keep her close for the next couple of weeks. From what I've discovered, Mr Levison is not a patient man. He won't want to wait to execute his plan. The longer you thwart him, the more likely it is that he'll make a mistake - and that's when we'll catch him."

"We'll get him, " I said, with more conviction than I felt.

"Yes." Khalil did not sound convinced either, and that was very bad news indeed.

Chapter Seventeen - Jennifer

"Oh shit, oh shit, oh shit, oh shit."

Mark chose that moment to enter the room, and I knew my spanking tally was about to hit astronomical numbers. Giving me one of his darkest looks, he said, "Right young lady, no sex for you for the next week."

"You'll suffer more than me," I fired straight back. Wriggling into a bright orange skater dress with a flared skirt, I checked my reflection in the mirror. It would do. I looked a bit worse for wear, and Mark hadn't let me have a lot of sleep last night, but on the plus side I was still in one piece, and there was a lot to be said for that. Unfortunately, after mum had learned about the recent incident at Escape, she immediately called to inform me she would be straight over. This was bad. Usually I went to see her, as there was still some friction between her and my husband, but today that had been taken out of my hands.

"I'll have you know I can go a week without sex." He couldn't.

"Fine. We'll do a week of domination, and you can wear a chastity belt for me. You'll be crying within a day." That was no word of a lie, either.

"Young lady..." His face darkened further, into the ice cold dominant expression I knew and loved, but we didn't have time for that right now.

"Mum's coming over." Mark's jaw opened in shock.

"Oh shit, oh shit, oh shit, oh shit." Interestingly, we shared the same sentiment but for entirely different reasons.

"No sex for you for a week, either," I said, grinning.

"Why's she coming here?" Mark hissed. His fingers were now in his hair, and it was clear he was agitated. Poor baby.

"To check I'm still alive." Putting a bright slash of peach lipstick on my lips and plenty of blusher on my cheeks, I did my best to try and look the picture of health. I felt anything but. And after all the spankings yesterday, I'd be lucky not to wince when I sat down.

"Oh, Christ. Maybe I could dash into town for a little while and give you guys some time to catch up?" Mark looked hopeful, as well he might. There was then a loud and persistent knock at the front door. "Is that her?" His face was aghast, and it would have been comical if I'd had more sleep. I nodded. "How is that possible?"

"She texted me five minutes ago to say she was in the area. She's worried."

"Fuck."

"Go and answer the door."

"You go and answer the door."

"What happens if it's Kyle?"

"Kyle is not going to knock on our front door."

"Fine, I'll go and answer the door."

"No, I'll do it." It was nice to see my husband's protective side won out, even against the mother-in-law. Following quickly in his footsteps, I crossed my fingers behind my back and hoped this meeting wasn't going to be the disaster it usually was.

When Mark got to the front door he winced at the camera that depicted it was indeed his mother-in-law, and even worse, she had a face like thunder. Opening the door cautiously he said, "Good morning, Laurel," but he might as well have saved his breath because she waltzed straight past him, without even looking in his direction.

"Jennifer, thank God you're okay." She kissed me once on each cheek, and I followed her into the lounge.

"Did you want some tea or coffee, mum?"

"Tea, please. Only dreadful Americans drink that coffee rubbish." Mark stuck his tongue out at her back and glowered. I resisted the urge to laugh.

"Mark, darling, would you mind?" I asked in my sweetest voice.

"Absolutely, darling," he said in an equally saccharine tone. He looked relieved that he was escaping for a while, though, and I suspected we weren't going to get our drinks anytime soon.

Taking off her black leather gloves and chiffon scarf, mum placed them neatly in her Dior handbag. Leaning towards me, she then said, "Are you sure you want to remain married to that man, darling? We can soon sort out a divorce if you need one." My mother was still not convinced Mark was the man for me. Although I'd been doing my damndest to tell her he was, the message hadn't sunk home for some reason.

"I'm quite attached to him now, Mum. He really is adorable when you get to know him. You should give him a chance." My mother frowned and looked unconvinced.

"He put you in danger yet again last night. What were you thinking of going back to that awful place?" The arched angle of her eyebrow suggested she knew exactly what went on in Escape, and knowing her contacts, there was a good chance that she did.

"Kyle's been out of the picture for over a year now, we thought the danger had passed," I said defensively.

"It hasn't, although you're safe for today at least. I have it on official authority that the man is out of the country. He left early hours this morning."

My breath whistled out in a rush. "Thank God for that. Now what?"

"We keep you safe."

Mark chose that moment to enter with a tray full of drinks, and after setting them down carefully on the coffee table, he began pouring the tea for both of us. "Milk or sugar?" he enquired.

"Just milk," my mother barked, obviously put out to have to talk to him.

Seriously, what was their problem?

"You're sweet enough as it is? I should have figured that out for myself." Mark was being obnoxious, but I wasn't about to draw attention to the fact, or he would act ten times worse for the sheer hell of it. Handing out our drinks, he grabbed his espresso and sat in the corner, as far away from my mother as he could manage.

"What are you drinking?" Laurel's eyes narrowed in on him as she took in the tiny cup suspiciously.

"Coffee, of course. Apparently, I'm one of those dreadful Americans you so despise. Cheers." He raised his cup and gave her a malicious grin. Here we go again, I thought. World war three was about to kick off, and I would be right in the middle of it.

"Stop it you two," I said angrily. "Have either of you figured out how to get in contact with Michael? Kyle's his lapdog, so if we can talk to him we might be able to solve this." Mum gave me a swift shake of the head. Mark also held his hands up in defeat.

"I am not going to remain a prisoner in this house forever," I stated mutinously, putting my cup down and crossing my arms over my chest.

"You will do whatever you're told," said my mother, and Mark piped up with something similar in the background. I could have screamed. "I have my people on it, and we'll figure out something very shortly. For now, you just have to do as you're told."

Mark snorted. "You obviously don't know your daughter very well. She finds it nearly impossible to do *anything* she's told."

"I think you'll find I've been exceptionally good this week and intend to be for the remainder of it," I remarked casually, giving my husband a sly wink. My mother looked at us both, wondering what the hell the inside joke was, and we sobered up abruptly.

"What do you recommend we do, Laurel?" Mark was trying his best, I'd give him that. He'd made an effort to speak to Laurel twice, and that was more than he usually did. Unfortunately, my mother ignored him.

Turning to me, she said, "I think we need to keep you under twenty-four-hour surveillance until we can get a location on Kyle. We monitor all roads coming in and out of the estate, and if you do need to go out in an emergency, you need a security detail of at least three men. I'll send mine over."

"Mine are perfectly adequate. If they can guard British diplomats they are more than equipped to ensure Jennifer's safety." Mark's voice was terse. My mother was trying to tell him that his men weren't good enough, and Mark was not going to take that lightly.

"You will use mine. Otherwise, there will be consequences."

What kind of consequences? I looked nervously from one to the other and wondered what the hell they were playing at now.

"So shoot me. I am not going to bow down to you. Jennifer is my wife, and I take it as my personal responsibility to take care of her. As it happens, it's a job I take very seriously, and Jennifer will happily tell you that."

I nodded quickly and pleaded inwardly for them both to stop fighting. Nothing good would come of this.

"I disagree. A mother and daughter have a more open and honest relationship. It's important to be frank with one another when lives ride in the balance. There can be no room for error or *lies*." I didn't miss the emphasis on lies and wondered what mum was getting at.

"Mark and I share everything together, Mother. We have no secrets." I was proud of the fact, too.

Laurel looked thoughtful for a moment, and then said, "So you are aware that just before you were married this man was fucking his entire office?" Her eyes were upon me and the black, sinking feeling of despair I thought I'd been rid of was back to suffocate me.

"Now just a fucking minute..." Mark roared.

I didn't hear any more. Running off upstairs, I reached the Velvet room and slammed the door behind me. This time I put chairs under both door handles so I would be left alone.

Dear God. I remembered Bella Rose saying something about my husband doing exactly what my mother had just accused him of. It was during our first visit to Escape when I'd been up on stage ready to receive my award. At the time I'd been devastated, but I'd later chalked her statements up as lies, especially after she'd claimed she was involved with him. What if they weren't? Was my husband still seeing those women behind my back? Admittedly he didn't go into the office anywhere near as much as he used to, but there was every chance he had them stashed away nearby. He was probably just waiting to get me pregnant, and then he'd be off.

Oh fuck. My pill. I hadn't taken my pill for the entire weekend, and I'd had lots of sex - lots and *lots* of sex. Oh, what if? No, I wasn't going to think about that. First thing tomorrow I was going to see my doctor, and I would sort this problem out. After I summoned up enough energy to murder my husband, of course. What sort of monster had I married?

The door handle began to move, but I knew it wouldn't get far. All I could think about was my husband in bed with an army of women. Although I am generally not the jealous type, that was a little tough to swallow.

"Jennifer, let me in." Mark's voice was soft, and the pleading tone he used sounded desperate to my ears. I didn't care. At the moment my misery was inconsolable, and it didn't require company. Flinging myself on the bed I grasped hold of the soft, dark velvet cover and buried my face in it. Not wanting to feel the tears that were coursing down my cheeks or be reminded of my own stupidity, all I wanted to do was sleep and fall into blissful blackness. The picture my mother had just presented to me needed to be erased from my mind because the images it was producing right now danced in my head with a lurid, far too colourful intensity that made me want to scream.

The other handle to the Velvet room rattled, and I ignored that too. The chairs were sturdy, metal, and they weren't budging. Unless my husband got a chainsaw out, I was safe here for the time being, although there was probably little chance of me getting any sleep.

"Let me in." The door handle stopped turning, and my husband had gone back to begging. "Jennifer, you knew what I was before I was married, and let's face it, the marriage was a sham. Your father saw to that. I haven't lied to you. If you let me in, I'll explain."

How did someone explain fucking an entire office full of women? It wasn't like explaining why you were late for work, or why you'd accidentally forgotten to bring the groceries back. *Oh, darling, I just happen to have a load of gorgeous secretaries in my office who are happy to lift up their skirts for me and bend their asses over the table whenever I click my fingers. You don't mind, do you? I've been doing it for years.*

It's no wonder the bastard hadn't had any long term relationships. I couldn't imagine any woman standing for that. There's liberal, and there's absolutely crazy. I let out a howl of misery. I couldn't help myself.

"You need to let me in, Jen. Please let me in." His fist thumped against the wood four or five times, and then the flat of his palm once or twice. Fear crept into my husband's voice, and I could feel his panic. He hated it when I cried. Once upon a time I'd thought the man as hard as nails, but the past year had taught me differently. Was there hope for us? Could we talk through something like this?

All the noise stopped, and I could hear him walking away. Was he giving up on us? Was he going to walk away from this that easily? Would I let him?

Rolling over on to my back, I frantically wiped my tears away. It did no good. They refused to stop. How many women was Mark cheating on me with, anyway? Ten, twenty, fifty, or could it be more? Knowing Mark, he probably had a huge office with hundreds of women in it. All of whom were sure to be supermodel thin and stunningly gorgeous. How could I compete with that? Mark was handsome, intelligent, amazing in bed, and a bloody billionaire to boot. There wasn't a woman in the world who would refuse him - but could I share him with others? I didn't know the answer to that. Inside my head, my husband was fucking everything that moved, and I couldn't focus worth a damn. Had he meant it when he said "I love you"? Or did he say that to everyone? Was Mark Matthews just a rich playboy who would never grow up? Perhaps I was just some interim amusement that would dull with time. How much time, though?

In the end my hysterics finally exhausted me, sending me into the oblivion I craved.

"Jen. Jen, can you hear me? Are you awake?" The voice was quite soft, but was annoyingly persistent, and no matter how many times I rolled over or tried to stuff the pillow in my ear, it would not go away. "Jen, please wake up, we need to talk."

The day's events came rushing back to me in a horrible black fog that instantly swamped my head. Propping myself up on the pillows, I felt horribly dizzy as I tried to listen to what Mark was saying.

"Jen, I have soup, and I have a club sandwich. I also have chocolate, crackers, cheese, some fruit salad, and if none of that works, I promise I'll find something that does. There's water, gin, and a bottle of wine, too. Please let me in, Jen. Don't make me do the chainsaw thing."

Rubbing my eyes with my fingertips didn't make them any less sore, but I guessed I had to face the music. I couldn't stay locked up in here forever, and it was bad enough knowing I would be a prisoner in this house for the foreseeable future, so I might as well make use of the little freedom I had.

"Wait a minute. I'll let you in." My throat was dry and scratchy. I desperately needed some water. Getting to my feet a little unsteadily, I had to yank at the chair twice to get it to budge. Eventually it did, and then my husband came charging through the door like a whirlwind, picking me up in his arms and taking me straight back to bed. Now, wait just a minute.

"You said you had water," I said accusingly, "along with all manner of other goodies. I hope you weren't lying."

"They're just outside the door. You want them now?"

"Just the water." I agreed we needed to talk. After the talk, I might need the wine and the gin, but I'd stick to the soft stuff for now.

"How about a couple of crackers, too? You haven't eaten all day, Jen." He looked worried, but that was too bad.

"It's difficult to build up an appetite after you've learned that not only is your husband cheating behind your back, but he's doing so with a small arsenal of women he's got conveniently stashed away in his office."

"I can exp—"

There was no way I was going to let him get a word in edgeways.

"That's not something you can explain away. Now I know why you married me, and I still feel guilty about that, but I can't live in a marriage of convenience. I'm not a toy. You can't play with me one moment, and then decide to play with someone else a couple of hours later. It doesn't work like that. Relationships are hard work, and they require trust. If you can't give me that, then I want out."

Mark sat down on the edge of the bed and handed me a bottle of water. "Are you asking me for a divorce?"

"If you want to keep your office harem, then yes, I'm asking for a divorce. Every time you're late back from the office, I don't want to imagine you in bed with all those women. It will destroy me. Being the good little wife safely stashed at home, never questioning your whereabouts is not something I can do. I deserve more than that."

"If I let you go, who will keep you safe from Kyle and your father?" It was a good question and one I hadn't thought of.

"I'll figure something out," I said tiredly. "I have friends I can go to."

"None who will keep you safe against that pair, I'll bet." He was right. That didn't mean I was going to stay married to him, though.

"I don't need your protection." My face was mutinous. I was giving my husband a chance here. I loved Mark too much to toss away what we had without at least trying to save our relationship, but as yet all he was throwing at me were curveballs. All I wanted to hear was that he was going to get rid of all those women and start afresh. But even if I did hear that, I didn't know if it would make me feel any better. Knowing he'd been going behind my back was a knife wound that would take years to repair.

"What if you're carrying my child?" My eyes flew open at that sentence, and I growled at him and reached for the lampshade.

"Don't even think of throwing that at me, young lady. If you do you'll get a spanking right here and now, even though you still haven't managed to hear my end of the story - and there are always two sides to a story. You especially should know that." My fingers reluctantly returned to the bed, but I glowered at him.

"Why didn't you stop me? Did you plan this on purpose?" There were fresh tears in my eyes. I was shortly about to be divorced, homeless, pregnant, and on the run from two psychopaths. That was a little too much for me to handle all at once.

"Don't cry, Jen. Please don't cry."

Mark's face became very serious as he gathered me up and cuddled me to his chest. I was having none of it. Pummelling my fists against him, I wailed, "How could you do this to me? You're a monster." I said it over and over, and he did nothing. He let me cry myself out again, and he tolerated my fists for a while, before he pulled my body closer to him, giving me no room to do anything except breathe. That made everything worse. The bastard smelled so good I wanted to eat him, and here I was supposed to be getting rid of him. Dissolving into a fresh fit of tears, Mark sighed heavily and pulled a hankie from his pocket. "You need to stop crying, so I can explain."

"I can't stop crying," I howled again, and a couple of fist shots went out before I was restrained once more.

"Fine, I'll just talk really loudly until you get the message." His voice was now deafening, and I think the tears stopped in shock. "I am not having sex with all the women in my office. I am not even having sex with half of them. In fact, I am not having sex with *any* of them. If it makes you feel better, there's only three women and two men who work there at the moment. Of the women, Cynthia is nearing retirement age, her sister isn't far behind her, and Francis may be young, but she is also my cousin. You have my solemn word, hand on heart, that I am not having sex with any of them."

My head began to pull away from where it had been restrained against his chest and this time he let it, but he kept a tight hold of me, just in case.

"But you did have sex with them? That wasn't a lie, was it?" Now I didn't know who to believe. Mum wasn't lying to me, was she?

He sighed. "Yes, I did, and lots more besides, else you wouldn't have met me. I abused my power over women back then in any way I could, which was probably a direct result of Sophia wielding so much power over me. I was out of control for a while, and I'm not proud of the fact." I could understand that. After the state Sophia had left Mark in last year, I was only surprised he hadn't gone completely off the rails.

"When did you give them up?"

"Shortly after we got together, and I realised that you weren't the vicious, scheming, manipulative bitch I thought you were." I guess I deserved that.

"If I find out that you're lying to me..." My voice growled with a thousand unspoken words.

"I swear on my life I am not lying." He put his hand on his chest as if to emphasise the fact. "Hell, you can come and work for me if you like; that way you'll be able to keep tabs on everyone, and we're rather short staffed at the moment. There must be something useful you can do around there." Mark looked at me doubtfully, which wasn't very flattering so I couldn't resist pointing out all the things I *would* be able to do for him.

"What you mean like answering the phones in English, German, French, Spanish, and Mandarin? Or perhaps you mean typing one hundred and twenty words per minute? I believe I have an adequate range of computer skills with experience in Word, Excel, Powerpoint, Sage..."

"Point taken. You can start on Monday. It would be especially helpful if you could work through your lunch breaks, in my office, behind closed, lockable doors." Mark gave me a knowing look, and my eyes rolled up inside my head. "That's another fifty spanks," he said.

"And I suppose you want to deliver them at lunchtime, too?"

"I hadn't thought of that. What a good idea. This is getting better by the minute." He rubbed his hands together in mock glee.

"Don't think you're off the hook yet, Matthews." I poked a finger into his chest. "What happens if I'm pregnant? And that will be your fault, by the way."

My husband looked torn for a moment. I had a feeling I knew what he wanted to say, but he was battling the impulse for a change. This should be good, I thought.

"That will be your decision, Jennifer. If you want my opinion I will happily provide it, but it is ultimately your decision, and I will stand by and support you, whatever you decide." It was more than I had expected. Nodding, I sighed.

"Will you eat something now?" he pleaded. I ignored him. Food was not high on my list of priorities.

"First thing tomorrow I am going to visit my doctor," I said firmly.

"Over my dead body; he can come here," Mark said, just as firmly.

"You can send your security detail out with me. Mother will be watching the roads, making sure no one's around. I think I can visit my doctor, darling, and if I can't, I might have to stamp my feet and cry lots."

"That is blackmail, Mrs Matthews."

"Take it or leave it," I replied.

"Will you eat something if I let you go?"

"There you are; you can compromise. That's the way to a healthy and happy marriage, so the experts say." This was probably pushing my luck at the minute, but I was on a roll. "Yes, I will eat something."

"Your butt is going to be so sore this evening you won't be able to sit down at the doctor's," said Mark, as he brought in armfuls of food for me to eat. He was smiling as he thought he'd had the last word. I had news for him.

"You're not going to be allowed to have sex until I'm back on the pill, darling, so you might as well get your kicks where you can."

Chapter Eighteen - Mark

Bringing the soup back upstairs, which I had now reheated, Jen was happily munching through everything I had brought her. Now able to breathe again, I'd had a glass of red to calm myself down and thanked my lucky stars that my wife was relatively easy going. Our conversation could easily have gone the other way, had she not been.

"What did you say to get rid of my mother so quickly?" Jen held her hands out for the soup tray, and I swapped it for the one she already had on her lap. For someone who wasn't hungry five minutes ago, she was doing a marvellous job of contradicting herself.

"I might have told her that if she didn't want you running around on the streets unprotected, her best bet was to be nice to me. If, however, she wanted us to divorce, she might as well get the papers drawn up, and sort out her spare bedroom."

Jen snorted. "That didn't get rid of her."

She was right, it hadn't. "No, but when I called her something very rude and demanded she get the hell out of my house before I wrapped my hands around her neck, she decided it was time to go."

Jen looked at me, horrified. "You didn't," she whispered.

"I absolutely did," I confirmed, and I didn't even pretend to look contrite. The nerve of that woman astounded me. While I knew she was just looking out for her daughter, there were ways and means to do so a little more delicately than she had. The woman had wanted to make a point, and she hadn't minded steamrolling me in the process. Damned if I was going to tolerate that.

"You need to at least try to get along - for me," Jen wailed.

"What would you have done in my place after she dropped the bomb?"

Jen scrunched her top and bottom lip together, making her look both comical and adorable, and then shook her head and shrugged her shoulders. "She did cross a line," she admitted. Well, thank God someone was on my side, I thought dryly.

"You do know that when we have children, you'll be seeing a lot more of her." Jen was trying her hardest to keep a straight face. I was not amused.

"I have to confess I hadn't considered that. You're right. We should never, ever, *ever* have children. We can both become workaholics instead." At that moment, I was deadly serious.

"About that, I'm not sure working together would be a very good idea."

"But how will you be able to check up on me if you're not at my side every second of the day?" I asked innocently. A spoon was thrown in my direction, which I dodged effortlessly. I was getting good at this husband and wife lark.

"Just you wait until I have you tied up next week, Matthews. Your butt is going to be redder than a tomato." She made practice swishing motions with her left hand until I caught it tightly in mine and gave her *the look*.

"You should be more concerned about *your* butt at this moment in time, Mrs Matthews. You get an hour, and then you're draping yourself over my lap."

"What have I done wrong now?" she said, batting her eyelashes coquettishly. Seriously, my spankings used to be feared, and now look where we were at.

"You mentioned the 'D' word, you don't trust me, you don't want to work with me, you wouldn't eat when told, you roll your eyes repeatedly, say cuss words, and your mother is a demon from hell. Need I say more?"

The infuriating woman stuck her tongue out at me. Oh, I was going to have some fun this evening. Yes, lots and lots of fun. Jen would need a padded rubber ring to sit on tomorrow, and lots of Aspirin.

"We any closer to finding out if Kyle is actually in the country or not?" My voice might have been a little bit terse, but it was nothing Khalil hadn't heard before.

"No. I want to know how Laurel's getting her intel, too. We didn't even catch him going out of the country." Khalil sounded irked. There wasn't much that got by him, but Jen's mum was in a whole other league. It was a pity we weren't on speaking terms, else she really could have come in handy.

"I think we both know how Laurel is getting her intel, and you won't be able to compete with her methods." Well, I certainly hoped he wouldn't. If he could, I didn't ever want to get on the wrong side of him.

"Maybe it's time you started sleeping with the enemy then." Nearly spitting my coffee out at that sentence, I choked on bile for a minute or two before I could get my breath back.

"She's my *mother-in-law*, Khalil," I said, incredulously. Not to mention the fact that Laurel looked like the kind of lady that would dissect your testicles while she made you watch, so I think it was safe to say we were never doing that.

"Figuratively speaking, Mark, not literally. Good grief." I could almost hear Khalil thump his head on the desk, even though the office was at least thirty miles away, and I shook my head to try and clear it.

"Sorry. My thoughts are all over the place. Jen is going out this morning. I know I shouldn't worry, but I can't help it." That was deflection, but hell, I was going with whatever worked.

"Laurel's got all the roads covered. She'll let us know if anything looks suspicious."

"She'd know," I remarked caustically. The latest wound she'd inflicted was still festering nicely. It could very easily have cost me my marriage - and I had Marianna to thank for that.

"How many men are you sending with her?"

"As many as will fit in the car comfortably, which is three."

"I'd still advise against it. Can't the doctor come to her?" It was a sensible question, and though I'd asked my wife the same thing several times, the answer was apparently "no". Normally I'd have put my foot down, but I didn't want to make any more waves after yesterday's antics.

Looking at the second hand on my Rolex slide down, I tipped my head back against my leather chair and tried to relax. My neck muscles felt like they had seized solid this morning. Not only did I have a mountain of work to catch up with, but I also needed to keep tabs on my wife, lest she disappear.

"Apparently not, and to be fair, I can't keep my wife a prisoner forever, much as I'd like to. If we haven't been able to get a whereabouts on either Redcliff or Kyle in a year, it's unlikely they're going to show up on the radar now. How do we get around this?"

"I don't think we do. The ball is in his court, and you can only make your move once he's made his, and by that time it will probably be too late. My only suggestion is to start mending bridges with the mother-in-law and work together. If we can work together, perhaps we can find some sensible way out of this mess."

The word "perhaps" did not sit well with me. There were no assurances of success coming my way, and everywhere I went I found huge, looming potholes with no end in sight. There had to be a way to dig ourselves out of this. We couldn't live like this indefinitely. The whole situation was intolerable. An if Khalil thought I was going to go off and make friends with Laurel, he was much mistaken. That woman wouldn't help me if I were the last man on earth. I had no idea why she hadn't killed me when she had the chance because the woman made no secret of the fact that she loathed me.

"Laurel nearly got me divorced yesterday. I'm not sure I'm up to speaking to that woman just yet, but I'll keep what you've said in mind. For now, just keep on doing what you're doing and let me know if you find anything."

Jen got to the doctors and came back in one piece. Although she'd only been gone for an hour, I'd been a total wreck, expecting thugs to pop out at every turn and whisk her away from me. Realistically, I knew I needed to give her some freedom, but the cost to my mental health was going to be high. We would need to take this one small step at a time until I could feel almost comfortable with the arrangement.

Oh God, what happened when I had to go away for work? Should I place her under house arrest? Pinching the bridge of my nose, I reminded myself that I needed to breathe. It wouldn't always be like this. Life was going to throw us many hurdles as a couple, and we were going to have to combat them together. For now, I just wanted her nailed to my side. The last encounter with Kyle had been too close for comfort.

Banging the alarm down with my fingertips, I winced as daylight streamed into the room. As I clearly remembered drawing the blinds last night, there was something wrong. Snapping my eyes open, it was to find my gorgeous wife at the foot of our bed, dressed in something black and incredible, with high heels to boot.

"What are you doing?" I said groggily, rubbing my eyes to make sure the siren in front of me was not an apparition.

"Coming with you to work. You said I could. Now get up sleepy head. There's coffee and breakfast already on the table for you." When my eyes could just about focus, they got to witness a very delectable ass, tightly encased in black satin, happily wiggling its way out of my bedroom. It sashayed in just the right places, and if it was coming to work with me, it was going to keep me preoccupied all day. Jesus Christ. What had I done?

Getting up and showered in record time, I quickly donned my suit and tie and gathered up my laptop. Wondering if there was any way I could wriggle out of my earlier invitation, it didn't take a genius to realise that not only was I up the proverbial creek without a paddle, but the boat had a bloody big hole in it, too. If I told her she couldn't come, she'd suspect me of lying yesterday. Then we'd be back to square one, and the dreaded 'D' word would be flying about. It would be much easier to take her to work and bore her senseless. Yes, she'd distract the hell out of me for a day or two, but everything could go back to normal after that.

Taking the stairs two at a time towards the kitchen, I wondered what my wife had managed to burn this morning. I couldn't smell anything awful, but that didn't mean I was out of the woods yet. Making a mental note of where the fire extinguishers were stashed, I sauntered into the kitchen and prepared to smile at whatever monstrosity she presented to me. Whenever she decided to cook, I always took my life into my own hands as I did my best to eat it, and she'd given me no reason to suspect that today would be any different. Looking down at the latest offering with suspicion, I noted that once again it had not been burnt. Oh, happy days.

"Scrambled eggs on toast?" I looked up towards Jen for affirmation. It was never a good idea to be too confident around these parts.

"Well, of course it is, silly. Now eat up." She waved a spatula at me, indicating I had better get a move on, and that earned her fifty spanks immediately, although I'd tell her about it later.

Cutting a small square off the edge of the toast and chewing it carefully, there was no question that Jennifer had finally learnt the art of toasting bread. At least that was one breakfast I could suggest if this one went pear-shaped. Now for the part I was most concerned about - the eggs. Last time it had been a bit like eating a mouthful of sand and gravel, as she'd left half the egg shell in there, and I wasn't overly excited about dicing with death a second time. It was probably only luck that she'd managed to cook the eggs through last time, too.

As Jen was looking at me expectantly, I nervously cut off a small square of both toast and egg and brought it to my lips. Making a mental note to get my staff back in here soon, I took the plunge and began chewing. The trouble was, you couldn't walk around naked when there were people all over the place. It was also difficult explaining why your wife was tied up all over the house. Then there'd be the inevitable stumble upon a sex toy I'd placed in the dishwasher for cleaning, and all hell would break loose. Having thoroughly enjoyed the house to ourselves for the past year, bar a gardener and bi-weekly cleaning on Tuesday and Friday evenings when we made sure to behave ourselves, I was loath to go back to having a full staff. Privacy was a wonderful thing.

"Well?" Jen looked at me, smiling proudly, as well she might. There wasn't a crunchy mouthful in sight, and the lack of anything blackened and burnt was a pleasant surprise.

"It's really good," I said with more confidence than I felt. Just because I had taken one mouthful without obvious risk to my health didn't mean I would get through two.

"Well, hurry up darling. We don't want to be late." There was that "we" again. Today had disaster written all over it, and I'd practically invited the beast along. It was time to face the music. Cutting off a large square of egg and toast, I shovelled the thing into my mouth and was surprised to find no ill effects from doing so. Trying another and another, I began to build up some enthusiasm for the meal. When I'd finished, I was rather impressed. It was hardly haute cuisine, but it wasn't a bad effort. The best my wife had made to date, in any case.

"That was lovely darling. Your cooking skills are coming along wonderfully." In my opinion that was a bit overly optimistic, but as I had to work with Jen all day, it made sense not to put her in a bad mood before we'd even got out of the door.

"I know," she said. "I've been Googling. You'd be amazed at what you can learn on some of these cooking sites." Oh, good God, was I going to be subjected to more of this on a regular basis? Making a mental note to make sure my wife was tied to the bedpost tomorrow morning, we quickly cleared the kitchen up and made our way out to the car.

When I put Mozart on, shortly after I started the engine, that was code for I want a quiet and peaceful drive to work. Unfortunately, Jennifer had no understanding of such a code and just talked over it. She seemed to want to learn all the inner workings of Zystrom, which was sweet but entirely unnecessary, as she wouldn't last longer than a week. I'd make sure of that.

"Darling, can you fetch me a cup of coffee?" I was nestled in my office, a safe haven from all outside distractions, and ready to get to work. Although I was perfectly capable of getting my own coffee I hadn't done so for decades, and knowing the request would annoy Jen made it all the sweeter.

"If you think I'm here to..." She rounded on me, exactly as I'd thought she would, and there was thunder and lightning flashing in those bright blue eyes of hers. All I wanted to do was bend her over the desk and fuck the living daylights out of her, but there was a good chance she'd like that, and I didn't want to make today a pleasurable experience.

"Uh-uh-uh," I said, wagging my finger at her. "If you want your night of femdom you have to play the game, young lady. Are you obeying my every order or being difficult?" Throwing her hands up in the air and turning around abruptly on the point of a stiletto, it was clear I had won this round as she flounced from the office - actually, maybe not. Salivating over her retreating ass, I wondered if I'd be able to keep my hands off her until lunchtime, let alone the rest of the day. What the hell was wrong with me? Once upon a time I ruled everything I touched, and now I had been reduced to a dribbling mess. Damn it. What the hell had happened to my hormones in the past year?

When the coffee arrived it came just how I like it, which was basically a double espresso shot of the strongest variety available with a cup and saucer. Mugs are inelegant, and I refuse to tolerate them. "Thank you, darling. If you see Cynthia, she'll find you something simple to do. That way you can ease yourself in gently and find your niche." That was all lies of course. I'd instructed Cynthia to give her a heap of filing which should have her cross-eyed in no time at all. She'd be begging me to take her home in an hour or two.

"Oh, by the way, what should I call you when we're at work? Mark sounds too informal, and Mr Matthews just sounds wrong, although if you want me to use it, I will." Jen hovered by the door, her hand tightly grasped around the handle to make ready her escape.

"My lord and master will do fine," I said, without cracking a smile. I was mightily proud of myself. If that didn't irk her, nothing would.

"You are *very* funny," she said sarcastically, although she managed to control the eye-rolling thing. The girl was learning.

"And you can obey or not; doesn't make any difference to me."

There was still no eye rolling as Jen said, "Yes, my lord and master. Anything that amuses you amuses me, my lord and master. Oh, until this week is up, that is. Then everything is going to amuse me, *my lord and master*."

I ignored that comment. "Oh and darling, can you ring up Starbucks and get them to deliver a tuna melt Panini and latte for my lunch? I'm going to work right through today. Cynthia has the number."

"As you wish." She then retreated without a murmur, which made me instantly suspicious. What was my wife playing at? And that "As you wish" comment was strangely familiar. I'd seen it in a film somewhere, I was sure. Racking my brains for the better part of ten minutes, I finally Googled it. *The Princess Bride.* I vaguely remembered it. There was definitely some significance behind those words, but I was damned if I could remember it. About to waste valuable office time by doing yet more Googling, the telephone rang. Thank God for that.

Twenty minutes later, Cynthia came in with a great big smile on her face. That in itself was unusual, and I couldn't help but wonder what had put it there. Were my wife's dreadful antics that entertaining? It was time to find out.

"Why Cynthia, you look radiant. What has put you in such a good mood?" Cynthia's grey hair was artfully styled into a chic bob today, and she wore a string of large pearls around her neck. Her black jacket was tailored to taper gently at her waist, and her skirt was perfectly matched. In all the years I had known her she never had a hair out of place, and today was no different.

"Actually, it's your wife. She's an absolute gem around the office. Why did you not bring her in before? Did you know she can speak several languages fluently - and one of them includes Mandarin? She took over the call to Wang Li, who's curious about our new cell phone, and the pair rattled on for about ten minutes before she put down the phone and said he'd like to order two hundred thousand of them when they come online. That's two weeks of my life going back and forth among a translator she's just saved me - and she sold the package to boot. The woman's a genius!"

A stream of explicit cuss words exploded in my head. Extricating Jen out of this office was going to be harder than I thought if I wasn't careful.

"How did she know any of the specifics of the Strontium X?" I admit I was at a complete loss at this point. How did my wife manage to sell something she had virtually no knowledge of?

"I can assure you she did. When they began the call, it was in English. They were talking tech right from the start. Hadn't you briefed her on it beforehand?" Cynthia looked confused, as well she might. I hadn't briefed my wife on anything. Either the woman was going through my briefcase, or she'd managed to hack into my computer. It was one or the other.

"I must have, but for the life of me I can't remember doing so." I smiled. "So you're pleased with her so far?" Say no woman. Please say no.

"Yes. She's a dream. Everything you tell her to do gets done in record time, and she can type like the wind. She managed to whizz up your dictaphone tapes in seconds, and every single one is completely error-free. If only we had more office staff like her. We desperately need to employ some more people, Mark. When are you going to start hiring?"

"Soon," I said, but I didn't want to think about that right now. I wanted to find out if my wife had been snooping and I wanted her ass over my desk for two reasons. The first was because she always deserves a good spanking, and the second was that I couldn't resist her any longer. If I couldn't thrust myself inside Jennifer in the next thirty seconds I was going to go crazy, and I didn't see why I should deny both of us exactly what we wanted.

Nodding, Cynthia left a pile of papers on my desk for me to sign and went back to her office. Leaving her just enough time to get inside and close the door, I then went in search of my wife.

Typically the woman was nowhere to be found. I'd employed her for less than a day, and already she was bored witless. Maybe Cynthia's praise had been exaggerated. My second-in-command was hardly going to say something horrible about my wife, was she? Expecting to find her in the kitchen playing on her cell or painting her nails, I was somewhat surprised to find that room empty, too. That only left the ladies, so I waited patiently outside for five minutes before I stormed in and told her to hurry up. That might have worked if there was someone in one of the cubicles, but it was completely empty. Where the hell was she?

Marching into Cynthia's office, I asked her if she had seen Jen.

"Ah, no dear. She's just nipped out to Starbucks for your lunch. There seems to be a problem with the phone line at the moment, we can't dial out for some reason, so I asked her if she wouldn't mind walking over there instead." Cynthia saw my face lose all its colour and said, "That is okay, isn't it?"

I'd forgotten that Cynthia wasn't up to speed on current events.

"She's not supposed to go anywhere without a security detail. We've had death

110

threats." It was easier and quicker than explaining the whole sorry story. "You didn't know, don't worry. Which Starbuck's did she go to?"

Cynthia gave me the address, and I ran all the way there in less than three minutes. My lungs were screaming by the time I'd arrived, and I got a few odd stares, but I didn't give a flying fuck. My eyes were desperately searching around the café to see if Jen was still there, and having scanned the room from top to bottom three times, I could pretty much safely say that she wasn't.

Pushing my way to the front of the till, angering nearly every single customer in the line, I caught the attention of an extremely frazzled barista and explained that I was searching for someone. I gave a brief description of my wife, and what she might have ordered and waited to see if anyone could remember serving her.

Most of the staff shook their heads, but one gentleman then piped up that he had served her, describing her perfectly. When I asked him how long ago she'd been in, he said no more than five minutes. So why the hell hadn't I seen her? Had she decided to go shopping on her way back? It was unlikely. She had a large cup of coffee in her hand and a bag of sandwiches to lug about. Thanking the man I dashed out of the store, canvassed the area for ten minutes, and when she didn't materialise, I headed back to the office.

"Any sign?" I asked when I could breathe again. Cynthia was waiting for me, and shook her head.

"No, none. The phones are now working again, though. How odd."

I didn't like the sound of that at all. Something here was very wrong. Thinking quickly, my stomach took a nosedive as my heartrate exploded. The bastard had her. I was sure of it. Now I just had to get her back before it was too late. Oh fuck, where did I start?

With a feeling of dread slowly washing down my entire body, I said, "Cynthia, get the police on the line."

Chapter Nineteen - Jennifer

When Cynthia asked me to go out and get the Starbucks, I jumped at the chance. Although Fountaine Bleu is an incredible cage complete with beautifully manicured gardens, it's still a cage, and I was beginning to feel claustrophobic. I knew I would be in trouble once I got back if Mark found out, but I was going to try my best to make sure he didn't. As he'd sequestered himself tightly in his office all day so far, there was a good chance I'd get away with it.

Besides, how was Kyle going to find me in the centre of London? As long as I made sure I wasn't being followed, I would be fine. Pulling the hood of my coat up tightly over my head, I marched off, delighting in the little scrap of forbidden freedom that had presented itself.

Walking into the coffee shop, I smiled brightly and took in a good gulp of freshly roasted coffee bean air. God, I love that smell. Given half a chance, I could sit there all day. Unfortunately, I daren't stay for more than five minutes because if the alarm was somehow raised back at the office there would be all hell to pay, and after last night's session, it was going to hurt. Not that I minded too much, of course.

Freedom wasn't the only reason I was running off into the great unknown, though. After Mark's incredibly irresponsible actions with my birth control pills, there was a very real possibility I could be pregnant. So I was going to hightail it over to the nearest pharmacy and get a morning after pill. I wasn't sure if I'd be able to take it because the idea of killing a baby is abhorrent to me, but I wanted to keep my options open. I would give myself twenty-four hours to consider what I should do, get the advice of a few good friends, and then talk to Mark. It was a decision I should never have had to make, and a part of me blamed my husband for putting me in this position. Shaking my head, I swore at myself. We were both to blame. I could have said stop. We're both adults, and it takes two to tango.

"What would you like?" The lad behind the great big chrome monstrosity that was pumping out clouds of steam and churning up frothy brown bubbles at an impressive rate of knots smiled at me.

"Can I have a tuna melt and a latte to go, please?" I thrust out Mark's stainless steel travel mug, and it was whisked away from me.

"Sure thing. Be a couple of minutes." The guy handed me a small receipt and moved on to the next in line.

Shuffling to the ridiculously small table where all orders eventually appeared without being told, I did a bit of people watching. There were some students in the corner, judging from the workbooks all over the table, but they were doing more chatting than studying. It was early though, so I'd give them the benefit of the doubt. There were a couple of suits and briefcases, both sat alone on tables for two, and each looked as harassed as the other. I made a mental note never to get a briefcase. Then there was an Italian couple, obviously much in love, and animatedly talking to each other with large hand gestures. They could barely keep their hands off each other. It was adorable to watch. Lastly, sitting with their backs to the toilet, a couple of young mums sat side by side with their strollers next to each other. They looked tired and weary, and they clutched their coffee so tightly to their chest you'd have thought they were holding the crown jewels. It had obviously been a rough night. My eyes strayed to the babies who were curled up asleep in their makeshift beds. Both were little boys, and they looked adorable. One had tight blond curls, and the other had wispy tufts of dark brown fluff. Blondie had most of his fist stuffed inside his mouth and was happily sucking away at it in his sleep, while tufty had both hands up on either side of his head and was making adorable snuffling noises. My fingers suddenly had the itch to pick him up, and I wondered what the hell was happening to me. Geez. I must have been having an out of body experience or something. One day of work and my brain was already going to mush.

"One latte, one melt." Jumping at the sound of my order, I quickly grabbed my goodies and rushed back outside, jerking myself back into reality.

Hurry. You need to hurry. Scanning the area for a pharmacy, I eventually saw a tell-tale green cross flashing in the distance. Getting a wriggle on, I was just about to burst through the doors when something grabbed hold of my arm. Spinning around to give whoever it was a piece of my mind, I was suddenly wrenched back into a side alleyway and slammed against the wall. Both the sandwich and the cup of coffee crashed to the ground. Before I could regain my breath, my attacker reached into the pocket of his coat and pushed something small and blunt directly into my stomach. Though it was hidden from my view, there was no question in my mind it was a gun. I didn't need to look upwards to confirm the person wielding it was Kyle, but I did so anyway, recognising his features even though they were mostly shrouded by the hooded jacket he wore.

"Well, well, well. Fancy meeting you here."

I tugged at his arm, testing the strength of his grip. Unfortunately it was tight, and I went nowhere.

"You try that again and I pull the trigger." His face was now up close and personal with mine, and I could feel his spittle on my lips. Trying to pull away the back of my head came up hard against a brick wall, and I grimaced. Then I heard the click of a safety being released. "Now we can do this the hard way or the easy way, Jen. Which do you fancy?"

"How on earth did you find me?" I spat. This could not be happening. Mark had assured me we were not being followed on the way to work, and this wasn't part of my normal routine. How had the bastard managed to catch up with me so quickly?

"The hard way it is. I much prefer the hard way, Petal." Bringing a white cloth out of his pocket, he smothered it over my face. The smell was a bit like acetone. It was pungent, with a slightly sweet edge, and I had a fair idea this was nothing I wanted to breathe in. Struggling like mad, while trying to hold my breath, I did my best to get out of that alleyway, while making as much noise as I could. All I needed was for one person to come walking by, and the chances were they would raise the alarm. Frantic glances to either side of me revealed no such luck, and my desperate attempts to dislodge the creep were worthless. He was far too big and strong for me to get past. Kyle had me neatly backed up against the wall, and this encounter was only going one way - south. My head began to reel as the fumes of the drug started to work their way inside me, and I felt my legs wobble. Trying my best to scream behind the back of Kyle's hand I managed to bite him, once, before my vision started to blur.

As I sank into unconsciousness, my last waking thought was that if Kyle didn't somehow manage to kill me, Mark would.

When I awoke my head had a lightning storm of pain to contain. Gasping at the agony wreaking havoc behind my eyes, it took a moment or two before I could bear to open them. Where was I? What had happened? It didn't take long before it all came flooding back to me. Kyle. That miserable bastard.

Trying to bring my arm up to my head, I swore as I realised that not only was I naked but I was hogtied up tight in a ball. Rocking backwards and forwards a couple of times, it became apparent I was going nowhere fast. *Don't panic*, I tried to tell myself, but that's kind of hard when you find yourself naked and tied up. To make matters worse, Kyle was completely nuts. There was no telling what he'd do with me, and whatever it was, it was guaranteed to involve suffering - and lots of it.

As reality began to set in, I started shivering all over as panic and fear took over my body. This was not good. I needed to focus, make note of my surroundings, and use any little thing I could find to my own advantage. Swallowing against the all-consuming pain that was raging fires inside my head, I tried to figure out where I was being held. Any clues to my whereabouts would be helpful, especially if a chance to escape presented itself.

Take this one step at a time and remember to breathe. Breathing was very important. Blinking a couple of times to get my eyes used to the dim light, the first thing I saw was the bare wooden floorboards beneath me. They looked old and worn and were scratchy against my naked flesh. Looking higher, and wincing through blinding flashes of pain, I discovered I was in an almost empty room with peeling wallpaper. Lots of leaves and grand flourishes adorned it, and once upon a time, it would probably have been gold in colour. Now it had been bleached by the sun and rendered a dull yellow, and the pattern was reminiscent of an old damask bedspread I'd once had. Michael loved old things. He collected antiques as if they were going out of fashion, pun intended.

This was probably a townhouse he'd just bought, and if I had to make a bet, I'd say I'd been stashed in the attic. There was little else of note in the room. It had been stripped of furnishings, and there were darkened rectangles on the wall where artwork had once been hung. The windows were shuttered, there was an old tasselled velvet lampshade above my head, and an old brass handle adorning the single wooden door. Not much had probably changed since Victorian times, bar a couple of plug sockets that looked decidedly incongruous with my current surroundings.

Desperately needing some water I wondered whether to shout, but thought better of it. Kyle never played nice. He would want me to suffer, and as soon as I was awake I would be fair game. If I had any sense I'd remain as quiet as a mouse for as long as I could. My husband would be looking for me, as well as my mother with any luck. Between them, maybe they could beat Kyle at his own game. That was probably wishful thinking, but I was in a very tight spot, and I needed to cheer myself up. If I was honest with myself, there was a ninety-five percent chance this was not going to end well, and they weren't good odds in anyone's book. No one had seen me being abducted. It might have been an hour or more before the alarm was raised. There would be no clues to my whereabouts bar the probability that Kyle was involved, but no one had been able to find him before, so why should that change now?

The urge to bawl my eyes out was strong, but it was hardly likely to help my headache or anything else for that matter. *Stay strong.* It was easier said than done, though.

What did Kyle and Michael want? What did it have to do with me? Wheels within wheels spun inside my head. For lack of anything else to do, I began rocking my way towards the door, which I knew would be locked. It begged the question what did I expect to do with it if I made the journey, as my limbs were tied, but I needed to do something. Inactivity would have me delving deep into the realms of panic, and I didn't see why Kyle should win the war just yet.

Footsteps sounded on creaky wooden stairs, and I decided to play dead once more. *Talk of the devil and he shall appear.* There was the sound of a key in the lock, confirming my earlier suspicions, and the old wooden door moaned and groaned as it was pushed inwards. More heavy thuds of footfalls sounded, stopping just inches away from my body. I didn't bat an eyelid, though.

"You can stop the pretence because I have hidden cameras all over this room."

I didn't believe him. How could you conceal cameras in a room that housed no furniture?

"Fine. Have it your way." Kyle's booted foot found its way to my exposed ribcage with a swift kick and I gasped in shock. "Want to play 'let's pretend' again, Petal?"

Funnily enough, I didn't. Glaring up at him I hissed, "What do you want?"

Staring down at me, his hands crossed over his chest, he dropped his head to the side as he leered at my body. There wasn't a thing I could do about it, so I didn't bother trying. I was damned if I'd give him the satisfaction of watching me struggle.

"I thought you'd never ask." He pulled something out of the back pocket of his jeans, and though I could barely move a muscle, all instincts screamed that I retreat. Pulling an iPhone up to his chest, he tapped it against his black shirt as he gave me a crude whistle. "It's time to wind your husband up, Petal. I'm going to take some photos." He messed about with a few buttons on his cell, and then I heard the familiar click of the camera app being pressed over and over. He took shots of me from all angles and got several close-ups of my face. Obviously these were going to be sent to Mark, but to serve what purpose? Ransom?

"Do you want money? Is that what this is all about?" I whispered, still too mad to feel violated. That would come later.

"Dad wants money. I just want to play. You know how I like to play, Petal."

Oh yes, I knew that all too well.

"Are these photos for a ransom then?" What I was trying to say was: is there any chance I'm going to get out of here alive? Unfortunately he didn't answer me; he was too absorbed in rifling through his latest snaps.

"Ah, yes, this one should do it. Just the right amount of fear and loathing. I think Mark will love it." I didn't.

"He'll kill you if you try and pull another stunt," I threatened. Mark probably would too, given half a chance.

"Not if I kill him first. Right, what's hubby's number? Better get this across to him so he can stop worrying."

"You're an asshole, you know that?" I glared at him and I was so angry my whole body shook, not that it did much good, tied up as I was.

"Want another boot in the ribs, Petal, or are you going to give me that number?" By the light dancing in Kyle's eyes, it was clear he was enjoying himself.

"Go to hell," I spat, then paid for my outburst as his foot crashed into my body. My eyes squeezed tightly shut as pain ricocheted all through me. There was going to be a massive bruise there shortly.

"It's not a problem. I can always have it blown up on a poster and delivered by courier. Of course, you'll have to wait another three or four days for this to be sorted, but I'm more than happy to have some extra playtime. You don't know how long I've been looking forward to this moment, Petal. I have so much planned." He rubbed his hands together in glee. "Maybe I should start a few of my projects now and take some more photos, seeing as how you aren't particularly keen to get the ransom thing going. I think I could change your mind fairly quickly you know."

All the courage and bravery of earlier fled after that threat. I remembered what had happened in the depths of Albrecht's dungeons with the pinwheels and electricity. He'd threatened to use chilli salves on me internally, but Mark had thankfully stepped in to stop him. This time, with no one around, he could do what he liked to me, and I had a feeling it wouldn't bother him overly much if he killed me.

There was no point in using delaying tactics. All that would do was increase my suffering by a few days. If Mark was going to be involved anyway, we might as well get this over with. Reluctantly reeling off my husband's cell phone number I took a moment to wonder if he'd pay the ransom. I had no doubt Mark would if he could, but what if Kyle asked for a crazy amount of money? One that he didn't have? What would happen then? Would Kyle start cutting body parts off until he got what he wanted? I wouldn't put it past him.

Hearing the bleep of a text message being sent, a cold sliver of fear wedged itself deep inside my chest. There was a very real chance I wasn't getting out of this mess alive. It was entirely possible Kyle would take the money and run. After he got what he wanted, he wouldn't need me. All I'd be then was a liability - one who could rat on him to the police. Would Michael allow him to kill me? I wouldn't put anything past him. Christ, how had I ever got myself tangled up in this mess?

Replacing his cell back in his pocket, Kyle got down on his haunches so he could hover over me. It wasn't a friendly move. The man probably wanted to see my reaction to whatever bombshell he was about to drop next, so I steeled my expression to make sure he wouldn't get a whimper out of me. It might only be a small victory, but against this man every one would count.

Smoothing a strand of my hair away from my cheek, he brought his face so close to mine I wanted to vomit, but somehow I managed to keep it together. It wouldn't do to piss him off if I could avoid it, and I was pretty sure that splattering the contents of my stomach over him wasn't going to make his day. The sooner he got the hell away from me, the better.

"Well, you'll be pleased to know that's done. He's got twelve hours to come to your rescue, otherwise he's never going to see you again. I think that was blunt enough, don't you? Do you think he'll come for you, Petal? Does he love you, or are you merely one of his numerous playthings? It'll be interesting to find out, won't it?" Kyle grabbed a handful of my hair and yanked so hard I saw stars.

"What about the ransom? How much did you ask him for?" I'm not sure why I wanted to know the sordid little details, but I just wanted to convince myself that Mark would be able to pay it. Mind you, even if he didn't have the money he'd find a way. Mark was nothing if not resourceful.

"Oh, did I forget to mention that this isn't about ransom, Petal? I'm only inviting him over so I can kill him, after I've played with him for a bit, of course." Kyle got up and stretched himself out, looking down at me with eyes that were blazing with a crazy blend of insanity and excitement. "We're going to have such fun, you and I."

My face recoiled in horror. If I'd heard him correctly, I'd just signed my husband's death warrant. "You fucking asshole," I screamed before I could stop myself, and Kyle's face lit up with obvious delight. This was worse than waving a red rag to a bull. I lost it there and then, uncaring of the consequences. Rolling towards him, my mouth latched on to his ankle and bit as hard as it could. Although the bite was through jeans, there was no question the bastard felt it because he jumped back in shock. Then I watched his foot lash out towards my temple in slow motion, and I did my best to wrench my head back as far as I could. But I wasn't quick enough. I heard the sickening thud as his boot connected with my head, and then... nothing.

Chapter Twenty - Mark

Talking to the metropolitan police officer, I gave him a brief outline of what had happened and why I was so concerned. The officer wrote up the details on a large form and asked me a few questions of his own. Had I done anything that might have upset my wife? Had we had an argument of any kind? Was she happy when she'd left the office? Those kinds of questions were aimed at ascertaining whether I might have hopped out in my lunch hour to murder my wife. The husband is usually always the first suspect for that kind of thing, and I'd had my fair share of grief when Jen was poisoned last year.

Cynthia stepped in, thankfully, confirming that she had seen Jen leave the office, and more importantly, she also stated that I hadn't. The officer seemed satisfied for the time being and said he'd assign a team to the case and keep me updated. Meanwhile, he advised me to stay at the office, just in case she turned up. It happened, I was told.

Just before he left, he asked me if I had any idea where she might have gone if Kyle had taken her, as I suspected. I shook my head helplessly. The last time they'd abducted me they'd gone to an abandoned warehouse, but they wouldn't use the same place twice. Reeling off those details would only arouse awkward questions that I'd rather not answer. Maybe I would send some of my security guys around there just to make sure, though. There was a possibility she might have been taken to Albrecht, too, but again I thought it unlikely. Michael and Kyle weren't going to go anywhere I might catch them. They weren't stupid.

Anyway, after a forty-five minute chat I'd given the officer all the details he needed, and he reiterated what he'd said before about keeping me updated. I shook his hand and watched him leave. What now? There was little chance the police were going to bring my wife back, but I'd take any chance rather than none. Now I needed to figure out a way of getting her back, and I was prepared to sell my soul to do so. There were no bridges I wouldn't cross to see the safe return of my wife. *You need to talk to your mother-in-law.* Khalil's words were going to come back to haunt me - but he was right. I needed to speak to Laurel. She had contacts I could only dream of, and if we put our heads together, perhaps we'd come up with answers.

Warily pulling my cell phone out of my pocket, I looked at her number and grimaced. There was nothing for it; this had to be done.

Sucking in a deep breath, I tapped her number. My hand was shaking around the phone, and I suspected it was due to a combination of Jen's disappearance and the prospect of having to be civil to my mother-in-law. Bolstering myself for imminent annihilation, I prepared for the worst. She wasn't likely to be friendly to me, and she was even less likely to want to help, but I'd never forgive myself if I didn't at least try. Jen's life was probably hanging in the balance, and I needed to try everything - and this, in my eyes, was a last resort.

"Hello." The voice on the other end of the line was not female, and it put me completely off my stride. Having been all psyched up to do war with Laurel, all the air in my body left me suddenly and I felt like a deflated beachball.

"Is Laurel there, please?" I decided to be as polite as I could. My beef was with the mafia lady and no one else.

"Who's calling?" The gentleman sounded slightly bored, and it was clear he had better things to do with his time than chat to strangers.

"Mark Matthews, her son-in-law." I wasn't confident that was going to get results, but I thought I'd try and be civil for the first two minutes. The man put his hand over the speaker as I heard him call out Laurel's name. I had to take the phone away from my ear for a bit until he'd finished yelling back and forth with the antichrist; which was my new nickname for Laurel.

"She doesn't want to speak to you." Although I knew that, it ticked me off a teensy bit more than I was already, and I was near breaking point as it was.

"Tell her she will, so she'd better get her ass over here right now before I make it my mission in life to make hers miserable." Civility went flying out of the window. Was it wise threatening my wife's mother who could have me killed in an instant? Damned if I cared right now.

"Oh." The man sounded quite taken aback, as well he might. There probably weren't too many people who spoke their mind to the antichrist. More yelling followed, and I grimaced once more as I gave my cell phone a wide berth.

"No, it's official, she still doesn't want to speak to you. She says you called her a bitch last time you spoke to her. She also says that if you don't fuck off, she'll send someone over to take care of the job." The man growled at me menacingly, to make sure I got the message.

Figuring I'd get him on the right track before he hung up on me, I said, "Her daughter's been kidnapped, and I need her on the line now." If that didn't bring Laurel running, nothing would, and then I'd be back at square one with no leads, no ideas, and no hope in hell.

"You have my attention, Mr Matthews." Laurel's formal address was nothing new. She avoided talking to me wherever possible, but when she did have to, she made it clear it was under sufferance.

"Jen went missing from my office just before midday. She hasn't been seen since."

"I see." There was a long pause, which she used expertly to make me feel as small as she possibly could. "How could this have happened with her three-strong security detail?" That was an excellent point. Shit.

"My secretary asked her to go out and get coffee, and Jen did, knowing full well she wasn't supposed to." There was no way I was going to say she'd been sent out to get my lunch. I liked my testicles attached to my body, thank you very much.

"My daughter is very wilful and has a strong personality. One would think you would be aware of this after a year of marriage. Why did you not place one of your security guards on the door to make sure that something like this didn't happen?" I'd been asking myself that same question for the last five hours, but it was always nice to have your nose rubbed in it.

"I should have, but I trusted her to be sensible. It's a mistake I won't make again in a hurry." When I got my wife back - not if - we were going to have a conversation on ditching security guards. It would involve only me speaking, and lots and lots of spanking, whipping, flogging and anything else unpleasant I could think of.

"If she's dead you won't be able to make that mistake again, will you?" Laurel's voice was clipped, and her scathing tone was not lost on me. Yes, I probably deserved that, but there was only so much of this I could take.

"Well, at least I didn't abandon her for the first twenty odd years of her life. So no one's perfect. Are you going to help me or not, Laurel?" Grabbing my tie, I yanked it off and threw it on the floor. The walls around me began to close in, and the room felt suffocating. Though the day had already been an incredibly long one, I was no closer to achieving anything and I couldn't deal with the inactivity. There must be something I could do, but what?

"I'm hardly going to let my daughter die, am I? I'll call in some favours," she said frostily. "If you have any updates, let me know. I'll give you my personal cell number." She reeled it off quickly, but thankfully I had a pen and paper nearby. It did beg the question: who's bloody number had she given me the first time around? We'd discuss that another time.

"Thank you."

"Now, are you going to apologise for your earlier behaviour?"

Was she kidding? Were we back to this? I had the mother-in-law from hell. It was official. "You want me to apologise to you for what happened yesterday morning?" My wife had nearly left me after Laurel's crazy stunt, so I really didn't know what I had to be sorry about.

"Yes. Get to it. We haven't got all day." There was a pad of paper in front of me, and I began stabbing the nib of my pen through it while imagining it was the antichrist. It didn't make me feel any better, but it was a good outlet for a little of my pent-up rage.

Gritting my teeth I said in my sweetest voice, "I'm very sorry for calling you a bitch yesterday morning, Laurel. It was completely uncalled for. I'm also sorry that you came round at all, and I'm doubly sorry that your antics didn't end in divorce, as you probably hoped they would. You need to get used to the fact that Jen loves me, and we are happy together." I took another deep breath. "If that apology results in you not helping me find my wife, then I'm just sorry. Are you happy?"

Laurel's voice was dangerously quiet as she said, "If I don't find Jennifer alive, you are next on my hitlist."

I hung up on her.

After six o'clock had come and gone, I left the office and headed back home. I knew Jennifer wasn't going to waltz back in as the police had suggested, but if she did, Cynthia would be there until eight.

Driving home, all alone in the car, it felt like my world had been blown apart. There on the passenger seat was Jen's handbag, and right now, that was all I had left of her. I was so close to losing it I shouldn't even be driving, but I had not the time or patience to wait for anyone else to do it for me.

What should I do now? The question had been going over and over in my head. I'd already been through Jen's bag, and there was nothing in it that would help me find her. Enraged to discover she hadn't even taken her cell phone with her, I went through it just in case, but she'd received no calls or texts so far today, so it was another dead end. If she'd had it on her I could have had it tracked, or at least tried to call it, but she'd taken nothing with her bar a coat. *Please be okay*, I begged to anyone that would listen. *Please be okay*.

When I got home I called Khalil again to see if he'd had an update, but there was nothing new to report. But Laurel had been in touch with him, so at least she was on our side. It annoyed me that she had somehow managed to find Khalil's number, which was not listed anywhere that I knew of, without my help. But I guess I should have been pleased. The more resourceful my mother-in-law was, the more likely it was that we'd find Jen in one piece.

Dumping my briefcase in my home office, I checked my emails and phone for any messages that I might have missed. There was nothing that couldn't wait, so I headed off to the kitchen to get myself a drink. Pulling out a bottle of a twenty-one-year-old malt whisky, I poured myself two fingers and downed the whole lot in one. The resulting burn worked its way through limbs which felt frozen and wooden, helping to warm me up somewhat, but it did little to ease the panic circulating through me. Nothing was going to help with that, bar knowing my wife was safe.

Sitting down on the sofa in the lounge, I have no idea how long I sat there rocking backwards and forwards, berating myself for not having kept a closer eye on Jennifer. Misery and loathing consumed me, and I didn't know what to do with myself. At the back of my mind I knew I needed to keep it together, but I didn't know how much longer I'd be able to cope. My life seemed to be one big drama after another, and there are only so many times you can work through your wife being tortured, poisoned or kidnapped. Everything inside me felt broken and fragile.

My cell phone chose that moment to bleep, and I picked it up automatically. The number came up as unrecognised, but that didn't necessarily mean anything. Most of my work colleagues and associates had access to my number, and they called from all four corners of the globe. Having said that, my fingers still shook as I entered my password. It took me three times to open the damn message, and then when I did, I dropped the phone in horror. That fucking bastard. He'd got her - but how? How did he know where she'd be? Was he watching us? Were there people trained on this house all the time? Or just the office? I was going to kill him.

Standing up, I snatched the phone up from the floor to confirm what I'd just seen. For a second I stared at Jen's face, while trying to ignore the fact that she was tied up and naked. She had an odd expression on her face. It was somewhere between scared and furious.

When I could bear to tear my eyes away from her, I saw the message he'd sent me underneath.

If you want to see your wife again, meet me at Hyde Park at 11pm. We have all the entrances covered. If you are followed, I will kill the girl. If you tell anyone, I will kill the girl. If you don't show, I will kill the girl - but not before I've played with her a bit. You know how that turns me on, Matthews.

Roaring out loud, I flung the phone to the other side of the room where it hit the wall with a thud. It clattered to the floor, but I had more important things to worry about. What did I do next? Did I risk telling someone? What if he had the place bugged? Surely that wouldn't be possible with the surveillance I had installed here, but what if it was? He had managed to snatch Jennifer from right under my nose with very little trouble. That alone spoke volumes. Better to proceed with caution than do anything that might leave Jen's life hanging in the balance. Besides, I could be smart about this. While I didn't intend to phone anyone to tell them my whereabouts, I wasn't going to leave them all completely clueless.

Retrieving my phone, and snatching a pen and paper from my office, it didn't take long to jot down this evening's events. Leaving my cell phone on top of the notepad next to my laptop would allow them to try and trace the whereabouts of the caller when the alarm was raised. That wouldn't be until tomorrow when I was expected to go into work, but better late than never. I then picked up the small

GPS tracker I'd bought to track Jen's whereabouts but had never used because she never wore the same thing twice. Instead we'd had one installed in her phone, which was also utterly useless, seeing as how she hadn't taken it with her. The device was no bigger than a ten pence coin, and I could easily hide it somewhere. Khalil would be able to track it, so that was one more thing that went in my favour.

A glance at my watch told me I had an hour to kill before I needed to drive back into London. At least the traffic would have died down by now. I shook my head. What the fuck was I worried about traffic for? I was about to drive off to my death, wasn't I? If the poison of last year had been meant for me, then sure as hell death was in my imminent future. That was a friendly thought. I'd just have to hope that Laurel or Khalil managed to find me in time. Fuck. I was placing my hopes of rescue in the hands of my mother-in-law? I must be certifiably insane. There was nothing for it, though. I wouldn't risk Jennifer's life. If that meant mine was forfeit, then so be it. If she'd been prepared to sacrifice her own for mine last year, then the least I could do was return the favour. Besides, she'd been through enough.

Going back to my notepad, I added a message for Laurel at the end. It went something along the lines of *If I end up dead please end both Kyle and Michael's life in the most unpleasant way possible*. I even put a thank you in there for good luck.

Now, what did one wear to meet one's death? I figured I'd go with jeans, a black sweater, a padded jacket, and a pair of sneakers. Can't beat comfy clothes to die in. The GPS tracker could be hidden in my coat. The hood was stored in the collar, so I just opened the flap and pushed the thing inside. It wouldn't be easily recognisable because there were lots of poppers to keep the fold in place. In any case, Khalil would be able to track my whereabouts until Kyle found the device, and hopefully that would be later rather than sooner.

So, did I have any last requests before I went to meet my maker? The whisky had been done and dusted, but it probably made sense to eat something. When he got me right where he wanted me it was highly likely there would be some form of torture involved, and that always went down better on a full stomach. I suspected he'd surpass Sophia on the pain score unless a miracle happened and someone managed to intervene, but I wasn't overly optimistic. I'd known this was coming for a year now, and quite honestly I just wanted to get it over with. At least I'd finally figure out what Redcliff wanted. Hopefully.

The drive back to London was completed in silence. Only this morning I had been grumping about all the noise on the commute into work, and now I would have given anything to have it back.

Why did Redcliff want me dead? Obviously it had something to do with money, and the fact that Jennifer would inherit mine was probably a driving factor. Did Michael think he could control her after I was gone? Of course he did. I don't think he'd factored on Laurel being in the equation, though. Did he know about her mafia connections? It would be interesting to find out.

Parking my car at the office, which was another sure-fire way to sound the alarm tomorrow when they found it there without me, I got a taxi to Hyde Park. I knew I was all kinds of crazy for doing this, but I also knew that I couldn't do anything else. Needing to see Jennifer myself, to make sure she was okay, was my number one priority right now.

When the taxi dropped me off at the Queen Elizabeth gate, Sophia sprang to mind. Although it was where we first met, that wasn't what I was thinking about. Jen's obvious jealousy and animosity towards her were uppermost in my thoughts. Although I could understand why she had a problem with what had happened, she knew that I'd instigated it. Sophia hadn't done anything that I'd not asked for, and as such, I was at fault. Things had gone too far, though. Although she'd been reluctant I had encouraged her to do more than she was comfortable with, and as she'd had company, Sophia felt duty-bound to see the session through. It had been a mistake and one I never intended to repeat. Making a promise to myself, I vowed that if Jennifer and I managed to get through this next ordeal in one piece, I would allow her a night of domination. If that put us back on the right track it was a small price to pay. Besides, it would be interesting to see if she could wear the trousers for an evening. Thinking it and actually doing it were two different things entirely. *You're getting distracted. Pay attention.*

Hyde Park was mostly deserted at this time of the evening, which was probably why Kyle had chosen the location. There weren't too many people who would venture out on their own at this time of night, although I saw a few. Mostly happy revellers who wanted to walk off their dinner, though there was the odd young couple who were out seeking a little privacy for themselves. Walking along the Serpentine lake, watching the moon reflect upon the water in patterns of silvery lace, I scoured the area looking for Kyle. No one was near me, so there was little left to do but amble along and wait for the inevitable.

Stopping at one of the little placards that were dotted around, I discovered that the lake was created in 1730 at the request of Queen Caroline. It also hosted a one hundred yard swimming race every Christmas morning for souls braver than me. The lake achieved notoriety in 1816 when the pregnant wife of poet Percy Bysshe Shelly was found drowned in its depths. I sincerely hoped that wasn't where I was headed.

The sound of footsteps upon gravel alerted me to someone else's presence, and I looked over my shoulder to discover that there were now three gentlemen coming towards me. All of them were wearing dark jeans and sweatshirts, with the hoods pulled down low over their faces. Squinting in the darkness, I just about made out Kyle's features, which meant the theatrics were about to begin.

"Hands out to the side where I can see them, Matthews." The order was barked out, and I complied. The two gentlemen with him came up to pat me down, and they did a thorough job that any airport official would have been proud of.

"He's got nothing on 'im." The cockney accent was unmistakable, so these must have been the hired help.

"Not even a cell phone?" Kyle sounded a little disbelieving, as well he might, but I had plans for my phone.

"You would have only tossed it in the lake, so what was the point?" Looking Kyle directly in the eye I went on, "We're wasting time. Take me to my wife."

"You don't call the shots around here, Matthews. I do. All you need to worry about is obeying every fucking word that comes out of my mouth. Got it?"

The two thugs he'd brought with him flanked me on either side, and we began walking up West Carriage Drive. Kyle stayed behind them.

"Is Jen okay? Where are you keeping her?" I turned my head to get his attention, but the guys in front yanked me forward sharply.

"No questions. Shut the fuck up and do as you're told. If you cooperate you'll see her soon enough."

Kyle was not in a talking mood by the looks of things, and there was no point pushing the issue. All I'd do was delay things and probably get a black eye in the process. *Be patient.*

Before long we were headed into Bayswater. After no more than ten minutes we ducked into a parking lot where a plain white Ford transit was waiting.

"Get in and strip." One of the thugs unlocked the back of the van and ushered me inside. If he thought I was getting naked he was much mistaken. I was just about to protest when three guns were trained on me.

"Now just a fucking minute..." I growled.

Kyle's pistol was in front of my face in a heartbeat. "You want to come with us, you get naked. We are dumping those clothes, Matthews. You could have planted a tracker or transmitter inside something, and I haven't got time to mess about. There are clothes in the truck for you. Get on with it, or I'll knock you out and do it for you."

Kyle waved the butt of his gun about, so I got the message. That was enough of an incentive for me to do as I was told. The thought of Kyle's hands on me had me coming out in a cold sweat. Getting undressed quickly, I tossed my clothes back to him and searched around for what he'd left me. It turned out to be a plain black t-shirt and a pair of boxer shorts. Great. I wasn't going to be able to conceal much in those, not that it mattered. Kyle had his eyes on me the whole time, so there was no chance I could slip the tracker out and shove it down my pants. Now what? That was one bridge burned. Could Laurel work with virtually nothing to go on? I sure hoped so. She was my last hope, and I wasn't very happy about it. Putting your life in someone's hands is one thing, but putting your life in the hands of someone who openly despises you is another. God help me.

When I'd got dressed, if you could call it that, Kyle told me to turn around and put my hands behind my back. He then used zip ties to fasten my wrists and ankles together. Usually I'd enjoy this kind of kinky stuff, but I just wasn't feeling up to it right then. Hey, you laugh, but my sense of humour was about the only thing I had left because my dignity had just flown out of the window.

Kyle yanked the zip ties nice and tight as if I was some kind of Houdini who made a habit of escaping from moving vehicles. I wish.

"You afraid I might get loose?" I asked dryly after he nearly cut off the circulation in my wrists. Testing the bonds, as soon as he'd let me go, I found I could barely separate one wrist from the other.

"I don't think you're going anywhere in a hurry, Matthews." He gave me a smug grin as he slammed the door of the van shut, much harder than he needed to.

I didn't either. The bastard had me right where he wanted me.

Chapter Twenty-One - Somewhere in Iran

I'd seen enough bad guys in my line of business to know that the bloke in front of me was one mean motherfucker. I don't mean the kind of guy who'd mug your grandmother in her own home and then punch her lights out, either. This guy was a special kind of asshole, and by *special,* I mean he was quite content to blow up ninety percent of the world's inhabitants so he could rule the remaining ten. He was also a nuclear arms dealer, but the two kind of went hand in hand.

Having been deep undercover in the depths of hell, otherwise known as Mashhad, for what seemed like forever, I was starting to get sick and tired of this shit. It was all very nice making sure that a few select assholes didn't get out of line and try and blow everyone up, but these last few years I'd gotten a bit tired with the whole saving-the-world thing. It was time someone else stepped up. My ability to speak eleven different languages rather fluently had kept me deep undercover in some hole or another for the last twenty-five years, and it really was past time I threw in the towel. Having an IQ of over two hundred points is not to be recommended. They work you like slave drivers in these parts, and the perks aren't all that great.

So, where was I? Oh yes, Iran. Well, the negatives are that the heat in summer often tops forty degrees centigrade, you can't cross the road because drivers are nuts, the public toilets haven't been upgraded since the sixteenth century, and alcohol is virtually non-existent. They're some pretty serious negatives, I'm sure you'll agree, but Iran is not without its charms. Everyone who isn't a terrorist is normally very friendly, they have some of the best open-air markets in the world, the women are absolutely, jaw-droppingly stunning, if you need a good carpet someone always knows a man, and the history and culture aspects are pretty astounding.

Anyway, back to the subject in hand; the guy in front of me. He was currently holding four world-renowned scientists hostage, with the hopes that they'd be able to help him assemble his payload. They had adequate encouragement to do so; he'd already executed one that didn't want to play ball. To cut a long story short, he'd been sold a half-completed nuke, and he needed to know how to put the rest of it together to make a decent profit from his endeavour. Being a terrorist, he decided his best course of action was to kidnap a few people and hope for the best. His plan was all going swimmingly well until we found out that his buyer was in North Korea. We get a bit touchy in these parts when the North Koreans want nukes, and then I have to step in and clean up the mess. It was quite a spectacular one, too.

We had a guy on the inside working for him, and we rated his survival chances at a seventy/thirty combo. Navid Hassani wasn't known for his patience or his benevolent temperament. You remained in his employ while he considered you useful, and you took a bullet between your eyes as soon as you weren't. Now I've seen a lot of people die in my line of work, so I'm a bit desensitised to it all, but I was quite good friends with the guy on the inside this time, and I was going to be very put out if he came back in several pieces. Which was looking increasingly likely as I hadn't heard from him in twenty-four hours. There was a chance his cover could have been blown, and if that was the case, he was probably having a bit of unnecessary dentistry done at the moment. Still, I might be overreacting. It was possible the asshole had just shut operations down for the time being, or our guy might have copped a black eye or worse from one of the delightful gentlemen down there. They weren't known for playing nice.

Our last transmission had details of the trade that was due to take place today, and I hoped the intel was still good. We were about to bust in there and send most of the nasties up to meet their maker. If our cover had been blown we should have seen some movement as they tried to get the hell out of there. Either way, it was going to be a super fun day.

Currently briefing a team of SAS soldiers, who were decidedly upbeat considering the delightful day they had in store, we went through several different scenarios, all of which ended in us winning the day. There couldn't really be any other conclusion. Too much was at stake. Batting a wave of flies away with my hand, I wiped a trail of sweat from my forehead. This was going to be a long day.

When my phone vibrated in my pocket I immediately suspected the worst and bent to pick it up. If I found out Hawk had been murdered I was going to be in a very bad mood for the rest of the day.

"Hello." The call was unrecognised, which immediately sent warning bells hammering in my overheated brain. Christ, I needed to go somewhere that had air-conditioning. My internal circuits were being fried.

"Darling. Long time no see. How goes the international world of crime and espionage?" The voice was female and strangely familiar. It still took a few seconds for me to place it, and when I did I nearly dropped my phone.

It is usually quite hard to shock me, but getting a call from your ex-wife who you haven't heard from in twenty odd years can do that to a person. Fortunately, I recovered quickly.

"Laurel, darling. It's been ages. What's the matter? Is crime not paying these days? I can't see that it pays any less than working for the government, but I'll ship you some cash if I can find some."

"You're very funny, Rupert." Laurel's tone was rather curt, but that was nothing new so I didn't take offence.

"What's the problem then, darling?"

"Redcliff has kidnapped your daughter."

"Nah. The old boy hasn't got it in him. That's why we picked him. He dotted all the Is and crossed all the Ts. When I got his file I went over it with a fine tooth comb. Actually, there wasn't very much of a file, if I remember rightly. Investment

126

banker, dull, boring, a bit of golf, not a whiff of scandal. That sort of thing."

"Did you have anyone follow him for a bit?" Laurel's tone was dry, and I didn't appreciate it.

"Why would I have an investment banker followed? I know you think I sit about on my ass all day long and play silly games, but actually, some of this stuff is quite important..."

"Rupert. This is serious. She's been taken hostage. I think he's hoping to get some money out of the deal, which should give him plenty of cash to get rid of both of us. At least, that's how I see this playing out unless you have a better theory."

I didn't. The guy was a fucking moron, though. You don't tangle with the mafia and Her Majesty's Secret Service unless you've got a death wish or a screw loose. I wondered which it was. "Is he still in love with you?" It could explain a few things if he was. A woman scorned was one thing, but a man scorned who had access to a lot of cash was another.

"Of course he is. So are you for that matter."

"Says who?" I grinned. You had to love Laurel's sass. Besides, she was probably right; I just hadn't had enough time lately to give the matter any real thought. Slapping an annoying mosquito on my arm, I was most pleased with myself when I got it the first time.

"Okay, Laurel, what do you want me to do?" I sure as hell hoped that whatever it was, she didn't want me to do it immediately. Things would be a little sticky here for at least the next eight hours or so.

"Finish up whatever international emergency you're in the middle of and get your ass back to the UK, so we can extract your daughter and her husband."

I blinked. "She's married? When did that happen?" Rolling my eyes skywards, I wondered how long I'd been off the grid and what else had happened since I'd been away.

Laurel sighed as if the weight of the world was upon her shoulders. "She's been married a year. If you were contactable I'd have sent you the photos, but no, you always have to be squirreled away somewhere secret where no one can get a hold of you."

"It comes with the territory, Laurel," I said, with my tongue firmly in my cheek. "It would be a little pointless being in the secret service if I announced my presence to everyone. Can you imagine how that would go? Hi nuclear arms dealer, I'm a spy, and I'm about to blow you and your operation to bits. Fancy telling me everything you know?" Laurel was clucking impatiently on the other end of the line, but I'd just hit my stride. "I also take umbrage to 'squirreling'. I don't *squirrel* anywhere." I nodded to myself. That told her. "Oh, and it can't be that secret because you got a hold of me, so stop complaining."

"I had to threaten the head of MI6 to get your number."

Bursting out laughing, I said, "God, I wish I'd been there." Daniel Winchester was a real pain in the ass at the best of times, and I have often wished for his swift demise. Unfortunately, the man is very robust and rules our little office with an iron fist. "Care to tell me what you threatened him with?" This I needed to know.

"Concentrate, Rupert. There's a very real chance Redcliff is going to kill Jennifer's husband, whose name is Mark Matthews."

"Would I like him?" I was curious. As soon as Laurel put down the phone I was going to do some research. Getting some dirt on your son-in-law is always good fun.

"I don't." Laurel sounded a little petulant. Something had happened between them, that much was obvious, and it would be fun to find out exactly what had tugged her chain.

"That probably means I will." Smiling to myself I added, "So what do you want, Laurel? I have thirty minutes until I get to go wild with an underground terrorist cell, and I haven't even loaded my assault rifle yet. Get to the point, woman." Having always loved tormenting her, today I was enjoying myself even more than normal. Retirement was becoming a more appealing prospect by the second.

"Fine. Find out where Redcliff is hiding, get over there, and rescue Jennifer. If you can get Mark out then do so, but only if it's not too much trouble. That succinct enough for you?"

"Reading you loud and clear, boss lady. Be there as soon as I can. Right, gotta go. I've things to do, people to kill." She grunted and hung up on me. That was the Laurel I knew and loved. She was such a feisty thing. Would our daughter take after her? Did she have balls of steel just like her mother? If she did, I pitied her poor husband. He was going to have his work cut out for him.

Heading back to base to finish my talk with the boys, I thought wistfully back to our brief spell together. Having had no time lately for anything bar the odd one night stand - mainly because most of them didn't get to live longer than that - I thought it would be quite fun to take up where we left off. Laurel might not see it the same way, of course, but I can be very persuasive when I want to be. Mind you, so can she, and it doesn't pay to annoy her. She's a very accomplished killer, probably nearly as good as me, and I wouldn't want to go up against her. Actually, scrap that. Crossing swords with Laurel would probably be more fun than I'd had in a very long time, and I was due some. For the first time in ages, I was excited at the prospect of returning home.

Turning to the soldiers who were waiting patiently for my return, I decided I'd probably briefed them enough. "Right, come on you lot. We haven't got all day. Get your asses in the truck." We could chat about our latest assignment and all the other glorious details on the journey down. I'd just have to hope that my daughter and new son-in-law could make it twenty-four hours without my help. A spot of torture here and there was good for the soul, anyway. Built character, so it did. So trusting that Laurel wouldn't let anyone die until I got there, I concentrated on the job in hand. It wouldn't do to get killed just before I got to meet the happy couple, now would it?

Chapter Twenty-Two - Mark

The journey seemed endless, and without my watch there was no way I could keep track of time. I hadn't bothered putting it on because Kyle wouldn't have let me keep it, and he'd probably have delighted in smashing the thing to pieces in front of me. I wasn't going to give him the satisfaction.

Unfortunately, that meant I was left in the dark. We could be driving out of town, or we could be going around in circles to disorientate me, there was no way of knowing. I just hoped he didn't take too long about it. Desperately needing to set eyes on Jen, to convince myself she was okay, I hoped the ride wouldn't take too long. My brain was going into overdrive, thinking about all the horrendous scenarios that might be waiting for me when we arrived, and there was no point dwelling on that just yet.

Needing something to do, I searched around the van for anything that might help weaken the hold of my makeshift handcuffs. After ten minutes of scrambling about trying to find something sharp, banging around in the back like a ping pong ball, I realised my search was hopeless. It was a new van, there was nothing in the back except me, and all I was doing was wasting energy. There was a good chance I'd need plenty of that in a bit, so I might as well lie back and brace myself for whatever ugliness was to come.

When the van finally came to a lurching halt my body shot forward, and I cracked my head on the bulkhead. Swearing, I listened intently for any signs of life outside. Were we there yet? Was someone coming to get me? Was this where Jen was being held? All these questions and more knocked about in my brain, and I was literally jumping with adrenaline, desperate to get out of this tin can. When I finally heard footsteps thump down onto the tarmac I waited for them to come and get me, but after a couple of seconds I realised they were travelling in the other direction.

Shit. Were they going to leave me here? Please tell me this wasn't how I was going to die. If they were going to leave me abandoned somewhere while they had my wife, I would go insane. Resisting the urge to bang on the back of the van and yell as loud as I could, I sat there for several minutes, with beads of sweat dripping down my neck. When I finally heard some footsteps coming back, I wanted to sob in relief.

The van door wrenched open and the two thugs I'd met earlier placed a thick black hood over my head. Between them, they then dragged me out of the van and onto a concrete path. At least, I assumed it was because my feet made odd scraping sounds over it. The guys then lumped me up into some kind of doorway, and I was hoisted up some stairs. As I didn't have the use of my feet or hands I was entirely reliant on the two goons, and they were none too gentle. Smacking my head on a doorframe as they tried to manoeuvre me inside a room, I swore viciously. By the time they'd finished with me I was going to be black and blue.

"Where do you want 'im, Boss?"

"Just shove him over there. I've got a couple of things to get ready before we need him downstairs. Just make sure those wrist and ankle ties are tight, and that he's pinned to the floor. I don't want him wandering off until we're ready for him."

"Gotcha." I was flung in a corner, and some rope was wound around my wrists and ankles, over the cuffs, and attached to some eyebolts in the floor. It was a little overkill in my opinion, but nobody was worried what I thought.

"I want to see Jennifer," I demanded. The hood was still over my head, but I was positive she wasn't in the same room as me. The only bodies I could hear scuffling around belonged to Kyle and the goons.

Kyle walked up to me and ploughed a right hook into my face. My head went crashing sideways as pain splintered through my cheek. "No one cares what you want, so shut the fuck up or we'll gag you. You'll get your chance to see your wife in a bit. Be a good boy and stay quiet in the meantime." The fist in the face should have been warning enough, but I couldn't let the matter rest.

"Just let me see her. I need to see she's okay. It won't take—"

"Boys, knock him out for fuck's sake. His whining is driving me mad." Kyle sounded disgusted with me, and the boys in front of me sniggered. I didn't care. If I thought it would have made any difference, I'd get down on my hands and knees and beg to see Jen, but I knew my pleas would fall on deaf ears.

One smash with the butt of a gun into my face and I was out like a light. Three, two... gone.

When I woke up I did not have a hood over my head. This much I could figure out with my left eye. My right was swollen shut. The two thugs had done some damage between them, and I felt pain radiating down my cheekbone. Blinking dazedly, it took me a moment to discover that my feet were in water. Freezing cold water. Jesus. Jerking my feet upward it didn't take long to learn they were also chained to the floor. Looking down, I found out I was sitting on a long wooden plank that had been suspended in the middle of a swimming pool. Rocking from side to side, I realised that my hands were still tied behind me, and fastened to a wooden bar. Grabbing it tightly, I used it to steady myself. I was sitting on some kind of platform in the water, but it seemed stable enough, provided I didn't move about too much.

"Mark, you're okay. Thank God." The voice made me snap my head up, and there, on the opposite side of the plank was Jennifer, in much the same predicament as me. She looked fine, bar a particularly ugly bruise on her face, in a similar place to mine. Kyle had been busy.

"Are you all right? Has he hurt you?" My words tumbled all over each other in a rush. I can't begin to describe the relief I felt at seeing she was alive, but it was certainly enough to make me forget about the sub-arctic temperature of the water.

"I'm fine. What about you? What did he do to your face?" Her eyes glistened with tears, and I could see she was trying her best to hold them back. "Mark, I'm so sorry. This is all my fault. When Cynthia asked me to go out for coffee, I didn't think—"

"This is not your fault, Jen. He would have got to us sooner or later. He was playing a waiting game. We couldn't hide forever." That much was true.

Stifling a sob, she nodded, though her lip wobbled dangerously. "Does anyone know we're here?"

I shook my head. Technically they didn't, but hopefully they'd know we were missing soon enough. Khalil would be able to trace my whereabouts to central London, and hopefully he could catch some kind of trail from that. It was a long shot, but he'd come through for me before. We had Jen's mother, too. That had to count for something.

"Don't panic. I called Laurel. If she can't get us out of here, no one can." Thank God I had. We needed some kind of light at the end of the tunnel, and right now she was probably our only hope.

"That must have hurt."

Jen looked at me knowingly, and I smiled back ruefully. "She still doesn't like me very much, but at least she talked to me."

Jen would have said something then, but Kyle burst in on us, and he looked very pleased with himself. Striding up and down the length of the pool, he surveyed us both with unconcealed delight. Back and forth he strutted, his black trainers thudding against the tiled floor as he inspected the results of his scheming. Neither of us looked at him.

"How are you two lovebirds doing? Is it a little cold in there?" He was appropriately dressed with a warm fleece, jeans, and a thick wool jacket. How long had the bastard been planning this? A year? Longer? It made my blood run cold.

"Go to hell," I yelled at him. "It's only a matter of time before the police will be crawling all over here." One could hope, at any rate.

"Oh, I don't think so, Matthews. We've been very careful about concealing both of your whereabouts. No one is coming to get you." Kyle shook his head in mock pity, looking first at me and then at Jennifer. "I'm supposed to kill you right now, as it happens, but I figure I've earned me a little bit of fun, and you know how I like to play games."

Looking the bastard square in the eye, I said something unrepeatable. Even Jennifer winced, but Kyle looked amused.

"I'd save your energy if I were you, Matthews. You're gonna need it in a minute." He walked back down the length of the pool and stopped in front of Jen. Thankfully someone had put her in a black T-shirt because if she'd been naked I'd have torn the man's eyes out. When, not if I got free of these restraints, Kyle was going to need some serious facial reconstruction surgery.

"Wanna know the rules of the game, sweetheart?" By now Jen's teeth were chattering, and only half of our bodies were submerged in the pool. If this stunt went the way I thought it was going, there was going to be a good deal of suffering involved.

"Not particularly." Although the sentence came out in a pained, frozen stutter, I couldn't help but be proud of my wife. If Kyle did manage to kill me he was going to have to deal with a hellcat, and I didn't think she'd leave too many parts of him intact.

"Suit yourself. You can figure it out as you go along." Kyle pulled out some kind of remote control from his coat pocket and pressed a button. "There. That should get it going in a minute or two." He beamed at us. "Well, I'd love to stay and chat, but I think things are going to get pretty wet and nasty in here. I'm going to watch you from the comfort of a room upstairs - a very warm room as it happens. Good luck, lovebirds. You're going to need it." With that parting shot, he was off.

"Wh-wh-what's happening?" Jen's stutter was getting worse. I didn't think she'd last long when we were fully submerged, but I was going to be the one to take the brunt of most of this. Reasonably confident that Kyle didn't want to kill us just yet, we'd just have to endure to the best of our abilities.

"Take big, deep breaths, honey. The next part isn't going to be very pleasant, but we can get through this." Breathing was going to become a very important commodity in the next few minutes.

The platforms that held the plank stable at both ends began to sink into the water, and my end started swiftly plummeting downwards. Now we were suspended on a single pivot in the middle, which meant we were about to play seesaw.

"Mark!" Jen saw me begin to sink and she panicked, wriggling all over the place. The last thing we needed was for her to fall off the damn plank, or I'd be permanently underwater with no way to get up.

"Jen stop moving about, else there's a very real chance you'll kill me. If you fall off your side without a counterweight I won't be able to bounce back up. This is going to work just like a seesaw. I'll go underwater for a bit, and then it will be your turn. This is nothing we can't handle," I said optimistically, as I was now up to my neck in water and bloody freezing. Taking a huge gulp of air I got ready for the journey down and closed my eyes. The wait seemed endless, and everything seemed to move much slower as soon as the water covered my head. Up above I knew Jen would be panicking, but she'd be fine once she saw I was okay. Blowing out a long stream of bubbles as I plummeted my feet finally hit the tiles, and when I had enough leverage I used them to bounce me back up again.

Springing up out of the water I barked at Jen, 'Lean as far back as you can; it will give me a little more time to breathe!" She immediately complied, but I was already on the way down again. There was only time to suck in another big breath of air before I went tumbling under the surface again.

Since I was so much heavier than my wife, my weight was going to continually drag me down to the pool floor. Jen wasn't likely to get more than her stomach wet. This was good. The pool was so cold had she had her body immersed for any length of time the effects of hypothermia would set in, and there was no way you wanted to fall asleep in a pool full of water. I would be able to last a bit longer than her, and I could hold my breath for longer, but this wasn't a game I was going to be able to play for long. If Kyle wanted to kill me this would probably do it.

In the beginning I tried to talk to her each time I rose to the surface, to reassure her I was okay. Her face was by now bleached white with fear, and each time I went below I could tell she was wondering if I'd manage to make it back up again. Sharing her concerns, I tried my best not to let them show. Counting on the fact that Kyle would have more games in store for us, I did my best to ignore my chattering teeth and shivering body and tried to concentrate on staying alive.

Again and again I went plummeting down into arctic water, and each time was a little bit worse than the last. My thighs began to ache, my lungs were burning and my body was a stiff block of ice that could barely move. What I needed to do was start bouncing about to try and keep warm, but that would take energy I didn't have.

After twenty minutes things were getting serious. My eyes were getting heavy, my heartrate was slowing, my movements were very uncoordinated, and my speech was beginning to slur. It was becoming an almost insurmountable effort just to drag in air.

Jen looked stricken each time I managed to get to the surface, and I knew she was wondering how much longer I could last. There was now no way I could speak to her to calm her down because I needed to concentrate on breathing. Talking used up valuable air and time I didn't have, not to mention energy. We both knew I wasn't going to last much longer.

"Mark, don't you dare die on me, I'll never forgive you." Jen was yelling at me every time I reached the surface, trying her best to keep me going. It was sweet of her, but she didn't have to worry. I'd do my best to stay alive until my body gave up on me. I owed her that much. Besides, if I left her she'd be on her own with Kyle, and the thought terrified me.

Down, and down I went, over and over, until I barely knew which way was up. Now when I hit the bottom I could scarcely summon the energy to push back up, and my legs were shuddering so hard they could barely accomplish the task. I was falling apart, and there was nothing I could do about it. Lightheaded due to lack of oxygen, I got to the part where I almost didn't care whether I lived or died, and that spelt disaster. It was all over. About to die at the hands of a madman, while leaving my wife's fate in his hands. Fuck.

The next time I went under I hadn't finished sucking in my breath of air and took a mouthful of water down with me. Jennifer saw this and screamed, but I was past caring. My energy reserves had been used up, I had no oxygen left in my body, and I didn't have the strength or coordination in my legs to push myself up. This was it. This time, when I landed on the bottom of the pool, the seesaw stopped moving.

The water all around me swirled for a bit, and then settled, and everything seemed very calm and serene. Letting my eyes drift shut, I decided to hold my breath until I passed out and judging by the state of my trembling body, that wouldn't take very long. Feeling my hair flapping about in the water, I wondered when the bright lights would hit. Everyone who had a near-death experience reported them. It looked like today was my chance to find out whether they were right.

My lungs were just nearing the end of their usefulness when I felt a flicker of movement behind me. Something grabbed my hands and I felt the chains rattling behind me. The chains on my feet then began to move. Just as I was about to pass out I felt myself being pushed upwards towards the surface, and as my head broke free I took in a frantic gasp of air.

The two thugs from earlier had rescued me, now dressed in black wetsuits, and they dragged me up over the side of the pool and placed me on my side. My lungs burned and my body shook so hard I thought I might fall apart. It seemed that Kyle didn't want me dead just yet, after all. Jennifer was a constant noise in the background, sobbing and screaming, but there was nothing I could do to make her feel any better. I was a wreck, and I wasn't out of the woods yet.

"Get him in a hot bath, or he's going to die on us before I'm ready. Quick sharp. Meanwhile, I'll take care of his lovely wife." Kyle waved his arm, ushering them to move past him.

Even that snide comment didn't raise an ounce of defiance in me because I was too exhausted.

"Stop, where are you taking him? I need to go with him. Let me go, you bastard. Let. Me. Go."

I heard Kyle swear in the background, so my wife was obviously giving him some trouble. In the dazed fog that surrounded me, I almost managed a smile.

Hearing Kyle roar, "You bite me again, missy, and I'll give you a matching bruise on the other eye," wasn't quite so amusing.

The two thugs made short work of dragging me to the bathroom. I was of no use to them because I was trembling so hard none of my muscles functioned. Thankfully the cuffs had been cut, as they thought I didn't pose much of a threat, but they'd be back soon.

The bathroom was an antiquated affair. There was a claw-footed tub with old Victorian copper taps, and a large, ornate, gilt-edged mirror. The basin was cracked in a few places, the wooden floorboards rough and uneven, and the floral wallpaper had seen better days. If I had to guess, I'd say Kyle was stashing us in an abandoned house somewhere, judging by the lack of heating, and I didn't think we were far out of London. Whether we were there with the owner's permission or not remained to be seen. Kyle would have done his homework, though, so I knew they wouldn't be anywhere nearby.

"You run the bath, Harry, and I'll make sure he doesn't get into any trouble."

"Gotcha."

The taps squeaked when Harry turned them on, and I wasn't convinced we'd have any hot water, but sure enough, a few moments later steam began rising. Thankfully I wasn't in pain yet, but I knew I had that to look forward to. Once they got my circulation going again my body was going to be in agony for a bit. Still, I couldn't complain. I'd been given a reprieve, I was still alive, and hopefully a chance to escape would present itself soon. Honestly, I couldn't handle any more ordeals like the one I'd just experienced. That man was one sick bastard. How many other people had he played with before me? The question didn't bear thinking about. I just hoped that we'd be his last.

Lurching sideways without warning, the guy who was supposed to be holding me upright was having a hell of a job keeping me still. He managed to rescue me before I hit the floor, but it was a close-run thing. To make matters worse, I nearly fell asleep on him twice, but a couple of swift slaps to the face kept me almost compos mentis.

When the bath had a few inches of water in it the boys flipped my legs over its side, and I landed in the bottom with a thud. Then I screamed. The water was scalding hot, it was more pain than I could take right now, and I was going to continue screaming until they put some cold in. I just hoped Jen couldn't hear me. She'd assume the worst.

"What's the matter with him now, Freddie?" Harry winced as my screaming got louder.

"Cold tap," I yelled. "Put some cold in!" Freddie shrugged but did as I asked. My legs felt like someone had driven a thousand cigarette ends into them, and the pain was indescribable. Christ, Sophia had nothing on this lot.

When I'd stopped yelling, Freddie went downstairs to change, while Harry babysat. They allowed me to take control of the temperature as soon as I was able, and I increased the flow of hot water in small increments, taking as much pain as I could handle, but not enough to send me into meltdown. I was aware that I needed to get back to Jen as soon as possible, and the thought of what Kyle might be doing to her made me physically sick. Mind you there was another school of thought that said as soon as I got back to Jen, the games would begin anew. Maybe it would be better to take my time. If round two was anything like round one, I didn't have long left in this world.

Speak of the devil, Kyle chose that moment to barge into the room. "How's he doing, Harry?"

"Well, he's not dead," said Harry helpfully.

"I can see that," replied Kyle sarcastically. Turning to me, he then said, "You lasted longer than I thought you would."

The urge to punch his lights out was so strong I had to clutch my hands together to prevent myself from doing something stupid. Two against one was not good odds, especially in the state I was in, and they only had to yell for another to come running. My chance would come; I just had to hang on in there.

As if sensing my struggle, Kyle winked at me. "How long do you think it will be until you're begging me to kill you?" Kyle pretended to think about his question. "A day, maybe two if you're really determined. You won't last longer than that." He made a slashing motion across his neck, just in case I was completely stupid and hadn't figured out what he was talking about. "I am very much looking forward to killing you, Matthews."

That was it. I'd had enough. I was going to stand up so I was eye to eye with the bastard, even if it killed me. Lurching to my feet, every limb screaming in protest while spraying water in all directions, I eyeballed that bastard to the best of my ability. Harry stood up, flexing his knuckles and getting ready to have some fun. I didn't care. If he wanted to knock me out Kyle wouldn't be able to play any of his games, and that suited me just fine.

"Maybe I'll surprise you." Grabbing a towel, I gave my hair a good rub and waited for the bastard to get out of my way. "Maybe, just maybe, you've underestimated my resources." If he didn't move backwards he was going to get wet in a minute.

He did move, backing out of the doorway like the coward he was. He'd been on the receiving end of my fist before, and it seemed that he didn't fancy another round with it. That was too bad. Freddie was now waiting just outside the door, ready to back up his boss should the need arise.

"Cuff him and bring him back down to the pool room, Harry. It's Jen's turn to go underwater this time." He was trying to goad me into a reaction, and this time he'd hit the right button.

Pitching forward, my fist already arcing through the air, it connected with nothing as Kyle smartly moved out of my way. Harry and Freddie stepped in as I stumbled, flanking either side of me. In seconds they both had an arm each and were twisting them cruelly behind me. Roaring my displeasure I called Kyle every foul name I could think of as I watched him retreating. The bastard did not glance back at me once.

Nearly crippled with pain, I crouched there seething with hatred as I wondered what new form of torture awaited me.

Chapter Twenty-Three - Jennifer

After the pool fiasco, Kyle had dragged me upstairs and flung me back in my room.

"You even think of biting me again, bitch, and I'll beat you black and blue."

Pushing my hands against the wooden floor, so I could prop myself up and get a good look at the asshole, I eyed him with fearsome contempt. My eyes burned like fire as I said, "Don't tempt me." I made no further move to take a chunk out of him, though. If he wanted to beat me he would, so I didn't see why I should make it easy for him.

"What have you done with my husband? I want to see him. Now." Growling like a feral animal, I made my way towards him on my hands and knees, with water dripping off me and pooling on the floor. Walking was beyond me. Every nerve vibrated with anger, but even that wasn't enough to warm the block of ice my body had become. I must have looked a state. The black T-shirt I was wearing clung to every curve, but Kyle had already seen me naked, so I didn't see why I should let that bother me. For the first time in my life I wanted to kill someone, and the beast inside needed to be sated. All I needed was a weapon, and the man in front of me would be dead.

"What is it with you two and all this touching concern for each other? The marriage was a sham. You're just a number to Matthews. He's had more women than you've had hot baths. Trust me. He doesn't give a damn about you." Kyle sneered, but I didn't care. I knew differently.

"If he didn't care about me he wouldn't be here. You know that, and I know that. Stop beating about the bush and tell me what you want." My eyes searched the room for anything I could use to bash him over the head with, but I already knew there would be nothing. Kyle was far too thorough.

"Patience is a virtue, darling. You'll find out soon enough. You've got half an hour to recover before I come for you again, so I'd make the best of that time and try to come to terms with your husband's imminent demise. I've been looking forward to killing him for years, and I'm going to do it real slow and make you watch, Petal. *Real* slow." Lunging for him again - because a bite was better than nothing - he shut the door smartly in my face and locked it. Coward. Once again I was on my own, and this time it was worse than before. This time he had my husband, and if he killed him I was going to tear his heart out with a nail file.

Pacing up and down my small room, as Kyle hadn't bothered to tether me this time, I wondered what was going to happen next. Was this the part where he killed someone or was he saving that for later? Surely someone was going to come for us? What was the point of having a mother in the mafia if she couldn't throw her weight around when her daughter got kidnapped? Would anyone find us? Or was the clock just ticking down until D-day?

I screamed and began pounding my fists against the locked door. It wasn't to attract anyone's attention, for I knew no one would come running, but I needed an outlet for the rage that had overtaken me. Watching Mark nearly drown had killed something inside me, something I would never get back. If he had died I would have been responsible, and that on my conscience wasn't something I'd be able to drag around with me. Would the end game be worse? Almost certainly. Was there any way we could play Kyle at his own game? Unlikely.

More fist pounding ensued. It was either that or bawl my eyes out, and if I started that I wasn't going to be able to stop. This wasn't how my life was going to end. God couldn't be that cruel, could he?

I was shivering in a bedraggled wet heap in the corner when Kyle and one of his goons came for me. Shoving a hood over my head, they twisted my hands behind my back and fastened them with metal cuffs. I couldn't have posed much of a threat to them with the blindfold, but they were taking no chances apparently.

"Where are we going? Where's Mark? What have you done with him?" My questions were met with deaf ears. Marched down the stairs with little idea of what I was doing, in the end the pair practically carried me as I was more of a hindrance than help. That was their problem.

They led me through a series of rooms, which smelled old and musty, confirming what I'd already thought. The house was abandoned. No one knew we were there and no one was coming for us unless my mother was a mind-reader. Mark and I were on our own. Hoping he had some excellent ideas on how to get out of the place, I stumbled along blindly until the smell of chlorine hit my nose. Oh God, no. Not again.

Struggling instinctively my body used its remaining strength in trying to break the hold of my captors. If they thought they were dunking me in that icy pool again they had another think coming. If I had my hands free I'd have gouged out some eyeballs by now, but unfortunately they were firmly twisted behind my back. *Think, Jennifer, think.* There were no answers to my problem, though.

Pushed into a chair the cuffs were removed, but before I had a chance to lash out my wrists were tightly bound. This time the restraints felt thicker. A belt, perhaps? When I flexed my wrists there was a little give in the material, so leather was probably a good guess. Waiting patiently for them to take the hood off, I realised it was very quiet in the room. There wasn't a murmur or footstep to be heard. Nothing.

"Hello?" I yelled. There was no answer, and the only sound that filtered through my ears was that of the water dripping over the edge of the pool and back into the filter. They'd left me? Why? Were they waiting for something? And then it clicked. They were getting Mark. Nothing would begin without my husband in attendance. But why keep me blindfolded? Had they done something awful to him? My mind ran riot as I started thinking about the worst things that could have happened. With Kyle in charge anything was possible.

As the minutes ticked by I began to assume the worst. My adrenaline levels were already jacked up to an all-time high, and there was a looming threat in the back of my mind that Kyle was going to kill my husband. I knew it wasn't an idle threat. I just hoped he hadn't already done it. What had Mark been thinking, coming to rescue me? If this got him killed I would never forgive myself. Ever.

"Oh my God. Jen. Get her out of there now, you bastards. Get. Her. Out. Now." Some kind of scuffle ensued, and I heard Mark grunt in pain before he roared, "Get off me!"

"Stop it, don't hurt him!" I screamed.

"Shut up both of you, before I decide to gag you. And for one of you that would be almost certain death, so I'd keep those lips zipped if I were you."

Mark shut up immediately, and as I had no idea what we were dealing with I figured it would be sensible to do the same.

An eerie silence settled over the pool and the hairs on my body began to stand up on end. It felt suffocating beneath the dark, damp interior of the hood, and I struggled to breathe. My body wanted to kick out and struggle, but I knew the effort would be wasted and would only upset Mark. This was a waiting game, and I'd just have to sit tight.

All of a sudden my hood was whipped off and Kyle stood next to me, his trademark sneer plastered all over his face. Glancing around in panic, all I could see was water all around me. The chair I was sitting on was suspended on one of the platforms from earlier, and this didn't look good. What was he going to do to me? My eyes anxiously swept the outskirts of the pool, looking for Mark. I found him on the far side, right in front of me, tied to a similar wooden chair. He wasn't in the pool, though. What was going on?

"You two lovebirds enjoying being reunited?" Kyle stroked his knuckle down the side of my cheek, and I winced. Mark's eyes flared with hatred and he shot forward in his seat, but there was nowhere for him to go. "I thought so." Kyle put his hand behind me, and I turned to find two large chains attached to the arms of my chair. "Your turn to get dunked, Jen. It's only fair, right? How long do you think you'll last? As long as your husband? I very much doubt it. Know this, though; I'm not coming back into this room until twenty minutes is up at the very least, so if you want to live you'd better give it your best shot, or say your goodbye's now. Any last words?"

If there were, Kyle didn't want to hear them. He walked over the little wooden footbridge he'd placed upon the platform and when he got to the other side, pulled it towards him. His retreating back could then be seen, as he and his goons left the room. There were no escape routes left for me. This was happening, and there was nothing I could do about it. You need to stay calm, Jen. If Mark managed to get through his ordeal, the least I could do was try to get through mine.

"Mark, I..."

"Save your energy, Jen. You're going to need it. Concentrate on taking deep breaths, and when you go under blow out bubbles really slowly, so you're ready to take another breath as soon as you come up. You need to stay as still as possible and don't talk. This isn't goodbye, you just need to concentrate, okay?"

The sound of the platform underneath me whirring into motion made my eyes flutter downwards. My chair began rocking as the platform started to sink beneath the water. The chair tipped forward slightly, dunking the tips of my feet into the pool and I sucked in a gasp. It was so cold. So damn cold. I didn't think I could do this again.

The next noise I heard was the sound of the chains beside me being lowered, and my face bore a horrified expression as the water began to slowly creep up around my waist. Already chilled to the bone, I wasn't relishing the thought of going under. Could I last twenty minutes? Did I have it in me?

"You can do this, Jen. Don't think about it. All you need to worry about is breathing." Mark tried to keep his expression calm as I began to descend into the water, but I could see lines of angst tightening his features. I guess he had a rough idea of what I was in for, having been through it first-hand.

When the water reached my neck I began to stutter in panic, nearly losing the plot, as I waited for the water to crawl over my face. *This can't be happening. This can't be happening.* The words repeated themselves over and over in my head, but it did no good. It was happening, and I had to deal with it.

"Tip your head up and breathe, Jen. One last big breath. You can do it. Breathe!"

Following orders I did as he said, and then closed my lips tight as the water closed in all around me. It sucked the light and colour out of my world in an instant. There was no sound down there, just the gentle lapping of tiny waves as the chair continued on its journey to the bottom of the pool. My hair flapped all around me, twisting in never-ending circles around my face, but I kept my eyes tightly closed. I didn't want to see this. If I somehow managed to survive my ordeal, I didn't want any images of this nightmare to haunt my dreams.

The chair took its time hitting the bottom of the pool, and there was a moment of stillness when its journey was complete. I had expected it to rise immediately, and when it didn't my heartrate began to increase. A few seconds ticked by as caterpillars crawled all over my skin and butterflies tried to escape from my insides. I thought I would explode from fear, but the chair then began moving upwards again with a jerk, making me release a stream of bubbles from my lips in relief.

When I got to the surface my lungs were screaming. Tilting my head to its highest point I waited for the water to run down my face before opening my jaws for a giant mouthful of air. Sucking in painful breaths, over and over, I didn't hear Mark. I knew he would be shouting out words of encouragement, but I didn't have time for that now. All I wanted to do was get air into my lungs.

I felt the moment as the chains tightened and jerked to their highest point. Another moment of stillness, where I swung about in mid-air, contemplating the descent back into the artic unknown.

"Laurel won't let you die here. She'll come for us. Just hang in there, Jen." His hands were working the leather straps that held him, but there was no chance they would give. "Head back Jen, get in as much air as you can."

The chains jerked again, and that meant the descent had begun. Mark kept shouting words of encouragement, but he was sounding frantic. I didn't hear what he was saying; too traumatised by what was about to happen.

This time Mark didn't have to tell me to tip my head back because I was desperate to get as much oxygen into me as possible before the ride began again. The journey up and down probably wasn't any longer than a minute, but I found it impossibly hard to hold my breath for that length of time. On my first try I hadn't taken a deep enough lungful, so I wasn't going to make the same mistake again.

As I went under I counted the seconds in my head. *One and two and three.* Once I knew roughly for how long I had to hang on it would give me something to aim for. This time around the fear wasn't as bad, but the cold was worse. The water bit into my skin like tiny shards of glass, each burrowing as far as they could to do the maximum amount of damage possible. Icy cold water is quite an impressive tormentor, all by itself. *Twenty and twenty-one.* It wouldn't be long before my fingers and toes were completely numb and after that, my body would start shutting down whatever it could, in order to keep my heart beating. A pleasant thought. Think of something else. *Thirty and thirty-one.* My lungs were burning. Think of something other than that. You could still be pregnant. *Christ almighty.* You want to think of that now? For some reason being pregnant didn't scare me as much as it had earlier. I could probably put that down to the near-death experience that was coming. *Forty-one, forty-two.* My chest was now so tight all I could think about was air and the last ten seconds of my ride seemed like an eternity.

Bursting up through the water, I took in great wheezing breaths as I tried to replenish what I'd lost. Mark was still talking in the background, but I was oblivious. My ears were full of water, and I didn't have the energy to shake it out. Instead, I opened my eyes and feasted upon him. He would get me through this. If I gave up, not only would I let Kyle win, but I'd lose the only thing I'd ever cared about. I couldn't let that happen. I had to remind myself what was at stake. Laurel would come for us. She'd get us out. We just had to hang in long enough for her to find us.

Up and down I went. Up and down. The count from one to fifty became very familiar as the icy graveyard tried to claw its way into my body. At first I focused on Mark, my happy place, trying to forget my surroundings and predicament. This worked for a time. Then lack of oxygen got the better of me. I tried to gasp for air before my face was above the waterline, and I'd come up coughing, spluttering and choking. Mark's face now appeared haunted, as if he was bracing himself for the worst. I couldn't bear to see him like that.

Although I hadn't counted how many times I'd been under, I was sure I must have been halfway by now. Not that it mattered. There was no way I was going to make it past twenty minutes. My lungs weren't equipped to deal with this kind of stress, and I was now lightheaded. My face weaved around in the water, this way and that, and a pleasant euphoria began to settle over me. I didn't need anyone to tell me that was bad. These were all signs of hypoxia, and proof that I was getting nowhere near enough oxygen into my blood.

Up and down, up and down. My teeth were chattering so hard it was painful to keep my jaw clamped together. When would this end? I couldn't feel anything any more, either, because everything was numb. My eyes were now tightly closed too. Opening them would require me to face what was happening, and I wasn't ready to do that. What should I do? Did I say goodbye? Tell him I loved him? I should probably do one of those before I gave up. It seemed the right thing to do.

Up and down. Up and down. This time when I came up, Kyle was standing over Mark with a gun, pointing it at his head. There was the soft snick of the safety being removed, and then he turned around to face me, his eyes burning brightly with a rabid look of crazy excitement. So the moment had come. I heard a loud bang that echoed around the room. Screaming my head off I rode back underwater, unable to see any more. That was when I realised I still had my eyes closed. I hadn't seen a thing. This was in my head. I was going mad. The lack of oxygen was causing hallucinations; the beginning of the end. Although I'd never expected my grave to be a watery one, there were worse places to die, I guessed. If there was ever a good place to die, that was.

The next time I came up breathing would be the last. I was choking so badly there was barely any opportunity to take a breath, but I did what I could. Mark was yelling desperately in the background, but my head couldn't piece together a single coherent word. He then tipped his chair over, struggling to get out, but the restraints wouldn't budge and there was nothing he could do. There were tears in his eyes as he pleaded with me not to give up, but there was no fight left in me. Everything was too cold and exhausted. What kind of sick bastard made a husband watch while he killed his wife in front of him?

It hadn't been twenty minutes. This was it. The next time I came up I would not be breathing. Blinking my eyes open one last time, I drank him in before diving to my death.

Chapter Twenty-Four - Mark

I remember screaming. I screamed so loud I made myself hoarse, but I kept on making as much noise as I could, hoping against hope that someone would come running. They didn't.

I would have given anything in the world to trade places with my wife. Watching her suffer had been the cruellest torture imaginable, made even worse because I was utterly helpless to prevent it. I just sat there, watching her choke and freeze to death. The last time she came up she'd coughed up a lungful of water, so I knew she wasn't coming back. She hadn't had enough time to take any air in. Besides, she'd be so cold by this time she'd barely be able to keep her eyes open. I knew exactly what she was going through, and how much effort it took to stay alive under that kind of pressure. Even so, I anxiously watched the waterline, hoping that somehow she was still breathing while praying for a miracle.

It was the longest minute of my life watching those chains move up and down, and I'm not ashamed to admit tears were pouring down my cheeks. This was more than any human being should have to endure, and there were no limits to the lengths I would go to in order to reap my revenge. If Kyle killed my wife I would make it my mission in life to kill him or die trying.

When the chair came up my eyes were blurry, and I had to blink several times for them to clear enough so I could see again. I was now sideways on the floor, having managed to knock my chair over, and my head was resting in a shallow pool of cold water. I didn't care. My eyes were focused on the top of the chair that was now being pulled out of the water.

As soon as I saw her slumped shoulders and head I screamed in agony. Jen's skin had taken on a bluish pallor, and she looked like a ghost, with her wet hair whipped all around her face.

"Know what this is?" Kyle barged into the room with a large yellow case and waggled it in front of my face on the floor. I went mad, kicking and clawing at the restraints that held me, needing to get my hands around the bastard's neck.

"Pay attention, Mark. This little box might bring your wife back to life. It's important that you listen to me because every second you waste will mean there's less chance of getting her back."

I shut up immediately. It was a defibrillator pack, judging by the big green medical symbol on the box. As the water had been bloody cold there was a very real chance that little box could get her back for me.

"You need to sign over all of your worldly possessions to Jennifer. We have a will drawn up; all that's required is your signature. As soon as you've done that we'll do what we can about bringing her back to life." Kyle looked at Jennifer's slumped body and shook his head. "I wouldn't think too long about it, though. She doesn't look good, does she?" The concerned expression he was trying to adopt made me see red, but thankfully sense and reasoning somehow managed to win the day.

"I'll sign anything you want and right now, just get her back," I yelled.

Kyle motioned for Harry and Freddie, who had just got Jennifer out of the chair, to commence CPR and he set the box down beside them. Righting my chair, he then held out a sheaf of papers in front of me and pointed to several places where I had to sign. I did so as quickly as I could, with a hand that was shaking so badly I feared it would fall off.

Meanwhile the thugs had dragged Jen's T-shirt up and were applying electrodes to her chest. They'd pulled her clear of the pool and had her on the deck at the end of the room. One was doing chest compressions and breaths, while the other switched on the device and began following the computerised instructions. The whole thing felt completely surreal, like an out of body experience, but unfortunately I knew for a fact it wasn't.

Signing on the last dotted line I handed the papers back to Kyle, but I didn't take my eyes off Jennifer for a second. *Please come back*, I begged silently. *Please come back*. We'd been here once before, Jennifer and I. She'd come back to me then, but could she do it again? The law of averages were probably against it, but I wasn't going to think of that now.

When it was time for them to begin the first series of shocks they stood well back and waited for the machine to do its job. Waiting on the opposite side of the room with my heart in my mouth, I watched her body anxiously for any kind of response, but there was nothing. *No, no, no*. The next series of shocks began and ended with the same result. This was it. I had better brace myself for the worst.

"This is the last round, Matthews. Doesn't look good, does it?" Kyle clucked his tongue in mock sympathy. I roared and knocked the chair from one leg to the other as the bastard chuckled. My grief was all-consuming, and the little spark of hope that had begun inside me slowly began to extinguish itself. Still, I couldn't give in to the murderous rage that wanted to eat me up alive. Jen still had a chance. A small one, but there was still a chance.

The third and final shock was delivered. The silence afterwards was deafening as all eyes and ears turned to examine the prone form on the floor. There was nothing. The longest two seconds of my life passed, but I waited for some kind of sound. There would be a sound. There had to be. More seconds ticked by. One after the other. Then the boys closed the sliding door at the back of the pool room, and everything went quiet. I was aware of what that meant. I just wasn't going to face it right now.

Turning to Kyle, I went ballistic, screaming and shouting every fucking swear word I could come up with. With a burst of almost inhuman effort I managed to get a single arm free from one of the leather restraints, and I dived for the bastard. I missed him by less than a hair's breadth, but it was a close-run thing. He wasted no time in diving for my arm so he could get me back where he wanted me, but I was too fast. I was already working the restraint on the other hand, and with a sharp crack of my elbow I caught him square in the eye and sent him flying. That was just a taster. All I wanted to do was wrap my hands around his neck and watch the life slowly drain out of him. Getting out of the chair I advanced towards him, but before I knew what was happening there was a gun in his hand.

"On your knees, hands on your head."

If Kyle thought I gave a flying fuck about dying after what he'd just done, he was sadly mistaken.

"Go fuck yourself," I roared, and with my head down in front of me I made to ram him in the stomach. If he shot me I'd land on him like a dead weight, and so help me God, if I had enough strength left in my arms I'd do my damndest to make sure the bastard never walked the face of the earth again.

The gun went off, but I didn't feel a thing. Ploughing headfirst into Kyle I did my best to make sure my head splintered a rib or two, and when I landed on top of him I whipped my wrists around his neck. My need for revenge overtook any rational part of my brain, and all I wanted to do was kill. In my opinion I was doing an excellent job of it, because a few seconds later he was making the sweetest strangling noises I'd ever heard.

"Tell me why I shouldn't gut you and pour your entrails out all over the place?" I hissed. "Tell me why I shouldn't let you die slowly and painfully - because watching you try and scoop your innards up and shove them back in your body is an absurdly entertaining vision right now. Why, asshole? Why?" I shook him like he was a leaf, and his head rattled all over the place. He didn't respond to my question, due to the fact my arms were still wrapped firmly around his neck, and I didn't care. The time for questions was over. I just wanted him dead.

Alas, this was not my day. The two goons burst in, and I couldn't fight three people off at once. That didn't mean I didn't have a damn good try, though. Lashing out with my limbs, I had a toxic adrenaline overload inside my body that needed to be expended. Using my feet and arms to the best of their ability, I made sure everyone felt my displeasure. There was a good chance there were going to be some fractured bones around shortly.

Eventually they got me under control. They cuffed me hand and foot and shoved me in a room with a hood over my head. It took a further half hour before the rage and anger left me, and all that remained was pain and grief. Mostly because Kyle had just killed my wife, but I realised later that he'd shot me too. Thankfully his aim was crap and he'd only managed to take a chunk out of my arm, but it didn't make me feel any better. Nothing was going to make me feel any better, and I wished he'd just get on with it. If he was going to kill me, I wanted to be put out of my misery sooner rather than later because there was sod all left to live for now. Once again I had everything I could have ever possibly wanted in my hands, and once again I'd let it all slip away. To do it once was stupid, to repeat the same mistake twice was just plain sloppy. Now death was the only thing left, and I would happily fall into its dark embrace. Yes, it was a coward's way out, but the alternative was even worse. Life without Jen was not living at all. The first real tear of grief slipped its way out of the corner of my eye, and then the floodgates opened. The tears didn't help in the slightest, but they put a name to my pain.

Lying there on the floor, my blood slowly dripping on to the splintered wood beneath me, I dropped in and out of consciousness. It had been an exhausting day, my body had been taxed to the max, and I hadn't slept in twenty-four hours. Besides, what else could I do except sleep? Kyle would come for me eventually, and when he did he'd better put an end to this nightmare. If he didn't, I'd take matters into my own hands.

"Get him up." I had no idea what time it was when Kyle barged into the room, but it was light. Though the hood I wore didn't let me see very much, there were subtle differences between night and day, and right now it was somewhere nearing midday.

"You've got my money. Just shoot me already. Why is it so important to play with your toys?" Stumbling forward as they yanked me upright, I swayed all over the place as they led me back down the creaky wooden stairs. What new kind of torture awaited me today? What could be worse than yesterday? I was about to find out.

"Want to know what's in store for you, Matthews?" Kyle sounded particularly pleased with himself as he pushed me with a hand in my back, making me stumble a little more than I was already.

"Hell no. I love surprises." The words contained no inflection. Kyle wasn't getting any more emotion from me. I'd cried my tears yesterday and made peace with my maker. Today he was dealing with a robot.

"Suit yourself, Matthews. But I should warn you that Redcliff is here, in a roundabout way. He's going to tell you a little story."

"Sounds fascinating. Can't wait." Desperately needing water, I refused to give in to the urge to ask for some. Kyle wasn't likely to grant my request, so I didn't see the point. My stomach was also rumbling in protest because I hadn't eaten in a while, and it was just reminding me that I was still alive. Ignoring it, I figured I wouldn't be for too much longer. These were just small inconveniences, and very soon none of them would matter.

Kyle and his thugs herded me into one of the downstairs rooms, slamming me into a chair where they then used my handcuffs to restrain my wrists to the wooden arms. Clearly they weren't going to trust leather after yesterday's fiasco. It didn't matter to me in any case. I had no intention of escaping. I just wanted Kyle to finish what he'd started.

When they had me in place they pulled the hood off my head, and I found I was in a darkened room with no windows. A basement, probably. The floor beneath me was concrete, the walls made of grey uneven stone, and there was a series of archways leading off to the right. Above my head were old decaying wooden beams, peeling white paint. The air smelled musty and damp. There hadn't been a lot of life down here for some time.

Harry and Freddie were wheeling in a trolley, on top of which sat a laptop. Ah, this was how I was going to speak to Redcliff. God forbid he came to see me in person. He wouldn't want to reveal his hidey-hole, now would he? Come to that, I bet Kyle wasn't in the country legally either. Redcliff would make sure he had an alibi, too. The thought that both of them would get away with this monstrosity would normally have made my blood boil, but I felt so numb it would be difficult for anything to penetrate the cold shell that resided around my body.

The laptop was fired up, and the necessary connection was made. In less than three minutes Redcliff's yellowing, watery eyes were staring at me intently, and he seemed pleased with what he saw. I didn't care. If the smug, self-righteous bastard thought I was going to beg for my life, he was much mistaken.

Clearing his throat, he coughed and said, "You don't look so good, Mark."

I bared my teeth in a vicious smile. "It's due to your son's careful handling, Michael. You don't *sound* so good." He didn't look good, either, and I suspected he didn't have long left in this world. It was a comforting thought.

"How are you feeling?" The wrinkly old bastard raised an eyebrow at me.

"Let's dispense with the pleasant chitchat, Michael. What do you want?" There had to be a reason for this call, and I figured we might as well get it over with. I also couldn't bear to look at the bastard for any longer than necessary, so he needed to get on with it.

"Well, it's your funeral, I suppose. If you're in a hurry, I'll get straight to the point." Redcliff looked amused, as well he might, although I didn't understand how he could have lived with Jennifer for all those years and then been able to order her death so mercilessly. Did the guy not have an ounce of compassion? Did family mean nothing?

"I'm in a hurry," I confirmed. "Death waits for no one." Oh yes, I couldn't wait to hear this story. It had better be good.

"Fine. Have it your way." Redcliff pulled a pair of black-rimmed spectacles off his face and made a great show of cleaning them. I waited patiently. We'd get where we were going eventually, and to be fair, I was in no rush to be tortured.

Looking up at me, he said, "Do you remember a company you purchased a while back? I think it went by the name of Amatech."

I shook my head. I'd purchased a lot of companies in my time, and though it was more than possible I'd bought this one, I didn't remember the exact details of the acquisition.

"That's too bad." Redcliff gave me a lazy smile. "It was my company, as it happened. We made AI chips for cell phones. You know, the ones that can learn things outside their original programming."

I did. "I know what you mean. Zystrom develops them for the Strontium X," I said.

"Yes, I'm aware of that, but I wasn't when you bought Amatech. I thought you'd grow the brand, put a little money in the research and development side of things and generally do wonders for the product. At least, that's what your guy assured me you'd do."

Things were now beginning to slot into place. One thing bothered me though. "Who runs this company? It isn't you, is it?" If Redcliff's name had been anywhere on the company files Khalil would have found it. Whoever ran this company was not directly associated with Redcliff in any way.

"It's a sister company of mine, run by a close friend, although I haven't actually seen him in years."

That would explain it then.

"Anyway, we're veering off course. You bought it, and you liquidated it. Immediately. You went back on your word, and not only did you destroy a company of mine, but you managed to destroy all the credibility for the new cell phone I was creating that would use that chip. Overnight three of my most profitable businesses had turned to dust. Just like that." He clicked his fingers to send his point home. "Of course, I understood your business acumen. You annihilated the competition to pave the way clear for your tech, and in doing so quickly rose to the top of the charts, staying there for the past five years or so, I believe?"

I nodded. What he was saying was correct - well, for the most part. "As I didn't attend the meeting I have no idea what my representative said, but I can't imagine he would have lied to the owner. We are usually upfront about what we plan to do." Although there had been a case a while back where I'd had to fire one of our representatives because he'd gone rogue, only motivated by the money he'd earn on each commission. Although Zystrom makes it clear that honesty and loyalty rule the day if they want to have a long and promising career, there are some that just want to make a quick buck, but we usually weed them out pretty quickly. My heart sank. So all of this was just a case of sour grapes? By the look of things I'd sliced off a large chunk of his fortune and credibility, and now he felt honour bound to have his revenge.

"Let me assure you that Zystrom was not *upfront* in this case. Your man, Timothy Greene, managed to half the value of my stocks with just a day's work, and in less than a month they'd dived to rock bottom."

Fuck. Tim Greene was the man in question. "You aren't going to believe me when I say I had no knowledge of that, but that is the case. I do remember Tim Greene later being fired for misconduct, though. I'm afraid my organisation is just too big for me to keep tabs on everyone." Zystrom was a minefield. We had over five thousand employees in hundreds of different divisions. I couldn't keep tabs on my own personal staff, let alone everyone else.

"You nearly bankrupted me. I had to call in a lot of favours after that little fiasco, one of which means that I'm indebted to some very unpleasant people. They want their money. I don't have it, but I will. Shortly, after I get rid of you."

Something didn't add up. If I died all my money would go to Jennifer, not Redcliff. As Jennifer was no longer alive, it would go to my family, unless there was something else in that will I was unaware of. If there was, I was pretty sure someone would smell a rat. I change my will and then immediately disappear and die? It wasn't going to look good.

"How much do you owe them?" I didn't need to know, but I was curious.

Redcliff smiled. "A lot. That's not a problem, though, because I don't intend to pay them back. I intend to get rid of them, but I need the funds to do so."

Adding the dots up, one by one, I came to a rather ghastly conclusion. "You borrowed the money from Laurel?" There was no money in the world that would get rid of Laurel without extremely unpleasant consequences. Surely Redcliff had to know that? I mean, I didn't think much of my mother-in-law, but I did at least realise that killing her would not be the answer to my problems.

Redcliff's face was now suffused with anger, and I could feel the rage bubbling up inside him. "I've babysat her bloody daughter for years. You'd think it was the least she owed me, but oh no. All favours have to be repaid, apparently. It doesn't look good for the mob, elsewise. I was in love with that bloody woman, and look how she repays me!" Redcliff's face was mottled with fury, and his hands were waving about like a madman. Everything was falling into place; Jennifer's visit to Albrecht, for instance. Daddy dearest was out for revenge, and doing his best to get Laurel's attention. The pair of them were ideally suited for each other. And here was me thinking the old man was clueless.

"So, do you think this will annoy Laurel?" I had a feeling it might.

"I do, and I think she'll be mightily put out when we kill you."

I didn't. He was probably doing her a favour. "There are just a few small problems with your plan, old boy," I said, giving him a long look. "How do you intend to lure Laurel to her death?" I didn't think Redcliff could have all that much collateral now, after what happened yesterday.

"We'll threaten to kill her daughter, of course."

Which brought me to the second problem and the fact that something didn't quite add up.

"Won't that be rather tricky, seeing as how she's dead?" The word felt hollow in my throat. I still hadn't accepted the fact that my wife was not with us any more, although it was more a case that I didn't want to believe. The eyes did not lie, though. "It'll be a little hard to get your hands on my money, now that my wife is no longer of this earth. The money will not revert to you on her death; it will go to my family." This had been chewing at the back of my mind for a few minutes now. What was going on here?

Redcliff looked confused for a moment. "What gave you that idea?" he said, narrowing his eyes. "She's alive and well, dear fellow, and I hear she's quite excited about watching your execution in a few minutes' time." If the old man was playing with me this was downright cruel.

"I watched her die yesterday," I countered, although I desperately wanted to believe what he was saying.

"Kyle, have you been playing with your toys again?" Redcliff's voice was stern, and he sounded unimpressed. I failed to see how Kyle could fake someone's death.

Kyle came around behind me, so his face was in full view of the screen. "She's fine, Dad. You'll see her in a few minutes. We just had a little fun yesterday. You said I could, remember?"

"Not that much fun. We will talk about this later." Redcliff nodded at Kyle and then motioned for him to get out of the way. "Right, we're wasting time. Any last words, Matthews?"

"I want to see my wife." If she was alive, and I didn't know who to believe.

"Oh, you'll definitely be seeing her. She's going to need years of therapy after what we have planned for you today. I will have my revenge on Laurel. Even if it's mostly through her daughter." He began coughing repeatedly and waving his hand decisively at the screen, which went blank. I'd take that as goodbye.

"Well, what are we waiting for?" Kyle said, striding forward so he could stick his face in mine. "It's time for the finale."

Chapter Twenty-Five - Jennifer

As I sank to the bottom of the pool for the last time, I remember a peaceful feeling settling over me. Maybe lack of oxygen does that to a person, I don't know. Then I remember a blanket of white crossing my vision, and a tugging feeling as if I was being pulled somewhere else. My life didn't flash before my eyes, and for that I was thankful. I had no wish to recount my early years with Michael. All I wanted to think about was Mark, but he was so far away right now. The tugging continued as if something was trying to rip my soul apart from my body, but I was stubborn. I clung on to it for dear life, and nobody was going to get the essence of what was essentially "me" without a fight. I had too much to live for.

Lights and mists continued to swirl around me, and I thought I could see someone walking towards me in the distance, but they were too far away for me to recognise. Still, they seemed familiar. I was almost positive it was someone I knew. The mist around me slowly began to evaporate, and a field was then revealed. It was a lush green field, complete with summer flowers, blue skies, and warm sunshine. It was somewhere peaceful and relaxing, and I felt like I could have stayed there forever, so it was a bit of a shock when the bright light was suddenly ripped away from me.

The reality of my situation hit me like a hammer on the head, and it was not pleasant. For starters my lungs were trying to cough up an ocean of water, and it was nearly impossible to breathe while I was doing this. My chest felt sore, bruised even, and each time I choked searing pain lodged itself in my throat. Over and over little puddles of water came out of my mouth until my throat was so sore I almost wished it would stay inside me. As the great heaves gradually began to subside, I opened my eyes and looked around me.

Holy hell. Harry and Freddie were beside me with a great big yellow box, and judging by the wires trailing everywhere, they had just jumpstarted my heart. Looking frantically from right to left I realised I was still in the pool room, but a much smaller section of it, at the back. It had been closed off by some sliding doors. Where was Mark?

"Need. To. See. Mark." Trying to say those words took almost more energy than I had, but I got them out there. Mark would think I was dead. Kyle had surpassed himself this time.

Harry shook his head. "Bed rest for you, young lady. For a minute there we didn't know whether we would get you back. Just as well that water's bloody cold, huh?" Freddie laughed, but I was not amused. Kyle had to be unhinged to pull a stunt like that. What if he hadn't been able to get me back? Then again, perhaps Kyle didn't care if I lived or died. We were just toys, but eventually he'd grow bored of us, and when that happened he wouldn't let us go. It would be too dangerous having witnesses walking around.

When they shoved me in a warm bath to bring my body temperature up, I had to clamp my teeth together to stop from screaming out loud. Was this what Mark had gone through? Would this day never end? Raising the temperature gradually, my skin tone finally went from a bluish grey back to light pink. The process was pretty horrific, but I was glad to be alive. If I was alive there was a chance, if I was dead, it was all over, and I wasn't ready to die just yet.

When the goons were satisfied I was almost back to normal, they took me to my room and chained me up. No food or water was provided, but then, I hadn't expected anything else. Left alone in the dark, there was little for me to do except sleep and wait to see what tomorrow would bring. Praying it would be rescue, I tossed and turned all night, hoping against hope that there would be a way out of there for both of us.

The following morning I was dragged out of my restless stupor and marched downstairs. Making no complaint at the rough treatment I moved as fast as my legs could carry me, anxious to set eyes on Mark. Nearly every part of my body hurt, and it was tough just to move one foot in front of the other, but all that barely registered. My thoughts were solely focused on my husband.

Trudging down some stone steps in a file, with me wedged firmly in the middle even though I was in chains, the guys were taking no risks. Reaching the bottom, we entered a large room with stone walls that was dark and smelly. Although my eyes frantically ran from left to right, there was no sight of Mark yet.

"Sit." A plastic chair was pulled forward for me to sit on, and I sank onto it warily. Although my legs could barely support me, this was not a good thing. If they wanted me to watch something, I knew from experience it was bound to be unpleasant.

As soon as the thought entered my head, Kyle's face popped into view. My fingers itched to tear into the soft skin of his face and rip his flesh to ribbons, but I'd seen the guns on the guys beside me. The move would not be a smart one, and if my husband was alive I needed to try and stay alive too.

"Good morning, Petal. I trust you slept well?" Glaring at Kyle I declined to answer his question, but he wasn't at all concerned, for he continued, "Today's the day we set about killing your husband. I thought you should be here to watch. It's only fitting, after all." Kyle watched my face carefully, but I refused to give anything away. That man lived on fear, and he wasn't getting anything from me just yet. He'd taken far too much yesterday.

"Does dad know you tried to kill me?" I bet he didn't. While there was no love lost between Michael and me, I didn't think he'd kill me, at least, not with Laurel lurking in the background. It was Kyle's turn to ignore me, so that gave me my answer.

"Don't think you'll get any money from me if you kill my husband. Albrecht isn't the threat it used to be, Kyle." If they thought I'd use Mark's money for their gains, they were much mistaken. I'd rather kill myself.

"You'll do anything you're told," Kyle hissed, and he grabbed hold of my hand and twisted my little finger backwards so hard I thought he'd break it. Looking up at him defiantly I told him to do his worst. It would take more than a few broken bones if he wanted to get me to toe the line.

Pointing to the middle of the room he beckoned someone forward. "Bring him on. Let's get this over with."

When Harry and Freddie began wheeling some wooden contraption out, I wanted to close my eyes. What horrors would they expect me to watch now? The only reason I didn't was because I needed to assure myself that my husband was still alive.

Setting my eyes centre stage, everything was still shrouded in darkness. Straining, I tried to make out the figure before me, and although I was sure it was Mark, I couldn't be certain. Then the lights came up, and my worst fears were confirmed. There he was, completely naked except for a noose around his neck, with his arms tied in front of him. The wooden platform he was on had been fashioned into gallows, and he had to stand on tiptoe to avoid putting any tension on the rope. All that stood between him and a gruesome death was a wooden slab resting two metres above the floor on metal stilts. If it was taken away, it didn't take a genius to figure out what would happen next. Right then and there I should have gone into meltdown mode. The only reason I didn't was because there was no energy left in me for hysterics. Besides, that was what Kyle wanted. I had to be strong for my husband. Tears weren't going to help him. If there was any chance I could get us out of this mess, I needed to think and quickly.

"What are you going to do to him?" Somehow I managed to keep my voice calm and measured.

"Kill him, of course," Kyle said, looking at me as if I'd grown two heads. "But we're going to whip him first. Let's see how long he can stand on those tippy toes with a bullwhip coming at him."

Mark stared at me as if he'd seen a ghost. It was almost as if he didn't trust his own eyes, and he had to blink several times to make sure I wasn't a figment of his imagination. His lips twitched as if he wanted to speak, but it took several attempts before he could get a word past his constricted throat.

"I watched you die." He shook his head, and I could tell he was having a hard time trying to figure out what was going on.

Kyle walked up to him and pinched his cheek, shaking his head this way and that in the process. "You watched as Harry and Freddie used a training unit as a defibrillator. That unit had no power. They didn't actually use the real one until the doors were closed. It was a bit of a risky move, but it was worth it to see the look on your face."

"Why you miserable fucking bastard," Mark hissed, and lurched forward, only to be cut short by the rope throttling his neck. Losing his balance for a second, I went rigid on my seat because one wrong move on that platform could mean something terrible, but somehow he managed to get upright once more. "When I get my hands on you..."

"Shut up. The game's over, Mark. After I've finished whipping your hide I'm going to remove that platform beneath your feet, and you will fall to your death rather abruptly in front of your wife. This time there will be no second chances. A snapped neck is a bit difficult to fix." Kyle threw his hands up in the air and gave a caricature of a frown. I wanted to vomit. "Apologies, but Jen won't inherit your moolah if you don't die, and time, as we know, is money. Let's get on with it, shall we?"

"What would have happened if you'd killed Jen yesterday?" Mark had a good point. If Kyle had killed me off, and it was a pretty close run thing, he'd be back to square one right now.

"I'd have ransomed you off, got the money, and then killed you. Dad would have been pissed, but as I'm doing his dirty work for him, that would be his problem. I needed to see you brought as low as you could go, and you were grovelling on the floor yesterday, Matthews. I've got it on camera. I'm going to watch that tape over and over again."

"Why don't you untie me and we can have this out, man to man," Mark growled, the lines on his face standing out as he went nearly apoplectic with rage. My husband was about to blow, and that was never a good thing with a noose around your neck.

"Just do as you're fucking told, Matthews. I'm running this show, and you'd better get used to it." To demonstrate his point, Kyle swung his fist at Mark's jaw and the retching, choking noises that followed had me flying off the chair, only to be smacked back down onto it. As I watched Mark struggle to retain his balance yet again I knew I had to do something, *anything* to make this stop.

"What do you want, Kyle? We'll do anything. Just let us go. You can have money, cars, houses, businesses, anything you want. You don't need to kill anyone. If you do, eventually you'll get caught, and then you'll spend the rest of your life rotting in jail. Why would you risk that?" I was getting desperate. Trying to negotiate with Kyle was like trying to make a deal with the devil, but there didn't seem to be too many other options floating around.

"Shut up little lady, or you'll be next. Besides, I'm not murdering anyone. I'm not even in the damn country. Dad made sure of that."

Kyle disappeared behind one of the arches to the right of me, and I was left staring helplessly ahead.

"Jen, are you okay?" Mark had regained his balance, and had eyes only for me. Watching his chest heave, I knew he was under a colossal amount of strain, but he had to hang in there.

"Don't die on me, Matthews," I warned, but my voice was all choked up and there were tears in my eyes. I'd gone past the point where I could handle everything that Kyle threw at me. I knew what that bastard was capable of, and it wasn't pretty.

Mark closed his eyes and tipped his head back to alleviate some of the pressure from the rope. "I'll try my best."

"Promise me you won't die." I had no idea why I wanted him to make promises he had no way of keeping. Mark was going to die, right in front of me, and I was going to watch. No amount of therapy was ever going to get me through this, and I was never going to forgive my mother for not finding us in time.

Mark saw the first tear dribble from my left eye. He caught his breath. "Don't cry, Jen," he pleaded. "Save those tears for later. Don't give that bastard what he wants."

I nodded, wiping away little trails of moisture from each eye, trying my best to stop the waterworks. I would be strong. If Mark could stand up there and take what was coming, the least I could do was support him.

"She will come," I said, nodding. My voice lacked conviction, but I'd just have to hope he wasn't paying too much attention. "Promise me you won't die," I repeated, waiting for my answer.

"How about I promise you that I'll fight until my very last breath? I won't leave you alone with these bastards unless I have to, you can count on it."

"That will have to do," I whispered, although it wouldn't. If Kyle continued with this madness he would destroy me from the inside out. Even if we did get through today, and that was looking extremely unlikely, I would constantly be looking over my shoulder for the rest of my life, and that was being optimistic. Michael would probably have me shipped off somewhere as a slave, and I would never see the light of day again. Racking my brains to try and figure out what I could do to stop this, I came up with nothing - absolutely nothing. They had guns. They could easily overpower me. The only thing I could do was try and get myself killed at the same time, and I was seriously considering it. But we weren't at that point yet. Laurel still had time. Not much time - but some. She had to come through for us. There weren't any other options left.

"I can't believe you're alive. Thank God you're alive." Mark's voice broke on the last word, and I wanted to break down with him.

"What should I do?" I whispered. Hoping against hope that he'd have some idea that would get us out of there, I looked up into his eyes, only to watch him shake his head. This was hopeless. My lip wobbled and I stifled a sob.

"Promise me you won't cry, Jen. If you cry he'll do it all the more. Give him a blank stare. Look at him with contempt. Hell, I don't care what you do, but don't cry okay?" Mark looked at me pleadingly.

I nodded and squared my shoulders. "I'll do my best." There was nothing else I could do.

When Kyle swaggered back in, with a vicious looking bullwhip, I looked away. Keeping my promise for any length of time was going to be nigh on impossible, but for Mark's sake I had to try.

Kyle came up to where I was sitting and rubbed the leather handle of the whip against my cheek. I flinched. Having the bastard anywhere near me made my skin crawl. While I am not the murdering type, I figured I might make an exception for the lowlife standing in front of me. Unfortunately I'd already scoped out Harry and Freddie, and while I knew they were carrying, they kept their guns behind them. As badly as I wanted to shoot Kyle, it was too risky a move to take.

"Ready to see your husband beg for mercy?"

My head snapped up to meet the monster's eyes. "What do you think will be your punishment when you go to see the man upstairs? Tell me what's the worst thing you think will happen to you."

Kyle laughed. "Don't tell me you believe in all that shit, Mrs Matthews? I'm not a big fan of it myself."

My eyes pinned him with a glare so deadly it made Ebola look tame. "I'd never of guessed," I spat. "Just know that whatever the devil has planned for you, my plans are far worse. That's all you need to know."

Kyle backed away from me automatically but was immediately annoyed with himself. It was my turn to smile.

"Get her on the floor. I want her on her knees." The order was barked out, and less than ten seconds later, that was where I was. I didn't struggle. My body was sore and broken enough as it was.

"Are you going to beg for your husband's life before we begin, Petal?"

"Would it do any good?" My eyes were blank as I looked up at him, utterly devoid of emotion. The rage bubbling inside me had seen to that.

"No, but it might be sweet to see you try. Go on, Petal. You never know, it might work."

"Please let my husband go." The words were flat because I refused to give him what he wanted. If Kyle could risk killing me to witness Mark's reaction, he was unlikely to pay any attention to a little pleading. All I was doing was stalling for time.

Kyle frowned, as I thought he might. "You can do better than that, Petal. Remember your husband's life depends on it."

"Oh well, in that case I'd better give you the Oscar award-winning performance. Hang on a minute." Composing my features for a few more precious time-wasting seconds, I prostrated myself on the floor and began wailing and begging for mercy. It was only half an act, but I knew the performance would now be ruined for Kyle, and that was all I cared about.

Yanking me up by a handful of hair he ordered me to stop, and I immediately obeyed him.

"You're playing a dangerous game, Petal," he whispered. "I just need to remove that wooden board and you'll be writing your husband's epitaph." He clicked his fingers to demonstrate how quickly that would happen, and I flinched.

"How did you find me?" It was a redirect, aimed at buying more time, but Kyle would love talking about anything that made him look clever and important.

Sure enough he paused, and then smiled. "You think I followed you, don't you? I bet you think I've been trailing you for days." I nodded. That's what I'd thought initially, but now I had my doubts. "Remember your night out at Escape, when I came to see you?" Nodding, I waited for him to continue. "Well, when I spanked you there was a pinch. Did you feel it?" Another nod. I had. My mind had relived that episode last night, and the pinch had bothered me. "You now have a small GPS chip inside you that lets me trace you all over the place. All I had to do was wait for the right moment and *boom*. I knew as soon as I had you your husband would come trailing after you like a whipped puppy. It was all so easy." Great. I had now a piece of floating electronic debris lodged in my body that would never let me escape this monster. My day was getting better and better.

"And when..." My voice trailed off because Kyle had a fierce grip on my hair and was yanking it hard.

"Shut up. Don't think I don't know you're stalling. We need to get this over with, don't we?" He let go of me so abruptly my head bounced like a ball on my chest. Swearing under my breath, I watched Kyle mount the platform. I was already shivering. There was no heating in the place and the thin cotton T-shirt I'd been given provided no warmth whatsoever. It was also stiff as a board after the pool and bath combo.

"Ready for this, Matthews? Dad will be watching via webcam, so put on a good performance, won't you?" Mark didn't acknowledge the taunt, and neither did I.

Raising my eyes slowly to the platform above I watched Kyle walk behind my husband, raising his whip hand as he did so. As much as I wanted to stare at the concrete floor beneath me and try to ignore this next bout of torture, my eyes refused to cooperate. They were glued to my husband, still perched precariously on his tiptoes, about to be whipped so severely he would probably choke himself to death.

The first crack rang through the basement like a lightning bolt, the sound ricocheting off the walls. It made my ears sting, so God only knew what it had done to Mark's body, but he took it well. He barely wobbled. Perhaps I did have something to thank Sophia for, after all.

Kyle was brutal with the whip, as I knew he would be, and his aim had improved considerably since our last encounter. He'd obviously been practicing. The whip flew with precision, grace and style - all words I would not normally associate with the psychopath in front of me. By the look on Mark's face, it was clear he was thinking the same thing.

Lash after lash flew through the air, and each sickening thud sliced into flesh with the ease of a knife sinking through hot butter. It was only a matter of seconds before the tang of blood was in the air.

So far I had kept my promise of no tears, but I was pretty sure Mark didn't trust me. He hadn't looked at me once, but to be fair, he had to keep his wits about him just to retain his balance. One wrong move and it could all be over very quickly. There was only so much of this he could stand, especially as we'd had no food or water in over twenty-four hours. Even though he was as stubborn as they came, I didn't see him lasting more than an hour. Blood loss, dehydration and exhaustion would get the better of him eventually.

Kyle paused every now and again to take a look at me. When he didn't get what he wanted he simply continued his game, knowing I'd crack eventually. And I would. Watching Mark writhe in pain would be my undoing, and he knew it.

The first stumble came after twenty minutes or so, and my attention was then glued to the stage. Mark wobbled one way and then teetered back the other, but eventually he managed to find his balance once more. Kyle gave another glance my way, but I held my nerve. The second stumble came not long after, but this time Kyle continued to swing the whip, making it nearly impossible for Mark to recover his footing as he was swung this way and that. Five vicious cracks of the whip, all at once, sent my husband reeling and I had to choke back a sob. This was the beginning of the end.

It continued like this for another twenty minutes, and now Mark was slipping all over the place in his own blood. My poor husband was beginning to flag. He didn't get more than a few seconds on his feet at any one time, and was wheezing in air whenever he could. The lack of oxygen would make it difficult to do anything, and he probably couldn't even think straight. When a particularly nasty blow smashed into him I'd had enough.

"Stop it. Just stop it," I pleaded. "There must be something you want. Anything. Name it and I'll do it; just leave him alone," I sobbed. "If you want to kill someone kill me, but let him go." The tears were falling freely. Memo to me: never make promises you don't have a chance of keeping.

Mark must have heard me because he roared out his displeasure for all to hear, using valuable oxygen that he didn't have.

Kyle immediately stopped what he was doing and turned to stare at me. "Well, well, well. You do have a heart. I was beginning to wonder." Pausing, his eyes narrowed, and I could see the cogs beginning to turn. I knew what that meant. He wanted to have some fun with me. It was unlikely I'd save my husband this way, but I might buy him a few seconds worth of air.

"What do you want?" I croaked.

"Hmm, what do I want?" His index finger came up to rub his top lip as he appeared deep in thought. I knew better. He'd already planned for this and was just waiting for a chance to watch me squirm. Whatever he was about to suggest would be absolutely horrific, but it couldn't be any worse than the carnage I was witnessing.

Kyle walked up and down the platform in front of Mark as he pretended to consider my proposition, his shoes making terrible sucking noises as they stepped through blood. "I think there may be something I want. Jennifer, how about you come up here."

He beckoned me with his index finger, and I shakily got to my feet even as Mark yelled out, "No!"

I didn't care. I couldn't watch any more. Mounting the platform, putting one foot in front of the other with equal amounts of terror and dread, I came to stand before him, trembling like a leaf.

"You'll do anything, huh?" His calculating look was beyond creepy, and I had a feeling I knew where this was going, but there was no turning back now.

"Anything," I confirmed.

"Then you'd better bend over and roll that T-shirt up around your waist."

"You fucking bastard," Mark spat, earning himself another slice of the whip which sent him skittering across the other side of the platform, gasping for breath once again.

Meanwhile I closed my eyes and did as ordered. If this was what it took I was willing to pay the price. Bending over from my waist, I began rolling the T-shirt up. There were no feelings of embarrassment. I was too terrified for that.

Harry and Freddie were watching us with their tongues hanging out. That should have repulsed me, but again I was too far gone to care. My head was not in a good place.

"Jen, you do this and I'll never forgive you," Mark yelled, and his last attempt to save my soul was duly noted. But if I didn't do it I'd never forgive myself, and that was all that concerned me right now. Do or die. There was no time for thinking.

Kyle moved towards me, running his hand up my inner thigh. I shuddered. There was another hand, curling around my waist as he pulled me into him, and I heard Mark screaming in the background. Blocking the sound out I concentrated on the stone wall in front of me. Kyle ran a finger down my backside and plunged into my anus with no warning.

"What say I take her in the ass, Matthews? Think she'd like that?" Mark came barrelling across the stage, hoping to knock Kyle over, but he managed to move to the side of the platform just in time, out of his reach. My stubborn husband then spent a stupid amount of time trying to strangle himself in order to reach us.

"Yes, I think that's exactly what I'm going to do, Mark." He slowly unzipped his pants, and the rasp of his zipper rang loudly in my ear. Feeling a cock being pressed up close and personal with my backside, I stared at the stone wall and started counting in my head. A weird coping mechanism, I grant you, but I had to do something other than scream. When he grabbed hold of my hair and pushed my head forward to bend me over a little further I wanted to pass out, but I held my nerve. If it meant saving the life of my husband, it was a small price to pay.

Chapter Twenty-Six - Mark

When Kyle bent Jennifer over I wanted to gut him like an animal. Scrap that. Gutting him would be too quick. I wanted to peel every inch of skin off his body while the bastard was still alive and then let him admire my efforts after I'd finished.

Although I admired my wife's courage, she was playing right into the bastard's hands. He would still kill me, but now she'd get a sick and twisted memory of the event to take with her. I couldn't let that happen.

Working desperately to try and loosen the rope around my wrists, I nearly tore the flesh off my hands in my attempts to get free. No matter how hard I struggled the cord was wound too tightly, and there was no way I was going to budge it. What was I going to do now? There had to be something. If I had to watch this I was going to go crazy.

Just as that thought entered my head the sound of splintering glass tore through the building, and every head in the room whipped round to see where the noise was coming from. If my ears hadn't deceived me, it sounded like there was someone upstairs. A few seconds later heavy booted footsteps could be heard, and there were several pairs of them. I prayed they were on our side. We really needed a miracle right now. My head swung back to Kyle to see what he was up to.

"What the fuck was that?" Kyle had immediately stopped what he was doing and was zipping himself up rather quickly. Shoving Jennifer off the platform so abruptly she nearly went headfirst, I winced. Somehow she managed to land on her feet, and at first glance it didn't look like she'd hurt herself. My eyes darted back to Kyle, who was now also on the floor. Watching as he grabbed hold of the wooden platform, I realised things were about to go south very quickly.

With a vicious yank he tore the platform away and my bound hands shot towards the noose, trying to cushion my neck on the dive downwards, so it didn't bloody break. The jarring impact of the fall nearly severed my fingers, but at least it didn't kill me. Jennifer immediately ran to me, clinging to my body like a limpet and trying to prop me up as best she could. But Kyle had other ideas. Grasping her around the elbow he tried to yank her away, but she wouldn't let go.

"Come on you silly bitch, we have to get the hell out of here!" Kyle pulled his gun out of his back pocket, aimed it at me and released the safety.

"Over my dead body," she screamed, still trying her best to hold me up, and then she turned and slammed her knee in his groin. Atta girl. It slowed him down for a moment or two, but when he'd recovered he wrenched her away sharply, leaving me hanging as he made to aim his gun once more.

He wasn't fast enough. The room filled with men in black and they all looked terrifying armed with machine guns and grenades. They turned to focus on Kyle, Freddie, and Harry, who instantly dropped their weapons as soon as they were ordered to. Unless you want to die you don't fuck with the SAS, and unless I was much mistaken, this was them.

Someone cut me down and provided Jen with a foil blanket. She sank to the floor with it, shivering and sobbing uncontrollably. I would have given anything in the world to go down there to comfort her, but there was no way I could bend my back after what had happened.

"Jen, sweetheart. It's all over now. Don't cry." I tousled her hair with my fingertips, but she only sobbed harder. It was going to take a little while to come down from the horrors of today, so I decided to let her cry it out for a while.

Meanwhile, one of the guys took a look at my back and whistled. Speaking into a walkie-talkie at the top of his belt, he ordered an ambulance.

"Christ, you should be in agony right now. How come you're still standing?" He looked rather in awe of my injuries, and that probably wasn't good. Right now I barely felt them, but I knew I would in a couple of hours.

"Because sitting down would be too painful." I smiled tightly. "Thanks for coming to our rescue. Did Laurel send you?"

He looked confused for a moment. "I don't know. We just follow orders. You'd have to ask the man in charge." He pointed to someone who was currently using cable ties to restrain Kyle hand and foot. He was none too gentle about it, of which I thoroughly approved. When he'd finished he walked towards us, pushing the goggles he was wearing over his head before yanking his balaclava off.

"Mark Matthews, isn't it? Hang in there and we'll get you an ambulance in a jiffy." He had short grey hair, blue eyes, and looked like a reasonably intelligent fellow. Was he in charge?

"Just need to get my knife out. Ah, there it is." Although the man was talking to me he had eyes only for Jennifer. Who was he? Jennifer hadn't paid him any attention until he'd started talking to me but was now looking him up and down with eyes that were red-rimmed with tears. She didn't stop staring at him, then her head tilted and her eyes narrowed as if she recognised him. I was definitely missing something. The man then began sawing at the ropes that still held my hands together, and it didn't take him long to cut through them.

"How long have you been here, Dad?" she whispered.

Fuck, no. The man in front of me was her father? This was fucking great. He worked for the intelligence service and was a crack shot. I'd probably been rescued from one disaster, straight as I was about to dive into another. This could not be happening. Oh, and let's not forget I was stark bollock naked. That's always a good impression to make on your first meeting with your father-in-law.

"A while. I like to do my homework before I start taking people out. We have protocols to follow and all that." The wry grin on his face told me I'd been hung out to dry for the past hour or so, while the bastard decided to see what I was made of. I made a strangled sound and it was an effort not to punch him, even though he was currently trying to untie me.

He didn't seem at all phased by it. Just pushed my hand out of the way and continued with what he was doing. "You didn't do too badly up there, old son. I was almost positive Jen had married a pussy at the beginning, but you seemed to come through admirably."

This was the last straw. I was going to kill him. It might have to wait until I wasn't naked and tied up, but it was definitely on the cards.

"Jen, darling, I can't tell you how extraordinarily good it is to see you. I know I'm that asshole who hasn't been in your life since forever, but the security of the country was at stake, and any association with me or your mother would have probably got you killed, which is why your mother remarried. Redcliff had enough money to keep you safe, and she severed all ties with him as soon as she was able. When she married him he was quite the respectable gentlemen and she seemed certain he would remarry someone nice, but it seems we both fucked up, doesn't it? The man's an absolute animal. Your mum and I are going to have good fun with him soon, though. Rest assured. I'm Rupert by the way." He shook her hand briefly, by way of introduction.

My head was reeling. "So let me get this straight. You're SAS, and you married the leading lady of the Mafia?" This could not be true. Someone, somewhere had to be having a laugh. I mentally crossed out trying to kill him. That would be a big mistake... and then all the dots connected. This was why Redcliff had wanted me dead. He needed all my money to kill the pair of them. Putting a hit on a member of the SAS was certifiably insane - but I could almost sympathise with the bastard. I shook my head in disbelief.

159

Rupert turned to Jen and rolled his eyes. "He's not too quick this one, is he darling?" He gave me a withering look that had me itching to punch his lights out, but I kept myself in check. Family relations were already strained enough as it was.

"MI6 actually, but yes, that's about it, old boy. Well done for keeping up." Rupert slammed his palm onto my shoulder, sending shards of pain all through my body. I was beginning to see why Redcliff wanted the man assassinated, and I wondered whether I did have enough money to get the job done.

"What better wife than one who knows everything about everyone? There's not a stone that goes unturned without Laurel noticing. Is she still going by that name, by the way? I can never keep up."

Neither could I, and that was saying something.

The ambulance chose that time to arrive, and we were all herded outside, where I was bundled facedown onto a stretcher. It was a position I was getting a little too familiar with. Don't get me wrong, I was thrilled to be alive, but my masochistic streak had been well and truly sated because I never wanted to go through anything like that ever again. Jennifer settled in beside me and grabbed my hand, squeezing it as if it were a stress ball. Squeezing back, I turned to face her and drank her in. I'd come so close to losing her. So, so, close. It didn't bear thinking about.

"Thank God you're okay," I whispered.

Jen whistled through her teeth. "Me? It was you who was swinging there, up on that block." She put a hand on her chest and took a deep, shuddering breath.

"It's all over now. We don't have to think about him ever again." Well, except what we were going to do with him, to make him atone for his many sins. That monster had better not be being shipped off to prison. I had a lot of ideas on how to punish him, but keeping him nice and cosy under Her Majesty's close observation was not one of them.

Jen gave me a quick smile and kissed my cheek. She then turned to her father, who had also got in the ambulance with us. There was no getting rid of him for the time being, it seemed.

"So where have you been for the past twenty-odd years?" Her voice was small, and I could tell she was suffering. Both parents had been reintroduced to her in a short space of time, and it looked likely that the pair of them were quite intelligent but completely nuts - which was a rather dangerous combination.

He coughed a little contritely, as well he might. "Ah, all over the place really, darling. I was in the US at the time of September 11, I've had some fun in Ireland with the IRA, and I've spent a lot of time in Russia, Syria, and Iran as well. My work is all undercover, and I feel like I haven't seen the light of day for years. You'll be pleased to know that I'm about to retire in two weeks, though, and I'd love to catch up with you and your family if you'll let me. Although I'll understand if you don't." Rupert gave her a pleading look and beamed at her. He went for a goofy expression that was cunningly brilliant. My wife was reduced to a puddle almost instantly. Fuck.

"I think I'd like that," she said softly. I knew I wouldn't. I wondered how far we'd have to move away to prevent more than yearly visits from her parents. Brazilian rainforest, Sahara desert, Outer Mongolia, or even the Arctic Circle were now on my list of favourite places to relocate; the less access there was by sea, land or air, the better.

"Yes, I'm going to have a lot of free time on my hands very shortly, so whenever you want to catch up, darling, you just let me know. I'll be round straight away. I may not have been there in your younger years, but if you'll have me, I'll do my best to make up for lost time.

Over my dead body. I was going to build a twenty-foot, electrified barbed wire fence around my whole estate, and plant land mines in my garden. Maybe I'd employ some snipers, too.

It was about time I changed the conversation. "How were you able to locate us? My phone would have led you to Hyde Park, but you wouldn't be able to get here with that, surely? And where were we being held?" I still had no idea, but it appeared to be in London, as I'd previously thought.

"Ah, that. You're very lucky I work where I do. If I didn't you'd be dead about now."

I had a feeling that might be the case, but I was not going to feel beholden to the man. He'd left my wife high and dry without a parachute for the past twenty years, and so what if the security of the country had been at stake. Damned if I was going to forgive him that easily, even if my wife seemed to pool into a puddle at his feet. Looking at him expectantly, I waited for him to continue.

"When our experts were trying to track you down, we watched the footage of Jen leaving your office, but no one appeared to be tailing her. Several other cameras on her walk down to the café confirmed the same thing, which meant someone nabbed her out of nowhere. At first we figured they'd hacked her phone until we were told she didn't have it on her. Then we guessed someone had planted a tracker on her, but someone would have had to get very close to her for that, and she didn't even have a handbag on her; the obvious place to drop a tracking device. It was unlikely her attacker would have planted it on clothing because it's too risky. So that led me to digging up dirt on your recent exploits, and your visit to Escape."

Oh, fantastic. Jen's father, who kills people legally for a living, now knows I like to spank and whip my wife, as well as torment her... I was going to die a horrible, *horrible* death. I went so pale then that the medic who was monitoring my statistics asked if I was okay. I wasn't, but I nodded.

"Jen takes after her mother in that respect. She was always into the kinky stuff." Rupert looked thoughtful for a moment, and I bit my tongue. If that was how he wanted to play it, I wasn't going to enlighten anyone. "Anyway, we spotted Kyle on camera and managed to catch him injecting Jen with a tiny little tracker which is not much bigger than a grain of rice. Impressive, eh? Modern technology never fails to astound me." Rupert shook his head in awe. "After that, of course, it was all plain sailing. We had one of our hackers find the device, thankfully there aren't too many of them in circulation at the moment, and hey presto; there you were at an abandoned house on the outskirts of London." He looked at Jen and then jumped. "Oh, that reminds me. I'd better text your mother and tell her you're okay. She's been going crazy this past half hour and has threatened to decapitate me at least twice. I wouldn't put it past her to have a go at it, either."

Letting my head drop face first into the thin mattress of the stretcher, I prayed that the morphine would kick in quickly. This was all too much to take. Way too much.

Chapter Twenty-Seven - Jennifer

Mark spent three days in hospital as they assessed the extent of the damage he had suffered under Kyle. Thankfully it was nothing that wouldn't heal, which took a good deal of weight off both our minds. They insisted on checking me over, too, even though I protested. I was also given the all clear.

For the first two days, both of us did little except catch up on missed sleep, fluids and food. There was only so much trauma either of us could deal with. Eventually we managed to fight off the miasma of exhaustion that had penetrated our room and were finally able to say a string of more than three words to each other.

Sitting at my husband's bedside on the third day of his treatment, I was pleased to hear he was feeling much better and was almost entirely off his pain meds. This, unfortunately, gave us a lot of time to talk - we hadn't done much of that lately - and he had plenty of things to say about my very dysfunctional family.

"Holy fuck, you've got a mother who's in the Mafia and a father who's in MI6? Can this get any worse?" He looked horrified, as well he might.

Settling in bed beside him, which was strictly against hospital policy, I put an arm around his neck and whispered in his ear, "Is this going to interfere with your world domination plans, darling?"

He pulled me in close to him and buried his fingers in my hair. "No, but it might interfere with my plans to dominate you. I like my testicles firmly attached to my body." My husband had a frown on his face, and it was clear he was concerned. I resisted the urge to laugh.

"Well you'll just have to hope my father is a reasonable human being, won't you?" I flicked my hair back over my neck and grinned at him.

"If he's related to you there's no chance of that!" Mark had a point.

"Let's not talk about my family now. That's a conversation for another day. We don't even have to invite them back into our lives if we don't want to—"

Mark was quick to interrupt. "Then let's not."

"Let me finish. We don't have to invite them back into our lives, but it might seem a touch ungrateful after they rescued us from a fate worse than several deaths. They might be handy people to have around, just in case. You never know who might want to kidnap one of us next."

Mark bit the bottom of my earlobe and growled. "That's not even funny."

"It wasn't meant to be. I had no idea how exciting being married to you was going to be."

"You haven't seen anything yet, darling." Mark moved from my earlobe to nuzzle and nip my neck, and I moaned before he stopped abruptly.

"Oh shit, I completely forgot. You could be pregnant, right? The drowning incident..." Mark tailed off, and he didn't need to say any more.

"I talked to the nurse about that. She said that if I miss my period, then she'd schedule an appointment with a specialist and we could take it from there, but I don't think I am."

"How would you know? If you were, the baby wouldn't even be as big as a pea right now." Mark squeezed his thumb and forefinger together to illustrate just how tiny the baby would be, and I smiled.

"I'll know when I'm pregnant." I nodded and looked smug.

He rolled his eyes. "And you think I'm the control freak?"

"You are - but I'm learning."

"Well, we'll take it one step at a time. Right now I just need to get out of here."

"Funny you should say that. Doctor Einheld spoke to me a couple of hours ago and said you could be released today. Sound good?"

"Halle-fucking-lujah. Now that *is* good news. Can I have sex today too?"

"Don't push it, Mr Matthews. There is to be no exertion for the next week or two. We don't want to open up any of those nasty lacerations on your back, now do we?"

"I'm willing to take that risk if you are." Mark grinned up at me adoringly.

"You get nada from me until you've been given the all-clear." I gave him my most fearsome look, put my hands on my hips, and shook my head to emphasise my point. Getting up off the bed, and ignoring his loud groan of protest, I decided we both needed a cup of really bad coffee in order to change the direction of this conversation.

"That will mean at least three million spanks will be added to your tally, Mrs Matthews," Mark bit out as I left the room.

"Good job I'm in this relationship for the long haul then," I shot back.

Two weeks later and my husband was nearly certifiably insane. I'd kept my word on the no sex thing, following the advice of Mark's physician, but my poor darling was a self-confessed addict, and the withdrawal symptoms were nearly his undoing.

"I'm not an invalid, you know." Mark was constantly trying to wheedle me into ignoring the doc's instructions, but it was not happening.

"Actually you are. That's what happens when you get whipped to within an inch of your life."

"The doctor didn't actually say 'no sex' though, did he?" This wasn't the first time he'd tried that tactic, either.

"Actually, he did, which is why we aren't going to have any until he says it's okay."

"What if I ring him today? Give me his number." Mark reached for the phone beside him, and there was a devilish gleam in his eyes. I extinguished it right away.

"I wouldn't trust you to tell me the truth. You'll just have to wait until I get his say so in person."

"But that could be days from now, and I might die in the meantime." He flung the phone across the room in exasperation.

"I haven't heard of anyone dying from lack of sex before. But if you want to be the first I'll see if I can get you a slot in the Guinness Book of World Records." My eyes twinkled.

"I'm serious here."

"So am I. On another note of seriousness, I did everything you said for seven days, and you owe me a night of domination."

"You did not! I've been telling you to have sex with me every day for the last two weeks, and you haven't! How is that obeying me?" Mark looked flabbergasted, which was really quite endearing.

"Instructions that are against doctor's orders cannot be taken into consideration. However, if you allow me my night, and I have earned it," I said, pointing at my chest, "I might ring Doctor Einheld today and see if he can clear you for various naughtiness."

"No way. That's blackmail." Mark narrowed his eyes and gave me a dark look. I didn't even blink.

"Fine by me. You aren't scheduled to have another appointment for two weeks, so you can just suck it up and wait till then." I held the sheet of paper up with Einheld's number and began to rip it in two.

"Give me that number now," he said, glowering at me. I immediately ripped the sheet to shreds.

"I can get his number any time I like by—"

"Calling the hospital information line. Absolutely. That should keep you busy for a good hour or so. You have fun with that. I know from experience that they enjoy hanging up on people. Catch you later." I began to remove the robe I was wearing, revealing a red silk chemise, and then I sashayed slowly from the room.

"You can't do this!" My husband's face was a picture, and I was enjoying myself immensely.

"You're right. Maybe I shouldn't leave. Maybe I should just walk up and down the room several times in my sexy red lingerie. I wouldn't want to leave you unattended."

I got to do two deliciously slow laps of the room before Mark leapt out of bed and pounced on me, slamming me into the floor.

"Finally—" That was the only word I managed to get in for some time. When he eventually let go of my lips, and there was enough air in my lungs for a sentence, I sighed blissfully. "It's about time."

"What's about time?" He frowned at me.

"I asked the doctor yesterday when you could start walking around, and he said you'd let me know when you were ready."

Mark rolled his eyes heavenward and gave me a filthy look. "If you'd have told me that I'd have been up and walking about a week ago."

"That's why I didn't let you know earlier. And you're still not getting any until I get my night. I died for you, Mark Matthews. It's the least you owe me." I didn't exactly die *for* him, but it sounded good, and anything that was going to sway the odds in my favour had my vote.

"Can we have sex this instant if I agree to this silliness?"

"Right now," I confirmed. I'd been desperate to get my clothes off and slide underneath my husband for days. No encouragement was needed.

"Fine. You get your night, but I have one condition."

"What's that?" I raised an eyebrow of my own. This should be good.

"My blood stays in my body. You can do what you like, other than that, but I can't cope with any more blood." He shoved a thumb behind him to indicate his back.

I shuddered. "I wouldn't be capable of that."

"Good to know. You get your night. Oh, and one more question, which I hardly dare ask, but I need to be a responsible adult every now and again."

I looked up at him, puzzled. "What now? Don't even think of trying to wriggle..."

"Relax. I agreed. What I need to know now is if you're back on the pill? If you aren't we'll need to get some condoms, and I'm going to get the bastard things couriered over here in under an hour. There'll be someone I can find who'll do it."

Laughing, as I imagined that rather terse phone conversation, I nearly choked. We would be getting a reputation around these parts if we weren't careful. "This is something I have to see," I said, through bursts of giggles.

"Give me the phone and my iPad. I need to Google motorbike courier services. Go, go, go; this is an emergency." Mark had already flung me off him and was scrambling to get up. I laughed so hard I couldn't speak for a good minute and a half. Seriously, I had tears pouring down my face.

"Steady on, darling. Are you okay?"

Mark slowed down enough to sit back down on the floor and reach for my hand. I gripped it tightly. Tugging him towards me, I whispered, "Actually, that's something I wanted to talk to you about."

"You want to talk to me about motorcycle couriers?" There was the familiar, deadly twinkle in Mark's eyes that told me he probably knew what I was about to say before I did.

"No, I want to talk to you about pills." I finally managed to stop laughing.

"What about them?" He was once again nuzzling my neck, and I was finding it difficult to think, let alone speak, but this was important, so I did my best.

"I don't want them."

Mark stopped nuzzling my neck abruptly. He thought carefully about what he was going to say, bringing his face up to mine and looking very serious. "So we use condoms. It's not a problem." He scoured my face from left to right, wondering if this conversation was going to go the way he wanted it to. I saw concern etched on his features, and I heard him clear his throat as if to speak before he thought the better of it.

"I don't want them either."

"Stop beating around the bush, Jen. If you're saying what I think you're saying, please spit it out. If you're not, don't get me excited. You're not to do this for me, either. We have plenty of time. We can take it slowly and see how you feel in a few months. I'd never forgive myself if I thought I'd coerced you into this before you were ready."

"I. Want. Babies. Your babies. At least two, but no more than four. I don't want to wait. No one knows how much time they have on this earth, and more than anything else in the world right now, I want to be pregnant with your child - our child. I hope I already am, but if I'm not, I'm confident you'll give it your best shot in the next few months, Mr Matthews."

By now Mark's eyes were glistening with tears. He was staring at me, not sure if he could believe what I was saying. Who knew the word babies could totally destroy one of London's most famous dominants? I would have to mention it more often.

"Babies, babies, babies," I whispered, nibbling on his ear while rubbing my silk chemise firmly into his body.

"Stop that. I can't think. Are you sure?"

"Yes," I said happily.

He looked at me through narrowed lids. "Are you *sure* you're sure?"

"Yes," I yelled, laughing. "I had a lot of time to think in that cold little room that Kyle put me in. I can't think of anything more precious than having a baby with you. I've gone from being scared of the idea, to needing to have one yesterday. It's utterly bizarre but completely enchanting."

"Life and death experiences can do that, I hear." He pulled my arms up over my head and lifted my silk shift over my head. "Are you sure, though? You can't change your mind once we start this." He frowned. "Well, you can, but it's not to be recommended. I want you to be certain."

"I'm certain. Stop stalling and fuck my brains out, darling. I've been waiting two weeks for this." I pulled my hair out of the loose ponytail I was wearing and shook my blonde mane around my head.

"Fuck. I can't think when you look like that."

"Then don't," I said, and thankfully, he didn't.

Michael Redcliff was caught three weeks after my father had begun to interrogate Kyle. Whatever tactics my father used, they must have been pretty good. I didn't expect Kyle had talked easily.

Rupert was sitting in our lounge, nursing a cup of coffee that immediately made him Mark's friend for life, and my mother was sitting alongside him. Miracle of miracles, Mark had not run screaming from the building.

We were currently snuggled together on the sofa, and he had his arm protectively around my stomach as if afraid someone might shoot me at any second. Rupert was amused by this, Laurel not so much, but at least she was now on speaking terms with him. Whatever Rupert had told her about the incident something must have attracted her attention, for she looked at Mark with newfound respect in her eyes.

"What do you want us to do with them?" We'd been talking about Michael's arrest for some time, and how they'd caught him hiding out in the Caribbean with Katrina. Mark had been listening intently. I knew he wouldn't have been able to rest until Redcliff was caught, so at least now we could lay another demon to rest.

"The worst thing you can possibly think of," Mark said, without a moment's hesitation. "Although legally, I don't think there's anything you can do to him that will even touch on what's he done to both of us, unfortunately."

Rupert coughed and glanced sideways at Laurel. They shared a long look together. "Well, that's why Laurel and I didn't put either of their arrests on the books. If I hand everything over to my stunningly beautiful and incredibly cunning ex-wife, I'm pretty sure she can do something even you'd approved of. The mafia have some quite ingenious torments, so I've heard." Rupert tried to look innocent and failed miserably. By the look on Mark's face, my father had just made a friend for life.

"Can you string him upside down by his testicles and wait for them to drop off?" Mark and Rupert looked expectantly at my mother, while I wanted to bury my way under the table. If they were going to talk about blood, death and gore, I wanted to go in the other room. I'd had enough of that just lately.

My mother looked bored at my husband's suggestion and waved it away with her hand. "Oh please. We can do much better than that. Why don't you let me do my thing, and I'll keep you updated?"

Rupert gave Mark a huge grin and gave him the thumbs up. Christ almighty. What was the world coming to? I wanted to bury my head in my hands.

Mark did not feel the same way. "That works for me. If I think of anything truly disgusting in the meantime, I can always get back to you. Besides, Jennifer and I are going to be very busy in the next couple of weeks." Mark began stroking my stomach, and I elbowed him sharply in the ribs. Laurel pursed her lips and looked suspiciously at my husband, but she wisely kept quiet. Rupert did no such thing.

"Oh yes, son? What are you guys planning on doing?"

"We're going to be making babies," said Mark smugly, looking directly at my mother.

I don't remember much after that. Laurel dived for her purse and my father jumped in front of us both. Mark took this as an opportunity to yank me away from the lounge as quickly as he could, and we ran upstairs as fast as our legs could carry us. We could still hear them talking for several minutes afterward - until we locked ourselves in the bedroom, anyway.

"They're joking, Laurel. You need to be able to take a joke." Rupert was trying to persuade my mother not to kill my husband, which was appreciated.

"That's not funny, Rupert. He needs to be respectful." Laurel was not amused and sounded very terse.

"Calm down and put the gun away. Mark isn't an employee, he's your daughter's husband. It would be a good idea to stay on the right side of them both. You do want grandchildren, right, Laurel? If you kill him that's not going to happen for a while, trust me."

"Couldn't I just string him up for a while instead? Our relationship would improve tenfold if I just had a half hour alone with him."

"You don't want to do that, Laurel. Mark's a rich man. He could make it very difficult for you to see your daughter if he wanted to."

"He wouldn't dare."

"Laurel, if you're going to shoot me, just shoot me. Otherwise, I think we'd better get out of here and put all that rage to good use somewhere."

We didn't hear too much after that. Mark was ripping my clothes off, and his fingers were already pumping away happily inside me. Ever since I'd mentioned the idea that I'd like to get pregnant, Mark had taken his role in the matter *very* seriously. We were having sex approximately ten times a day, and if he didn't stop I might murder him - let alone my mother.

"After I fall pregnant, will I get a break from all this exertion?" I asked, giggling away in a tangled heap of black satin sheets.

"No way. After you fall pregnant I will find you even more sexy than I do now and you will have to beat me off with a stick."

"Oh, Good Lord," I wailed.

"And he's not going to be able to save you either," said Mark, ruining the third pair of my panties that day, as he ripped them from my body and flung them across the room, which earned a cross glare from me in the meantime.

"I only have three pairs left now. What is wrong with you? You're a barbarian."

Mark shrugged his shoulders. "Panties are highly overrated. When I bust them all you won't be able to wear any."

Ah, so that was his plan. It was all making sense now. My husband the master schemer. It was about time I wiped that smug smile off his face.

"Don't forget that it's your turn to be dominated tomorrow, darling. I have booked my slot, and you will be present and correct, or there'll be trouble. Maybe I can trash your pants for a change," I grumbled.

"By all means," he said grinning, "and feel free to do your worst. I think I'm actually looking forward to this."

Picking up the hardback book I was reading from the bedside table, I lumped him over the head with it. While it was unlikely to knock any sense into him, it made me feel a little better.

Chapter Twenty-Eight - Jennifer

The following day nearly every one of my muscles groaned in torment as I struggled out of bed. I didn't care because nothing was going to wipe the smile off my face. I'd had a fantastic evening, about eleven orgasms and a decent spanking. If that wasn't enough, tonight was going to be the night that I got to dominate my husband, and the excitement rippling through my body was almost too much to contain. I had planned it all out in my head for weeks. All I needed was to put my thoughts into action.

Mark had been relatively good-humoured yesterday. He'd given in to my demands with good grace, and that in itself was a little strange because I'd thought I stood no chance, but something had certainly happened. Maybe it was our near-death experience, perhaps it was something else, but he didn't seem too concerned with the baptism of fire I was going to put him through this evening.

When he came down for breakfast I beamed at him and laid out my famous microwave omelette, which I had now perfected. I'd even made him a breakfast smoothie, having grasped the basics of the blender. Blenders are great. You chuck all kinds of fruit and veg in them and voila. You just have to remember to make sure the lid is locked down. My first attempt had sadly failed to ascertain this and resulted in the redecoration of the kitchen. Blackberry stains are almost impossible to remove from magnolia walls, take my word for it.

"Are you nervous?" Yes, I was teasing him, but it was nice to get my own back once in a while.

"Not particularly," he said calmly, as soon as he'd finished a mouthful of non-crunchy omelette. "Should I be?" His eyes caught mine over the table, and they were twinkling. He wasn't going to let me ruffle his feathers just yet. I'd get there, though. The day was young.

"Yes, you absolutely should be," I said, trying for my sternest, disciplinarian look. Mark could always do dark withering looks so well, but I have to confess I struggled with them. Tonight was going to be a challenge, but one that I wholly intended to embrace.

"You realise that if it's really bad, I'll just get my own back the next day?" There was the merest glimmer of a smile around his lips, but other than that - nothing. Trying to ruffle the feathers of my husband was nearly impossible - well unless you were Kyle, that was, but thankfully we'd seen the end of him. My mother and father had promised to keep Mark in the loop about that, but I'd told him I didn't want to know, and I'd meant it. It was bound to be something truly awful, and sometimes you're better off not knowing. I had better things to think about.

"I don't care. I'll just find another opportunity to get my own back at a later date."

"Good luck with that. I might just keep you chained and locked up in my naughty room after this. Spread-eagled on my wall, flogged hourly, and ready for sex at any and every opportunity." He drank a sip of his very green smoothie and winced. "What the hell is in this?"

"Wheatgrass, spirulina, celery, broccoli, spinach, and kale."

He pulled a face at me. "Forget domination. If you ever want to *really* torture me, just make me drink this revolting crap on a regular basis." He held the glass at arm's length as if it were a grenade about to explode.

I beamed. "It's good for you. Drink it up. If you're going to be a dad you need to stay healthy for at least the next twenty years or so." I gave him the you'd-better-do-as-you're-told look that I'd been perfecting over the last few days and waited to see if it would work. After a long deliberation and several scowls at me, he drank the thing down in one and pulled another face.

"God, that is awful. You can't do that to me every morning."

"Watch me."

"I am. You look gorgeous. That frowny face you just loosed on me is adorable, by the way." He waved his knife at me and grinned.

I rolled my eyes in annoyance. I should have known that was coming.

"That's another fifty spanks." He shook his head and gave me a mocking glance.

I had a reply ready and waiting for him. "You've just gained yourself a hundred by being cheeky, and I'm going to use the rubber flogger."

"Lucky me. Are you going to dress up for me?" His eyes lit up at the thought.

I was, but I wasn't about to tell him that.

"You'll just have to wait and see." I winked at him.

He smirked at me. "It's going to be fun to watch you wear the trousers for a change." He then got up, placed his plate and utensils in the dishwasher, and came back to the dining table to lay a kiss upon my head. "I'll be in the office as I'm working from home today, and I'm going to work straight through lunch, so you can have me for an early start at six p.m. Does that fit in with your plans?" I felt him bury his face in my hair, breathing in my scent. Mark had always been touchy-feely, but after the event with Kyle he couldn't seem to keep his hands off me. Whether that was because he was glad I was alive, or because he kept thinking about getting me pregnant was anybody's guess, but if he kept up with this attentive behaviour there was a distinct chance I might have ten kids after all.

"Perfectly. Thank you for being so thoughtful," I purred. Oh God, I couldn't wait until six. This was going to be the longest day ever.

"You need to make yourself available for a lunchtime quickie at twelve, though." His hands dipped from my face to my breasts, and he caressed them gently. My nipples immediately peaked, and the rest of my body pleaded for some of the good stuff. *No Jennifer. Control.*

"No can do, darling. You aren't getting a thing from me until this evening." There. I'd said it. It hurt, but I'd said it.

"What? How am I supposed to go all day without sex? You can't do that to me," he moaned pitifully. Slipping his hand between my legs, as if to emphasise his point, he rested his chin on the top of my head and growled.

"You've just managed to go two weeks without sex. The next nine hours or so should be a cinch." Standing up, I blew him a kiss and then disappeared from view.

"Tomorrow your ass is mine, young lady," he yelled after me.

"That's another one hundred spanks, darling," I said breezily, almost skipping from the room.

Six o'clock could not come fast enough. Although I was helping Mark work from home by typing up his correspondence and dealing with a few calls, my mind couldn't focus on anything worth a damn. Thankfully all the tasks I'd been set I could almost do with my eyes closed, so that was something.

When I'd finished the allotted assignments, which was a couple of hours after lunch, I went to work on preparing myself for the evening ahead.

We would start in the bedroom. I'd need a rubber flogger, a paddle, a crop, and a blindfold. Now, how was I going to restrain my husband? Rope seemed like a good idea, but did I want rough hessian rope that would leave marks, or smooth, soft bondage rope? We had lots of either variety and more in between.

Deliberating over this, I laid my outfit for the evening out on our bed. It was designed in black leather and had an adorable headband to match. Mark was going to love it. It also came with a little bullwhip for decoration, although I didn't intend to use it. My problem would be stamina. Having been working my arms in the gym all week, it didn't take an idiot to realise that I wasn't going to be able to wield any kind of whip for long. But with frequent breaks I reckoned I could do some pretty impressive damage. My husband was going to remember our night together for at least a couple of days to come; I would make sure of it.

Hmm. Hessian rope, I decided. The more reminders he had of me, the better. I'd need cuffs, too. Next question: should I gag him? Yes, absolutely. He was sure to get cheeky at some point and hearing him moan for a change would turn me on something fierce. A ball gag would do nicely - a big fat one. What else? Damn, there were so many things to think about.

Rooting through the bottom drawer of my lingerie I found the last couple of things I was looking for. They'd been delivered by mail order a couple of days ago, in anticipation for tonight, and I was very excited by them. One was a strap on dildo, and the other was a stainless steel chastity device. He didn't know what was going to hit him, but whatever it was, it was going to hit him hard.

"Hello, darling. How's work going?" I peered around the door to my husband's office, hoping he'd be sweating buckets, but no, still cool as a cucumber, finalising a couple of accounts on Excel, by the looks of things. Lucky him. I was as jumpy as a March Hare. It was now ten to six and the minutes had ticked down ridiculously slowly.

"Nearly finished, sweetheart." He looked at his watch and whistled. "Am I up for the chop yet? Where and how do you want me?" I wanted him kicking and screaming, but we'd get to that later.

"We're going to start in the bedroom, and I want you at the door, naked and on your knees at six p.m. sharp. Failure to do so will, of course, result in punishment. Am I clear?" He raised his eyebrows at me, tried his best not to laugh, and then nodded. The man was in serious trouble. I gave him my most disdainful look and sauntered from the room without waiting for a reply. The dance had begun. Would he obey me? The jury was out on that, but we'd soon find out.

Surprisingly I heard him outside the door, bang on time, just as I'd begun doing my make-up. He'd have to wait a few minutes, but as I'd been told before, anticipation is the mother of desire.

"Are you naked, slave?" My voice carried through the closed door, and it was masterful and terse. There was a lot more to this being dominant than I'd previously thought, and holding it together for a whole evening was going to be a challenge for me. *You can do this.*

"I am."

"Get on your knees and place your forehead on the floor. I'll come and get you when I'm ready." There was no sound from outside the door, so I'd find out later whether my instructions had been followed. When I finally opened the door, twenty minutes later, it was to find Mark in the position I'd said, waiting patiently for my arrival. He didn't look up at me as I stood there in my robe, and this was when I realised that my husband was probably a better trained submissive than I would ever be. Sophia must have been one very skilled mistress. One day I'd try and get him to talk about it, but not now. We needed some time without drama for the next couple of months - anything but sexual drama, that was.

Raising the thick leather collar I held in my hands, I brought it out in front of me. Tapping the top of his head, I spoke to him sharply. "Sit upright on your knees, eyes on the floor." He obeyed instantly, his body straight and stiff, although some parts were stiffer than others. If I had worried that he wouldn't be turned on by tonight's proceedings, my fears were put to rest.

Fastening the collar around his neck, I buckled it firmly behind him. "There are cuffs on the bed. Fasten your ankles together, and then do your wrists in front of you. When you're finished, lie on your back on the bed. I'll be back shortly." My black silk robe fluttered behind me as I marched from the room.

When I was satisfied with the results of my make-up in the bathroom mirror, I removed my robe and picked up the headband I'd left in there earlier. Placing it gently upon my head, I arranged my hair carefully around it. That was it. I was ready and feeling quite confident. Fairly sure I'd soon get in the swing of things, I decided all we needed now was a little background ambience.

As one of Mark's favourite pastimes was to dominate me to the accompaniment of classical music, I thought I'd return the favour to make him feel right at home. Cranking up the stereo as loud as it would go, the delicate strain of something melodious and endearingly beautiful wafted through the room. It was a famous piece, and I was positive he'd recognise it; I just wondered how long it would take him to get the joke. The answer was not long.

"You can turn that off right now, young lady, or you're not going to be able to sit down for a week when tomorrow morning dawns." My man was not amused.

Ah, finally. I had my husband back. I'd wondered when he was going to pipe up and say something. The Nutcracker by Tchaikovsky was a very apt piece, I thought. Too bad he didn't appreciate my sense of humour.

"Slaves should be seen and not heard, darling," I purred, entering the room in a leather catsuit, complete with side cut-out panels that revealed almost as much of my figure as they hid. Black opera gloves snaked up each arm, and on my head I wore a leather headband complete with kitten ears. In my right hand I carried a bullwhip. Five-inch spike heels and a push-up bra completed the look. I was popping out all over the place. *Meow*. Call me vain, but I looked awesome. Now it was time to wreak havoc upon my poor husband's body.

"Holy fuck, you look incredible," Mark stuttered, before remembering where he was and what was about to happen. Doing his best to look stern he added, "Just you wait until tomorrow. A bullwhip will be the least of your worries, darling."

"I don't think so," I drawled. "Both Mummy and Daddy have promised to get rid of you if you prove problematic." I fluttered my eyelashes at him and waggled my whip in the air.

"They did not!" he said, clearly horrified.

"They absolutely did," I said, lying through my teeth. "If I want to dominate you every day for the next twenty years, there's not a thing you can do about it."

"And do you?" Mark's voice was soft and dangerous. If I wanted to push my husband like this he would become a lethal weapon, and I did not want to be his target; we'd been there before.

"No. I like the status quo exactly like it is. The odd night of domination is nice, though, so let me have my fun."

"Duly noted, Mistress Matthews." Mark lifted his cuffed hands in front of his face and raised an eyebrow. "So what do you want this evening? Do you want an obedient slave, one that obeys your every order immediately, or do you want *something* else?" The emphasis on something else went on forever. I frowned.

"I don't want a doormat if that's what you're asking. I want my husband. Feel free to be as sarcastic as you like, just be aware that I'm going to have some fun at your expense for a change." Tapping the whip in my gloved hand I gave him a long, searing look that spoke volumes.

"Then let the fun begin," he said.

Straddling my husband's face and ordering him to make me come three times in a row was a gratifying experience - for me at least. It also relaxed me. When I got off the bed my eyes lingered on his cock, which was straining for attention, and I fluttered a gloved fingertip up and down its length. He didn't make a sound. Mark was going to play tough guy for the evening, that much was obvious.

Leaning towards his face, I whispered, "How much do you want to come right now, darling?"

He blinked once, twice, and then his cuffed hands grabbed my arms and swung me down on the bed, and all of a sudden he was lying on top of me.

"Just a thought," he bit, "but when you're trying to dominate someone who's bigger, faster, and stronger than you are, make sure they're restrained properly before you tease them." He took my bottom lip in his mouth, bit it gently, and heard me moan.

"So you don't want to come then?" I batted my eyelashes at him seductively, and my fingers found his cock nestling between my legs. I gripped it tightly and pumped it very gently.

"If you think I'm begging you for an orgasm, Jennifer, you have a very long evening ahead of you." My husband was getting a little irked. This was perfect.

"We'll see," I whispered seductively. "Now get off me and let me finish, else I'll call mum." I bit his ear and heard him let out a hiss. He deserved it.

"You can't do that from here. I could just lie on you all evening and fuck you senseless, and there isn't a thing you could do about it." Mark's eyes were glowing brightly and damned if I didn't nearly melt into a puddle on the spot.

"Think again, tough guy. I enabled voice recognition on my phone. Dial mum," I called out, and sure enough my phone heard and in a female voice said, "Calling mum. Yes or no?" Looking expectantly at my husband, I waited for his response.

"You wouldn't," he said tightly.

"Want to test that theory?" I teased, wriggling beneath him.

Rolling off me, his lips flattened in evident frustration.

"You agreed to this. Be a good boy now," I said sweetly. "Right. I think it's time we put this on you." Pulling a black rubber cockring out of my pocket, I slid it down the length of his erect cock. "That should keep you nice and hard for what I'm about to do next."

"And what's that?" he growled.

"Put your hands above your head, roll over on your stomach, and I'll show you," I murmured in his ear.

"Fine." He did as I instructed and I watched him slowly relax into the bed. The bastard knew what I was about to do once again and was preparing himself in advance. Was this how he managed to amass his fortune? Always being one step ahead of the opposition? It wouldn't surprise me.

Kneading his magnificent ass for a minute or two, I then moved on to the paddle. There was no point trying to spank him with my hand. It would hurt me more than it would hurt him, of that I was almost certain. At least he'd feel it if I used the paddle. The one in my hand was made of bamboo, with holes cut into its surface to help decrease air resistance. The end result meant it was light and easy to swing but still packed a very solid punch. I would also be able to wield it for some considerable time, and I did. Mark didn't say a word. His backside was blisteringly red by the time I'd finished, but I didn't hear a single noise, moan or whimper. What was his secret? I'd be in hysterics by now.

"Do you want the flogger or the crop next, darling? Or perhaps you want to beg for mercy?" I leaned over his body to whisper all that in his ear, and a throaty aroused sound came out. Even though I had orgasmed three times in the last hour, I was already craving more of the same, but it would have to wait. There was no way my husband was sitting down tomorrow, and I intended to make sure of that.

"Both, and put a bit of effort into it, darling. This may be the only chance you get to dominate me, so try and make it memorable, sweetheart." He sounded bored and completely unaffected by my recent paddling as if I'd barely scraped the surface of what he could take. Compressing my lips together and curling my fingers into fists, I resisted the urge to fling the paddle at his head. Fine. If he wanted to play tough guy, I could work with that.

The gloves came off as I used the flogger, and I flung that thing down as if I were trying to tame a wild beast. My arm was by this time killing me, but I was damned if I'd stop until I gave it my best shot. When my tendons were screaming for a rest I ran the tendrils up and down his sensitised flesh and wiped a few beads of sweat away from my forehead.

"It's not as easy as it looks, is it?" I could tell Mark was amused by the tone of his voice, but I refused to let him get to me. He was trying to rile me, and it wasn't going to work. Besides, I would have the last laugh. There was no way he was getting an orgasm this evening.

"Ready for the crop, darling?" Purring sweetly in his ear, I ran a single fingernail sharply down his left buttock. I heard him suck in a breath, but nothing more. Still, it was a start.

"Absolutely," he confirmed enthusiastically. "And I'll bet you one hundred pounds your whipping arm hasn't got more than ten minutes left in it." Wanting to scream, mostly because my husband was a smug, sanctimonious bastard, I decided that it was probably better to save my breath. Besides, I could still get even.

"That's actually excellent news, sweetheart, because as soon as I'm finished with the crop I'm locking your cock in a teeny weeny little cage, and taking your ass. There is no way you're getting an orgasm this evening, and by the time I'm finished with you, you'll be so revved up that sleep will be an impossible dream. Now open wide for me, darling, because I've had just about enough of your attitude this evening."

Pressing the black ball gag firmly to his lips, I waited for him to open before I yanked the straps tightly behind his head and buckled it up.

Now I was really going to have some fun.

Chapter Twenty-Nine - Mark

My wife did a real number on me yesterday evening and then left me tied hand and foot to the bed all night. Blue balls didn't even begin to describe the agony of her sexy little body writhing all over me with no sign of relief in sight, and she knew it. She'd have to untie me eventually though, and when she did I was going to even up our scoresheet. So far this morning she'd been conveniently absent, but I could hear her bustling about downstairs, so I knew she was just putting off the inevitable. The longer she made me wait, the worse it would be for her. She should know that by now.

Hearing the phone ring, and unable to answer it, I heard the dial tone disappear as Jen picked up. Then the sound of her feet on the stairs, and she walked into the bedroom in her robe with a mug of coffee in her hand. If she thought that would appease me, she was much mistaken.

"Hang on Rupert, I'll just go and get him for you." She laid the phone and mug of coffee down while she went to work untying my right hand. Hurrah. Vengeance would shortly be mine, and I could almost smell its tantalising fragrance on the air. When I had the use of my hand back I picked up the phone and scowled at her. She immediately dashed from the room. Smart woman.

Rupert talked pleasantries for a few minutes until the conversation moved back to Kyle. "Have you decided what you're going to do to him yet?" I asked. Putting the phone on speaker, I made short work of untying my other wrist and then got to work on my ankles. The rope marks were going to be with me for a few days, but they would be a fantastic reminder of the fact that my wife needed to pay for every single thing she'd done to me last night, and then some.

"Ah, about that. There's a special wing at Albrecht where we do 'experimental things'. I was wondering if you'd be interested in something like that?" Rupert sounded very chipper, and if my ears weren't deceiving me, someone was snoring in the background. A female. I wondered if he'd got back together with Laurel or if it was a new squeeze. Interesting.

Quickly donning a pair of jeans and a black shirt, I began walking down the stairs. "Define 'experimental'," I replied. I wanted all the details of what would happen to that miserable bastard, and he was lucky I didn't want him dead because if I did, I'm sure Rupert and Laurel would have taken care of it for me. The only reason I decided against it was because death was too quick. I wanted Kyle and Redcliff to suffer for what they'd done, not just to me, but to Jennifer; and for most of her life.

"Gender reassignment. They'll get boobs, lose other *important* parts of their anatomy, and be given a horrible cocktail of hormones. That sort of 'experimental'. What do you think? Laurel's all for it. She says she could do with a new housemaid."

Holy hell. As far as punishments went, not even I could have come up with that. It was truly monstrous and probably perfect for them both.

"They'll be assigned a master or mistress at the end of the surgery, and I have a feeling Laurel will probably want to play with them for a bit, so I can pretty much guarantee you they'll suffer in all the ways that matter."

Pushing the door to my office wide, I could barely sit down on what used to be a very comfortable leather chair, but I gritted my teeth and took the plunge. There was no way I was letting Jennifer know she'd put me through the wringer last night, and she was bound to come in with another cup of coffee at any moment.

"Jesus Christ," I whispered.

"Or we could put them in a cell if you prefer. It's your call."

There was silence down the end of the phoneline for a minute. I didn't know if I could do that to a person. It was too horrific, even for me.

"Laurel says if you can't decide, she's happy to make the decision for you. She is pretty cross at the moment." A grunt could be heard somewhere in the background, so I had my answer about who Rupert was sleeping with. He was a brave son of a bitch, I'd give him that.

Letting out a long slow breath, I pursed my lips together and sighed. "I'll leave it in Laurel's hands. Tell her she can do what she wants with them."

Rupert laughed. "She thought you'd say that. You've just made her really happy." Yeah, and she was going to call me a pussy as soon as I put the phone down, but what the hell.

"Remind me never to annoy Laurel, okay?"

I could almost see Rupert's face creasing up as he said, "Hell no. That's the fun part. You'll understand all about that in a few years." Ha. That's what you think, I thought.

We then said our various goodbyes and I decided I'd lay the past to rest. This was the end of a chapter for Jennifer and me, and one we were glad to say goodbye to. We would shortly be embarking on another, and it would probably be no less challenging, but hopefully far more rewarding in every way. I couldn't wait. We were going to have sex constantly until she was pregnant, and if you think I'm joking, you'd be wrong.

But before I started getting even with my wife, I had a small present to give her. It was currently resting in my top bedside drawer, and it was a navy velvet box, the inside of which held a soft velvet collar in the same colour. On the front of the collar rested an emerald cut, one-carat diamond, to celebrate our first year of marriage. On the rear of the collar was a little disc that had both of our initials engraved on it. I intended to make her wear the thing all the time, to help her remember who was boss around these parts.

As if she'd read my thoughts, she chose that moment to saunter in a cream babydoll dress that was pretty much see-through all over. Thrusting a cup of coffee in my face I nearly dropped it, far too intent on other things that were also thrusting out towards me.

"Fuck," I whispered throatily. To add to my woes I promptly spilled hot coffee all over myself.

"The word is thank you, and you're welcome," she said sweetly. "By the way, how's your ass this morning?" She gave me a mock frown and pretended to be extremely concerned for my welfare.

"Not as sore as yours is going to be this evening," I replied, with a knowing smile.

Thanks for reading!

Want to be notified when Christina releases a new book? Sign up to her newsletter here: **http://bit.ly/1MVubkR**.

If you'd like to find out how Mark and Jenny met, the first book is called **The Riding School**, and is book one of a six-book series called **Pony Tales**.

Please Help a Starving Author by Leaving a Review

Ok, so I lied about the starving part, but books need reviews, particularly on Amazon, in order to sell. Without them they wither and die, and so do the authors. Honest.

You don't have to say much, and you can stay anonymous - just set your Amazon reviewer name to something like *Amazon Reviewer 3982*. Anyway, here are a few examples of what you could write if you were a truly wonderful person who didn't mind doing a good deed every now and again:

This book was so awesome I forgot to feed my kids. Thankfully they reminded me, over and over again, so I haven't managed to kill them yet. Phew.

This book sucked. It was even worse than a certain president's infamous hairdo, and that is saying something.

Mark and Jennifer are so hot I want a threesome with both of them. As long as I'm allowed a safe word - because Mark is a little bit on the seriously freaky crazy side.

I would rather read War and Peace than this ridiculous smutty drivel and nonsense. Seriously, all Mandara talks about is orgasms, sex, and hot blokes. Who wants to read about that?

Ms Mandara does not write quickly enough. I need her to release a book every month at the very least, and she keeps me waiting for months - and worse - ends everything on a horrendous cliff-hanger. I have a love/hate relationship with this author. She should probably be spanked.

This is not a good book to read on the train. Especially when the hot guy sitting next to me kept trying to read it over my shoulder.

Don't ever read this book to your wife. She will demand sex for days on end and will suddenly become insatiable in bed. Seriously, I have been considering divorce...

Any of these will do (I'm more partial to the nice ones...) and it will give you extra karma points that will be returned to you in due course in the form of cookies, money, hugs, and wine. Honest.

Thank You!

I just need to say a big thank you to all my wonderful beta readers who always step up to the rather tricky task of reading my books before they've had a good edit. Without you, my books would probably be unreadable as you manage to figure out that my heroine can't see things when she's wearing a blindfold, and that it's tough for her to talk if she's gagged. You also help me to correct my numerous errors and give me your honest opinions, which are more valuable than pixie dust. (The stuff that makes you fly without wings). (That is what pixie dust does, right?)

So, for everyone who's helped me along the way, thank you, thank you, thank you! I am particularly indebted to Debenpac from Texas who told me Tesla cars do not 'roar' they 'whine' - must be something to do with the fact they're electric, right? And for those of you who are curious - that actual car won't be on the market until 2020 - so how was I to know? He also provided me with the spectacular punishment for both Kyle and Michael at the end. I usually don't like to name names, given the dark nature of my books, so I am sending virtual hugs to everyone instead. They are valid for the next twenty-four hours only, though. So grab 'em quick ;)

For those of you who are wondering if there will be any more Mark and Jen, I haven't decided yet. I've toyed with the idea of telling Leyland and Marianna's story, too. Next up, I'll be writing the third book in my latest special agent BDSM series, **Flames**, so watch this space.

Love 'n hugs to all xxx

Bio

Christina Mandara was born in the UK but has spent most of her life travelling the world. She speaks three languages and has been chiefly employed in the fields of finance and travel. Her favourite city is Sydney, and her favourite holiday destination is the south of France.

She loves keeping fit and enjoys running, cycling, and water sports. Think surfing or sailing. She's a big fan of BDSM in all its glorious forms, and her favourite item in the toy closet (a box simply isn't big enough) is her riding crop.

In her spare time, she's usually cuddled up with a good book, exploring the countryside, or baking in the kitchen. In fact, she loves her kitchen so much she's one of few women who wouldn't mind being tied to it! Her first and foremost love is writing, however, and more often than not you'll find her on a laptop spinning tales of romance, erotica, or dark paranormal fantasies.

Christina's Social Media Hangouts:

C.P. Mandara's Facebook Street Team:
www.facebook.com/groups/1021736604577782
FaceBook: **www.facebook.com/CPMandara**
Twitter: **twitter.com/cpmandara**
Website: **christinamandara.com**
GoodReads: **www.goodreads.com/author/show/7113521.C_P_Mandara**
Amazon Author Page: **http://author.to/CPMandara**